THE BLACK PYRAMID OF ALASKA

Michael James

KDP

Copyright © 2025 Michael James

All rights reserved

The characters and events portrayed in this book are fictitious. Any similarity to real persons, living or dead, is coincidental and not intended by the author.

No part of this book may be reproduced, or stored in a retrieval system, or transmitted in any form or by any means, electronic, mechanical, photocopying, recording, or otherwise, without express written permission of the publisher.

ISBN-13: 9781234567890
ISBN-10: 1477123456

Cover design by: Art Painter
Library of Congress Control Number: 2018675309
Printed in the United States of America

CONTENTS

Title Page
Copyright
The Black Pyramid Of Alaska   1
Introduction   2
Prologue   3
Chapter 1: The Vanishing Light   5
Chapter 2: The Summons   19
Chapter 3: Gathering Shadows   32
Chapter 4: The Raven's Warning   44
Chapter 5: The Slab and the Seal   57
Chapter 6: Descent into the Unknown   69
Chapter 7: The Pyramid's Heart   81
Chapter 8: The Shaman's Arrival   92
Chapter 9: The First Sacrifice   103
Chapter 10: The Government's Hand   113
Chapter 11: The Ritual Chamber   124
Chapter 12: The Opening   135
Chapter 13: The Other Side   145
Chapter 14: The Bargain   156
Chapter 15: The Return   166
Chapter 16: The Cover-Up   176

Chapter 17: The Survivors	186
Chapter 18: The Cultists	199
Chapter 19: The Little People	208
Chapter 20: The Aurora's Song	217
Chapter 21: The Gathering Storm	226
Chapter 22: The Siege	236
Chapter 23: The Final Ritual	246
Chapter 24: The Shaman's Sacrifice	255
Chapter 25: The Aftermath	264
Chapter 26: The Raven's Legacy	273
Chapter 27: The Spirits' Return	280
Chapter 28: The New Generation	288
Chapter 29: The Unanswered Questions	296
Chapter 30: The Black Pyramid Endures	303
Epilogue: Beneath the Ice	311
About The Author	317
Books By This Author	319

THE BLACK PYRAMID OF ALASKA

By: **Michael James**

To find all of my books scan QR Code on back of the book or you can visit website below.

THANKS 4 READING

INTRODUCTION

The land remembers.

Beneath the endless snows of Alaska, where the aurora burns like fire across the sky, stories linger in silence. Elders whisper of wounds carved into stone, of guardians buried beneath ice, of forces too vast for human hands to hold. The wilderness is not empty—it breathes, it watches, it endures.

Explorers came once, chasing anomalies and shadows. Shamans prayed, scientists measured, hunters listened to the wind. They found spirals etched into rock, voices carried in dreams, and a pyramid blacker than night itself. Some sought knowledge, others balance, but all were changed.

The land took its toll. Sacrifices were made, visions endured, balance restored—yet never fully healed. The pyramid sank beneath ice, its presence dormant but unbroken. Ravens circled, caribou moved, little people laughed at the edges of vision. The cycle continued.

Now, generations later, the story begins again. A young seeker will find journals buried in frost, artifacts wrapped in cloth, chants preserved in ink. She will hear voices in the aurora, footsteps in the snow, warnings in the wind. The land will call, and she will answer.

This is not a tale of conquest. It is a tale of humility, of awe, of wounds that never close. It is the story of the black pyramid—guardian and danger, mystery and truth. It endures, and so must those who walk its shadow.

PROLOGUE

The ice cracked like bone beneath the weight of silence. In the heart of Alaska's wilderness, where the sun vanished for months and the stars burned like cold fire, something waited. It was not alive, not dead, but something in between—a geometry that defied reason, a shape that gnawed at the edges of thought. The pyramid was not seen so much as felt, a pressure behind the eyes, a vibration in the marrow.

Those who dreamed of it awoke screaming. They spoke of corridors that stretched forever, of walls that pulsed like flesh, of voices that whispered in languages no human throat could form. The dreams were not dreams but invitations, and each invitation carried a price. Some resisted, some succumbed, but all were marked.

The land itself bent around the pyramid. Rivers froze in unnatural patterns, trees twisted toward the north, animals fled without reason. Hunters found tracks that led nowhere, circles burned into the snow, shadows that moved against the wind. The wilderness was no longer wilderness—it was a labyrinth, and the pyramid was its heart.

Government agents came with machines and weapons, confident in their authority. They left with madness. Reports spoke of hallucinations, of soldiers turning on one another, of instruments recording voices that did not exist. Files were sealed, names erased, missions forgotten. But the pyramid remembered.

The aurora was its herald. Green and violet flames danced

across the sky, forming symbols that no scientist could explain. Some saw eyes, others saw mouths, still others saw entire cities rising and collapsing in the span of seconds. The aurora was not light but language, and the pyramid spoke through it.

Villagers told stories of Raven, of Wolf, of Bear, each drawn to the pyramid and consumed. They said the spirits themselves feared it, that even the trickster could not escape its hunger. Rituals were performed, offerings made, but nothing silenced the whispers. The pyramid was not a god, not a demon, but something older, something that made gods and demons alike tremble.

And still, people came. Curiosity is a sickness, and the pyramid was its cure and its cause. Explorers, scientists, wanderers—all drawn north, all swallowed by the silence. Their names became footnotes, their bodies became bones beneath the ice.

The prologue unfolds as a litany of warnings, each paragraph a descent deeper into dread. The reader is pulled into a world where history, myth, and horror converge, where the pyramid is both symbol and reality, both wound and weapon. By the end, the stage is set: the black pyramid waits, and those who seek it will not return unchanged.

CHAPTER 1: THE VANISHING LIGHT

The twilight clung to the horizon like a bruise, refusing to yield to either day or night. Lena Sorensen stood at the edge of the outpost, her breath crystallizing in the air, watching the aurora ripple in unnatural patterns across the sky. The colors bled into shapes that seemed deliberate—triangles, spirals, jagged lines that mirrored the seismic readings she had been analyzing. She told herself it was coincidence, a trick of the atmosphere, but the thought gnawed at her. The silence of the wilderness pressed against her ears, broken only by the occasional crack of ice shifting in the river. Even the wolves had vanished, their absence more unsettling than their howls. She returned inside, the warmth of the generator barely holding back the cold, and tried to bury herself in data.

The charts spread across her desk told a story she did not want to believe. The seismic readings were too precise, too symmetrical, forming angles that nature did not create. She traced the lines again, her pencil trembling as she sketched what appeared to be a pyramid buried beneath the permafrost. The idea was absurd, yet the evidence refused to bend. She whispered to herself, trying to rationalize, but the words sounded hollow in the empty room. Her rational mind clashed with instinct, and instinct whispered that something vast and unnatural lay beneath her feet. The generator hummed weakly, its rhythm faltering like a heartbeat on the verge of collapse.

She tried the radio, but static swallowed her voice. The equipment had been unreliable for weeks, as though the air itself resisted transmission. Lena adjusted the dials, listening for any sign of life, but only the hiss of interference answered. She leaned back, exhaustion settling into her bones, and stared at the frost creeping across the window. Outside, the aurora pulsed brighter, casting shadows that moved in ways the light should not allow. For a moment, she thought she saw a figure —tall, indistinct, neither human nor animal—standing at the edge of the snowfield. When she blinked, it was gone.

Fear was not unfamiliar to Lena; isolation bred its own demons. But this was different, sharper, as though the land itself had turned against her. She remembered stories told by the local villagers, warnings about places where the earth swallowed men whole, where lights lured travelers into the ice. She had dismissed them as folklore, remnants of a mythic past, yet now they returned with unsettling clarity. Her rational mind fought to dismiss the visions, but her instincts whispered otherwise. She scribbled notes in her journal, her handwriting jagged, her words fragmented. The more she wrote, the less sense they made.

The generator failed with a final sputter, plunging the outpost into darkness. Lena froze, listening to the sudden silence, her breath loud in her ears. She reached for the emergency lantern, fumbling with numb fingers, but before she could light it, she heard movement outside. Slow, deliberate, crunching footsteps in the snow. Her pulse quickened, every nerve screaming at her to stay still. She forced herself to the radio, sending a garbled distress signal, her voice breaking as static devoured her words. The last thing she saw before the lantern flickered to life was a shadow pressed against the window, its shape impossible, its presence undeniable.

The lantern's glow was weak, casting long, trembling shadows across the walls. Lena clutched it like a talisman, her knuckles white, her breath shallow. The silence outside was worse than the footsteps, as though the world itself had paused to listen. She tried to convince herself it was her imagination, but the frost on the window began to spread in geometric patterns, spirals and triangles etched by unseen hands. She backed away, her journal clutched to her chest, her mind racing with questions she could not answer. The outpost felt smaller, suffocating, as though the walls were closing in.

She thought of her colleagues back in Anchorage, of the skepticism they would greet her findings with. They would laugh, dismiss her data as error, her visions as fatigue. But Lena knew what she had seen, and she knew the land was hiding something. She whispered to herself, repeating fragments of equations, trying to anchor her mind in science. Yet the numbers twisted, forming symbols that matched the patterns outside. She dropped the pencil, her hands trembling, her breath uneven.

The aurora intensified, flooding the sky with unnatural light. Lena stepped outside, lantern in hand, drawn by a compulsion she could not resist. The cold bit into her skin, but she barely felt it. The snowfield stretched endlessly, the shadows shifting with each pulse of the aurora. She saw the figure again, closer now, its outline blurred, its movements deliberate. It raised an arm, pointing toward the horizon, where the land seemed to ripple like water. She stumbled back, her lantern flickering, her heart pounding.

She ran inside, slamming the door, her breath ragged. The outpost felt no safer, its walls thin against whatever pressed in from the wilderness. She collapsed at her desk, clutching her journal, scribbling furiously. Her words were incoherent, fragments of equations, symbols, and warnings. She wrote of triangles, of spirals, of a pyramid buried beneath the ice. She wrote of shadows that moved against the light, of footsteps that echoed in silence. She wrote until her hand cramped, until the lantern sputtered, until exhaustion claimed her.

Sleep came reluctantly, dragging her into dreams she could not escape. She dreamed of corridors that stretched forever, of walls that pulsed like flesh, of voices whispering in languages no human throat could form. She dreamed of a pyramid, vast and black, its surface etched with symbols that burned into her eyes. She woke screaming, her breath ragged, her body trembling. The lantern had gone out, and the outpost was silent.

She lit the lantern again, her hands shaking, her eyes darting to the window. The frost patterns had grown, covering the glass in spirals and triangles. She pressed her hand against the cold surface, feeling a vibration beneath her skin. She pulled back, her breath uneven, her mind racing. She whispered to herself, trying to anchor her thoughts, but the words dissolved into silence.

The radio crackled suddenly, a burst of static that made her jump. She rushed to it, adjusting the dials, listening desperately. A voice emerged, faint, distorted, speaking words she could not understand. She leaned closer, straining to hear, but the voice dissolved into static. She slammed the radio, frustration and fear boiling over. She screamed into the microphone, her voice breaking, her words swallowed by interference.

The aurora pulsed again, brighter than ever, flooding the outpost with unnatural light. Lena shielded her eyes, but the patterns burned into her vision. She saw triangles, spirals, and a pyramid rising from the ice. She stumbled back, her lantern flickering, her breath ragged. She whispered to herself, repeating fragments of equations, trying to anchor her mind.

But the numbers twisted, forming symbols that matched the patterns outside.

She collapsed at her desk, clutching her journal, her breath uneven. She wrote furiously, her words incoherent, her handwriting jagged. She wrote of shadows, of footsteps, of voices whispering in silence. She wrote of a pyramid buried beneath the ice, of symbols etched into the frost. She wrote until her hand cramped, until the lantern sputtered, until exhaustion claimed her.

Sleep came again, dragging her into dreams she could not escape. She dreamed of corridors, of walls, of voices. She dreamed of a pyramid, vast and black, its surface etched with symbols. She woke screaming, her breath ragged, her body trembling. The lantern had gone out, and the outpost was silent.

She lit the lantern again, her hands shaking, her eyes darting to the window. The frost patterns had grown, covering the glass. She pressed her hand against the cold surface, feeling a vibration. She pulled back, her breath uneven, her mind racing. She whispered to herself, trying to anchor her thoughts, but the words dissolved.

The radio crackled again, a burst of static. She rushed to it, adjusting the dials, listening. A voice emerged, faint, distorted. She leaned closer, straining to hear, but the voice dissolved. She slammed the radio, frustration boiling over. She screamed into the microphone, her voice breaking.

The aurora pulsed again, brighter than ever. Lena shielded her eyes, but the patterns burned. She saw triangles, spirals, and a pyramid. She stumbled back, her lantern flickering. She whispered to herself, repeating fragments. But the numbers twisted, forming symbols.

She collapsed again, clutching her journal. She wrote

furiously, her words incoherent. She wrote of shadows, of footsteps, of voices. She wrote of a pyramid buried beneath the ice. She wrote until her hand cramped, until the lantern sputtered. Exhaustion claimed her.

Sleep dragged her into dreams. She dreamed of corridors, of walls, of voices. She dreamed of a pyramid, vast and black. She woke screaming, her breath ragged. The lantern had gone out. The outpost was silent.

The twilight was not merely the absence of sun but the presence of something older, something that had lingered long before Lena Sorensen arrived at the outpost. The sky was a canvas of shifting colors, the aurora bending into shapes that resembled eyes, wings, and spirals. To Lena, trained in the language of science, these were anomalies of solar wind and magnetic fields. Yet she could not shake the feeling that the lights were speaking, whispering in a tongue she did not know but somehow understood. The silence of the wilderness pressed against her, heavy and deliberate, as though the land itself was listening.

The people of Tanana had warned her, though she had dismissed their words as folklore. They spoke of a mountain that was not a mountain, a shadow beneath the ice that swallowed hunters whole. They told her of Raven, the trickster, scorched by forbidden light when he flew too close to the sleeping stone. Lena had smiled politely, recording their stories as cultural artifacts, but now those words returned with unsettling clarity. The aurora above her seemed to echo their warnings, its colors bleeding into symbols that matched the seismic readings she had been analyzing.

Her charts told a story she did not want to believe. The lines were too precise, too deliberate, forming angles that nature did not create. She traced them again, her pencil trembling, sketching what appeared to be a pyramid buried beneath the permafrost. The thought was absurd, yet the evidence refused to bend. She whispered equations to herself, trying to anchor her mind in science, but the numbers twisted, forming symbols that matched the patterns outside. It was as though the land itself was rewriting her language, bending her tools to its will.

The generator hummed weakly, its rhythm faltering like a heartbeat. Lena adjusted the radio, listening for any sign of life, but only static answered. She leaned back, exhaustion settling into her bones, and stared at the frost creeping across the window. The patterns were not random; they were spirals, triangles, glyphs etched by unseen hands. She pressed her palm against the glass, feeling a vibration beneath her skin, as though the ice itself was alive. She pulled back, her breath uneven, her mind racing.

Outside, the aurora pulsed brighter, casting shadows that moved in ways the light should not allow. For a moment, she thought she saw a figure—tall, indistinct, neither human nor animal—standing at the edge of the snowfield. It raised an arm, pointing toward the horizon, where the land seemed to ripple like water. Lena stumbled back, her lantern flickering, her heart pounding. She whispered to herself, repeating fragments of equations, trying to anchor her mind, but the numbers twisted again, forming symbols that matched the patterns outside.

She remembered the elders' warnings, their voices trembling as they spoke of hunters who vanished, of shamans who went mad, of dreams that bled into waking life. She had dismissed them as superstition, remnants of a mythic past, but now they returned with unsettling clarity. Her rational mind fought to dismiss the visions, but her instincts whispered otherwise. She scribbled notes in her journal, her handwriting jagged, her words fragmented. The more she wrote, the less sense they made.

The generator failed with a final sputter, plunging the outpost into darkness. Lena froze, listening to the sudden silence, her breath loud in her ears. She reached for the emergency lantern, fumbling with numb fingers, but before she could light it, she heard movement outside. Slow, deliberate, crunching footsteps in the snow. Her pulse quickened, every nerve screaming at her to stay still. She forced herself to the radio, sending a garbled distress signal, her voice breaking as static devoured her words.

The lantern's glow was weak, casting long, trembling shadows across the walls. Lena clutched it like a talisman, her knuckles white, her breath shallow. The silence outside was worse than the footsteps, as though the world itself had paused to listen. She tried to convince herself it was her imagination, but the frost on the window began to spread in geometric patterns, spirals and triangles etched by unseen hands. She backed away, her journal clutched to her chest, her mind racing with questions she could not answer.

She thought of her colleagues back in Anchorage, of the skepticism they would greet her findings with. They would laugh, dismiss her data as error, her visions as fatigue. But Lena knew what she had seen, and she knew the land was hiding something. She whispered to herself, repeating fragments of equations, trying to anchor her mind in science. Yet the numbers twisted, forming symbols that matched the patterns outside. She dropped the pencil, her hands trembling, her breath uneven.

The aurora intensified, flooding the sky with unnatural light. Lena stepped outside, lantern in hand, drawn by a compulsion she could not resist. The cold bit into her skin, but she barely felt it. The snowfield stretched endlessly, the shadows shifting with each pulse of the aurora. She saw the figure again, closer now, its outline blurred, its movements deliberate. It raised an arm, pointing toward the horizon, where the land seemed to ripple like water. She stumbled back, her lantern flickering, her heart pounding.

She ran inside, slamming the door, her breath ragged. The outpost felt no safer, its walls thin against whatever pressed in from the wilderness. She collapsed at her desk, clutching her journal, scribbling furiously. Her words were incoherent, fragments of equations, symbols, and warnings. She wrote of triangles, of spirals, of a pyramid buried beneath the ice. She wrote of shadows that moved against the light, of footsteps that echoed in silence. She wrote until her hand cramped, until the lantern sputtered, until exhaustion claimed her.

Sleep came reluctantly, dragging her into dreams she could not escape. She dreamed of corridors that stretched forever, of walls that pulsed like flesh, of voices whispering in languages no human throat could form. She dreamed of a pyramid, vast and black, its surface etched with symbols that burned into her eyes. She woke screaming, her breath ragged, her body trembling. The lantern had gone out, and the outpost was silent.

She lit the lantern again, her hands shaking, her eyes darting to the window. The frost patterns had grown, covering the glass in spirals and triangles. She pressed her hand against the cold surface, feeling a vibration beneath her skin. She pulled back, her breath uneven, her mind racing. She whispered to herself, trying to anchor her thoughts, but the words dissolved into silence.

The radio crackled suddenly, a burst of static that made her jump. She rushed to it, adjusting the dials, listening desperately. A voice emerged, faint, distorted, speaking words she could not understand. She leaned closer, straining to hear, but the voice dissolved into static. She slammed the radio, frustration and fear boiling over. She screamed into the microphone, her voice breaking as static devoured her words.

The aurora pulsed again, brighter than ever, flooding the outpost with unnatural light. Lena shielded her eyes, but the patterns burned into her vision. She saw triangles, spirals, and a pyramid rising from the ice. She stumbled back, her lantern flickering, her breath ragged. She whispered to herself, repeating fragments of equations, trying to anchor her mind. But the numbers twisted, forming symbols that matched the patterns outside.

She collapsed at her desk, clutching her journal, her breath uneven. She wrote furiously, her words incoherent, her handwriting jagged. She wrote of shadows, of footsteps, of voices whispering in silence. She wrote of a pyramid buried beneath the ice, of symbols etched into the frost. She wrote until her hand cramped, until the lantern sputtered, until exhaustion claimed her.

Sleep came again, dragging her into dreams she could not escape. She dreamed of corridors, of walls, of voices. She dreamed of a pyramid, vast and black, its surface etched with symbols. She woke screaming, her breath ragged, her body trembling. The lantern had gone out, and the outpost was silent.

She lit the lantern again, her hands shaking, her eyes darting to the window. The frost patterns had grown, covering the glass. She pressed her hand against the cold surface, feeling a vibration. She pulled back, her breath uneven, her mind racing. She whispered to herself, trying to anchor her thoughts, but the words dissolved.

The radio crackled again, a burst of static. She rushed to it, adjusting the dials, listening. A voice emerged, faint, distorted. She leaned closer, straining to hear, but the voice dissolved. She slammed the radio, frustration boiling over. She screamed into the microphone, her voice breaking.

The outpost was a skeleton of steel and ice, its walls groaning against the weight of the Alaskan winter. Lena Sorensen paced the narrow corridor, her boots crunching on frost that had crept inside despite the heaters. The aurora outside bled through the windows, painting the walls in shifting green and violet. She stopped, staring at the flicker, her breath catching. It wasn't random—it was pulsing, rhythmic, almost like a signal. She whispered to herself, "No... no, it's just solar wind." But the words didn't convince her.

Her instruments told a different story. Seismic charts spread across the desk revealed angles too clean, too deliberate. She traced them with a trembling finger, whispering, "This isn't natural." The lines converged into a shape she didn't want to see: a pyramid buried beneath the permafrost. She leaned back, rubbing her temples, trying to dismiss the thought. But the data was undeniable. Every reading pointed to something massive, something impossible.

The radio hissed with static, drowning her attempts to call Anchorage. "Sorensen to base... Sorensen to base..." Nothing. She slammed the receiver down, frustration boiling. The silence pressed in, heavier than the snow outside. She glanced at the window, and for a heartbeat, she thought she saw movement. A shadow, tall and indistinct, sliding across the snowfield. She blinked, and it was gone.

Her breath quickened. She grabbed her journal, scribbling notes, equations, fragments of thought. The handwriting was jagged, uneven. "Triangles... spirals... resonance..." She stopped, staring at the words. They weren't hers. Or at least, they didn't feel like hers. She dropped the pencil, her hands shaking.

The generator sputtered, coughed, and died. Darkness swallowed the outpost. Lena froze, listening. The silence was absolute, broken only by the faint crunch of snow outside.

Footsteps. Slow. Deliberate. She reached for the emergency lantern, fumbling with numb fingers. The flame flickered to life, casting long shadows across the walls.

She moved to the radio, desperate. "Sorensen to base, emergency—" Static devoured her words. A faint voice emerged, distorted, speaking in a language she didn't recognize. She leaned closer, straining to hear. The voice dissolved, leaving only silence. She slammed the radio, her breath ragged.

The lantern's glow trembled. Frost spread across the window in spirals and triangles, etched by unseen hands. Lena backed away, clutching her journal. "No... no, this isn't real." But the patterns grew, covering the glass, pulsing with the rhythm of the aurora. She pressed her palm against the cold surface, feeling a vibration beneath her skin. She pulled back, her heart pounding.

She thought of the villagers' warnings, their voices trembling as they spoke of hunters who vanished, of shamans who went mad. She had dismissed them as superstition, but now they returned with clarity. "The sleeping stone," they had called it. "The mountain that is not a mountain." She whispered the words, her voice breaking.

The aurora intensified, flooding the sky with unnatural light. Lena stepped outside, lantern in hand, drawn by a compulsion she couldn't resist. The cold bit into her skin, but she barely felt it. The snowfield stretched endlessly, shadows shifting with each pulse of the aurora. She saw the figure again, closer now, its outline blurred, its movements deliberate. It raised an arm, pointing toward the horizon. The land rippled like water.

She stumbled back, her lantern flickering. "No... no..." Her breath came in ragged gasps. She turned, running inside, slamming the door. The outpost felt no safer, its walls thin against whatever pressed in from the wilderness. She collapsed at her desk, scribbling furiously. Her words were incoherent, fragments of equations, symbols, warnings.

Sleep clawed at her, dragging her into dreams she couldn't escape. Corridors stretched forever, walls pulsed like flesh, voices whispered in languages no human throat could form. She saw the pyramid, vast and black, its surface etched with burning symbols. She woke screaming, her breath ragged, her body trembling. The lantern had gone out.

She lit it again, her hands shaking. The frost patterns had grown, covering the glass. Spirals. Triangles. Glyphs. She pressed her hand against the cold surface, feeling the vibration. She pulled back, whispering, "It's alive." Her voice cracked.

The radio crackled, sudden and violent. She rushed to it, adjusting the dials. A voice emerged, faint, distorted. "Sorensen…" Her name. She froze, listening. The voice dissolved into static. She screamed into the microphone, her words swallowed.

The aurora pulsed again, brighter than ever. Lena shielded her eyes, but the patterns burned into her vision. Triangles. Spirals. A pyramid rising from the ice. She stumbled back, her lantern flickering. "It's real," she whispered. "It's real."

Her journal lay open, pages filled with jagged handwriting. She wrote furiously, her words incoherent. Shadows. Footsteps. Voices. A pyramid buried beneath the ice. She wrote until her hand cramped, until the lantern sputtered. Exhaustion claimed her.

Sleep dragged her under again. Corridors. Walls. Voices. The pyramid, vast and black. She woke screaming, her breath ragged. The lantern had gone out. The outpost was silent.

She lit the lantern again, her hands shaking. The frost

patterns covered the glass. She pressed her hand against the cold surface, feeling the vibration. She pulled back, whispering, "It's waiting." Her voice broke.

The radio crackled once more. A voice emerged, faint, distorted. "Sorensen…" Her name again. She leaned closer, straining to hear. The voice dissolved. She slammed the radio, frustration boiling. She screamed into the microphone, her words breaking.

The aurora pulsed, flooding the sky. The patterns burned into her vision. Triangles. Spirals. A pyramid. She stumbled back, her lantern flickering. "It's here," she whispered. Her breath ragged. Her heart pounding.

The outpost was silent, but Lena knew she was not alone. The land itself was alive, watching, waiting. The pyramid beneath the ice had awakened, and its shadow stretched across the snow. She clutched her journal, her words incoherent, her breath uneven. The vanishing light was not the end of day but the beginning of something far older, far darker.

CHAPTER 2: THE SUMMONS

The classified alert arrived in Reed's inbox at 3:17 a.m., its subject line stark and unyielding: Transmission Intercept – Yukon Outpost. He rubbed his eyes, weary from another sleepless night, and opened the file. Lena Sorensen's garbled distress signal played through the speakers, distorted by static, but the urgency in her voice was unmistakable. Reed leaned back, his jaw tightening. He had heard voices like that before —voices of men and women who had seen something they couldn't explain, voices that haunted him long after the missions ended.

The briefing room was cold, fluorescent lights buzzing overhead as Reed's superior slid a folder across the table. "Anomalous structures. Unexplained disappearances. You've seen this language before." Reed flipped through the pages, his eyes narrowing at the photographs—snowfields, aurora distortions, blurred shadows. "We've had reports going back decades," his superior continued, "but they never make it past classification. Your job is containment. Assemble a team. Proceed discreetly." Reed nodded, though skepticism lingered in his eyes. He had chased ghosts before, and ghosts had cost him dearly.

He walked out of the briefing with the weight of failure pressing against his chest. Memories of past missions surfaced —operations that ended in silence, comrades lost to anomalies no one could explain. He had sworn never to chase shadows again, but here he was, ordered to march into the wilderness after another phantom. He lit a cigarette, the smoke curling in the cold air, and muttered, "Containment. Always containment." He knew what that meant: bury the truth, silence the witnesses, erase the evidence.

Meanwhile, in a village far from Anchorage, Taq knelt beside the fire, his breath steady as Elder Anana guided him through the ceremony. The drumbeat echoed in his chest, each strike a pulse that carried him deeper into vision. He closed his eyes, and the world dissolved into light and shadow. Ravens circled above him, their wings black against a storm that churned across the sky. Beneath the ice, a pyramid rose, vast and dark, its surface etched with symbols that burned into his mind. He gasped, his body trembling, but Anana's hand steadied him.

The vision deepened, pulling him into corridors that stretched forever, walls that pulsed like flesh, voices whispering in languages no human throat could form. He tried to turn away, but the pyramid loomed larger, its shadow swallowing the horizon. A darkness spread beneath the ice, seeping into rivers, forests, and mountains. He felt the weight of generations pressing against him, the voices of ancestors warning, pleading. He opened his eyes, sweat dripping down his face, his breath ragged. "Grandmother," he whispered, "it's waking."

Anana's gaze was steady, her voice calm but grave. "The spirits have spoken. The land is restless. You must go, Taq. You must see what stirs beneath the ice." He shook his head, fear tightening his chest. "I'm not ready." But Anana placed her hand on his shoulder, her grip firm. "None of us are ready. That is why you must go." Her words carried the weight of prophecy, and Taq felt the burden settle on his shoulders.

Back in Anchorage, Reed began assembling his team. He called Mei Chen, a seismologist whose curiosity often clashed with authority. He contacted Sergeant Tom Alvarez, a survival specialist with a reputation for keeping men alive in impossible conditions. Finally, he reached out to Dr. Sarah Kalluk, an Inuit anthropologist whose knowledge of local lore was unmatched. Each agreed reluctantly, drawn by duty, curiosity, or obligation. Reed knew they were capable, but he also knew capability meant little against the unknown.

He briefed them quickly, his words clipped, his tone sharp. "We're heading north. Outpost near the Yukon. Scientist went dark. Distress signal intercepted. Classified operation. Containment priority." Mei frowned, her curiosity piqued. "Containment of what?" Reed's jaw tightened. "That's what we're going to find out." Sarah exchanged a glance with Alvarez, her eyes filled with unease. She had heard stories of the silent mountain, stories that matched the whispers in Lena's transmission.

As Reed prepared the transport, he felt the weight of secrecy pressing against him. He knew the mission was not about rescue but about control. Lena's voice haunted him, her desperation echoing in his mind. He lit another cigarette, staring at the aurora flickering above Anchorage. The lights bent unnaturally, forming shapes that mirrored the photographs in the file. He muttered to himself, "Ghosts again."

Taq packed his belongings quietly, his grandmother watching from the doorway. He carried only what was necessary—warm clothing, a drum, a pouch of herbs, and a carved raven feather. Anana handed him a small bundle wrapped in cloth. "For protection," she said. He unwrapped it, revealing a stone etched with spirals and triangles. "It belonged to your grandfather. He carried it when he faced the silent mountain." Taq nodded, his throat tight, his heart heavy.

The journey ahead was uncertain, but Taq felt the urgency

pressing against him. The vision had been clear: the pyramid was waking, and its shadow was spreading. He whispered a prayer to the spirits, asking for guidance, for strength, for courage. The wind howled outside, carrying with it whispers older than the glaciers. He stepped into the night, his path set, his destiny entwined with forces he could not yet comprehend.

Reed's team boarded the helicopter, the rotors slicing through the cold air. The city lights faded behind them, replaced by endless snowfields and forests. Reed stared out the window, his reflection fractured by the aurora. He thought of Lena, alone in the outpost, her voice breaking through static. He thought of the shadows in the photographs, the anomalies buried in classified files. He thought of failure, of ghosts, of containment.

Taq walked alone through the forest, the raven feather clutched in his hand. The aurora shimmered above him, its colors bending into shapes that mirrored his vision. Ravens circled overhead, their cries echoing through the trees. He felt the land watching him, guiding him, testing him. Each step carried him closer to the source of the disturbance, closer to the pyramid buried beneath the ice.

Reed's team landed near the Yukon, the helicopter blades scattering snow into the air. The outpost loomed in the distance, half-buried, silent. Reed felt the weight of dread pressing against him, but he masked it with authority. "Stay sharp," he ordered. "We don't know what we're walking into." Alvarez adjusted his rifle, Mei checked her instruments, Sarah whispered a prayer in her native tongue.

Taq reached the river, its surface frozen, its currents silent. He knelt, pressing his hand against the ice, feeling the vibration beneath. The pyramid's shadow pulsed through the land, resonating in his bones. He whispered to the spirits, asking for guidance, but the only answer was silence. He stood, his breath ragged, his path clear.

Reed's team approached the outpost, their footsteps crunching in the snow. The silence was absolute, broken only by the wind. Reed raised his hand, signaling them to stop. He stared at the building, its windows frosted, its walls trembling against the cold. He felt the weight of Lena's voice pressing against him, her desperation echoing in his mind.

Taq continued north, his steps steady, his resolve firm. The aurora pulsed above him, its colors bending into symbols. Ravens circled, their cries sharp, their wings black against the storm. He felt the land guiding him, pushing him toward the source. He whispered to himself, "It's waking."

Reed's team entered the outpost, their lanterns casting long shadows across the walls. The silence was suffocating, the air heavy with dread. They found Lena's notebook, frozen, filled with frantic notes and geometric patterns. Mei frowned, tracing the symbols with her finger. "These aren't random," she whispered. Sarah's eyes widened. "They're warnings." Reed clenched his jaw, his skepticism faltering.

Taq reached the edge of the forest, the horizon stretching endlessly before him. The pyramid's shadow loomed in his vision, vast and dark, its presence undeniable. He whispered a prayer, clutching the stone his grandmother had given him. The wind howled, carrying with it whispers older than the glaciers. He stepped forward, his path set, his destiny entwined with Reed's team.

The summons came to Marcus Reed not as a request but as a command, wrapped in the sterile language of classified alerts. Yet beneath the bureaucratic phrasing, he sensed something older, something that had haunted the frozen north long before governments drew borders. The intercepted transmission was garbled, but the desperation in

Lena Sorensen's voice carried through the static like a warning from the past. Reed's superior spoke of anomalies, structures, and disappearances, but the words felt hollow compared to the weight pressing against Reed's chest. He had chased shadows before, and shadows had cost him dearly.

The folder slid across the table, its photographs blurred and indistinct, yet Reed felt their gravity. Snowfields bent unnaturally, auroras twisted into symbols, shadows stretched longer than they should. "Containment," his superior repeated, the word sharp and final. Reed nodded, though he knew containment meant silence, erasure, denial. He lit a cigarette afterward, staring at the aurora flickering above Anchorage. The lights bent into spirals, triangles, glyphs. He whispered to himself, "Ghosts again."

Far from Anchorage, in a village where the river froze into silence, Taq knelt beside the fire. Elder Anana's drumbeat echoed in his chest, each strike a pulse that carried him deeper into vision. He closed his eyes, and the world dissolved into shadow and light. Ravens circled above him, their wings black against a storm that churned across the sky. Beneath the ice, a pyramid rose, vast and dark, its surface etched with symbols that burned into his mind. He gasped, trembling, but Anana's hand steadied him.

The vision deepened, pulling him into corridors that stretched forever, walls that pulsed like flesh, voices whispering in languages no human throat could form. He tried to turn away, but the pyramid loomed larger, its shadow swallowing the horizon. A darkness spread beneath the ice, seeping into rivers, forests, and mountains. He felt the weight of ancestors pressing against him, their voices warning, pleading. He opened his eyes, sweat dripping down his face, his breath ragged. "Grandmother," he whispered, "it's waking."

Anana's gaze was steady, her voice calm but grave. "The

spirits have spoken. The land is restless. You must go, Taq. You must see what stirs beneath the ice." He shook his head, fear tightening his chest. "I'm not ready." But Anana placed her hand on his shoulder, her grip firm. "None of us are ready. That is why you must go." Her words carried the weight of prophecy, and Taq felt the burden settle on his shoulders.

Back in Anchorage, Reed began assembling his team. Mei Chen, a seismologist whose curiosity often clashed with authority. Sergeant Tom Alvarez, a survival specialist hardened by impossible conditions. Dr. Sarah Kalluk, an Inuit anthropologist whose knowledge of local lore was unmatched. Each agreed reluctantly, drawn by duty, curiosity, or obligation. Reed knew they were capable, but capability meant little against the unknown.

He briefed them quickly, his words clipped, his tone sharp. "We're heading north. Outpost near the Yukon. Scientist went dark. Distress signal intercepted. Classified operation. Containment priority." Mei frowned, curiosity piqued. "Containment of what?" Reed's jaw tightened. "That's what we're going to find out." Sarah exchanged a glance with Alvarez, her eyes filled with unease. She had heard stories of the silent mountain, stories that matched Lena's transmission.

Taq packed his belongings quietly, his grandmother watching from the doorway. He carried only what was necessary—warm clothing, a drum, a pouch of herbs, and a carved raven feather. Anana handed him a small bundle wrapped in cloth. "For protection," she said. He unwrapped it, revealing a stone etched with spirals and triangles. "It belonged to your grandfather. He carried it when he faced the silent mountain." Taq nodded, his throat tight, his heart heavy.

The journey ahead was uncertain, but Taq felt urgency pressing against him. The vision had been clear: the pyramid was waking, and its shadow was spreading. He whispered a prayer to the spirits, asking for guidance, for strength, for courage. The wind howled outside, carrying whispers older than glaciers. He stepped into the night, his path set, his destiny entwined with forces he could not yet comprehend.

Reed's team boarded the helicopter, the rotors slicing through the cold air. The city lights faded behind them, replaced by endless snowfields and forests. Reed stared out the window, his reflection fractured by the aurora. He thought of Lena, alone in the outpost, her voice breaking through static. He thought of shadows in the photographs, anomalies buried in classified files. He thought of failure, of ghosts, of containment.

Taq walked alone through the forest, the raven feather clutched in his hand. The aurora shimmered above him, its colors bending into shapes that mirrored his vision. Ravens circled overhead, their cries echoing through the trees. He felt the land watching him, guiding him, testing him. Each step carried him closer to the source of the disturbance, closer to the pyramid buried beneath the ice.

Reed's team landed near the Yukon, the helicopter blades scattering snow into the air. The outpost loomed in the distance, half-buried, silent. Reed felt dread pressing against him, but he masked it with authority. "Stay sharp," he ordered. "We don't know what we're walking into." Alvarez adjusted his rifle, Mei checked her instruments, Sarah whispered a prayer in her native tongue.

Taq reached the river, its surface frozen, its currents silent. He knelt, pressing his hand against the ice, feeling vibration beneath. The pyramid's shadow pulsed through the land, resonating in his bones. He whispered to the spirits, asking for guidance, but the only answer was silence. He stood, breath ragged, path clear.

Reed's team approached the outpost, footsteps crunching in

the snow. The silence was absolute, broken only by the wind. Reed raised his hand, signaling them to stop. He stared at the building, its windows frosted, its walls trembling against the cold. He felt Lena's voice pressing against him, her desperation echoing in his mind.

Taq continued north, steps steady, resolve firm. The aurora pulsed above him, colors bending into symbols. Ravens circled, cries sharp, wings black against the storm. He felt the land guiding him, pushing him toward the source. He whispered to himself, "It's waking."

Reed's team entered the outpost, lanterns casting long shadows across the walls. The silence was suffocating, the air heavy with dread. They found Lena's notebook, frozen, filled with frantic notes and geometric patterns. Mei frowned, tracing the symbols with her finger. "These aren't random," she whispered. Sarah's eyes widened. "They're warnings." Reed clenched his jaw, skepticism faltering.

Taq reached the edge of the forest, horizon stretching endlessly before him. The pyramid's shadow loomed in his vision, vast and dark, presence undeniable. He whispered a prayer, clutching the stone his grandmother had given him. The wind howled, carrying whispers older than glaciers. He stepped forward, path set, destiny entwined with Reed's team.

The alert came through Reed's secure line at 3:00 a.m., jolting him awake before the second buzz. He sat up, rubbed his eyes, and answered with the flat tone of a man who had been through too many false alarms. The voice on the other end was clipped, urgent: "Transmission intercepted. Yukon outpost. Scientist compromised." Reed swung his legs out of bed, already reaching for his clothes. He didn't need the details yet. He knew the drill—containment, silence, control.

By the time he reached the briefing room, the file was waiting for him. His superior didn't waste time.

"Sorensen's signal. Distorted, but she got something through. Electromagnetic anomalies. Possible structure." Reed flipped through the photographs, his jaw tightening. Blurred shadows. Aurora distortions. Patterns in the snow that looked too deliberate. "We've had reports like this before," his superior said. "They never make it past classification. You know why." Reed nodded. He knew exactly why.

"Containment," the man repeated. Reed lit a cigarette, exhaling slowly. "Always containment." He hated the word. It meant burying the truth, silencing the witnesses, erasing the evidence. He had done it before, and it had cost him pieces of himself he would never get back. But orders were orders. He stubbed out the cigarette and said, "I'll need a team."

Far away, in a village where the river slept under ice, Taq knelt beside the fire. The drumbeat was steady, his grandmother's voice low and rhythmic. He closed his eyes, letting the sound carry him. The vision came fast, sharper than before. Ravens wheeled overhead, their cries piercing the storm. Beneath the ice, a pyramid rose, black and immense, its surface alive with symbols that burned into his mind. He gasped, his body trembling, but Anana's hand steadied him.

The storm in his vision grew, swallowing the horizon. Darkness spread beneath the ice, seeping into rivers, forests, mountains. He felt the weight of ancestors pressing against him, their voices urgent, insistent. He tried to turn away, but the pyramid loomed larger, its shadow stretching across the land. He opened his eyes, sweat dripping down his face. "Grandmother," he whispered, "it's waking."

Anana's gaze was steady, her voice calm but grave. "The spirits have spoken. The land is restless. You must go, Taq. You must see what stirs beneath the ice." He shook his head, fear tightening his chest. "I'm not ready." Her grip on his shoulder was firm. "None of us are ready. That is why you must go."

Back in Anchorage, Reed began making calls. Mei Chen, seismologist. Tom Alvarez, survival specialist. Sarah Kalluk, anthropologist. Each answered reluctantly, their voices carrying curiosity, duty, or unease. Reed gave them the bare minimum. "Scientist missing. Outpost compromised. We leave tonight." He didn't mention pyramids, anomalies, or shadows. Not yet.

The team gathered in the hangar, their breath fogging in the cold air. Reed's briefing was short, sharp. "We're heading north. Outpost near the Yukon. Distress signal intercepted. Classified operation. Containment priority." Mei frowned. "Containment of what?" Reed's jaw tightened. "That's what we're going to find out." Sarah's eyes flicked to Alvarez, unease written across her face. She had heard stories of the silent mountain.

Taq packed his belongings quietly. A drum. A pouch of herbs. A carved raven feather. His grandmother handed him a bundle wrapped in cloth. "For protection," she said. Inside was a stone etched with spirals and triangles. "It belonged to your grandfather. He carried it when he faced the silent mountain." Taq nodded, throat tight. He slipped it into his pack.

The helicopter lifted off, rotors slicing through the night. Anchorage fell away, replaced by endless snowfields and forests. Reed stared out the window, the aurora flickering above. The lights bent unnaturally, forming spirals, triangles, glyphs. He muttered under his breath, "Ghosts again." Mei leaned forward, eyes on her instruments. Alvarez checked his rifle. Sarah whispered a prayer.

Taq walked alone through the forest, the raven feather clutched in his hand. The aurora shimmered above him, its colors bending into shapes that mirrored his vision. Ravens circled overhead, their cries sharp, insistent. He felt the land watching him, guiding him, testing him. Each step carried him closer to the source of the disturbance.

The helicopter touched down near the Yukon, snow whipping around them. The outpost loomed in the distance, half-buried, silent. Reed felt dread pressing against him, but he masked it with authority. "Stay sharp," he ordered. Alvarez adjusted his rifle. Mei checked her instruments. Sarah whispered another prayer.

Taq reached the river, its surface frozen, its currents silent. He knelt, pressing his hand against the ice. A vibration pulsed through him, deep and resonant. The pyramid's shadow was alive beneath the surface. He whispered to the spirits, asking for guidance. The only answer was silence.

Reed's team approached the outpost, their footsteps crunching in the snow. The silence was absolute, broken only by the wind. Reed raised his hand, signaling them to stop. He stared at the building, its windows frosted, its walls trembling against the cold. He felt Lena's voice pressing against him, her desperation echoing in his mind.

Taq continued north, steps steady, resolve firm. The aurora pulsed above him, colors bending into symbols. Ravens circled, cries sharp, wings black against the storm. He whispered to himself, "It's waking." His breath fogged in the air, his heart pounding.

Reed's team entered the outpost, lanterns casting long shadows. The silence was suffocating, the air heavy with dread. They found Lena's notebook, frozen, filled with frantic notes and geometric patterns. Mei traced the symbols with her finger. "These aren't random," she whispered. Sarah's eyes widened. "They're warnings." Reed clenched his jaw.

Taq reached the edge of the forest, horizon stretching endlessly before him. The pyramid's shadow loomed in his vision, vast and dark. He whispered a prayer, clutching the stone his grandmother had given him. The wind howled, carrying whispers older than glaciers. He stepped forward, path set.

Reed closed Lena's notebook, his expression grim. "We move at first light," he said. The team exchanged uneasy glances, the weight of the unknown pressing against them. Outside, the aurora pulsed, casting the outpost in unnatural light. Shadows stretched across the snow, reaching toward the horizon.

Taq lifted his eyes to the sky, the aurora burning above him. Ravens wheeled overhead, their cries echoing through the night. He felt the land guiding him, pushing him forward. His path was clear, his destiny entwined with Reed's team. The pyramid was waking, and its shadow was spreading.

CHAPTER 3: GATHERING SHADOWS

The helicopter blades slowed to silence, leaving Reed's team standing in the snow, staring at the outpost half-buried in ice. The building loomed like a tomb, its windows frosted, its walls trembling against the cold. Reed adjusted his coat, his jaw tight, his eyes scanning the perimeter. "Stay sharp," he muttered, though the words felt hollow against the vast silence. Alvarez gripped his rifle, Mei checked her instruments, and Sarah whispered a prayer in her native tongue. The aurora pulsed overhead, casting the outpost in unnatural light.

They approached cautiously, their footsteps crunching in the snow. The silence was absolute, broken only by the wind. Reed raised his hand, signaling them to stop. He stared at the building, its door half-frozen shut, its walls scarred by frost. He felt Lena's voice pressing against him, her desperation echoing in his mind. He clenched his jaw, forcing the thought away. "Let's move," he ordered.

Inside, the air was heavy, suffocating. Their lanterns cast long shadows across the walls, illuminating frost patterns that spiraled into triangles and glyphs. Mei frowned, tracing the symbols with her finger. "These aren't random," she whispered. Sarah's eyes widened. "They're warnings." Reed shook his head, skepticism faltering. He had seen strange things before, but this felt different—older, heavier, deliberate.

They found Lena's notebook frozen on the desk, its pages filled with frantic notes and geometric patterns. Mei flipped through it, her brow furrowed. "She was documenting something... seismic anomalies, electromagnetic fields." Sarah leaned closer, her voice trembling. "These symbols... they resemble Tlingit and Haida motifs, but twisted, distorted." Alvarez shifted uneasily, his eyes scanning the shadows. "Whatever happened here, it wasn't natural."

The team moved deeper into the outpost, their lanterns flickering. Evidence of a struggle lay scattered— overturned chairs, broken glass, blood frozen into the floor. Reed's jaw tightened. "She fought something," he muttered. Alvarez crouched, examining the tracks leading out the door. "Three-toed," he said, his voice low. "Not human. Not animal." The words hung in the air, heavy and undeniable.

Outside, the tracks led into the snowfield, disappearing into the darkness. Reed stared at them, his skepticism crumbling. "We follow them," he said, though his voice lacked conviction. Mei hesitated. "Are you sure? We don't know what we're dealing with." Reed's jaw tightened. "We don't have a choice." Sarah whispered another prayer, her voice trembling.

They followed the tracks, their lanterns casting trembling light across the snow. The aurora pulsed overhead, its colors bending into spirals and triangles. Mei's instruments crackled, detecting residual electromagnetic fields. "It's strong," she whispered. "Stronger than anything I've seen." Alvarez adjusted his rifle, his eyes scanning the shadows. "We're being watched," he muttered.

Sarah knelt, tracing the symbols etched into the snow. "These aren't just warnings," she said. "They're seals. Protective glyphs. Someone tried to contain whatever's here." Reed frowned, his skepticism faltering. "Containment," he muttered, the word echoing his orders. He felt the weight of secrecy pressing against him, the burden of silence.

The tracks led them to a partially unearthed stone slab, its surface etched with glyphs that pulsed faintly in the aurora's light. Mei's eyes widened. "It's… alive," she whispered. Sarah's voice trembled. "This is ancient. Pan-cultural. Tlingit, Haida, Athabaskan… and something else. Something older." Reed stared at the slab, his jaw tight. "What the hell is this?"

Alvarez adjusted his rifle, unease written across his face. "We shouldn't be here," he muttered. Reed ignored him, stepping closer to the slab. The glyphs pulsed, resonating with the aurora. He felt the vibration beneath his skin, deep and resonant. He clenched his jaw, forcing himself to stay calm. "We need answers," he said.

Mei set up her instruments, her hands trembling. "The energy source below is massive. Far beyond anything natural." Sarah whispered another prayer, her voice trembling. "This isn't just science. This is spirit. This is myth." Reed shook his head, his skepticism faltering. "It's both," he muttered. "And it's dangerous."

The team debated, tension rising. Mei pushed for discovery, her curiosity burning. "We have to know what's down there." Reed advocated caution, his voice sharp. "We don't rush into the unknown." Alvarez muttered, "Unknown? This is madness." Sarah's voice trembled. "We need protection. We need Raven."

Sarah performed a ritual, invoking Raven as a guardian spirit. She chanted softly, her voice steady, her hands tracing symbols in the snow. The aurora pulsed, responding to her words. Reed watched, his skepticism faltering. He felt the weight of belief pressing against him, the burden of faith. He clenched his jaw, forcing himself to stay calm.

Alvarez reported strange phenomena—compasses spinning, radios emitting distorted voices, shadows moving against the wind. "We're being watched," he muttered. Reed's jaw tightened. "Stay sharp." Mei's instruments crackled, detecting stronger fields. "It's below us," she whispered. "It's waking."

The slab trembled, the glyphs pulsing brighter. Reed stepped back, his breath ragged. "We're at the point of no return," he muttered. Sarah's voice trembled. "The wound in the world. That's what the spirits call it." Mei's eyes widened. "We have to see it." Alvarez shook his head. "We shouldn't."

The team prepared to descend, their lanterns flickering. Reed's jaw tightened, his voice sharp. "We move carefully. No mistakes." Alvarez adjusted his rifle, his eyes scanning the shadows. Mei clutched her instruments, her curiosity burning. Sarah whispered another prayer, her voice trembling.

The shaft yawned open, dark and endless. The glyphs pulsed, resonating with the aurora. Reed stared into the darkness, his breath ragged. "This is it," he muttered. "No turning back." The team exchanged uneasy glances, the weight of the unknown pressing against them.

They descended slowly, their lanterns casting trembling light across the walls. The air grew colder, heavier, suffocating. Mei's instruments crackled, detecting stronger fields. Sarah whispered another prayer, her voice trembling. Alvarez muttered, "We're being watched." Reed clenched his jaw, forcing himself to stay calm.

The shaft stretched endlessly, its walls etched with glyphs that pulsed faintly. Reed felt the weight of secrecy pressing against him, the burden of silence. He clenched his jaw, forcing himself to stay calm. "We keep moving," he muttered. The team descended deeper, their lanterns flickering, their breath ragged.

The descent marked a point of no return, both physically and psychologically. Reed felt the weight of Lena's voice pressing against him, her desperation echoing in his mind. Sarah whispered another prayer, her voice trembling. Mei's curiosity burned, her eyes wide. Alvarez muttered, "We shouldn't be here." The aurora pulsed above, casting the shaft in unnatural light.

The outpost lay silent beneath the aurora, its walls half-buried in snow, its windows frosted into opaque eyes. Reed's team approached cautiously, lanterns flickering, their breath fogging in the cold air. The silence was not emptiness but presence, heavy and deliberate, as though the land itself was listening. Sarah whispered a prayer in her native tongue, invoking Raven to guide their steps. Mei frowned, her instruments trembling in her hands. Alvarez muttered, "This place isn't right." Reed clenched his jaw, forcing himself to stay calm.

Inside, the air was suffocating, thick with frost and silence. Their lanterns cast trembling light across the walls, illuminating spirals and triangles etched into the ice. Sarah's eyes widened. "These are not random," she whispered. "They are seals, protective glyphs." Mei traced the symbols with her finger, her voice trembling. "They match Lena's notes. She saw this too." Reed shook his head, skepticism faltering. He had seen strange things before, but this felt older, heavier, deliberate.

They found Lena's notebook frozen on the desk, its pages filled with frantic notes and geometric patterns. Mei flipped through it, her brow furrowed. "She documented seismic anomalies, electromagnetic fields… but look at these symbols." Sarah leaned closer, her voice grave. "They resemble Tlingit and Haida motifs, but twisted, distorted. They are warnings, Reed. Warnings from the land itself." Alvarez shifted uneasily, his eyes scanning the shadows. "Whatever happened here, it wasn't natural."

Evidence of a struggle lay scattered— overturned chairs, broken glass, blood frozen into the floor. Reed's jaw tightened. "She fought something," he muttered. Alvarez crouched, examining the tracks leading out the door. "Three-toed," he said, his voice low. "Not human. Not animal. Something else." The words hung in the air, heavy and undeniable. Sarah whispered another prayer, her voice trembling.

Outside, the tracks led into the snowfield, disappearing into the darkness. Reed stared at them, his skepticism crumbling. "We follow them," he said, though his voice lacked conviction. Mei hesitated. "Are you sure? We don't know what we're dealing with." Reed's jaw tightened. "We don't have a choice." Sarah's voice trembled. "The spirits warned of this. The silent mountain. The wound in the world."

They followed the tracks, lanterns casting trembling light across the snow. The aurora pulsed overhead, its colors bending into spirals and triangles. Mei's instruments crackled, detecting residual electromagnetic fields. "It's strong," she whispered. "Stronger than anything I've seen." Alvarez adjusted his rifle, his eyes scanning the shadows. "We're being watched," he muttered. Sarah nodded. "The land is awake."

Sarah knelt, tracing the symbols etched into the snow. "These are seals," she said. "Protective glyphs. Someone tried to contain whatever's here." Reed frowned, his skepticism faltering. "Containment," he muttered, the word echoing his orders. He felt the weight of secrecy pressing against him, the burden of silence. Mei's eyes widened. "If these are seals, then something is trapped below."

The tracks led them to a partially unearthed stone slab, its surface etched with glyphs that pulsed faintly in the aurora's light. Mei's voice trembled. "It's alive." Sarah's eyes widened. "This is ancient. Pan-cultural. Tlingit, Haida, Athabaskan… and something older. Something not human." Reed stared at the slab, his jaw tight. "What the hell is this?" Alvarez muttered, "We shouldn't be here."

The glyphs pulsed, resonating with the aurora. Reed stepped closer, feeling the vibration beneath his skin. It was deep, resonant, alive. He clenched his jaw, forcing himself to stay calm. "We need answers," he said. Mei's instruments crackled, detecting stronger fields. "The energy source below is massive. Far beyond anything natural." Sarah whispered another prayer. "This is spirit. This is myth. This is the wound in the world."

The team debated, tension rising. Mei pushed for discovery, her curiosity burning. "We have to know what's down there." Reed advocated caution, his voice sharp. "We don't rush into the unknown." Alvarez muttered, "Unknown? This is madness." Sarah's voice trembled. "We need protection. We need Raven."

Sarah performed a ritual, invoking Raven as a guardian spirit. She chanted softly, her voice steady, her hands tracing symbols in the snow. The aurora pulsed, responding to her words. Reed watched, his skepticism faltering. He felt the weight of belief pressing against him, the burden of faith. He clenched his jaw, forcing himself to stay calm.

Alvarez reported strange phenomena—compasses spinning, radios emitting distorted voices, shadows moving against the wind. "We're being watched," he muttered. Reed's jaw tightened. "Stay sharp." Mei's instruments crackled, detecting stronger fields. "It's below us," she whispered. "It's waking." Sarah's voice trembled. "The wound in the world is opening."

The slab trembled, glyphs pulsing brighter. Reed stepped

back, his breath ragged. "We're at the point of no return," he muttered. Sarah's voice trembled. "The spirits warned us. The wound must remain sealed." Mei's eyes widened. "We have to see it." Alvarez shook his head. "We shouldn't."

The team prepared to descend, lanterns flickering. Reed's jaw tightened, his voice sharp. "We move carefully. No mistakes." Alvarez adjusted his rifle, eyes scanning the shadows. Mei clutched her instruments, curiosity burning. Sarah whispered another prayer, invoking Raven again.

The shaft yawned open, dark and endless. Glyphs pulsed, resonating with the aurora. Reed stared into the darkness, his breath ragged. "This is it," he muttered. "No turning back." The team exchanged uneasy glances, the weight of the unknown pressing against them. Sarah whispered, "The wound awaits."

They descended slowly, lanterns casting trembling light across the walls. The air grew colder, heavier, suffocating. Mei's instruments crackled, detecting stronger fields. Sarah whispered another prayer, her voice trembling. Alvarez muttered, "We're being watched." Reed clenched his jaw, forcing himself to stay calm.

The shaft stretched endlessly, walls etched with glyphs that pulsed faintly. Reed felt the weight of secrecy pressing against him, the burden of silence. He clenched his jaw, forcing himself to stay calm. "We keep moving," he muttered. The team descended deeper, lanterns flickering, breath ragged. Sarah whispered, "The wound is opening."

The descent marked a point of no return, both physically and spiritually. Reed felt Lena's voice pressing against him, her desperation echoing in his mind. Sarah whispered another prayer, invoking Raven. Mei's curiosity burned, her eyes wide. Alvarez muttered, "We shouldn't be here." The aurora pulsed above, casting the shaft in unnatural light.

The glyphs pulsed brighter, resonating with the aurora. Reed felt the vibration beneath his skin, deep and resonant. He clenched his jaw, forcing himself to stay calm. "We keep moving," he muttered. The team descended deeper, lanterns flickering, breath ragged. Sarah whispered, "The wound in the world is awake."

The helicopter touched down hard, snow whipping into the air as Reed's team disembarked. The outpost loomed ahead, half-buried, silent, its windows frosted into blind eyes. Reed adjusted his coat, jaw tight, scanning the perimeter. "Stay sharp," he ordered, voice clipped. Alvarez gripped his rifle, Mei checked her instruments, Sarah whispered a prayer. The aurora pulsed overhead, casting the building in unnatural light.

They moved in formation, boots crunching against the ice. The silence was absolute, broken only by the wind. Reed raised his hand, signaling them to stop. He stared at the door, frozen shut, scarred by frost. Lena's voice echoed in his mind, her desperation pressing against him. He clenched his jaw. "Let's move."

Inside, the air was heavy, suffocating. Lanterns flickered, shadows stretched long across the walls. Frost patterns spiraled into triangles and glyphs, etched by unseen hands. Mei frowned, tracing them with her finger. "These aren't random," she whispered. Sarah's eyes widened. "They're warnings." Reed shook his head, skepticism faltering. Alvarez muttered, "This place isn't right."

Lena's notebook lay frozen on the desk, pages filled with frantic notes and geometric sketches. Mei flipped through it, brow furrowed. "Seismic anomalies. Electromagnetic fields. She was documenting something massive." Sarah leaned closer, voice grave. "These symbols... they resemble Tlingit and Haida motifs, but twisted. Distorted." Alvarez shifted uneasily. "Whatever happened here, it wasn't natural."

Evidence of a struggle littered the room—chairs overturned, glass shattered, blood frozen into the floor. Reed's jaw tightened. "She fought something," he muttered. Alvarez crouched, examining tracks leading out the door. "Three-toed," he said, voice low. "Not human. Not animal." The words hung in the air, heavy and undeniable.

Outside, the tracks stretched into the snowfield, vanishing into darkness. Reed stared at them, skepticism crumbling. "We follow," he said, though his voice lacked conviction. Mei hesitated. "Are you sure? We don't know what we're dealing with." Reed's jaw tightened. "We don't have a choice." Sarah whispered another prayer.

They followed, lanterns casting trembling light across the snow. The aurora pulsed overhead, colors bending into spirals and triangles. Mei's instruments crackled, detecting residual fields. "It's strong," she whispered. Alvarez adjusted his rifle, eyes scanning the shadows. "We're being watched," he muttered. Sarah nodded. "The land is awake."

Sarah knelt, tracing symbols etched into the snow. "These are seals," she said. "Protective glyphs. Someone tried to contain whatever's here." Reed frowned, skepticism faltering. "Containment," he muttered, the word echoing his orders. Mei's eyes widened. "If these are seals, then something is trapped below."

The tracks ended at a partially unearthed stone slab, its surface etched with glyphs pulsing faintly in the aurora's light. Mei's voice trembled. "It's alive." Sarah's eyes widened. "This is ancient. Pan-cultural. Tlingit, Haida, Athabaskan... and something older." Reed stared at the slab, jaw tight. "What the hell is this?" Alvarez muttered, "We shouldn't be here."

The glyphs pulsed brighter, resonating with the aurora.

Reed stepped closer, feeling vibration beneath his skin. It was deep, resonant, alive. He clenched his jaw, forcing himself to stay calm. "We need answers," he said. Mei's instruments crackled, detecting stronger fields. "The energy source below is massive. Far beyond anything natural." Sarah whispered, "This is spirit. This is myth."

The team debated, tension rising. Mei pushed for discovery, her curiosity burning. "We have to know what's down there." Reed advocated caution, voice sharp. "We don't rush into the unknown." Alvarez muttered, "Unknown? This is madness." Sarah's voice trembled. "We need protection. We need Raven."

Sarah performed a ritual, invoking Raven as guardian. She chanted softly, voice steady, hands tracing symbols in the snow. The aurora pulsed, responding to her words. Reed watched, skepticism faltering. He felt the weight of belief pressing against him, the burden of faith. He clenched his jaw.

Alvarez reported strange phenomena—compasses spinning, radios emitting distorted voices, shadows moving against the wind. "We're being watched," he muttered. Reed's jaw tightened. "Stay sharp." Mei's instruments crackled, detecting stronger fields. "It's below us," she whispered. "It's waking." Sarah's voice trembled. "The wound in the world is opening."

The slab trembled, glyphs pulsing brighter. Reed stepped back, breath ragged. "We're at the point of no return," he muttered. Sarah's voice trembled. "The spirits warned us. The wound must remain sealed." Mei's eyes widened. "We have to see it." Alvarez shook his head. "We shouldn't."

The team prepared to descend, lanterns flickering. Reed's jaw tightened, voice sharp. "We move carefully. No mistakes." Alvarez adjusted his rifle, eyes scanning shadows. Mei clutched her instruments, curiosity burning. Sarah whispered another prayer, invoking Raven again.

The shaft yawned open, dark and endless. Glyphs pulsed, resonating with the aurora. Reed stared into the darkness, breath ragged. "This is it," he muttered. "No turning back." The team exchanged uneasy glances, weight of the unknown pressing against them. Sarah whispered, "The wound awaits."

They descended slowly, lanterns casting trembling light across the walls. The air grew colder, heavier, suffocating. Mei's instruments crackled, detecting stronger fields. Sarah whispered another prayer, voice trembling. Alvarez muttered, "We're being watched." Reed clenched his jaw, forcing himself to stay calm.

The shaft stretched endlessly, walls etched with glyphs pulsing faintly. Reed felt secrecy pressing against him, burden of silence. He clenched his jaw. "We keep moving," he muttered. The team descended deeper, lanterns flickering, breath ragged. Sarah whispered, "The wound is opening."

The descent marked a point of no return, both physical and psychological. Reed felt Lena's voice pressing against him, her desperation echoing in his mind. Sarah whispered another prayer, invoking Raven. Mei's curiosity burned, eyes wide. Alvarez muttered, "We shouldn't be here." The aurora pulsed above, casting the shaft in unnatural light.

The glyphs pulsed brighter, resonating with the aurora. Reed felt vibration beneath his skin, deep and resonant. He clenched his jaw. "We keep moving," he muttered. The team descended deeper, lanterns flickering, breath ragged. Sarah whispered, "The wound in the world is awake."

CHAPTER 4: THE RAVEN'S WARNING

The tundra stretched endlessly before Taq, a white desert broken only by the jagged silhouettes of distant mountains. His sled dog, Nanuq, padded steadily at his side, breath steaming in the frigid air. The silence was immense, pressing against his ears, broken only by the crunch of snow beneath his boots. He pulled his fur-lined hood tighter, whispering a prayer his grandmother had taught him. The aurora shimmered above, its colors bending into spirals that mirrored his vision. He felt the land watching him, guiding him, testing him.

Ravens appeared suddenly, black wings cutting across the sky. They circled overhead, their cries sharp, insistent, unnatural. Taq frowned, unease tightening his chest. Ravens were messengers, tricksters, guardians—but these moved erratically, as though driven by something unseen. Nanuq growled softly, ears pinned back. Taq whispered, "I know," his voice trembling. The birds wheeled, then vanished into the storm.

At the river's edge, the ice cracked, and a figure emerged from the water. Taq froze, breath catching. It was a Kushtaka, the land otter man of stories told around the fire. Its eyes gleamed, its body shifting between human and animal, its voice a whisper carried by the wind. "Turn back," it hissed. "The wound is not for you." Taq clutched the raven feather his grandmother had given him, whispering a prayer. The figure dissolved into mist, leaving only ripples in the ice.

The wind rose, carrying whispers that echoed his vision. Words he could not understand pressed against his ears, filling his mind with dread. He stumbled, clutching his chest, his breath ragged. Nanuq barked, snapping him back to the present. Taq whispered, "I hear you," though he wasn't sure if he spoke to the dog, the spirits, or himself. The tundra stretched endlessly, but he felt the pyramid's shadow pressing closer.

That night, he built a fire, its flames flickering against the snow. The warmth was fragile, a small defiance against the vast cold. He laid out his drum, his herbs, his raven feather. He whispered prayers, his voice steady despite the fear pressing against him. The aurora pulsed overhead, casting the camp in shifting light. He closed his eyes, letting the rhythm of the drum carry him.

The trance came quickly, pulling him into a dreamscape of shadow and fire. He stood on a plain of ice, the black pyramid rising before him. Its surface was etched with symbols that burned into his eyes, spirals and triangles twisting endlessly. Ravens circled above, their cries echoing like thunder. The ground trembled, splitting open, revealing corridors that stretched forever. He stepped forward, his body trembling, his spirit pulled.

Ancient spirits emerged from the shadows, their forms shifting, their voices a chorus. They spoke in languages older than the mountains, words that pressed against his mind like weight. He understood without understanding: the pyramid was a wound in the world, a place where realms bled together. It was not built, but born, a scar left by forces beyond comprehension. The spirits warned him: if the wound opened fully, the land would bleed, and the world would follow.

Cosmic entities loomed beyond the spirits, vast and

incomprehensible. Their forms were geometry and shadow, their presence unbearable. Taq fell to his knees, clutching his chest, his breath ragged. He whispered prayers, his voice breaking. The entities did not answer, but their silence was worse than words. He felt small, insignificant, a speck beneath their gaze. Yet the spirits pressed him forward, urging him to stand.

He rose, trembling, his raven feather clutched tightly. The pyramid loomed larger, its shadow swallowing the horizon. He whispered, "I will go," though his voice was barely audible. The spirits nodded, their forms dissolving into light. The ravens wheeled overhead, their cries sharp, insistent. The dreamscape dissolved, pulling him back into the firelight.

Taq gasped, his body trembling, sweat dripping down his face despite the cold. Nanuq whined softly, pressing against him. He whispered, "I saw it," his voice breaking. The fire flickered, casting long shadows across the snow. He clutched the raven feather, his resolve hardening. "I will go," he whispered again, stronger this time.

The wind howled, carrying whispers older than glaciers. The aurora pulsed, casting the tundra in unnatural light. Taq felt the land watching him, guiding him, testing him. He whispered a prayer, his voice steady. "I will go." The words echoed in the silence, carried by the wind.

He packed his belongings, his movements steady despite the fear pressing against him. The drum, the herbs, the raven feather—all went into his pack. Nanuq barked softly, ready to move. Taq whispered, "We go together." The dog wagged its tail, eyes bright. The bond between them was unspoken, but unbreakable.

The tundra stretched endlessly, but Taq felt the pyramid's shadow pressing closer. Each step carried him deeper into the unknown, deeper into the wound in the world. He whispered prayers, his voice steady. The aurora pulsed overhead, casting the snow in shifting light. Ravens wheeled in the distance, their cries sharp, insistent.

He thought of his grandmother, her voice steady, her hand firm on his shoulder. "None of us are ready. That is why you must go." The words echoed in his mind, guiding him. He whispered, "I will not fail." The wind howled, carrying whispers older than glaciers. He pressed forward, his resolve firm.

The land shifted beneath his feet, the snow cracking, the ice groaning. He stumbled, but Nanuq steadied him. He whispered a prayer, his voice steady. The aurora pulsed, casting the tundra in unnatural light. He felt the pyramid's shadow pressing closer. He whispered, "I will go."

The ravens returned, circling overhead, their cries sharp, insistent. They wheeled, then vanished into the storm. Taq whispered, "I hear you." The wind howled, carrying whispers older than glaciers. He pressed forward, his resolve firm. The pyramid loomed in his vision, vast and dark.

The night deepened, the cold pressing against him. He built another fire, its flames flickering against the snow. He whispered prayers, his voice steady. The aurora pulsed, casting the camp in shifting light. He closed his eyes, letting the rhythm of the drum carry him. The dream returned, the pyramid looming, the spirits warning.

He woke gasping, his body trembling, sweat dripping down his face. Nanuq whined softly, pressing against him. He whispered, "I saw it again." The fire flickered, casting long shadows. He clutched the raven feather, his resolve hardening. "I will go," he whispered.

The tundra stretched endlessly, but Taq felt the pyramid's shadow pressing closer. Each step carried him deeper into the

47

unknown. He whispered prayers, his voice steady. The aurora pulsed overhead, casting the snow in shifting light. Ravens wheeled in the distance, their cries sharp, insistent.

He thought of the spirits' warning: the pyramid was a wound in the world. If it opened fully, the land would bleed, and the world would follow. He whispered, "I will stop it." The wind howled, carrying whispers older than glaciers. He pressed forward, his resolve firm.

The raven feather glowed faintly in the aurora's light, a talisman against the darkness. Taq clutched it tightly, his breath steady. Nanuq barked softly, ready to move. The tundra stretched endlessly, but the pyramid's shadow loomed closer. He whispered, "I will go." The words echoed in the silence, carried by the wind.

The tundra was vast and endless, a white ocean stretching beneath the aurora's shifting veil. Taq walked steadily, Nanuq padding at his side, each step a rhythm against the silence. His grandmother's words echoed in his mind: The land remembers, even when people forget. He felt the weight of those words pressing against him, guiding his path. The aurora shimmered above, bending into spirals and triangles that mirrored the visions he had seen. He whispered a prayer, his voice steady despite the fear gnawing at him.

Ravens appeared suddenly, black wings cutting across the sky. They circled overhead, their cries sharp, insistent, unnatural. Taq frowned, unease tightening his chest. Ravens were messengers, tricksters, guardians—but these moved erratically, as though driven by something unseen. Nanuq growled softly, ears pinned back. Taq whispered, "I hear you," his voice trembling. The birds wheeled, then vanished into the storm.

At the river's edge, the ice cracked, and a figure emerged from the water. Taq froze, breath catching. It was a Kushtaka, the land otter man of stories told around the fire. Its eyes gleamed, its body shifting between human and animal, its voice a whisper carried by the wind. "Turn back," it hissed. "The wound is not for you." Taq clutched the raven feather his grandmother had given him, whispering a prayer. The figure dissolved into mist, leaving only ripples in the ice.

The wind rose, carrying whispers that echoed his vision. Words he could not understand pressed against his ears, filling his mind with dread. He stumbled, clutching his chest, his breath ragged. Nanuq barked, snapping him back to the present. Taq whispered, "I hear you," though he wasn't sure if he spoke to the dog, the spirits, or himself. The tundra stretched endlessly, but he felt the pyramid's shadow pressing closer.

That night, he built a fire, its flames flickering against the snow. The warmth was fragile, a small defiance against the vast cold. He laid out his drum, his herbs, his raven feather. He whispered prayers, his voice steady despite the fear pressing against him. The aurora pulsed overhead, casting the camp in shifting light. He closed his eyes, letting the rhythm of the drum carry him.

The trance came quickly, pulling him into a dreamscape of shadow and fire. He stood on a plain of ice, the black pyramid rising before him. Its surface was etched with symbols that burned into his eyes, spirals and triangles twisting endlessly. Ravens circled above, their cries echoing like thunder. The ground trembled, splitting open, revealing corridors that stretched forever. He stepped forward, his body trembling, his spirit pulled.

Ancient spirits emerged from the shadows, their forms shifting, their voices a chorus. They spoke in languages older than the mountains, words that pressed against his mind like weight. He understood without understanding: the pyramid was a wound in the world, a place where realms bled together. It was not built, but born, a scar left by forces beyond comprehension. The spirits warned him: if the wound opened fully, the land would bleed, and the world would follow.

Cosmic entities loomed beyond the spirits, vast and incomprehensible. Their forms were geometry and shadow, their presence unbearable. Taq fell to his knees, clutching his chest, his breath ragged. He whispered prayers, his voice breaking. The entities did not answer, but their silence was worse than words. He felt small, insignificant, a speck beneath their gaze. Yet the spirits pressed him forward, urging him to stand.

He rose, trembling, his raven feather clutched tightly. The pyramid loomed larger, its shadow swallowing the horizon. He whispered, "I will go," though his voice was barely audible. The spirits nodded, their forms dissolving into light. The ravens wheeled overhead, their cries sharp, insistent. The dreamscape dissolved, pulling him back into the firelight.

Taq gasped, his body trembling, sweat dripping down his face despite the cold. Nanuq whined softly, pressing against him. He whispered, "I saw it," his voice breaking. The fire flickered, casting long shadows across the snow. He clutched the raven feather, his resolve hardening. "I will go," he whispered again, stronger this time.

The wind howled, carrying whispers older than glaciers. The aurora pulsed, casting the tundra in unnatural light. Taq felt the land watching him, guiding him, testing him. He whispered a prayer, his voice steady. "I will go." The words echoed in the silence, carried by the wind.

He packed his belongings, his movements steady despite the fear pressing against him. The drum, the herbs, the raven feather—all went into his pack. Nanuq barked softly, ready to move. Taq whispered, "We go together." The dog wagged its tail, eyes bright. The bond between them was unspoken, but unbreakable.

The tundra stretched endlessly, but Taq felt the pyramid's shadow pressing closer. Each step carried him deeper into the unknown, deeper into the wound in the world. He whispered prayers, his voice steady. The aurora pulsed overhead, casting the snow in shifting light. Ravens wheeled in the distance, their cries sharp, insistent.

He thought of his grandmother, her voice steady, her hand firm on his shoulder. "None of us are ready. That is why you must go." The words echoed in his mind, guiding him. He whispered, "I will not fail." The wind howled, carrying whispers older than glaciers. He pressed forward, his resolve firm.

The land shifted beneath his feet, the snow cracking, the ice groaning. He stumbled, but Nanuq steadied him. He whispered a prayer, his voice steady. The aurora pulsed, casting the tundra in unnatural light. He felt the pyramid's shadow pressing closer. He whispered, "I will go."

The ravens returned, circling overhead, their cries sharp, insistent. They wheeled, then vanished into the storm. Taq whispered, "I hear you." The wind howled, carrying whispers older than glaciers. He pressed forward, his resolve firm. The pyramid loomed in his vision, vast and dark.

The night deepened, the cold pressing against him. He built another fire, its flames flickering against the snow. He whispered prayers, his voice steady. The aurora pulsed, casting the camp in shifting light. He closed his eyes, letting the rhythm of the drum carry him. The dream returned, the pyramid looming, the spirits warning.

He woke gasping, his body trembling, sweat dripping down his face. Nanuq whined softly, pressing against him. He whispered, "I saw it again." The fire flickered, casting long shadows. He clutched the raven feather, his resolve hardening. "I will go," he whispered.

The tundra stretched endlessly, but Taq felt the pyramid's shadow pressing closer. Each step carried him deeper into the unknown. He whispered prayers, his voice steady. The aurora pulsed overhead, casting the snow in shifting light. Ravens wheeled in the distance, their cries sharp, insistent.

The tundra stretched out like a battlefield, endless white broken only by jagged ridges of ice. Taq moved quickly, Nanuq trotting at his side, breath steaming in the cold. The aurora pulsed overhead, casting the snow in shifting green and violet. He kept his eyes forward, but the silence pressed against him, heavy, deliberate. His grandmother's words echoed in his mind: The land is restless. You must go. He clenched the raven feather in his hand, whispering, "I will."

Ravens appeared suddenly, black wings slicing across the sky. They circled overhead, cries sharp, insistent, unnatural. Nanuq growled, ears pinned back. Taq frowned, unease tightening his chest. Ravens were messengers, guardians, tricksters—but these moved erratically, as though driven by something unseen. He whispered, "I hear you," his voice trembling. The birds wheeled, then vanished into the storm.

At the river's edge, the ice cracked. A figure rose from the water, shifting between human and animal. Taq froze, breath catching. It was a Kushtaka, the land otter man of stories told around the fire. Its eyes gleamed, its voice a whisper carried by the wind. "Turn back," it hissed. "The wound is not for you." Taq clutched the raven feather, whispering a prayer. The figure dissolved into mist, leaving only ripples in the ice.

The wind rose, carrying whispers that echoed his vision. Words pressed against his ears, filling his mind with dread. He stumbled, clutching his chest, breath ragged. Nanuq barked, snapping him back. Taq whispered, "I hear you," though he wasn't sure if he spoke to the dog, the spirits, or himself. The tundra stretched endlessly, but the pyramid's shadow pressed closer.

That night, he built a fire, its flames flickering against the snow. The warmth was fragile, a small defiance against the vast cold. He laid out his drum, herbs, raven feather. He whispered prayers, voice steady despite the fear pressing against him. The aurora pulsed overhead, casting the camp in shifting light. He closed his eyes, letting the rhythm of the drum carry him.

The trance came fast, pulling him into a dreamscape of shadow and fire. He stood on a plain of ice, the black pyramid rising before him. Its surface was etched with spirals and triangles, symbols burning into his eyes. Ravens circled above, cries echoing like thunder. The ground trembled, splitting open, revealing corridors that stretched forever. He stepped forward, body trembling, spirit pulled.

Spirits emerged from the shadows, forms shifting, voices a chorus. They spoke in languages older than the mountains, words pressing against his mind like weight. He understood without understanding: the pyramid was a wound in the world, a place where realms bled together. It was not built, but born, a scar left by forces beyond comprehension. The spirits warned him: if the wound opened fully, the land would bleed, and the world would follow.

Cosmic entities loomed beyond the spirits, vast and incomprehensible. Their forms were geometry and shadow, presence unbearable. Taq fell to his knees, clutching his chest, breath ragged. He whispered prayers, voice breaking. The entities did not answer, but their silence was worse than words. He felt small, insignificant, a speck beneath their gaze. Yet the spirits pressed him forward, urging him to stand.

He rose, trembling, raven feather clutched tightly. The pyramid loomed larger, shadow swallowing the horizon. He whispered, "I will go," though his voice was barely audible. The spirits nodded, dissolving into light. Ravens wheeled overhead, cries sharp, insistent. The dreamscape dissolved, pulling him back into the firelight.

Taq gasped, body trembling, sweat dripping down his face despite the cold. Nanuq whined softly, pressing against him. He whispered, "I saw it," voice breaking. The fire flickered, casting long shadows across the snow. He clutched the raven feather, resolve hardening. "I will go," he whispered again, stronger this time.

The wind howled, carrying whispers older than glaciers. The aurora pulsed, casting the tundra in unnatural light. Taq felt the land watching him, guiding him, testing him. He whispered a prayer, voice steady. "I will go." The words echoed in the silence, carried by the wind.

He packed his belongings, movements steady despite the fear pressing against him. Drum, herbs, raven feather—all went into his pack. Nanuq barked softly, ready to move. Taq whispered, "We go together." The dog wagged its tail, eyes bright. The bond between them was unspoken, but unbreakable.

The tundra stretched endlessly, but the pyramid's shadow pressed closer. Each step carried him deeper into the unknown, deeper into the wound in the world. He whispered prayers, voice steady. The aurora pulsed overhead, casting the snow in shifting light. Ravens wheeled in the distance, cries sharp, insistent.

He thought of his grandmother, voice steady, hand firm on his shoulder. "None of us are ready. That is why you must go." The words echoed in his mind, guiding him. He whispered, "I will not fail." The wind howled, carrying whispers older than glaciers. He pressed forward, resolve firm.

The land shifted beneath his feet, snow cracking, ice groaning. He stumbled, but Nanuq steadied him. He whispered a prayer, voice steady. The aurora pulsed, casting the tundra in unnatural light. He felt the pyramid's shadow pressing closer. He whispered, "I will go."

The ravens returned, circling overhead, cries sharp, insistent. They wheeled, then vanished into the storm. Taq whispered, "I hear you." The wind howled, carrying whispers older than glaciers. He pressed forward, resolve firm. The pyramid loomed in his vision, vast and dark.

The night deepened, cold pressing against him. He built another fire, flames flickering against the snow. He whispered prayers, voice steady. The aurora pulsed, casting the camp in shifting light. He closed his eyes, letting the rhythm of the drum carry him. The dream returned, pyramid looming, spirits warning.

He woke gasping, body trembling, sweat dripping down his face. Nanuq whined softly, pressing against him. He whispered, "I saw it again." The fire flickered, casting long shadows. He clutched the raven feather, resolve hardening. "I will go," he whispered.

The tundra stretched endlessly, but the pyramid's shadow pressed closer. Each step carried him deeper into the unknown. He whispered prayers, voice steady. The aurora pulsed overhead, casting the snow in shifting light. Ravens wheeled in the distance, cries sharp, insistent.

He thought of the spirits' warning: the pyramid was a wound in the world. If it opened fully, the land would bleed, and the world would follow. He whispered, "I will stop it." The wind howled, carrying whispers older than glaciers. He

MICHAEL JAMES

pressed forward, resolve firm.

CHAPTER 5: THE SLAB AND THE SEAL

The slab was half-buried in snow, its surface etched with glyphs that pulsed faintly in the aurora's light. Reed stood over it, jaw tight, lantern casting trembling shadows across the stone. Mei crouched beside him, instruments humming, her breath fogging in the cold. "It's alive," she whispered, her voice trembling. Sarah knelt, tracing the symbols with her fingers. "These are warnings. Tlingit, Haida, Athabaskan... but twisted, distorted. And something older." Alvarez shifted uneasily, rifle in hand. "We shouldn't be here."

The glyphs pulsed brighter, resonating with the aurora. Reed stepped closer, feeling vibration beneath his skin. It was deep, resonant, alive. He clenched his jaw, forcing himself to stay calm. "We need answers," he muttered. Mei's instruments crackled, detecting stronger fields. "The energy source below is massive. Far beyond anything natural." Sarah whispered another prayer, invoking Raven. "This is spirit. This is myth. This is the wound in the world."

The team debated, tension rising. Mei pushed for discovery, her curiosity burning. "We have to know what's down there." Reed advocated caution, voice sharp. "We don't rush into the unknown." Alvarez muttered, "Unknown? This is madness." Sarah's voice trembled. "We need protection. We need Raven." Reed clenched his jaw, torn between skepticism and belief.

Sarah performed a ritual, invoking Raven as guardian. She

chanted softly, voice steady, hands tracing symbols in the snow. The aurora pulsed, responding to her words. Reed watched, skepticism faltering. He felt the weight of belief pressing against him, the burden of faith. He clenched his jaw, forcing himself to stay calm. "Do what you need," he muttered.

Alvarez reported strange phenomena—compasses spinning, radios emitting distorted voices, shadows moving against the wind. "We're being watched," he muttered. Reed's jaw tightened. "Stay sharp." Mei's instruments crackled, detecting stronger fields. "It's below us," she whispered. "It's waking." Sarah's voice trembled. "The wound in the world is opening."

The slab trembled, glyphs pulsing brighter. Reed stepped back, breath ragged. "We're at the point of no return," he muttered. Sarah's voice trembled. "The spirits warned us. The wound must remain sealed." Mei's eyes widened. "We have to see it." Alvarez shook his head. "We shouldn't." Reed clenched his jaw, forcing himself to decide.

The team prepared to descend, lanterns flickering. Reed's voice was sharp, clipped. "We move carefully. No mistakes." Alvarez adjusted his rifle, eyes scanning shadows. Mei clutched her instruments, curiosity burning. Sarah whispered another prayer, invoking Raven again. The aurora pulsed, casting the slab in unnatural light.

The shaft yawned open, dark and endless. Glyphs pulsed, resonating with the aurora. Reed stared into the darkness, breath ragged. "This is it," he muttered. "No turning back." The team exchanged uneasy glances, weight of the unknown pressing against them. Sarah whispered, "The wound awaits."

They descended slowly, lanterns casting trembling light across the walls. The air grew colder, heavier, suffocating. Mei's instruments crackled, detecting stronger fields. Sarah whispered another prayer, voice trembling. Alvarez muttered,

"We're being watched." Reed clenched his jaw, forcing himself to stay calm.

The shaft stretched endlessly, walls etched with glyphs pulsing faintly. Reed felt secrecy pressing against him, burden of silence. He clenched his jaw. "We keep moving," he muttered. The team descended deeper, lanterns flickering, breath ragged. Sarah whispered, "The wound is opening."

The descent marked a point of no return, both physical and psychological. Reed felt Lena's voice pressing against him, her desperation echoing in his mind. Sarah whispered another prayer, invoking Raven. Mei's curiosity burned, eyes wide. Alvarez muttered, "We shouldn't be here." The aurora pulsed above, casting the shaft in unnatural light.

The glyphs pulsed brighter, resonating with the aurora. Reed felt vibration beneath his skin, deep and resonant. He clenched his jaw. "We keep moving," he muttered. The team descended deeper, lanterns flickering, breath ragged. Sarah whispered, "The wound in the world is awake."

The shaft narrowed, walls pressing closer, glyphs glowing faintly. Mei's instruments crackled, readings spiking. "It's stronger," she whispered. Alvarez muttered, "Something's down here." Reed clenched his jaw, forcing himself to stay calm. Sarah whispered another prayer, invoking Raven. The aurora pulsed, casting the shaft in unnatural light.

The team reached a landing, stone etched with spirals and triangles. Mei crouched, examining the symbols. "They're converging," she whispered. Sarah's eyes widened. "It's a seal. A barrier." Reed frowned, skepticism faltering. "A barrier against what?" Alvarez muttered, "We don't want to know."

The glyphs pulsed brighter, resonating with the aurora. Reed stepped closer, feeling vibration beneath his skin. It was deep, resonant, alive. He clenched his jaw, forcing himself to stay calm. "We keep moving," he muttered. Mei's instruments crackled, detecting stronger fields. Sarah whispered, "The wound is opening."

The descent grew steeper, walls etched with glyphs glowing faintly. Reed felt secrecy pressing against him, burden of silence. He clenched his jaw. "We keep moving," he muttered. The team descended deeper, lanterns flickering, breath ragged. Sarah whispered another prayer, invoking Raven.

The shaft opened into a vast chamber, dominated by the base of the black pyramid. Its surface absorbed all light, casting the chamber in unnatural darkness. Mei's eyes widened. "It's here," she whispered. Sarah's voice trembled. "The wound in the world." Reed clenched his jaw, breath ragged. Alvarez muttered, "We shouldn't be here."

The pyramid loomed, vast and dark, its surface etched with spirals and triangles. Mei's instruments crackled, readings spiking. "It's stronger," she whispered. Sarah whispered another prayer, invoking Raven. Reed clenched his jaw, forcing himself to stay calm. "We keep moving," he muttered.

The chamber pulsed, resonating with the aurora. Reed felt vibration beneath his skin, deep and resonant. He clenched his jaw. "We keep moving," he muttered. The team descended deeper, lanterns flickering, breath ragged. Sarah whispered, "The wound in the world is awake."

The base of the pyramid absorbed all light, casting the chamber in unnatural darkness. Reed stared at it, breath ragged. "This is it," he muttered. "No turning back." The team exchanged uneasy glances, weight of the unknown pressing against them. Sarah whispered another prayer, invoking Raven. Mei's curiosity burned, eyes wide. Alvarez muttered, "We shouldn't be here."

The slab lay half-buried in snow, its surface etched with

glyphs that pulsed faintly in the aurora's light. Reed stood over it, jaw tight, lantern casting trembling shadows across the stone. Sarah knelt, her fingers brushing the carvings, her breath catching. "These are not just symbols," she whispered. "They are seals. Protective glyphs. Warnings from the land itself." Mei crouched beside her, instruments humming, eyes wide. "The readings are off the charts. This isn't natural." Alvarez shifted uneasily, rifle in hand. "We shouldn't be here."

The glyphs pulsed brighter, resonating with the aurora. Reed stepped closer, feeling vibration beneath his skin. It was deep, resonant, alive. He clenched his jaw, forcing himself to stay calm. "We need answers," he muttered. Sarah's voice trembled. "These are pan-cultural. Tlingit, Haida, Athabaskan... but there's something older. Something not human." Mei's instruments crackled, detecting stronger fields. "It's below us," she whispered. "It's waking."

Sarah closed her eyes, whispering a prayer. "Raven warned of this. The silent mountain. The wound in the world." Reed frowned, skepticism faltering. "Containment," he muttered, the word echoing his orders. He felt the weight of secrecy pressing against him, the burden of silence. Alvarez muttered, "We don't want to know what's down there." Mei's curiosity burned, her voice sharp. "We have to see it."

The team debated, tension rising. Mei pushed for discovery, her voice urgent. "This is history. This is science. We can't turn back." Reed advocated caution, his voice clipped. "We don't rush into the unknown." Alvarez shook his head. "Unknown? This is madness." Sarah's voice trembled. "We need protection. We need Raven."

Sarah performed a ritual, invoking Raven as guardian. She chanted softly, voice steady, hands tracing symbols in the snow. The aurora pulsed, responding to her words. Reed watched, skepticism faltering. He felt the weight of belief pressing against him, the burden of faith. He clenched his jaw, forcing himself to stay calm. "Do what you need," he muttered.

Alvarez reported strange phenomena—compasses spinning, radios emitting distorted voices, shadows moving against the wind. "We're being watched," he muttered. Reed's jaw tightened. "Stay sharp." Mei's instruments crackled, detecting stronger fields. "It's below us," she whispered. "It's waking." Sarah's voice trembled. "The wound in the world is opening."

The slab trembled, glyphs pulsing brighter. Reed stepped back, breath ragged. "We're at the point of no return," he muttered. Sarah's voice trembled. "The spirits warned us. The wound must remain sealed." Mei's eyes widened. "We have to see it." Alvarez shook his head. "We shouldn't." Reed clenched his jaw, torn between skepticism and belief.

The team prepared to descend, lanterns flickering. Reed's voice was sharp, clipped. "We move carefully. No mistakes." Alvarez adjusted his rifle, eyes scanning shadows. Mei clutched her instruments, curiosity burning. Sarah whispered another prayer, invoking Raven again. The aurora pulsed, casting the slab in unnatural light.

The shaft yawned open, dark and endless. Glyphs pulsed, resonating with the aurora. Reed stared into the darkness, breath ragged. "This is it," he muttered. "No turning back." The team exchanged uneasy glances, weight of the unknown pressing against them. Sarah whispered, "The wound awaits."

They descended slowly, lanterns casting trembling light across the walls. The air grew colder, heavier, suffocating. Mei's instruments crackled, detecting stronger fields. Sarah whispered another prayer, voice trembling. Alvarez muttered, "We're being watched." Reed clenched his jaw, forcing himself to stay calm.

The shaft stretched endlessly, walls etched with glyphs pulsing faintly. Reed felt secrecy pressing against him, burden of silence. He clenched his jaw. "We keep moving," he muttered. The team descended deeper, lanterns flickering, breath ragged. Sarah whispered, "The wound is opening."

The descent marked a point of no return, both physical and spiritual. Reed felt Lena's voice pressing against him, her desperation echoing in his mind. Sarah whispered another prayer, invoking Raven. Mei's curiosity burned, eyes wide. Alvarez muttered, "We shouldn't be here." The aurora pulsed above, casting the shaft in unnatural light.

The glyphs pulsed brighter, resonating with the aurora. Reed felt vibration beneath his skin, deep and resonant. He clenched his jaw. "We keep moving," he muttered. The team descended deeper, lanterns flickering, breath ragged. Sarah whispered, "The wound in the world is awake."

The shaft narrowed, walls pressing closer, glyphs glowing faintly. Mei's instruments crackled, readings spiking. "It's stronger," she whispered. Alvarez muttered, "Something's down here." Reed clenched his jaw, forcing himself to stay calm. Sarah whispered another prayer, invoking Raven. The aurora pulsed, casting the shaft in unnatural light.

The team reached a landing, stone etched with spirals and triangles. Mei crouched, examining the symbols. "They're converging," she whispered. Sarah's eyes widened. "It's a seal. A barrier." Reed frowned, skepticism faltering. "A barrier against what?" Alvarez muttered, "We don't want to know."

The glyphs pulsed brighter, resonating with the aurora. Reed stepped closer, feeling vibration beneath his skin. It was deep, resonant, alive. He clenched his jaw, forcing himself to stay calm. "We keep moving," he muttered. Mei's instruments crackled, detecting stronger fields. Sarah whispered, "The wound is opening."

The descent grew steeper, walls etched with glyphs glowing faintly. Reed felt secrecy pressing against him, burden of silence. He clenched his jaw. "We keep moving," he muttered. The team descended deeper, lanterns flickering, breath ragged. Sarah whispered another prayer, invoking Raven.

The shaft opened into a vast chamber, dominated by the base of the black pyramid. Its surface absorbed all light, casting the chamber in unnatural darkness. Mei's eyes widened. "It's here," she whispered. Sarah's voice trembled. "The wound in the world." Reed clenched his jaw, breath ragged. Alvarez muttered, "We shouldn't be here."

The pyramid loomed, vast and dark, its surface etched with spirals and triangles. Mei's instruments crackled, readings spiking. "It's stronger," she whispered. Sarah whispered another prayer, invoking Raven. Reed clenched his jaw, forcing himself to stay calm. "We keep moving," he muttered.

The chamber pulsed, resonating with the aurora. Reed felt vibration beneath his skin, deep and resonant. He clenched his jaw. "We keep moving," he muttered. The team descended deeper, lanterns flickering, breath ragged. Sarah whispered, "The wound in the world is awake."

The base of the pyramid absorbed all light, casting the chamber in unnatural darkness. Reed stared at it, breath ragged. "This is it," he muttered. "No turning back." The team exchanged uneasy glances, weight of the unknown pressing against them. Sarah whispered another prayer, invoking Raven. Mei's curiosity burned, eyes wide. Alvarez muttered, "We shouldn't be here."

Snow whipped across the slab, the aurora pulsing overhead like a living heartbeat. Reed's lantern cut a narrow cone of light across the stone, revealing glyphs that shimmered faintly. "It's not natural," Mei said, crouching, instruments buzzing in her hands. Sarah knelt beside her, tracing the carvings. "These are warnings. Tlingit. Haida. Athabaskan. But twisted. Something older." Alvarez shifted uneasily, rifle tight against his chest. "We shouldn't be here."

The glyphs pulsed brighter, resonating with the aurora. Reed stepped closer, jaw tight, feeling vibration beneath his skin. It was deep, resonant, alive. He clenched his jaw, forcing calm. "We need answers." Mei's instruments spiked, readings climbing. "The energy source below is massive. Far beyond anything natural." Sarah whispered, "The wound in the world." Alvarez muttered, "We should walk away."

The team argued, voices sharp against the silence. Mei pushed for discovery. "We have to know what's down there." Reed snapped back. "We don't rush into the unknown." Alvarez shook his head. "Unknown? This is madness." Sarah's voice trembled. "We need protection. We need Raven." Reed clenched his jaw, torn between skepticism and belief.

Sarah began a ritual, chanting softly, hands tracing symbols in the snow. The aurora pulsed, responding to her words. Reed watched, skepticism faltering. He felt the weight of belief pressing against him, the burden of faith. He muttered, "Do what you need." Alvarez scanned the shadows, unease written across his face. Mei's instruments crackled louder.

Alvarez reported strange phenomena—compasses spinning, radios emitting distorted voices, shadows moving against the wind. "We're being watched," he said flatly. Reed's jaw tightened. "Stay sharp." Mei's readings spiked again. "It's below us. It's waking." Sarah whispered, "The wound is opening."

The slab trembled, glyphs pulsing brighter. Reed stepped back, breath ragged. "We're at the point of no return." Sarah's voice trembled. "The spirits warned us. The wound must remain sealed." Mei's eyes burned with curiosity. "We have to see it." Alvarez shook his head. "We shouldn't." Reed clenched his jaw, forcing himself to decide.

The team prepared to descend. Reed's voice was clipped, sharp. "We move carefully. No mistakes." Alvarez adjusted his rifle, eyes scanning shadows. Mei clutched her instruments, determination etched across her face. Sarah whispered another prayer, invoking Raven. The aurora pulsed, casting the slab in unnatural light.

The shaft yawned open, dark and endless. Glyphs pulsed, resonating with the aurora. Reed stared into the void, breath ragged. "This is it. No turning back." The team exchanged uneasy glances, weight of the unknown pressing against them. Sarah whispered, "The wound awaits."

They descended slowly, lanterns flickering against the walls. The air grew colder, heavier, suffocating. Mei's instruments crackled, readings spiking. Sarah whispered another prayer, voice trembling. Alvarez muttered, "We're being watched." Reed clenched his jaw, forcing calm.

The shaft stretched endlessly, walls etched with glyphs glowing faintly. Reed felt secrecy pressing against him, burden of silence. He clenched his jaw. "We keep moving." The team descended deeper, lanterns flickering, breath ragged. Sarah whispered, "The wound is opening."

The descent marked a point of no return. Reed felt Lena's voice pressing against him, her desperation echoing in his mind. Sarah whispered another prayer, invoking Raven. Mei's curiosity burned, eyes wide. Alvarez muttered, "We shouldn't be here." The aurora pulsed above, casting the shaft in unnatural light.

The glyphs pulsed brighter, resonating with the aurora. Reed felt vibration beneath his skin, deep and resonant. He clenched his jaw. "We keep moving." The team descended deeper, lanterns flickering, breath ragged. Sarah whispered, "The wound is awake."

The shaft narrowed, walls pressing closer, glyphs glowing faintly. Mei's instruments spiked, readings climbing. "It's stronger," she whispered. Alvarez muttered, "Something's down here." Reed clenched his jaw, forcing calm. Sarah whispered another prayer, invoking Raven.

The team reached a landing, stone etched with spirals and triangles. Mei crouched, examining the symbols. "They're converging," she whispered. Sarah's eyes widened. "It's a seal. A barrier." Reed frowned, skepticism faltering. "A barrier against what?" Alvarez muttered, "We don't want to know."

The glyphs pulsed brighter, resonating with the aurora. Reed stepped closer, feeling vibration beneath his skin. It was deep, resonant, alive. He clenched his jaw. "We keep moving." Mei's instruments crackled, detecting stronger fields. Sarah whispered, "The wound is opening."

The descent grew steeper, walls etched with glyphs glowing faintly. Reed felt secrecy pressing against him, burden of silence. He clenched his jaw. "We keep moving." The team descended deeper, lanterns flickering, breath ragged. Sarah whispered another prayer, invoking Raven.

The shaft opened into a vast chamber, dominated by the base of the black pyramid. Its surface absorbed all light, casting the chamber in unnatural darkness. Mei's eyes widened. "It's here." Sarah's voice trembled. "The wound in the world." Reed clenched his jaw, breath ragged. Alvarez muttered, "We shouldn't be here."

The pyramid loomed, vast and dark, its surface etched with spirals and triangles. Mei's instruments crackled, readings spiking. "It's stronger," she whispered. Sarah whispered another prayer, invoking Raven. Reed clenched his jaw, forcing calm. "We keep moving."

The chamber pulsed, resonating with the aurora. Reed felt vibration beneath his skin, deep and resonant. He clenched his jaw. "We keep moving." The team descended deeper, lanterns flickering, breath ragged. Sarah whispered, "The wound is awake."

The base of the pyramid absorbed all light, casting the chamber in unnatural darkness. Reed stared at it, breath ragged. "This is it. No turning back." The team exchanged uneasy glances, weight of the unknown pressing against them. Sarah whispered another prayer, invoking Raven. Mei's curiosity burned, eyes wide. Alvarez muttered, "We shouldn't be here."

CHAPTER 6: DESCENT INTO THE UNKNOWN

The shaft gaped before them, a wound carved into the ice, its edges lined with glyphs that pulsed faintly in the aurora's light. Reed stood at the threshold, jaw tight, lantern casting trembling shadows across the stone. "We move carefully," he said, voice clipped. Alvarez adjusted his rifle, eyes scanning the darkness. Mei's instruments hummed, readings spiking. Sarah whispered a prayer, invoking Raven. The air was heavy, suffocating, as though the land itself resisted their entry.

They descended slowly, lanterns flickering against the walls. The shaft stretched endlessly, its walls etched with spirals and triangles. Mei crouched, examining the carvings. "These aren't random," she whispered. "They're deliberate. Ritualistic." Sarah nodded, her voice trembling. "Offerings. Totems. Bones. This was a place of ceremony. And fear." Reed clenched his jaw, forcing himself to stay calm.

The architecture was impossibly precise, angles and proportions defying Euclidean geometry. The walls bent in ways that made no sense, corridors twisting into shapes that hurt the eyes. Mei frowned, adjusting her instruments. "It's… wrong. The geometry is wrong." Alvarez muttered, "Feels like the walls are moving." Reed clenched his jaw, forcing himself to stay calm. "Keep moving."

The deeper they went, the colder the air grew. Their breath fogged, lanterns flickered, shadows stretched unnaturally.

Sarah whispered another prayer, invoking Raven. Mei's instruments crackled, detecting stronger fields. "It's stronger," she whispered. Alvarez muttered, "Something's down here." Reed clenched his jaw, forcing himself to stay calm.

Hallucinations began. Reed saw Lena's face in the shadows, her voice whispering his name. Mei gasped, clutching her head. "Patterns... equations... they're everywhere." Sarah trembled, eyes wide. "Voices. Ancestors. Spirits." Alvarez muttered, "We're being watched." Reed clenched his jaw, forcing himself to stay calm. "Focus. Keep moving."

Time distorted. Minutes stretched into hours, hours collapsed into moments. Memories bled into the present, boundaries between individuals blurring. Reed saw flashes of his childhood, his father's voice echoing. Mei whispered equations, her voice trembling. Sarah spoke in tongues, words older than the mountains. Alvarez panicked, breath ragged. "Something's stalking us."

The corridors twisted, geometry bending into impossible shapes. Lanterns flickered, shadows stretched unnaturally. Mei's instruments crackled, readings spiking. "It's stronger," she whispered. Sarah whispered another prayer, invoking Raven. Alvarez muttered, "We shouldn't be here." Reed clenched his jaw, forcing himself to stay calm. "Keep moving."

They reached a chamber, vast and dark, dominated by the base of the black pyramid. Its surface absorbed all light, casting the chamber in unnatural darkness. Mei's eyes widened. "It's here," she whispered. Sarah's voice trembled. "The wound in the world." Reed clenched his jaw, breath ragged. Alvarez muttered, "We shouldn't be here."

The pyramid loomed, vast and dark, its surface etched with spirals and triangles. Mei's instruments crackled, readings spiking. "It's stronger," she whispered. Sarah whispered another prayer, invoking Raven. Reed clenched his jaw, forcing himself to stay calm. "We keep moving." Alvarez muttered, "We shouldn't."

The chamber pulsed, resonating with the aurora. Reed felt vibration beneath his skin, deep and resonant. He clenched his jaw. "We keep moving." The team descended deeper, lanterns flickering, breath ragged. Sarah whispered, "The wound is awake." Mei's curiosity burned, eyes wide. Alvarez muttered, "We shouldn't be here."

Hallucinations intensified. Reed saw Lena, her voice whispering his name. Mei gasped, clutching her head. "Patterns... equations... they're everywhere." Sarah trembled, eyes wide. "Voices. Ancestors. Spirits." Alvarez panicked, breath ragged. "Something's stalking us." Reed clenched his jaw, forcing himself to stay calm.

Time fractured. Minutes stretched, hours collapsed. Memories bled into the present. Reed saw his father, his childhood. Mei whispered equations, trembling. Sarah spoke in tongues. Alvarez panicked, breath ragged. "We're being hunted." Reed clenched his jaw, forcing himself to stay calm.

The pyramid absorbed all light, casting the chamber in unnatural darkness. Mei's instruments crackled, readings spiking. "It's stronger," she whispered. Sarah whispered another prayer, invoking Raven. Reed clenched his jaw, forcing himself to stay calm. "We keep moving." Alvarez muttered, "We shouldn't."

The chamber pulsed, resonating with the aurora. Reed felt vibration beneath his skin, deep and resonant. He clenched his jaw. "We keep moving." The team descended deeper, lanterns flickering, breath ragged. Sarah whispered, "The wound is awake." Mei's curiosity burned, eyes wide. Alvarez muttered, "We shouldn't be here."

Hallucinations consumed them. Reed saw Lena, her voice

whispering his name. Mei gasped, clutching her head. "Patterns... equations... they're everywhere." Sarah trembled, eyes wide. "Voices. Ancestors. Spirits." Alvarez panicked, breath ragged. "Something's stalking us." Reed clenched his jaw, forcing himself to stay calm.

Time dissolved. Minutes stretched, hours collapsed. Memories bled into the present. Reed saw his father, his childhood. Mei whispered equations, trembling. Sarah spoke in tongues. Alvarez panicked, breath ragged. "We're being hunted." Reed clenched his jaw, forcing himself to stay calm.

The pyramid loomed, vast and dark, its surface etched with spirals and triangles. Mei's instruments crackled, readings spiking. "It's stronger," she whispered. Sarah whispered another prayer, invoking Raven. Reed clenched his jaw, forcing himself to stay calm. "We keep moving." Alvarez muttered, "We shouldn't."

The chamber pulsed, resonating with the aurora. Reed felt vibration beneath his skin, deep and resonant. He clenched his jaw. "We keep moving." The team descended deeper, lanterns flickering, breath ragged. Sarah whispered, "The wound is awake." Mei's curiosity burned, eyes wide. Alvarez muttered, "We shouldn't be here."

Hallucinations reached their peak. Reed saw Lena, her voice whispering his name. Mei gasped, clutching her head. "Patterns... equations... they're everywhere." Sarah trembled, eyes wide. "Voices. Ancestors. Spirits." Alvarez panicked, breath ragged. "Something's stalking us." Reed clenched his jaw, forcing himself to stay calm.

The chamber stretched endlessly, dominated by the base of the black pyramid. Its surface absorbed all light, casting the chamber in unnatural darkness. Reed stared at it, breath ragged. "This is it," he muttered. "No turning back." The team exchanged uneasy glances, weight of the unknown pressing against them. Sarah whispered another prayer, invoking Raven. Mei's curiosity burned, eyes wide. Alvarez muttered, "We shouldn't be here."

The shaft yawned before them like a wound in the earth, its edges lined with glyphs that pulsed faintly in the aurora's glow. Reed stood at the threshold, jaw tight, lantern trembling in his grip. Sarah whispered a prayer, invoking Raven, her voice steady despite the fear pressing against her. Mei crouched, instruments humming, eyes wide. "The readings are impossible," she whispered. Alvarez muttered, "We shouldn't be here." The air was heavy, suffocating, as though the land itself resisted their entry.

They descended slowly, lanterns flickering against the walls. The shaft stretched endlessly, its walls etched with spirals and triangles. Sarah's eyes widened. "These are seals," she whispered. "Protective glyphs. Warnings from the ancestors." Mei traced the carvings, her voice trembling. "They match Lena's notes. She saw this too." Reed clenched his jaw, forcing himself to stay calm.

The architecture was impossibly precise, angles and proportions defying Euclidean geometry. The walls bent in ways that made no sense, corridors twisting into shapes that hurt the eyes. Sarah whispered, "This is not human work. This is older. This is myth made stone." Mei frowned, adjusting her instruments. "It's... wrong. The geometry is wrong." Alvarez muttered, "Feels like the walls are moving." Reed clenched his jaw. "Keep moving."

The deeper they went, the colder the air grew. Their breath fogged, lanterns flickered, shadows stretched unnaturally. Sarah whispered another prayer, invoking Raven. Mei's instruments crackled, detecting stronger fields. "It's stronger," she whispered. Alvarez muttered, "Something's down here." Reed clenched his jaw, forcing himself to stay calm.

Hallucinations began. Reed saw Lena's face in the shadows, her voice whispering his name. Mei gasped, clutching her head. "Patterns... equations... they're everywhere." Sarah trembled, eyes wide. "Voices. Ancestors. Spirits." Alvarez muttered, "We're being watched." Reed clenched his jaw, forcing himself to stay calm.

Time distorted. Minutes stretched into hours, hours collapsed into moments. Memories bled into the present, boundaries between individuals blurring. Reed saw flashes of his father, his childhood. Mei whispered equations, her voice trembling. Sarah spoke in tongues, words older than the mountains. Alvarez panicked, breath ragged. "Something's stalking us."

The corridors twisted, geometry bending into impossible shapes. Lanterns flickered, shadows stretched unnaturally. Sarah whispered, "This is the wound in the world. The place where realms bleed together." Mei's instruments crackled, readings spiking. "It's stronger," she whispered. Alvarez muttered, "We shouldn't be here." Reed clenched his jaw. "Keep moving."

They reached a chamber, vast and dark, dominated by the base of the black pyramid. Its surface absorbed all light, casting the chamber in unnatural darkness. Sarah's voice trembled. "The ancestors warned of this. The silent mountain. The wound in the world." Mei's eyes widened. "It's here," she whispered. Reed clenched his jaw, breath ragged. Alvarez muttered, "We shouldn't be here."

The pyramid loomed, vast and dark, its surface etched with spirals and triangles. Mei's instruments crackled, readings spiking. "It's stronger," she whispered. Sarah whispered another prayer, invoking Raven. Reed clenched his jaw, forcing himself to stay calm. "We keep moving." Alvarez muttered, "We shouldn't."

The chamber pulsed, resonating with the aurora. Reed felt vibration beneath his skin, deep and resonant. Sarah whispered, "This is the wound. The place where the land bleeds." Mei's curiosity burned, eyes wide. Alvarez muttered, "We're being hunted." Reed clenched his jaw. "We keep moving."

Hallucinations intensified. Reed saw Lena, her voice whispering his name. Mei gasped, clutching her head. "Patterns... equations... they're everywhere." Sarah trembled, eyes wide. "Voices. Ancestors. Spirits." Alvarez panicked, breath ragged. "Something's stalking us." Reed clenched his jaw, forcing himself to stay calm.

Time fractured. Minutes stretched, hours collapsed. Memories bled into the present. Reed saw his father, his childhood. Mei whispered equations, trembling. Sarah spoke in tongues. Alvarez panicked, breath ragged. "We're being hunted." Reed clenched his jaw, forcing himself to stay calm.

The pyramid absorbed all light, casting the chamber in unnatural darkness. Sarah whispered, "This is the wound. The place where realms bleed together." Mei's instruments crackled, readings spiking. "It's stronger," she whispered. Alvarez muttered, "We shouldn't be here." Reed clenched his jaw. "We keep moving."

The chamber pulsed, resonating with the aurora. Reed felt vibration beneath his skin, deep and resonant. Sarah whispered, "The ancestors warned of this. The wound must remain sealed." Mei's curiosity burned, eyes wide. Alvarez muttered, "We're being hunted." Reed clenched his jaw. "We keep moving."

Hallucinations consumed them. Reed saw Lena, her voice whispering his name. Mei gasped, clutching her head. "Patterns... equations... they're everywhere." Sarah trembled, eyes wide. "Voices. Ancestors. Spirits." Alvarez panicked, breath ragged. "Something's stalking us." Reed clenched his jaw, forcing himself to stay calm.

Time dissolved. Minutes stretched, hours collapsed. Memories bled into the present. Reed saw his father, his childhood. Mei whispered equations, trembling. Sarah spoke in tongues. Alvarez panicked, breath ragged. "We're being hunted." Reed clenched his jaw, forcing himself to stay calm.

The pyramid loomed, vast and dark, its surface etched with spirals and triangles. Sarah whispered, "This is the wound. The place where realms bleed together." Mei's instruments crackled, readings spiking. "It's stronger," she whispered. Alvarez muttered, "We shouldn't." Reed clenched his jaw. "We keep moving."

The chamber pulsed, resonating with the aurora. Reed felt vibration beneath his skin, deep and resonant. Sarah whispered, "The ancestors warned of this. The wound must remain sealed." Mei's curiosity burned, eyes wide. Alvarez muttered, "We're being hunted." Reed clenched his jaw. "We keep moving."

Hallucinations reached their peak. Reed saw Lena, her voice whispering his name. Mei gasped, clutching her head. "Patterns... equations... they're everywhere." Sarah trembled, eyes wide. "Voices. Ancestors. Spirits." Alvarez panicked, breath ragged. "Something's stalking us." Reed clenched his jaw, forcing himself to stay calm.

The shaft opened like a wound in the ice, black and endless. Reed stood at the edge, lantern trembling in his grip. "We move," he said flatly. Alvarez adjusted his rifle, jaw tight. Mei's instruments buzzed, readings spiking. Sarah whispered a prayer, invoking Raven. The aurora pulsed overhead, casting the shaft in unnatural light.

They descended, boots crunching against stone and ice. Lanterns flickered, shadows stretched unnaturally. The walls bent at impossible angles, corridors twisting into shapes that hurt the eyes. Mei frowned, adjusting her instruments. "Geometry's wrong," she whispered. Alvarez muttered, "Feels like the walls are alive." Reed clenched his jaw. "Keep moving."

The deeper they went, the colder the air grew. Their breath fogged, lanterns sputtered. Sarah whispered another prayer, voice trembling. Mei's instruments crackled louder. "It's stronger," she whispered. Alvarez scanned the darkness. "Something's down here." Reed forced calm. "Stay sharp."

Hallucinations hit fast. Reed saw Lena's face in the shadows, her voice whispering his name. Mei gasped, clutching her head. "Patterns... equations... everywhere." Sarah trembled, eyes wide. "Voices. Ancestors. Spirits." Alvarez's breath came ragged. "We're being hunted." Reed snapped, "Focus. Keep moving."

Time fractured. Minutes stretched, hours collapsed. Memories bled into the present. Reed saw his father, his childhood. Mei whispered equations, trembling. Sarah spoke in tongues, words older than the mountains. Alvarez panicked, voice sharp. "Something's stalking us." Reed clenched his jaw. "Stay together."

The corridors twisted, geometry bending into impossible shapes. Lanterns flickered, shadows stretched unnaturally. Mei's instruments spiked again. "It's stronger," she whispered. Sarah whispered, "This is the wound in the world." Alvarez muttered, "We shouldn't be here." Reed forced calm. "Keep moving."

They reached a chamber, vast and dark, dominated by the base of the black pyramid. Its surface absorbed all light, casting the chamber in unnatural darkness. Mei's eyes widened. "It's here," she whispered. Sarah's voice trembled. "The wound." Reed clenched his jaw, breath ragged. Alvarez muttered, "We shouldn't be here."

The pyramid loomed, vast and dark, its surface etched with spirals and triangles. Mei's instruments crackled, readings spiking. "It's stronger," she whispered. Sarah whispered another prayer. Reed forced calm. "We keep moving." Alvarez muttered, "We shouldn't."

The chamber pulsed, resonating with the aurora. Reed felt vibration beneath his skin, deep and resonant. Sarah whispered, "The land bleeds here." Mei's curiosity burned, eyes wide. Alvarez muttered, "We're being hunted." Reed clenched his jaw. "Stay sharp."

Hallucinations intensified. Reed saw Lena, her voice whispering his name. Mei gasped, clutching her head. "Patterns... equations... everywhere." Sarah trembled, eyes wide. "Voices. Ancestors. Spirits." Alvarez panicked, breath ragged. "Something's stalking us." Reed snapped, "Focus."

Time dissolved. Minutes stretched, hours collapsed. Memories bled into the present. Reed saw his father, his childhood. Mei whispered equations, trembling. Sarah spoke in tongues. Alvarez panicked, voice sharp. "We're being hunted." Reed clenched his jaw. "Keep moving."

The pyramid absorbed all light, casting the chamber in unnatural darkness. Mei's instruments spiked again. "It's stronger," she whispered. Sarah whispered another prayer. Alvarez muttered, "We shouldn't be here." Reed clenched his jaw. "We keep moving."

The chamber pulsed, resonating with the aurora. Reed felt vibration beneath his skin, deep and resonant. Sarah whispered, "The wound is opening." Mei's curiosity burned, eyes wide. Alvarez muttered, "We're being hunted." Reed clenched his jaw. "Stay sharp."

Hallucinations consumed them. Reed saw Lena, her voice whispering his name. Mei gasped, clutching her head. "Patterns... equations... everywhere." Sarah trembled, eyes wide. "Voices. Ancestors. Spirits." Alvarez panicked, breath ragged. "Something's stalking us." Reed clenched his jaw. "Focus."

Time fractured again. Minutes stretched, hours collapsed. Memories bled into the present. Reed saw his father, his childhood. Mei whispered equations, trembling. Sarah spoke in tongues. Alvarez panicked, voice sharp. "We're being hunted." Reed clenched his jaw. "Keep moving."

The pyramid loomed, vast and dark, its surface etched with spirals and triangles. Mei's instruments spiked again. "It's stronger," she whispered. Sarah whispered another prayer. Alvarez muttered, "We shouldn't." Reed clenched his jaw. "We keep moving."

The chamber pulsed, resonating with the aurora. Reed felt vibration beneath his skin, deep and resonant. Sarah whispered, "The wound is awake." Mei's curiosity burned, eyes wide. Alvarez muttered, "We're being hunted." Reed clenched his jaw. "Stay sharp."

Hallucinations peaked. Reed saw Lena, her voice whispering his name. Mei gasped, clutching her head. "Patterns... equations... everywhere." Sarah trembled, eyes wide. "Voices. Ancestors. Spirits." Alvarez panicked, breath ragged. "Something's stalking us." Reed clenched his jaw. "Focus."

The chamber stretched endlessly, dominated by the base of the black pyramid. Its surface absorbed all light, casting the chamber in unnatural darkness. Reed stared at it, breath ragged. "This is it," he muttered. "No turning back." The team exchanged uneasy glances, weight of the unknown pressing against them. Sarah whispered another prayer. Mei's curiosity burned. Alvarez muttered, "We shouldn't be here."

CHAPTER 7: THE PYRAMID'S HEART

The chamber opened before them, vast and silent, its walls rising into impossible heights. The black stone absorbed all light, swallowing the glow of their lanterns. Reed stood at the threshold, jaw tight, eyes scanning the darkness. Mei's instruments buzzed, readings spiking wildly. Sarah whispered a prayer, invoking Raven, her voice trembling. Alvarez muttered, "We shouldn't be here." The air was heavy, vibrating with a low hum that pressed against their ears.

The pyramid's base dominated the chamber, its surface etched with spirals and triangles that shifted when viewed from different angles. Mei crouched, eyes wide. "It's geometry beyond Euclid," she whispered. "Angles that shouldn't exist." Sarah traced the carvings, her fingers trembling. "These are mythic motifs. Thunderbird. Raven. Spirits of the land." Reed clenched his jaw, forcing himself to stay calm. "We need answers."

The altar stood at the center, surrounded by concentric rings of bones and artifacts. Skulls, carved totems, animal bones, offerings frozen in time. Sarah's voice trembled. "This was a place of ceremony. Sacrifice. Fear." Mei adjusted her instruments, readings climbing higher. "It's an energy transceiver. Harnessing currents. Cosmic forces." Alvarez muttered, "It's death. That's what it is." Reed clenched his jaw, forcing himself to stay calm.

The glyphs pulsed faintly, resonating with the aurora above. Mei frowned, adjusting her instruments. "It's alive," she whispered. Sarah's eyes widened. "The ancestors warned of this. The wound in the world." Reed clenched his jaw, forcing himself to stay calm. "We keep moving." Alvarez muttered, "We shouldn't."

They approached the altar, lanterns flickering. The bones glowed faintly, resonating with the glyphs. Sarah whispered another prayer, invoking Raven. Mei crouched, examining the artifacts. "They're converging. Symbols from different cultures. Pan-cultural. Syncretic." Reed frowned, skepticism faltering. "A convergence of myth." Alvarez muttered, "Or madness."

The air vibrated, low-frequency hum pressing against their ears. Mei gasped, clutching her head. "It's resonating with us. With our bodies." Sarah trembled, eyes wide. "Visions. Rituals. Sacrifices." Reed clenched his jaw, forcing himself to stay calm. "Focus." Alvarez muttered, "We're being hunted."

The glyphs glowed brighter, walls shifting. Reed saw Lena's face, her voice whispering his name. Mei gasped, whispering equations. "Patterns... higher order... mathematics beyond comprehension." Sarah spoke in tongues, words older than the mountains. Alvarez panicked, breath ragged. "Something's stalking us." Reed clenched his jaw. "Stay sharp."

Visions consumed them. Reed saw his childhood, his father's voice echoing. Mei glimpsed mathematical patterns, fractals spiraling endlessly. Sarah saw ancestors, spirits, rituals. Alvarez saw shadows moving against the walls, eyes watching. Reed clenched his jaw, forcing himself to stay calm. "Focus."

The altar pulsed, resonating with the aurora. Mei's instruments crackled, readings spiking. "It's stronger," she whispered. Sarah whispered another prayer, invoking Raven. Reed clenched his jaw. "We keep moving." Alvarez muttered, "We shouldn't."

The chamber vibrated, low hum pressing against their bones. Reed felt Lena's voice pressing against him, her desperation echoing. Mei gasped, clutching her head. "It's knowledge. Forbidden knowledge." Sarah trembled, eyes wide. "The ancestors warned of this." Alvarez panicked, breath ragged. "We're being hunted." Reed clenched his jaw. "Stay sharp."

The glyphs glowed brighter, walls shifting. Reed saw Lena, her voice whispering his name. Mei whispered equations, trembling. "Patterns... higher order... mathematics beyond comprehension." Sarah spoke in tongues. Alvarez panicked, voice sharp. "Something's stalking us." Reed clenched his jaw. "Focus."

Visions intensified. Reed saw his father, his childhood. Mei glimpsed fractals spiraling endlessly. Sarah saw rituals, sacrifices, spirits. Alvarez saw shadows moving, eyes watching. Reed clenched his jaw, forcing himself to stay calm. "We keep moving."

The altar pulsed, resonating with the aurora. Mei's instruments spiked again. "It's stronger," she whispered. Sarah whispered another prayer. Reed clenched his jaw. "We keep moving." Alvarez muttered, "We shouldn't."

The chamber vibrated, low hum pressing against their bones. Reed felt Lena's voice pressing against him. Mei gasped, clutching her head. "It's knowledge. Forbidden knowledge." Sarah trembled, eyes wide. "The ancestors warned of this." Alvarez panicked, breath ragged. "We're being hunted." Reed clenched his jaw. "Stay sharp."

The glyphs glowed brighter, walls shifting. Reed saw Lena,

her voice whispering his name. Mei whispered equations, trembling. "Patterns... higher order... mathematics beyond comprehension." Sarah spoke in tongues. Alvarez panicked, voice sharp. "Something's stalking us." Reed clenched his jaw. "Focus."

Visions consumed them. Reed saw his father, his childhood. Mei glimpsed fractals spiraling endlessly. Sarah saw rituals, sacrifices, spirits. Alvarez saw shadows moving, eyes watching. Reed clenched his jaw, forcing himself to stay calm. "We keep moving."

The altar pulsed, resonating with the aurora. Mei's instruments spiked again. "It's stronger," she whispered. Sarah whispered another prayer. Reed clenched his jaw. "We keep moving." Alvarez muttered, "We shouldn't."

The chamber vibrated, low hum pressing against their bones. Reed felt Lena's voice pressing against him. Mei gasped, clutching her head. "It's knowledge. Forbidden knowledge." Sarah trembled, eyes wide. "The ancestors warned of this." Alvarez panicked, breath ragged. "We're being hunted." Reed clenched his jaw. "Stay sharp."

The glyphs glowed brighter, walls shifting. Reed saw Lena, her voice whispering his name. Mei whispered equations, trembling. "Patterns... higher order... mathematics beyond comprehension." Sarah spoke in tongues. Alvarez panicked, voice sharp. "Something's stalking us." Reed clenched his jaw. "Focus."

The chamber unfolded like a vision from myth, vast and silent, its walls rising into impossible heights. The black stone absorbed all light, swallowing lantern glow and aurora shimmer alike. Reed stood at the threshold, jaw tight, his skepticism faltering in the face of something older than history. Sarah whispered a prayer, invoking Raven, her voice steady despite the dread pressing against her.

Mei's instruments buzzed, readings spiking wildly. Alvarez muttered, "This isn't a place for us." The air vibrated, heavy with presence.

The pyramid's base dominated the chamber, its surface etched with spirals and triangles that shifted when viewed from different angles. Sarah's eyes widened. "These are Thunderbird motifs. Raven. Spirits of the land. But they're twisted, merged with something else." Mei crouched, her voice trembling. "It's geometry beyond Euclid. Angles that shouldn't exist. Proportions that defy comprehension." Reed clenched his jaw, forcing himself to stay calm. "We need answers."

At the center stood an altar, surrounded by concentric rings of bones and artifacts. Skulls, carved totems, animal bones, offerings frozen in time. Sarah's voice trembled. "This was a place of ceremony. Sacrifice. Fear. The ancestors came here to bargain with forces beyond them." Mei adjusted her instruments, readings climbing higher. "It's an energy transceiver. Harnessing telluric currents. Cosmic forces." Alvarez muttered, "It's death. That's what it is."

The glyphs pulsed faintly, resonating with the aurora above. Sarah whispered another prayer, invoking Raven. "The ancestors warned of this. The wound in the world." Mei frowned, adjusting her instruments. "It's alive," she whispered. Reed clenched his jaw, forcing himself to stay calm. "We keep moving." Alvarez muttered, "We shouldn't."

They approached the altar, lanterns flickering. The bones glowed faintly, resonating with the glyphs. Sarah traced the carvings, her fingers trembling. "These are syncretic. Tlingit. Haida. Athabaskan. But fused with something older, something not human." Mei crouched, examining the artifacts. "It's convergence. Cultures merging around a single myth. A single wound." Reed frowned, skepticism faltering. "A convergence of belief."

The air vibrated, low-frequency hum pressing against their ears. Mei gasped, clutching her head. "It's resonating with us. With our bodies. With our minds." Sarah trembled, eyes wide. "Visions. Rituals. Sacrifices. The ancestors are speaking." Reed clenched his jaw, forcing himself to stay calm. "Focus." Alvarez muttered, "We're being hunted."

The glyphs glowed brighter, walls shifting. Reed saw Lena's face, her voice whispering his name. Mei gasped, whispering equations. "Patterns... higher order... mathematics beyond comprehension." Sarah spoke in tongues, words older than the mountains. Alvarez panicked, breath ragged. "Something's stalking us." Reed clenched his jaw. "Stay sharp."

Visions consumed them. Reed saw his childhood, his father's voice echoing. Mei glimpsed fractals spiraling endlessly, patterns that hinted at a higher order. Sarah saw ancestors, spirits, rituals, sacrifices. Alvarez saw shadows moving against the walls, eyes watching. Reed clenched his jaw, forcing himself to stay calm. "Focus."

The altar pulsed, resonating with the aurora. Sarah whispered, "This is the wound. The place where realms bleed together." Mei's instruments crackled, readings spiking. "It's stronger," she whispered. Alvarez muttered, "We shouldn't be here." Reed clenched his jaw. "We keep moving."

The chamber vibrated, low hum pressing against their bones. Reed felt Lena's voice pressing against him, her desperation echoing. Mei gasped, clutching her head. "It's knowledge. Forbidden knowledge. It's trying to teach us." Sarah trembled, eyes wide. "The ancestors warned of this. Knowledge comes at a cost." Alvarez panicked, breath ragged. "We're being hunted." Reed clenched his jaw. "Stay sharp."

The glyphs glowed brighter, walls shifting. Reed saw Lena, her voice whispering his name. Mei whispered equations, trembling. "Patterns... higher order... mathematics beyond comprehension." Sarah spoke in tongues, words older than the mountains. Alvarez panicked, voice sharp. "Something's stalking us." Reed clenched his jaw. "Focus."

Visions intensified. Reed saw his father, his childhood. Mei glimpsed fractals spiraling endlessly, patterns that hinted at a higher order. Sarah saw rituals, sacrifices, spirits. Alvarez saw shadows moving, eyes watching. Reed clenched his jaw, forcing himself to stay calm. "We keep moving."

The altar pulsed, resonating with the aurora. Sarah whispered, "The wound is opening." Mei's instruments spiked again. "It's stronger," she whispered. Alvarez muttered, "We shouldn't." Reed clenched his jaw. "We keep moving."

The chamber vibrated, low hum pressing against their bones. Reed felt Lena's voice pressing against him. Mei gasped, clutching her head. "It's knowledge. Forbidden knowledge. It's trying to teach us." Sarah trembled, eyes wide. "The ancestors warned of this. Knowledge comes at a cost." Alvarez panicked, breath ragged. "We're being hunted." Reed clenched his jaw. "Stay sharp."

The glyphs glowed brighter, walls shifting. Reed saw Lena, her voice whispering his name. Mei whispered equations, trembling. "Patterns... higher order... mathematics beyond comprehension." Sarah spoke in tongues. Alvarez panicked, voice sharp. "Something's stalking us." Reed clenched his jaw. "Focus."

Visions consumed them. Reed saw his father, his childhood. Mei glimpsed fractals spiraling endlessly. Sarah saw rituals, sacrifices, spirits. Alvarez saw shadows moving, eyes watching. Reed clenched his jaw, forcing himself to stay calm. "We keep moving."

The altar pulsed, resonating with the aurora. Sarah

whispered, "The wound is awake." Mei's instruments spiked again. "It's stronger," she whispered. Alvarez muttered, "We shouldn't." Reed clenched his jaw. "We keep moving."

The chamber vibrated, low hum pressing against their bones. Reed felt Lena's voice pressing against him. Mei gasped, clutching her head. "It's knowledge. Forbidden knowledge. It's trying to teach us." Sarah trembled, eyes wide. "The ancestors warned of this. Knowledge comes at a cost." Alvarez panicked, breath ragged. "We're being hunted." Reed clenched his jaw. "Stay sharp."

The chamber opened like a wound in the earth, swallowing their lantern light. Reed stepped forward, jaw tight, eyes scanning the black stone walls. "Stay sharp," he muttered. Alvarez gripped his rifle, knuckles white. Mei's instruments buzzed, readings spiking wildly. Sarah whispered a prayer, invoking Raven. The air vibrated, low and steady, pressing against their bones.

The pyramid's base loomed, vast and dark, its surface etched with spirals and triangles that shifted when viewed from different angles. Mei crouched, eyes wide. "Geometry's wrong. Angles that shouldn't exist." Sarah traced the carvings, her fingers trembling. "These are Thunderbird motifs. Raven. Spirits of the land. But twisted." Reed clenched his jaw. "We need answers."

At the center stood an altar, surrounded by rings of bones and artifacts. Skulls, carved totems, animal bones, offerings frozen in time. Sarah's voice trembled. "This was a place of sacrifice. Ceremony. Fear." Mei adjusted her instruments, readings climbing higher. "It's an energy transceiver. Harnessing currents. Cosmic forces." Alvarez muttered, "It's death. That's what it is."

The glyphs pulsed faintly, resonating with the aurora above. Mei frowned, adjusting her instruments. "It's alive," she whispered. Sarah whispered another prayer. "The ancestors warned of this. The wound in the world." Reed clenched his jaw. "We keep moving." Alvarez muttered, "We shouldn't."

They approached the altar, lanterns flickering. The bones glowed faintly, resonating with the glyphs. Sarah traced the carvings, her voice trembling. "These are syncretic. Tlingit. Haida. Athabaskan. But fused with something older." Mei crouched, examining the artifacts. "It's convergence. Cultures merging around a single myth." Reed frowned. "A convergence of belief."

The air vibrated, low hum pressing against their ears. Mei gasped, clutching her head. "It's resonating with us. With our bodies." Sarah trembled, eyes wide. "Visions. Rituals. Sacrifices." Reed clenched his jaw. "Focus." Alvarez muttered, "We're being hunted."

The glyphs glowed brighter, walls shifting. Reed saw Lena's face, her voice whispering his name. Mei gasped, whispering equations. "Patterns... higher order... mathematics beyond comprehension." Sarah spoke in tongues, words older than the mountains. Alvarez panicked, breath ragged. "Something's stalking us." Reed snapped, "Stay sharp."

Visions consumed them. Reed saw his childhood, his father's voice echoing. Mei glimpsed fractals spiraling endlessly. Sarah saw ancestors, spirits, rituals. Alvarez saw shadows moving against the walls, eyes watching. Reed clenched his jaw. "Focus."

The altar pulsed, resonating with the aurora. Mei's instruments spiked again. "It's stronger," she whispered. Sarah whispered another prayer. Reed clenched his jaw. "We keep moving." Alvarez muttered, "We shouldn't."

The chamber vibrated, low hum pressing against their bones. Reed felt Lena's voice pressing against him. Mei gasped, clutching her head. "It's knowledge. Forbidden knowledge." Sarah trembled, eyes wide. "The ancestors warned of this." Alvarez panicked, breath ragged. "We're being hunted." Reed clenched his jaw. "Stay sharp."

The glyphs glowed brighter, walls shifting. Reed saw Lena, her voice whispering his name. Mei whispered equations, trembling. "Patterns... higher order... mathematics beyond comprehension." Sarah spoke in tongues. Alvarez panicked, voice sharp. "Something's stalking us." Reed clenched his jaw. "Focus."

Visions intensified. Reed saw his father, his childhood. Mei glimpsed fractals spiraling endlessly. Sarah saw rituals, sacrifices, spirits. Alvarez saw shadows moving, eyes watching. Reed clenched his jaw. "We keep moving."

The altar pulsed, resonating with the aurora. Sarah whispered, "The wound is opening." Mei's instruments spiked again. "It's stronger," she whispered. Alvarez muttered, "We shouldn't." Reed clenched his jaw. "We keep moving."

The chamber vibrated, low hum pressing against their bones. Reed felt Lena's voice pressing against him. Mei gasped, clutching her head. "It's knowledge. Forbidden knowledge." Sarah trembled, eyes wide. "The ancestors warned of this." Alvarez panicked, breath ragged. "We're being hunted." Reed clenched his jaw. "Stay sharp."

The glyphs glowed brighter, walls shifting. Reed saw Lena, her voice whispering his name. Mei whispered equations, trembling. "Patterns... higher order... mathematics beyond comprehension." Sarah spoke in tongues. Alvarez panicked, voice sharp. "Something's stalking us." Reed clenched his jaw. "Focus."

Visions consumed them. Reed saw his father, his childhood. Mei glimpsed fractals spiraling endlessly. Sarah saw rituals, sacrifices, spirits. Alvarez saw shadows moving, eyes watching. Reed clenched his jaw. "We keep moving."

The altar pulsed, resonating with the aurora. Sarah whispered, "The wound is awake." Mei's instruments spiked again. "It's stronger," she whispered. Alvarez muttered, "We shouldn't." Reed clenched his jaw. "We keep moving."

The chamber vibrated, low hum pressing against their bones. Reed felt Lena's voice pressing against him. Mei gasped, clutching her head. "It's knowledge. Forbidden knowledge." Sarah trembled, eyes wide. "The ancestors warned of this." Alvarez panicked, breath ragged. "We're being hunted." Reed clenched his jaw. "Stay sharp."

The chamber stretched endlessly, dominated by the altar and the base of the black pyramid. Its surface absorbed all light, casting the chamber in unnatural darkness. Reed stared at it, breath ragged. "This is it," he muttered. "No turning back." The team exchanged uneasy glances, weight of the unknown pressing against them. Sarah whispered another prayer, invoking Raven. Mei's curiosity burned, eyes wide. Alvarez muttered, "We shouldn't be here."

CHAPTER 8: THE SHAMAN'S ARRIVAL

The tundra stretched endlessly, a white expanse broken only by jagged ridges of ice and the flicker of aurora above. Taq moved steadily, Nanuq padding at his side, guided by the trail of ravens that wheeled overhead. Each cry echoed like a warning, sharp and insistent, urging him forward. His grandmother's words pressed against his mind: The land is restless. You must go. He clenched the raven feather tightly, whispering a prayer. The air was heavy, vibrating with presence.

At the outskirts of the site, Taq stopped, breath fogging in the cold. The pyramid loomed in the distance, its base swallowing all light. He crouched, watching the government team from afar. Lanterns flickered, shadows stretched unnaturally. He recognized the danger they were in, the weight pressing against them. His chest tightened. "I am only one," he whispered. "But I must go."

Nanuq growled softly, ears pinned back. Ravens circled overhead, cries sharp, insistent. Taq whispered, "I hear you." He felt the spirits pressing against him, guiding him. His internal struggle deepened. He feared his presence might not be enough to counter the forces at play. Yet duty and ancestral memory compelled him forward. He whispered another prayer, his voice steady.

He built a small fire, its flames flickering against the snow.

He laid out his drum, herbs, raven feather. He whispered prayers, invoking the aid of the Kushtaka and other spirit allies. The aurora pulsed overhead, responding to his words. Nanuq lay beside him, eyes bright, ears alert. The air grew heavy, vibrating with presence.

The ritual began. Taq drummed softly, rhythm steady, voice rising in chant. The scent of burning sage filled the air, smoke curling into spirals. Ravens wheeled overhead, cries echoing. The wind carried whispers, voices older than the mountains. Taq closed his eyes, letting the rhythm carry him. The trance came quickly, pulling him into vision.

He stood in a dreamscape of shadow and fire. The pyramid loomed, vast and dark, its surface etched with spirals and triangles. Spirits emerged from the shadows, forms shifting, voices a chorus. The Kushtaka appeared, eyes gleaming, body shifting between human and animal. "We will guide you," it whispered. "But the wound is deep."

Taq trembled, clutching the raven feather. "I am only one," he whispered. The spirits pressed against him, urging him forward. "You are bridge," they said. "Between worlds. Between realms. Between science and spirit." He nodded, breath ragged. "I will go." The dreamscape dissolved, pulling him back into the firelight.

He gasped, sweat dripping down his face despite the cold. Nanuq whined softly, pressing against him. He whispered, "I saw it." The fire flickered, casting long shadows. He clutched the raven feather, resolve hardening. "I will go," he whispered again, stronger this time.

At the pyramid's edge, Sarah trembled, lantern flickering. She whispered another prayer, invoking Raven. Her vision deepened, trance pulling her into shadow. She saw Taq, standing at the outskirts, raven feather in hand. She gasped, breath ragged. "He is bridge," she whispered. "Between worlds."

Reed frowned, skepticism faltering. "What did you see?" Sarah's voice trembled. "A shaman. Athabaskan. Guided by spirits. He is coming." Mei's eyes widened. "Another presence?" Alvarez muttered, "We don't need more ghosts." Reed clenched his jaw, forcing himself to stay calm. "Stay sharp."

Taq moved closer, steps steady, resolve firm. Ravens wheeled overhead, cries sharp, insistent. Nanuq padded beside him, ears alert. He whispered prayers, invoking Raven, Kushtaka, spirits of the land. The aurora pulsed, casting the pyramid in unnatural light. He felt the weight pressing against him, but he pressed forward.

Sarah's trance deepened. She saw visions of ancestors, spirits, rituals. She saw Taq, standing at the threshold, raven feather glowing faintly. She gasped, breath ragged. "He is healer. Mediator. Bridge." Reed frowned, skepticism faltering. "We'll see." Mei whispered, "We need him." Alvarez muttered, "We don't."

Taq reached the outskirts, crouching in the snow. He watched the team, lanterns flickering, shadows stretching. He recognized their danger, the weight pressing against them. His chest tightened. "I am only one," he whispered. "But I must go." Nanuq growled softly, ears pinned back. Ravens wheeled overhead.

He built another fire, flames flickering against the snow. He whispered prayers, invoking Raven, Kushtaka, spirits of the land. The aurora pulsed, responding to his words. The air grew heavy, vibrating with presence. He closed his eyes, letting the rhythm of the drum carry him. The trance came quickly, pulling him into vision.

He saw the pyramid, vast and dark, its surface etched with spirals and triangles. Spirits emerged, forms shifting, voices a chorus. The Kushtaka appeared, eyes gleaming. "We will guide you," it whispered. "But the wound is deep." Taq trembled, clutching the raven feather. "I will go." The dreamscape dissolved.

He gasped, sweat dripping down his face. Nanuq whined softly, pressing against him. He whispered, "I saw it again." The fire flickered, casting long shadows. He clutched the raven feather, resolve hardening. "I will go," he whispered. The aurora pulsed, casting the tundra in unnatural light.

Sarah's trance deepened further. She saw Taq, standing at the threshold, raven feather glowing faintly. She gasped, breath ragged. "He is bridge. Between worlds. Between realms." Reed frowned, skepticism faltering. "We'll see." Mei whispered, "We need him." Alvarez muttered, "We don't."

Taq pressed forward, steps steady, resolve firm. Ravens wheeled overhead, cries sharp, insistent. Nanuq padded beside him, ears alert. He whispered prayers, invoking Raven, Kushtaka, spirits of the land. The aurora pulsed, casting the pyramid in unnatural light. He felt the weight pressing against him, but he pressed forward.

The team sensed his presence, unease pressing against them. Sarah whispered, "He is coming." Reed clenched his jaw, forcing himself to stay calm. Mei's curiosity burned, eyes wide. Alvarez muttered, "We don't need him." The chamber pulsed, resonating with the aurora. The wound in the world awaited.

Taq whispered, "I will go." His voice was steady, his resolve firm. Ravens wheeled overhead, cries sharp, insistent. Nanuq barked softly, ready to move. The aurora pulsed, casting the pyramid in unnatural light. The spirits pressed against him, guiding him forward. He stepped into the darkness, path set.

The tundra stretched like a living memory, vast and silent beneath the aurora's shifting veil. Taq walked steadily, Nanuq padding at his side, guided by the trail of ravens that wheeled overhead. Each cry echoed like a warning, sharp and insistent, urging him forward. His grandmother's words pressed against his mind: The land remembers, even when people forget. He clenched the raven feather tightly, whispering a prayer. The air vibrated with presence, as though the ancestors themselves walked beside him.

At the outskirts of the site, Taq stopped, breath fogging in the cold. The pyramid loomed in the distance, its base swallowing all light. He crouched, watching the government team from afar. Lanterns flickered, shadows stretched unnaturally. He recognized the danger pressing against them, the wound in the world opening beneath their feet. His chest tightened. "I am only one," he whispered. "But I must go."

Nanuq growled softly, ears pinned back. Ravens circled overhead, cries sharp, insistent. Taq whispered, "I hear you." He felt the spirits pressing against him, guiding him. His internal struggle deepened. He feared his presence might not be enough to counter the forces at play. Yet duty and ancestral memory compelled him forward. He whispered another prayer, his voice steady.

He built a small fire, its flames flickering against the snow. He laid out his drum, herbs, raven feather. He whispered prayers, invoking the aid of the Kushtaka and other spirit allies. The aurora pulsed overhead, responding to his words. Nanuq lay beside him, eyes bright, ears alert. The air grew heavy, vibrating with presence.

The ritual began. Taq drummed softly, rhythm steady, voice rising in chant. The scent of burning sage filled the air, smoke curling into spirals. Ravens wheeled overhead, cries echoing. The wind carried whispers, voices older than the mountains. Taq closed his eyes, letting the rhythm carry him. The trance came quickly, pulling him into vision.

He stood in a dreamscape of shadow and fire. The pyramid loomed, vast and dark, its surface etched with spirals and triangles. Spirits emerged from the shadows, forms shifting, voices a chorus. The Kushtaka appeared, eyes gleaming, body shifting between human and animal. "We will guide you," it whispered. "But the wound is deep."

Taq trembled, clutching the raven feather. "I am only one," he whispered. The spirits pressed against him, urging him forward. "You are bridge," they said. "Between worlds. Between realms. Between science and spirit." He nodded, breath ragged. "I will go." The dreamscape dissolved, pulling him back into the firelight.

He gasped, sweat dripping down his face despite the cold. Nanuq whined softly, pressing against him. He whispered, "I saw it." The fire flickered, casting long shadows. He clutched the raven feather, resolve hardening. "I will go," he whispered again, stronger this time.

At the pyramid's edge, Sarah trembled, lantern flickering. She whispered another prayer, invoking Raven. Her vision deepened, trance pulling her into shadow. She saw Taq, standing at the outskirts, raven feather in hand. She gasped, breath ragged. "He is bridge," she whispered. "Between worlds."

Reed frowned, skepticism faltering. "What did you see?" Sarah's voice trembled. "A shaman. Athabaskan. Guided by spirits. He is coming." Mei's eyes widened. "Another presence?" Alvarez muttered, "We don't need more ghosts." Reed clenched his jaw, forcing himself to stay calm. "Stay sharp."

Taq moved closer, steps steady, resolve firm. Ravens wheeled overhead, cries sharp, insistent. Nanuq padded beside him, ears alert. He whispered prayers, invoking Raven, Kushtaka, spirits of the land. The aurora pulsed, casting the pyramid in unnatural light. He felt the weight pressing against him, but he pressed forward.

Sarah's trance deepened. She saw visions of ancestors, spirits, rituals. She saw Taq, standing at the threshold, raven feather glowing faintly. She gasped, breath ragged. "He is healer. Mediator. Bridge." Reed frowned, skepticism faltering. "We'll see." Mei whispered, "We need him." Alvarez muttered, "We don't."

Taq reached the outskirts, crouching in the snow. He watched the team, lanterns flickering, shadows stretching. He recognized their danger, the wound pressing against them. His chest tightened. "I am only one," he whispered. "But I must go." Nanuq growled softly, ears pinned back. Ravens wheeled overhead.

He built another fire, flames flickering against the snow. He whispered prayers, invoking Raven, Kushtaka, spirits of the land. The aurora pulsed, responding to his words. The air grew heavy, vibrating with presence. He closed his eyes, letting the rhythm of the drum carry him. The trance came quickly, pulling him into vision.

He saw the pyramid, vast and dark, its surface etched with spirals and triangles. Spirits emerged, forms shifting, voices a chorus. The Kushtaka appeared, eyes gleaming. "We will guide you," it whispered. "But the wound is deep." Taq trembled, clutching the raven feather. "I will go." The dreamscape dissolved.

He gasped, sweat dripping down his face. Nanuq whined softly, pressing against him. He whispered, "I saw it again." The fire flickered, casting long shadows. He clutched the raven feather, resolve hardening. "I will go," he whispered. The aurora pulsed, casting the tundra in unnatural light.

Sarah's trance deepened further. She saw Taq, standing

at the threshold, raven feather glowing faintly. She gasped, breath ragged. "He is bridge. Between worlds. Between realms." Reed frowned, skepticism faltering. "We'll see." Mei whispered, "We need him." Alvarez muttered, "We don't."

Taq pressed forward, steps steady, resolve firm. Ravens wheeled overhead, cries sharp, insistent. Nanuq padded beside him, ears alert. He whispered prayers, invoking Raven, Kushtaka, spirits of the land. The aurora pulsed, casting the pyramid in unnatural light. He felt the weight pressing against him, but he pressed forward.

The team sensed his presence, unease pressing against them. Sarah whispered, "He is coming." Reed clenched his jaw, forcing himself to stay calm. Mei's curiosity burned, eyes wide. Alvarez muttered, "We don't need him." The chamber pulsed, resonating with the aurora. The wound in the world awaited.

The tundra was alive with movement—ravens wheeling overhead, their cries sharp, insistent. Taq moved quickly, Nanuq trotting at his side, breath steaming in the cold. His eyes locked on the pyramid, its base swallowing all light. He whispered, "I am only one. But I must go." The aurora pulsed, casting the snow in unnatural light.

At the outskirts, Taq crouched low, watching the government team from a distance. Lanterns flickered, shadows stretched unnaturally. He saw Reed's jaw tight, Alvarez's rifle clenched, Mei's instruments buzzing, Sarah whispering prayers. He recognized their danger, the wound pressing against them. His chest tightened. "They don't see it," he whispered. "But I do."

Nanuq growled softly, ears pinned back. Ravens circled overhead, cries echoing like alarms. Taq whispered, "I hear you." He felt the spirits pressing against him, guiding him forward. His internal struggle deepened. He feared his presence might not be enough. Yet duty and ancestral memory compelled him. He clenched the raven feather tightly.

He built a fire, flames flickering against the snow. He laid out his drum, herbs, raven feather. He whispered prayers, invoking Raven, Kushtaka, spirits of the land. The aurora pulsed, responding to his words. Nanuq lay beside him, eyes bright, ears alert. The air grew heavy, vibrating with presence.

The ritual began. Taq drummed softly, rhythm steady, voice rising in chant. Smoke curled into spirals, carried by the wind. Ravens wheeled overhead, cries echoing. The trance came quickly, pulling him into vision. He saw the pyramid, vast and dark, its surface etched with spirals and triangles. Spirits emerged, forms shifting, voices a chorus.

The Kushtaka appeared, eyes gleaming, body shifting between human and animal. "We will guide you," it whispered. "But the wound is deep." Taq trembled, clutching the raven feather. "I am only one," he whispered. The spirits pressed against him, urging him forward. "You are bridge," they said. "Between worlds. Between realms." He nodded. "I will go."

He gasped, sweat dripping down his face despite the cold. Nanuq whined softly, pressing against him. He whispered, "I saw it." The fire flickered, casting long shadows. He clutched the raven feather, resolve hardening. "I will go," he whispered again, stronger this time.

Inside the pyramid, Sarah trembled, lantern flickering. She whispered another prayer, invoking Raven. Her trance deepened, pulling her into shadow. She saw Taq, standing at the outskirts, raven feather glowing faintly. She gasped, breath ragged. "He is bridge," she whispered. "Between worlds."

Reed frowned, skepticism faltering. "What did you see?" Sarah's voice trembled. "A shaman. Athabaskan. Guided by spirits. He is coming." Mei's eyes widened. "Another presence?" Alvarez muttered, "We don't need more ghosts." Reed clenched his jaw. "Stay sharp."

Taq moved closer, steps steady, resolve firm. Ravens wheeled overhead, cries sharp, insistent. Nanuq padded beside him, ears alert. He whispered prayers, invoking Raven, Kushtaka, spirits of the land. The aurora pulsed, casting the pyramid in unnatural light. He pressed forward.

Sarah's trance deepened further. She saw visions of ancestors, spirits, rituals. She saw Taq, standing at the threshold, raven feather glowing faintly. She gasped, breath ragged. "He is healer. Mediator. Bridge." Reed frowned. "We'll see." Mei whispered, "We need him." Alvarez muttered, "We don't."

Taq crouched again, watching the team. Lanterns flickered, shadows stretched. He recognized their danger, the wound pressing against them. His chest tightened. "I am only one," he whispered. "But I must go." Nanuq growled softly, ears pinned back. Ravens wheeled overhead.

He built another fire, flames flickering against the snow. He whispered prayers, invoking Raven, Kushtaka, spirits of the land. The aurora pulsed, responding to his words. The air grew heavy, vibrating with presence. He closed his eyes, letting the rhythm of the drum carry him. The trance came quickly, pulling him into vision.

He saw the pyramid, vast and dark, its surface etched with spirals and triangles. Spirits emerged, forms shifting, voices a chorus. The Kushtaka appeared, eyes gleaming. "We will guide you," it whispered. "But the wound is deep." Taq trembled, clutching the raven feather. "I will go." The dreamscape dissolved.

He gasped, sweat dripping down his face. Nanuq whined softly, pressing against him. He whispered, "I saw it again." The fire flickered, casting long shadows. He clutched the raven feather, resolve hardening. "I will go," he whispered. The aurora pulsed, casting the tundra in unnatural light.

Sarah's trance deepened further. She saw Taq, standing at the threshold, raven feather glowing faintly. She gasped, breath ragged. "He is bridge. Between worlds. Between realms." Reed frowned. "We'll see." Mei whispered, "We need him." Alvarez muttered, "We don't."

Taq pressed forward, steps steady, resolve firm. Ravens wheeled overhead, cries sharp, insistent. Nanuq padded beside him, ears alert. He whispered prayers, invoking Raven, Kushtaka, spirits of the land. The aurora pulsed, casting the pyramid in unnatural light. He pressed forward.

The team sensed his presence, unease pressing against them. Sarah whispered, "He is coming." Reed clenched his jaw. Mei's curiosity burned, eyes wide. Alvarez muttered, "We don't need him." The chamber pulsed, resonating with the aurora. The wound in the world awaited.

CHAPTER 9: THE FIRST SACRIFICE

The chamber was silent except for the low hum vibrating through the stone. Reed stood rigid, lantern trembling in his grip. Mei crouched near the altar, instruments buzzing, eyes wide with fascination. Sarah whispered prayers, her voice steady but strained. Alvarez paced, rifle clutched tight, eyes darting into the shadows. The pyramid loomed above them, its surface swallowing all light.

Alvarez muttered, "We shouldn't be here." His voice was sharp, ragged. Reed snapped, "Stay focused." Mei whispered, "The readings are incredible. This is knowledge beyond anything we've seen." Sarah trembled, whispering another prayer. Alvarez shook his head, breath ragged. "Something's watching us." Reed clenched his jaw. "Stay sharp."

The shadows shifted, moving against the lantern light. Alvarez froze, rifle raised. "There," he hissed. Reed turned, eyes scanning the darkness. Nothing. Mei frowned, adjusting her instruments. "No movement. Just interference." Sarah whispered, "It's spirits." Alvarez's breath came ragged. "It's hunting us."

He broke formation, moving into the shadows. Reed snapped, "Alvarez! Hold position!" Alvarez ignored him, rifle raised, eyes wild. Mei gasped, "Don't go alone!" Sarah whispered, "He's already gone." Reed clenched his jaw, forcing himself to stay calm. "Stay together."

Alvarez moved deeper into the darkness, lantern flickering. The walls bent unnaturally, shadows stretching. He muttered, "I see you." His voice trembled. The hum grew louder, pressing against his ears. He stumbled, breath ragged. "I see you."

The entity emerged, shifting between animal and human forms. Its body was shadow, its eyes gleaming. It whispered, voice distorted, echoing. Alvarez froze, breath catching. "What are you?" The entity shifted, form twisting, Kushtaka and something older. Alvarez raised his rifle, hands trembling.

The entity moved closer, shadows stretching. Alvarez fired, the shot echoing through the chamber. The bullet vanished into darkness, swallowed whole. The entity whispered, voice sharp. "Sacrifice." Alvarez stumbled back, breath ragged. "No." The shadows closed in.

The team heard the shot, echoing through the chamber. Reed snapped, "Alvarez!" Mei gasped, clutching her instruments. "He's gone too far." Sarah whispered, "The spirits have taken him." Reed clenched his jaw, forcing himself to stay calm. "We move."

They followed the sound, lanterns flickering. The shadows stretched unnaturally, walls bending. Mei whispered, "The geometry is shifting." Sarah trembled, whispering another prayer. Reed clenched his jaw. "Stay sharp." Alvarez's voice echoed faintly, distorted. "Help me."

They found his gear scattered on the ground. Rifle, lantern, pack. Blood smeared across the stone, trailing into darkness. Mei gasped, breath ragged. "He's gone." Sarah whispered, "Sacrifice." Reed clenched his jaw, forcing himself to stay calm. "We keep moving."

The shadows shifted, moving against the lantern light. Sarah whispered, "The wound demands blood." Mei trembled, clutching her instruments. "It's feeding." Reed clenched his jaw. "We don't stop." Alvarez's voice echoed faintly, distorted. "Help me."

Visions consumed them. Reed saw Lena, her voice whispering his name. Mei gasped, whispering equations. "Patterns... higher order... mathematics beyond comprehension." Sarah spoke in tongues, words older than the mountains. Alvarez's voice echoed, distorted. "Sacrifice." Reed clenched his jaw. "Stay sharp."

The altar pulsed, resonating with the aurora. Mei's instruments spiked again. "It's stronger," she whispered. Sarah whispered another prayer. Reed clenched his jaw. "We keep moving." Alvarez's voice echoed faintly, distorted. "Help me."

The chamber vibrated, low hum pressing against their bones. Reed felt Lena's voice pressing against him. Mei gasped, clutching her head. "It's knowledge. Forbidden knowledge." Sarah trembled, eyes wide. "The ancestors warned of this." Alvarez's voice echoed, distorted. "Sacrifice." Reed clenched his jaw. "Stay sharp."

The glyphs glowed brighter, walls shifting. Reed saw Lena, her voice whispering his name. Mei whispered equations, trembling. "Patterns... higher order... mathematics beyond comprehension." Sarah spoke in tongues. Alvarez's voice echoed, distorted. "Help me." Reed clenched his jaw. "Focus."

Visions intensified. Reed saw his father, his childhood. Mei glimpsed fractals spiraling endlessly. Sarah saw rituals, sacrifices, spirits. Alvarez's voice echoed, distorted. "Sacrifice." Reed clenched his jaw. "We keep moving."

The altar pulsed, resonating with the aurora. Sarah whispered, "The wound is awake." Mei's instruments spiked again. "It's stronger," she whispered. Alvarez's voice echoed faintly, distorted. "Help me." Reed clenched his jaw. "We keep moving."

The chamber vibrated, low hum pressing against their bones. Reed felt Lena's voice pressing against him. Mei gasped, clutching her head. "It's knowledge. Forbidden knowledge." Sarah trembled, eyes wide. "The ancestors warned of this." Alvarez's voice echoed, distorted. "Sacrifice." Reed clenched his jaw. "Stay sharp."

The chamber was vast, its walls etched with glyphs that pulsed faintly in rhythm with the aurora above. Reed stood rigid, lantern trembling in his grip, his skepticism eroding under the weight of myth made stone. Mei crouched near the altar, instruments buzzing, eyes wide with fascination. Sarah whispered prayers, invoking Raven, her voice steady but strained. Alvarez paced, rifle clutched tight, eyes darting into the shadows. The pyramid loomed, swallowing all light, its presence oppressive.

Alvarez muttered, "We shouldn't be here." His voice was sharp, ragged, echoing against the stone. Reed snapped, "Stay focused." Mei whispered, "The readings are incredible. This is knowledge beyond anything we've seen." Sarah trembled, whispering another prayer. Alvarez shook his head, breath ragged. "Something's watching us." Reed clenched his jaw, forcing calm.

The shadows shifted, moving against the lantern light. Alvarez froze, rifle raised. "There," he hissed. Reed turned, eyes scanning the darkness. Nothing. Mei frowned, adjusting her instruments. "No movement. Just interference." Sarah whispered, "It's spirits. The ancestors are restless." Alvarez's breath came ragged. "It's hunting us."

He broke formation, moving into the shadows. Reed snapped, "Alvarez! Hold position!" Alvarez ignored him, rifle raised, eyes wild. Mei gasped, "Don't go alone!" Sarah whispered, "He's already chosen." Reed clenched his jaw, forcing himself to stay calm. "Stay together."

Alvarez moved deeper into the darkness, lantern flickering. The walls bent unnaturally, glyphs glowing faintly. He muttered, "I see you." His voice trembled. The hum grew louder, pressing against his ears. He stumbled, breath ragged. "I see you."

The entity emerged, shifting between animal and human forms. Its body was shadow, its eyes gleaming. It whispered, voice distorted, echoing. Alvarez froze, breath catching. "What are you?" The entity shifted, form twisting, Kushtaka and something older. Alvarez raised his rifle, hands trembling.

The entity moved closer, shadows stretching. Alvarez fired, the shot echoing through the chamber. The bullet vanished into darkness, swallowed whole. The entity whispered, voice sharp. "Sacrifice." Alvarez stumbled back, breath ragged. "No." The shadows closed in, pressing against him.

The team heard the shot, echoing through the chamber. Reed snapped, "Alvarez!" Mei gasped, clutching her instruments. "He's gone too far." Sarah whispered, "The spirits have taken him." Reed clenched his jaw, forcing himself to stay calm. "We move."

They followed the sound, lanterns flickering. The shadows stretched unnaturally, walls bending. Mei whispered, "The geometry is shifting." Sarah trembled, whispering another prayer. Reed clenched his jaw. "Stay sharp." Alvarez's voice echoed faintly, distorted. "Help me."

They found his gear scattered on the ground. Rifle, lantern, pack. Blood smeared across the stone, trailing into darkness. Mei gasped, breath ragged. "He's gone." Sarah whispered, "Sacrifice. The wound demanded blood." Reed clenched his jaw, forcing himself to stay calm. "We keep moving."

The shadows shifted, moving against the lantern light. Sarah whispered, "The ancestors warned of this. The wound must be fed." Mei trembled, clutching her instruments. "It's feeding." Reed clenched his jaw. "We don't stop." Alvarez's voice echoed faintly, distorted. "Help me."

Visions consumed them. Reed saw Lena, her voice whispering his name. Mei gasped, whispering equations. "Patterns... higher order... mathematics beyond comprehension." Sarah spoke in tongues, words older than the mountains. Alvarez's voice echoed, distorted. "Sacrifice." Reed clenched his jaw. "Stay sharp."

The altar pulsed, resonating with the aurora. Mei's instruments spiked again. "It's stronger," she whispered. Sarah whispered another prayer. Reed clenched his jaw. "We keep moving." Alvarez's voice echoed faintly, distorted. "Help me."

The chamber vibrated, low hum pressing against their bones. Reed felt Lena's voice pressing against him. Mei gasped, clutching her head. "It's knowledge. Forbidden knowledge." Sarah trembled, eyes wide. "The ancestors warned of this. Sacrifice is the price." Alvarez's voice echoed, distorted. "Sacrifice." Reed clenched his jaw. "Stay sharp."

The glyphs glowed brighter, walls shifting. Reed saw Lena, her voice whispering his name. Mei whispered equations, trembling. "Patterns... higher order... mathematics beyond comprehension." Sarah spoke in tongues. Alvarez's voice echoed, distorted. "Help me." Reed clenched his jaw. "Focus."

Visions intensified. Reed saw his father, his childhood. Mei glimpsed fractals spiraling endlessly. Sarah saw rituals, sacrifices, spirits. Alvarez's voice echoed, distorted. "Sacrifice." Reed clenched his jaw. "We keep moving."

The altar pulsed, resonating with the aurora. Sarah whispered, "The wound is awake." Mei's instruments spiked again. "It's stronger," she whispered. Alvarez's voice echoed faintly, distorted. "Help me." Reed clenched his jaw. "We keep moving."

The chamber vibrated, low hum pressing against their bones. Reed felt Lena's voice pressing against him. Mei gasped, clutching her head. "It's knowledge. Forbidden knowledge." Sarah trembled, eyes wide. "The ancestors warned of this. Sacrifice is the cost." Alvarez's voice echoed, distorted. "Sacrifice." Reed clenched his jaw. "Stay sharp."

The chamber stretched endlessly, dominated by the altar and the base of the black pyramid. Alvarez was gone, consumed or transformed, his fate uncertain. Only his gear and blood remained. Reed stared at the darkness, breath ragged. "This is it," he muttered. "No turning back." Sarah whispered another prayer, invoking Raven. Mei's curiosity burned, eyes wide. The wound in the world awaited.

The chamber vibrated with a low hum, pressing against their bones. Reed scanned the darkness, lantern trembling in his grip. Mei crouched near the altar, instruments buzzing, eyes wide. Sarah whispered prayers, invoking Raven, her voice steady but strained. Alvarez paced, rifle clutched tight, eyes darting into the shadows. "We shouldn't be here," he muttered.

Reed snapped, "Stay focused." Mei whispered, "The readings are incredible. This is knowledge beyond anything we've seen." Sarah trembled, whispering another prayer. Alvarez shook his head, breath ragged. "Something's watching us." Reed clenched his jaw. "Stay sharp."

The shadows shifted, moving against the lantern light. Alvarez froze, rifle raised. "There," he hissed. Reed turned, eyes scanning the darkness. Nothing. Mei frowned, adjusting her instruments. "No movement. Just interference." Sarah whispered, "It's spirits." Alvarez's breath came ragged. "It's hunting us."

Alvarez broke formation, moving into the shadows. Reed

snapped, "Alvarez! Hold position!" Alvarez ignored him, rifle raised, eyes wild. Mei gasped, "Don't go alone!" Sarah whispered, "He's already gone." Reed clenched his jaw. "Stay together."

Alvarez moved deeper, lantern flickering. The walls bent unnaturally, glyphs glowing faintly. He muttered, "I see you." His voice trembled. The hum grew louder, pressing against his ears. He stumbled, breath ragged. "I see you."

The entity emerged, shifting between animal and human forms. Its body was shadow, its eyes gleaming. It whispered, voice distorted, echoing. Alvarez froze, breath catching. "What are you?" The entity shifted, form twisting, Kushtaka and something older. Alvarez raised his rifle, hands trembling.

The entity moved closer, shadows stretching. Alvarez fired, the shot echoing through the chamber. The bullet vanished into darkness, swallowed whole. The entity whispered, voice sharp. "Sacrifice." Alvarez stumbled back, breath ragged. "No." The shadows closed in.

The team heard the shot, echoing through the chamber. Reed snapped, "Alvarez!" Mei gasped, clutching her instruments. "He's gone too far." Sarah whispered, "The spirits have taken him." Reed clenched his jaw. "We move."

They followed the sound, lanterns flickering. The shadows stretched unnaturally, walls bending. Mei whispered, "The geometry is shifting." Sarah trembled, whispering another prayer. Reed clenched his jaw. "Stay sharp." Alvarez's voice echoed faintly, distorted. "Help me."

They found his gear scattered on the ground. Rifle, lantern, pack. Blood smeared across the stone, trailing into darkness. Mei gasped, breath ragged. "He's gone." Sarah whispered, "Sacrifice." Reed clenched his jaw. "We keep moving."

The shadows shifted, moving against the lantern light.

Sarah whispered, "The wound demands blood." Mei trembled, clutching her instruments. "It's feeding." Reed clenched his jaw. "We don't stop." Alvarez's voice echoed faintly, distorted. "Help me."

Visions consumed them. Reed saw Lena, her voice whispering his name. Mei gasped, whispering equations. "Patterns... higher order... mathematics beyond comprehension." Sarah spoke in tongues, words older than the mountains. Alvarez's voice echoed, distorted. "Sacrifice." Reed clenched his jaw. "Stay sharp."

The altar pulsed, resonating with the aurora. Mei's instruments spiked again. "It's stronger," she whispered. Sarah whispered another prayer. Reed clenched his jaw. "We keep moving." Alvarez's voice echoed faintly, distorted. "Help me."

The chamber vibrated, low hum pressing against their bones. Reed felt Lena's voice pressing against him. Mei gasped, clutching her head. "It's knowledge. Forbidden knowledge." Sarah trembled, eyes wide. "The ancestors warned of this." Alvarez's voice echoed, distorted. "Sacrifice." Reed clenched his jaw. "Stay sharp."

The glyphs glowed brighter, walls shifting. Reed saw Lena, her voice whispering his name. Mei whispered equations, trembling. "Patterns... higher order... mathematics beyond comprehension." Sarah spoke in tongues. Alvarez's voice echoed, distorted. "Help me." Reed clenched his jaw. "Focus."

Visions intensified. Reed saw his father, his childhood. Mei glimpsed fractals spiraling endlessly. Sarah saw rituals, sacrifices, spirits. Alvarez's voice echoed, distorted. "Sacrifice." Reed clenched his jaw. "We keep moving."

The altar pulsed, resonating with the aurora. Sarah whispered, "The wound is awake." Mei's instruments spiked again. "It's stronger," she whispered. Alvarez's voice echoed faintly, distorted. "Help me." Reed clenched his jaw. "We keep moving."

CHAPTER 10: THE GOVERNMENT'S HAND

The tundra trembled under the roar of engines. A convoy of snowcats and armored transports cut across the ice, headlights piercing the storm. Agent Victoria Hale stood at the front, her coat snapping in the wind, eyes locked on the pyramid's silhouette. She was Reed's former mentor, once his ally, now his rival. Her orders were clear: secure the site, retrieve artifacts, and silence witnesses if necessary. The aurora pulsed overhead, casting the convoy in unnatural light.

Hale's operatives disembarked, rifles slung, eyes scanning the horizon. Their movements were precise, disciplined, military. Behind them stepped a figure in black, tall, lean, his face obscured by a hood. He was known only as Mr. Black. His presence was unsettling, his knowledge of the pyramid disturbingly precise. Hale glanced at him, jaw tight. "Stay close," she muttered.

Taq watched from the outskirts, crouched low, Nanuq at his side. Ravens wheeled overhead, cries sharp, insistent. He whispered, "I hear you." His chest tightened. The spirits pressed against him, guiding him forward. He saw the operatives moving, rifles raised, eyes scanning. He whispered another prayer, clutching the raven feather tightly.

The operatives spotted him, rifles snapping up.

"Trespasser," one barked. Hale stepped forward, eyes narrowing. "Who are you?" Taq stood calmly, breath steady. "I am guided," he said. "The land remembers. The wound is awake." Hale scoffed, dismissive. "Superstitions." Mr. Black's eyes gleamed. "No," he whispered. "He matters."

Hale ordered her men to restrain him. Taq did not resist, his calm unsettling the operatives. Nanuq growled, but Taq whispered, "Peace." Hale frowned, jaw tight. "You'll stay out of our way." Mr. Black stepped closer, voice low. "He is a bridge. Between worlds. Between realms. We need him." Hale's eyes narrowed. "We'll see."

Inside the pyramid, Reed's team trembled, lanterns flickering. Sarah gasped, her trance deepening. She saw Taq, standing at the threshold, raven feather glowing faintly. "He is coming," she whispered. Reed frowned, skepticism faltering. Mei's eyes widened. "Another presence?" Alvarez was gone, consumed by sacrifice. The chamber pulsed, resonating with the aurora.

Hale's operatives moved with precision, securing the perimeter. Rifles gleamed, boots crunched against stone. Hale barked orders, voice sharp. "Secure the site. Retrieve artifacts. No mistakes." Mr. Black moved silently, eyes scanning the glyphs. He whispered, "It's alive." Hale frowned. "Focus."

Taq whispered prayers, invoking Raven, Kushtaka, spirits of the land. The aurora pulsed, responding to his words. Hale scoffed, dismissive. "Superstitions." Mr. Black's voice was steady. "He is conduit. He is necessary." Hale clenched her jaw, forcing herself to stay calm. "We'll see."

Sarah trembled, whispering another prayer. "He is healer. Mediator. Bridge." Reed frowned, skepticism faltering. Mei whispered, "We need him." Hale's operatives scanned the chamber, rifles raised. Mr. Black's eyes gleamed. "The wound demands balance." Hale muttered, "We'll take control."

The clash of agendas sharpened. Reed sought answers, Mei sought knowledge, Sarah sought protection, Taq sought healing. Hale sought power, Mr. Black sought something deeper. The chamber pulsed, resonating with the aurora. The wound in the world awaited.

Hale confronted Reed, eyes sharp. "You've gone too far." Reed clenched his jaw. "We're here for answers." Hale snapped, "You're here to die." Mei gasped, clutching her instruments. "The readings are incredible." Sarah whispered another prayer. Mr. Black's voice was steady. "The wound is awake."

Taq stood calmly, raven feather glowing faintly. Hale's operatives shifted uneasily, his presence unsettling. Hale scoffed, dismissive. "Superstitions." Mr. Black whispered, "He is bridge. He is necessary." Reed frowned, skepticism faltering. Sarah whispered, "He is healer." Mei whispered, "We need him."

The chamber vibrated, low hum pressing against their bones. Hale's operatives tightened their grip on rifles. Reed clenched his jaw, forcing himself to stay calm. Mei gasped, clutching her instruments. Sarah whispered another prayer. Taq whispered, "I will go." Mr. Black's eyes gleamed. "Yes."

The glyphs glowed brighter, walls shifting. Hale frowned, jaw tight. "Secure the site." Reed snapped, "You don't understand." Mei whispered, "It's alive." Sarah trembled, whispering another prayer. Taq whispered, "The wound is awake." Mr. Black's voice was steady. "It demands balance."

Visions consumed them. Reed saw Lena, her voice whispering his name. Mei gasped, whispering equations. Sarah spoke in tongues, words older than the mountains. Hale's operatives shifted uneasily, eyes wide. Taq whispered prayers, invoking Raven. Mr. Black's voice was steady. "It is prison. And power."

The altar pulsed, resonating with the aurora. Hale frowned,

jaw tight. "Retrieve artifacts." Reed clenched his jaw. "You don't understand." Mei whispered, "It's stronger." Sarah whispered another prayer. Taq whispered, "The wound must remain sealed." Mr. Black's eyes gleamed. "Or opened."

The chamber vibrated, low hum pressing against their bones. Hale's operatives tightened their grip on rifles. Reed clenched his jaw. Mei gasped, clutching her instruments. Sarah whispered another prayer. Taq whispered, "I will go." Mr. Black's voice was steady. "Yes."

The glyphs glowed brighter, walls shifting. Hale frowned. "Secure the site." Reed snapped, "You don't understand." Mei whispered, "It's alive." Sarah trembled, whispering another prayer. Taq whispered, "The wound is awake." Mr. Black's voice was steady. "It demands balance."

Visions consumed them. Reed saw Lena, her voice whispering his name. Mei gasped, whispering equations. Sarah spoke in tongues. Hale's operatives shifted uneasily. Taq whispered prayers, invoking Raven. Mr. Black's voice was steady. "It is prison. And power."

The chamber stretched endlessly, dominated by the altar and the base of the black pyramid. Hale's operatives stood rigid, rifles raised. Reed clenched his jaw, breath ragged. Sarah whispered another prayer. Mei's curiosity burned, eyes wide. Taq whispered, "I will go." Mr. Black's eyes gleamed. "The wound awaits."

The tundra stretched like a battlefield between worlds, the aurora shimmering above like a living omen. The pyramid loomed in the distance, its black stone swallowing all light. Into this silence came the roar of engines, a convoy of snowcats and armored transports cutting across the ice. Agent Victoria Hale stood at the front, her coat snapping in the wind, eyes locked on the pyramid's silhouette. She was Reed's former mentor, once his ally, now his rival. Her orders were clear: secure the site, retrieve artifacts, and silence witnesses if necessary.

Hale's operatives disembarked, rifles gleaming, boots crunching against stone. Their movements were precise, disciplined, military. Behind them stepped a figure cloaked in black, tall, lean, his face obscured by shadow. He was known only as Mr. Black. His presence was unsettling, his knowledge of the pyramid disturbingly precise. Hale glanced at him, jaw tight. "Stay close," she muttered. The aurora pulsed, casting them in unnatural light.

Taq watched from the outskirts, crouched low, Nanuq at his side. Ravens wheeled overhead, cries sharp, insistent. He whispered, "I hear you." His chest tightened. The spirits pressed against him, guiding him forward. He saw the operatives moving, rifles raised, eyes scanning. He whispered another prayer, clutching the raven feather tightly.

The operatives spotted him, rifles snapping up. "Trespasser," one barked. Hale stepped forward, eyes narrowing. "Who are you?" Taq stood calmly, breath steady. "I am guided," he said. "The land remembers. The wound is awake." Hale scoffed, dismissive. "Superstitions." Mr. Black's eyes gleamed. "No," he whispered. "He matters."

Hale ordered her men to restrain him. Taq did not resist, his calm unsettling the operatives. Nanuq growled, but Taq whispered, "Peace." Hale frowned, jaw tight. "You'll stay out of our way." Mr. Black stepped closer, voice low. "He is a bridge. Between worlds. Between realms. We need him." Hale's eyes narrowed. "We'll see."

Inside the pyramid, Sarah trembled, lantern flickering. Her trance deepened, pulling her into shadow. She saw Taq, standing at the threshold, raven feather glowing faintly. She gasped, breath ragged. "He is coming," she whispered. Reed frowned, skepticism faltering. Mei's eyes widened. "Another presence?" Alvarez was gone, consumed by sacrifice. The chamber pulsed, resonating with the aurora.

Hale's operatives moved with precision, securing the perimeter. Rifles gleamed, boots crunched against stone. Hale barked orders, voice sharp. "Secure the site. Retrieve artifacts. No mistakes." Mr. Black moved silently, eyes scanning the glyphs. He whispered, "It is alive." Hale frowned. "Focus."

Taq whispered prayers, invoking Raven, Kushtaka, spirits of the land. The aurora pulsed, responding to his words. Hale scoffed, dismissive. "Superstitions." Mr. Black's voice was steady. "He is conduit. He is necessary." Hale clenched her jaw, forcing herself to stay calm. "We'll see."

Sarah trembled, whispering another prayer. "He is healer. Mediator. Bridge." Reed frowned, skepticism faltering. Mei whispered, "We need him." Hale's operatives scanned the chamber, rifles raised. Mr. Black's eyes gleamed. "The wound demands balance." Hale muttered, "We'll take control."

The clash of agendas sharpened. Reed sought answers, Mei sought knowledge, Sarah sought protection, Taq sought healing. Hale sought power, Mr. Black sought something deeper. The chamber pulsed, resonating with the aurora. The wound in the world awaited.

Hale confronted Reed, eyes sharp. "You've gone too far." Reed clenched his jaw. "We're here for answers." Hale snapped, "You're here to die." Mei gasped, clutching her instruments. "The readings are incredible." Sarah whispered another prayer. Mr. Black's voice was steady. "The wound is awake."

Taq stood calmly, raven feather glowing faintly. Hale's operatives shifted uneasily, his presence unsettling. Hale scoffed, dismissive. "Superstitions." Mr. Black whispered, "He is bridge. He is necessary." Reed frowned, skepticism faltering. Sarah whispered, "He is healer." Mei whispered, "We need him."

The chamber vibrated, low hum pressing against their bones. Hale's operatives tightened their grip on rifles. Reed clenched his jaw, forcing himself to stay calm. Mei gasped, clutching her instruments. Sarah whispered another prayer. Taq whispered, "I will go." Mr. Black's eyes gleamed. "Yes."

The glyphs glowed brighter, walls shifting. Hale frowned, jaw tight. "Secure the site." Reed snapped, "You don't understand." Mei whispered, "It's alive." Sarah trembled, whispering another prayer. Taq whispered, "The wound is awake." Mr. Black's voice was steady. "It demands balance."

Visions consumed them. Reed saw Lena, her voice whispering his name. Mei gasped, whispering equations. Sarah spoke in tongues, words older than the mountains. Hale's operatives shifted uneasily, eyes wide. Taq whispered prayers, invoking Raven. Mr. Black's voice was steady. "It is prison. And power."

The altar pulsed, resonating with the aurora. Hale frowned, jaw tight. "Retrieve artifacts." Reed clenched his jaw. "You don't understand." Mei whispered, "It's stronger." Sarah whispered another prayer. Taq whispered, "The wound must remain sealed." Mr. Black's eyes gleamed. "Or opened."

The chamber vibrated, low hum pressing against their bones. Hale's operatives tightened their grip on rifles. Reed clenched his jaw. Mei gasped, clutching her instruments. Sarah whispered another prayer. Taq whispered, "I will go." Mr. Black's voice was steady. "Yes."

The glyphs glowed brighter, walls shifting. Hale frowned. "Secure the site." Reed snapped, "You don't understand." Mei whispered, "It's alive." Sarah trembled, whispering another prayer. Taq whispered, "The wound is awake." Mr. Black's voice was steady. "It demands balance."

Visions consumed them. Reed saw Lena, her voice

whispering his name. Mei gasped, whispering equations. Sarah spoke in tongues. Hale's operatives shifted uneasily. Taq whispered prayers, invoking Raven. Mr. Black's voice was steady. "It is prison. And power."

Engines roared across the tundra, headlights slicing through the storm. A convoy of snowcats and armored transports barreled toward the pyramid, their movements precise, military. Hale stood at the front, coat snapping in the wind, eyes locked on the black silhouette. She was Reed's former mentor, once his ally, now his rival. Her orders were clear: secure the site, retrieve artifacts, and silence witnesses if necessary.

Operatives disembarked, rifles raised, boots crunching against stone. Their discipline was absolute, their presence overwhelming. Behind them stepped a figure cloaked in black, tall, lean, his face obscured. He was known only as Mr. Black. His presence was unsettling, his knowledge disturbingly precise. Hale glanced at him, jaw tight. "Stay close," she muttered.

Taq crouched at the outskirts, Nanuq at his side. Ravens wheeled overhead, cries sharp, insistent. He whispered, "I hear you." His chest tightened. The spirits pressed against him, guiding him forward. He saw the operatives moving, rifles raised, eyes scanning. He whispered another prayer, clutching the raven feather tightly.

The operatives spotted him, rifles snapping up. "Trespasser," one barked. Hale stepped forward, eyes narrowing. "Who are you?" Taq stood calmly, breath steady. "I am guided," he said. "The land remembers. The wound is awake." Hale scoffed, dismissive. "Superstitions." Mr. Black's eyes gleamed. "No," he whispered. "He matters."

Hale ordered her men to restrain him. Taq did not resist, his calm unsettling the operatives. Nanuq growled, but Taq whispered, "Peace." Hale frowned, jaw tight. "You'll stay out of our way." Mr. Black stepped closer, voice low. "He is a bridge. Between worlds. Between realms. We need him." Hale's eyes narrowed. "We'll see."

Inside the pyramid, Reed's team trembled, lanterns flickering. Sarah gasped, her trance deepening. She saw Taq, standing at the threshold, raven feather glowing faintly. "He is coming," she whispered. Reed frowned, skepticism faltering. Mei's eyes widened. "Another presence?" Alvarez was gone, consumed by sacrifice. The chamber pulsed, resonating with the aurora.

Hale's operatives moved with precision, securing the perimeter. Rifles gleamed, boots crunched against stone. Hale barked orders, voice sharp. "Secure the site. Retrieve artifacts. No mistakes." Mr. Black moved silently, eyes scanning the glyphs. He whispered, "It is alive." Hale frowned. "Focus."

Taq whispered prayers, invoking Raven, Kushtaka, spirits of the land. The aurora pulsed, responding to his words. Hale scoffed, dismissive. "Superstitions." Mr. Black's voice was steady. "He is conduit. He is necessary." Hale clenched her jaw, forcing herself to stay calm. "We'll see."

Sarah trembled, whispering another prayer. "He is healer. Mediator. Bridge." Reed frowned, skepticism faltering. Mei whispered, "We need him." Hale's operatives scanned the chamber, rifles raised. Mr. Black's eyes gleamed. "The wound demands balance." Hale muttered, "We'll take control."

The clash of agendas sharpened. Reed sought answers, Mei sought knowledge, Sarah sought protection, Taq sought healing. Hale sought power, Mr. Black sought something deeper. The chamber pulsed, resonating with the aurora. The wound in the world awaited.

Hale confronted Reed, eyes sharp. "You've gone too far."

Reed clenched his jaw. "We're here for answers." Hale snapped, "You're here to die." Mei gasped, clutching her instruments. "The readings are incredible." Sarah whispered another prayer. Mr. Black's voice was steady. "The wound is awake."

Taq stood calmly, raven feather glowing faintly. Hale's operatives shifted uneasily, his presence unsettling. Hale scoffed, dismissive. "Superstitions." Mr. Black whispered, "He is bridge. He is necessary." Reed frowned, skepticism faltering. Sarah whispered, "He is healer." Mei whispered, "We need him."

The chamber vibrated, low hum pressing against their bones. Hale's operatives tightened their grip on rifles. Reed clenched his jaw, forcing himself to stay calm. Mei gasped, clutching her instruments. Sarah whispered another prayer. Taq whispered, "I will go." Mr. Black's eyes gleamed. "Yes."

The glyphs glowed brighter, walls shifting. Hale frowned, jaw tight. "Secure the site." Reed snapped, "You don't understand." Mei whispered, "It's alive." Sarah trembled, whispering another prayer. Taq whispered, "The wound is awake." Mr. Black's voice was steady. "It demands balance."

Visions consumed them. Reed saw Lena, her voice whispering his name. Mei gasped, whispering equations. Sarah spoke in tongues, words older than the mountains. Hale's operatives shifted uneasily, eyes wide. Taq whispered prayers, invoking Raven. Mr. Black's voice was steady. "It is prison. And power."

The altar pulsed, resonating with the aurora. Hale frowned, jaw tight. "Retrieve artifacts." Reed clenched his jaw. "You don't understand." Mei whispered, "It's stronger." Sarah whispered another prayer. Taq whispered, "The wound must remain sealed." Mr. Black's eyes gleamed. "Or opened."

The chamber vibrated, low hum pressing against their bones. Hale's operatives tightened their grip on rifles. Reed clenched his jaw. Mei gasped, clutching her instruments. Sarah whispered another prayer. Taq whispered, "I will go." Mr. Black's voice was steady. "Yes."

The glyphs glowed brighter, walls shifting. Hale frowned. "Secure the site." Reed snapped, "You don't understand." Mei whispered, "It's alive." Sarah trembled, whispering another prayer. Taq whispered, "The wound is awake." Mr. Black's voice was steady. "It demands balance."

Visions consumed them. Reed saw Lena, her voice whispering his name. Mei gasped, whispering equations. Sarah spoke in tongues. Hale's operatives shifted uneasily. Taq whispered prayers, invoking Raven. Mr. Black's voice was steady. "It is prison. And power."

CHAPTER 11: THE RITUAL CHAMBER

The secondary chamber opened like a hidden wound, its walls lined with ritual objects frozen in time. Masks stared from niches in the stone, their carved eyes wide and unblinking. Drums lay cracked, skins stretched taut as though they had been played only moments ago. Effigies of Raven, Thunderbird, and Kushtaka stood in a circle, their forms twisted, half-human, half-animal. Reed's lantern flickered, shadows dancing across the chamber. Sarah gasped, breath ragged. "This is a ritual chamber," she whispered.

Taq stepped forward, raven feather glowing faintly in the aurora's light. His eyes scanned the effigies, his voice steady. "These are guardians. Symbols of power. They tell a story." Sarah nodded, her trance deepening. "A catastrophe. A time when the pyramid was used to seal away something vast. Something that threatened the world." Reed frowned, skepticism faltering. "A prison?" Mei whispered, "Or a machine."

Mr. Black moved closer, his eyes gleaming. "It is both," he said. "Prison and power source. A sealed evil in a can. And we can open it." Hale's jaw tightened, her voice sharp. "Our orders are clear. Retrieve artifacts. Secure the site." Reed clenched his jaw, forcing himself to stay calm. "You don't understand what you're dealing with."

Sarah traced the carvings, her fingers trembling. "The

ancestors warned of this. The wound in the world. The spirits sealed it here." Taq whispered prayers, invoking Raven, Kushtaka, and Thunderbird. "They gave everything to contain it. Blood. Sacrifice. Ceremony." Mei's instruments buzzed, readings spiking. "It's stronger here. The energy is concentrated."

The chamber pulsed, resonating with the aurora. Reed felt vibration beneath his skin, deep and resonant. Sarah whispered, "The wound is awake." Taq's voice was steady. "It must remain sealed." Mr. Black's eyes gleamed. "Or harnessed." Hale muttered, "We'll take control."

Masks stared from the walls, their carved eyes glowing faintly. Sarah trembled, whispering another prayer. "They are watching us." Mei crouched, examining the effigies. "They're aligned. A circle of guardians. A seal." Reed frowned. "A seal against what?" Taq whispered, "Against the end."

Mr. Black stepped closer to the altar, his voice low. "We can activate it. Use the ritual. Harness the power." Hale's operatives shifted uneasily, rifles raised. Reed clenched his jaw. "You'll doom us all." Sarah gasped, breath ragged. "The ancestors warned of this." Taq whispered, "The wound must remain sealed."

The clash of agendas sharpened. Reed sought answers, Mei sought knowledge, Sarah sought protection, Taq sought healing. Hale sought power, Mr. Black sought control. The chamber pulsed, resonating with the aurora. The wound in the world awaited.

Sarah and Taq collaborated, voices steady. They traced the symbols, interpreting the narrative. "A catastrophe," Sarah whispered. "A cosmic entity sealed away. The pyramid was prison. Ceremony was key." Taq nodded. "The guardians gave everything. Blood. Sacrifice. Ceremony. It must remain sealed."

Mei's curiosity burned, her voice sharp. "But if we understand it, we can survive. Knowledge is power." Reed clenched his jaw. "Knowledge is death." Hale scoffed, dismissive. "Superstitions. We'll take control." Mr. Black's voice was steady. "We will activate it."

The chamber vibrated, low hum pressing against their bones. Sarah whispered another prayer. Taq whispered, "I will go." Reed clenched his jaw. "We keep moving." Mei gasped, clutching her instruments. "It's stronger." Hale's operatives tightened their grip on rifles. Mr. Black's eyes gleamed. "Yes."

Masks glowed faintly, effigies shifting in the flickering light. Sarah trembled, whispering, "They are alive." Taq whispered prayers, invoking Raven. Reed clenched his jaw. "Stay sharp." Mei whispered, "It's resonating with us." Hale frowned, jaw tight. "Secure the site." Mr. Black whispered, "Activate it."

Visions consumed them. Reed saw Lena, her voice whispering his name. Mei gasped, whispering equations. Sarah spoke in tongues, words older than the mountains. Taq whispered prayers, invoking guardians. Hale's operatives shifted uneasily. Mr. Black's voice was steady. "It is prison. And power."

The altar pulsed, resonating with the aurora. Sarah whispered, "The wound is awake." Taq's voice was steady. "It must remain sealed." Mei's instruments spiked again. "It's stronger." Reed clenched his jaw. "We keep moving." Hale muttered, "Retrieve artifacts." Mr. Black's eyes gleamed. "Or open it."

The chamber vibrated, low hum pressing against their bones. Reed felt Lena's voice pressing against him. Mei gasped, clutching her head. "It's knowledge. Forbidden knowledge." Sarah trembled, eyes wide. "The ancestors warned of this." Taq whispered, "The wound must remain sealed." Mr. Black's voice was steady. "It demands release."

Masks glowed brighter, effigies shifting. Sarah whispered another prayer. Taq whispered, "I will go." Reed clenched his jaw. "Stay sharp." Mei whispered, "It's alive." Hale frowned, jaw tight. "Secure the site." Mr. Black whispered, "Activate it."

Visions intensified. Reed saw his father, his childhood. Mei glimpsed fractals spiraling endlessly. Sarah saw rituals, sacrifices, spirits. Taq whispered prayers, invoking guardians. Hale's operatives shifted uneasily. Mr. Black's voice was steady. "It is prison. And power."

The altar pulsed, resonating with the aurora. Sarah whispered, "The wound is awake." Taq's voice was steady. "It must remain sealed." Mei's instruments spiked again. "It's stronger." Reed clenched his jaw. "We keep moving." Hale muttered, "Retrieve artifacts." Mr. Black's eyes gleamed. "Or open it."

The chamber vibrated, low hum pressing against their bones. Reed felt Lena's voice pressing against him. Mei gasped, clutching her head. "It's knowledge. Forbidden knowledge." Sarah trembled, eyes wide. "The ancestors warned of this." Taq whispered, "The wound must remain sealed." Mr. Black's voice was steady. "It demands release."

The chamber opened like a hidden memory, its walls lined with ritual objects that seemed to breathe with the aurora's pulse. Masks carved from bone and wood stared from niches, their eyes wide, unblinking, and alive with faint light. Drums rested in a circle, skins cracked but resonant, as though they had been played in ceremonies long forgotten. Effigies of Raven, Thunderbird, and Kushtaka stood sentinel, their forms half-human, half-animal, guardians of a story etched into stone. Sarah gasped, her voice trembling. "This is the place of sealing," she whispered.

Taq stepped forward, raven feather glowing faintly. His eyes scanned the effigies, his voice steady. "These are not idols. They are guardians. They tell of a time when the land bled and the sky broke." Sarah nodded, her trance deepening. "A catastrophe. A cosmic wound. The pyramid was built to contain it." Reed frowned, skepticism faltering. "Contain what?" Mei whispered, "Something vast. Something not human."

Mr. Black moved closer, his eyes gleaming. "It is both prison and power source," he said. "A sealed evil in a can. And it can be opened." Hale's jaw tightened, her voice sharp. "Our orders are clear. Secure the site. Retrieve artifacts." Reed clenched his jaw, forcing himself to stay calm. "You don't understand. This is not yours to control."

Sarah traced the carvings, her fingers trembling. "The ancestors warned of this. The wound in the world. The spirits sealed it here with blood and ceremony." Taq whispered prayers, invoking Raven, Kushtaka, and Thunderbird. "They gave everything to contain it. Sacrifice was the price." Mei's instruments buzzed, readings spiking. "It's stronger here. The energy is concentrated."

The chamber pulsed, resonating with the aurora. Reed felt vibration beneath his skin, deep and resonant. Sarah whispered, "The wound is awake." Taq's voice was steady. "It must remain sealed." Mr. Black's eyes gleamed. "Or harnessed." Hale muttered, "We'll take control."

Masks glowed faintly, effigies shifting in the flickering light. Sarah trembled, whispering another prayer. "They are watching us." Mei crouched, examining the effigies. "They're aligned. A circle of guardians. A seal." Reed frowned. "A seal against what?" Taq whispered, "Against the end."

Mr. Black stepped closer to the altar, his voice low. "We can activate it. Use the ritual. Harness the power." Hale's operatives shifted uneasily, rifles raised. Reed clenched his jaw. "You'll doom us all." Sarah gasped, breath ragged. "The ancestors warned of this." Taq whispered, "The wound must remain sealed."

The clash of agendas sharpened. Reed sought answers, Mei sought knowledge, Sarah sought protection, Taq sought healing. Hale sought power, Mr. Black sought dominion. The chamber pulsed, resonating with the aurora. The wound in the world awaited.

Sarah and Taq collaborated, voices steady. They traced the symbols, interpreting the narrative. "A catastrophe," Sarah whispered. "A cosmic entity sealed away. The pyramid was prison. Ceremony was key." Taq nodded. "The guardians gave everything. Blood. Sacrifice. Ceremony. It must remain sealed."

Mei's curiosity burned, her voice sharp. "But if we understand it, we can survive. Knowledge is power." Reed clenched his jaw. "Knowledge is death." Hale scoffed, dismissive. "Superstitions. We'll take control." Mr. Black's voice was steady. "We will activate it."

The chamber vibrated, low hum pressing against their bones. Sarah whispered another prayer. Taq whispered, "I will go." Reed clenched his jaw. "We keep moving." Mei gasped, clutching her instruments. "It's stronger." Hale's operatives tightened their grip on rifles. Mr. Black's eyes gleamed. "Yes."

Masks glowed brighter, effigies shifting in the flickering light. Sarah trembled, whispering, "They are alive." Taq whispered prayers, invoking Raven. Reed clenched his jaw. "Stay sharp." Mei whispered, "It's resonating with us." Hale frowned, jaw tight. "Secure the site." Mr. Black whispered, "Activate it."

Visions consumed them. Reed saw Lena, her voice

whispering his name. Mei gasped, whispering equations. Sarah spoke in tongues, words older than the mountains. Taq whispered prayers, invoking guardians. Hale's operatives shifted uneasily. Mr. Black's voice was steady. "It is prison. And power."

The altar pulsed, resonating with the aurora. Sarah whispered, "The wound is awake." Taq's voice was steady. "It must remain sealed." Mei's instruments spiked again. "It's stronger." Reed clenched his jaw. "We keep moving." Hale muttered, "Retrieve artifacts." Mr. Black's eyes gleamed. "Or opened."

The chamber vibrated, low hum pressing against their bones. Reed felt Lena's voice pressing against him. Mei gasped, clutching her head. "It's knowledge. Forbidden knowledge." Sarah trembled, eyes wide. "The ancestors warned of this." Taq whispered, "The wound must remain sealed." Mr. Black's voice was steady. "It demands release."

Masks glowed brighter, effigies shifting. Sarah whispered another prayer. Taq whispered, "I will go." Reed clenched his jaw. "Stay sharp." Mei whispered, "It's alive." Hale frowned, jaw tight. "Secure the site." Mr. Black whispered, "Activate it."

Visions intensified. Reed saw his father, his childhood. Mei glimpsed fractals spiraling endlessly. Sarah saw rituals, sacrifices, spirits. Taq whispered prayers, invoking guardians. Hale's operatives shifted uneasily. Mr. Black's voice was steady. "It is prison. And power."

The altar pulsed, resonating with the aurora. Sarah whispered, "The wound is awake." Taq's voice was steady. "It must remain sealed." Mei's instruments spiked again. "It's stronger." Reed clenched his jaw. "We keep moving." Hale muttered, "Retrieve artifacts." Mr. Black's eyes gleamed. "Or opened."

The chamber vibrated, low hum pressing against their bones. Reed felt Lena's voice pressing against him. Mei gasped, clutching her head. "It's knowledge. Forbidden knowledge." Sarah trembled, eyes wide. "The ancestors warned of this." Taq whispered, "The wound must remain sealed." Mr. Black's voice was steady. "It demands release."

The chamber stretched endlessly, dominated by masks, drums, and effigies. Hale's operatives stood rigid, rifles raised. Reed clenched his jaw, breath ragged. Sarah whispered another prayer. Mei's curiosity burned, eyes wide. Taq whispered, "I will go." Mr. Black's eyes gleamed. "The ritual awaits."

The chamber opened like a stage set for confrontation, lantern light cutting across masks and effigies. Reed's team froze, eyes wide, as Hale's operatives fanned out with rifles raised. Sarah gasped, her trance deepening, whispering prayers. Mei's instruments buzzed, readings spiking. Taq stood calm, raven feather glowing faintly. Mr. Black's eyes gleamed, fixed on the altar.

Masks stared from the walls, their carved eyes glowing faintly. Hale barked, "Secure the site." Reed snapped, "You don't understand." Mei whispered, "It's alive." Sarah trembled, whispering another prayer. Taq whispered, "The wound is awake." Mr. Black's voice was steady. "It demands release."

The effigies loomed, half-human, half-animal, their shadows stretching unnaturally. Sarah whispered, "They are guardians." Taq nodded. "They sealed the wound. They gave everything." Reed clenched his jaw. "It's a prison." Mei whispered, "Or a machine." Hale scoffed. "It's ours." Mr. Black whispered, "It is both."

The chamber pulsed, resonating with the aurora. Reed felt vibration beneath his skin, deep and resonant. Sarah whispered, "The wound is awake." Taq's voice was steady.

"It must remain sealed." Mei's instruments spiked again. "It's stronger." Hale muttered, "Retrieve artifacts." Mr. Black's eyes gleamed. "Or open it."

Hale's operatives shifted uneasily, rifles raised. Reed clenched his jaw, forcing calm. Mei gasped, clutching her instruments. Sarah whispered another prayer. Taq whispered, "I will go." Hale frowned, jaw tight. "You'll stay out of our way." Mr. Black's voice was steady. "He is conduit."

Visions consumed them. Reed saw Lena, her voice whispering his name. Mei gasped, whispering equations. Sarah spoke in tongues, words older than the mountains. Taq whispered prayers, invoking Raven. Hale's operatives shifted, eyes wide. Mr. Black's voice was steady. "It is prison. And power."

The altar pulsed, resonating with the aurora. Sarah whispered, "The wound is awake." Taq's voice was steady. "It must remain sealed." Mei's instruments spiked again. "It's stronger." Reed clenched his jaw. "We keep moving." Hale muttered, "Retrieve artifacts." Mr. Black's eyes gleamed. "Or opened."

Masks glowed brighter, effigies shifting in the flickering light. Sarah trembled, whispering, "They are alive." Taq whispered prayers, invoking guardians. Reed clenched his jaw. "Stay sharp." Mei whispered, "It's resonating with us." Hale frowned, jaw tight. "Secure the site." Mr. Black whispered, "Activate it."

The chamber vibrated, low hum pressing against their bones. Reed felt Lena's voice pressing against him. Mei gasped, clutching her head. "It's knowledge. Forbidden knowledge." Sarah trembled, eyes wide. "The ancestors warned of this." Taq whispered, "The wound must remain sealed." Mr. Black's voice was steady. "It demands release."

The clash of agendas sharpened. Reed sought answers, Mei sought knowledge, Sarah sought protection, Taq sought healing. Hale sought power, Mr. Black sought dominion. The chamber pulsed, resonating with the aurora. The wound in the world awaited.

Hale confronted Reed, eyes sharp. "You've gone too far." Reed clenched his jaw. "We're here for answers." Hale snapped, "You're here to die." Mei gasped, clutching her instruments. "The readings are incredible." Sarah whispered another prayer. Mr. Black's voice was steady. "The wound is awake."

Taq stood calmly, raven feather glowing faintly. Hale's operatives shifted uneasily, his presence unsettling. Hale scoffed, dismissive. "Superstitions." Mr. Black whispered, "He is bridge. He is necessary." Reed frowned, skepticism faltering. Sarah whispered, "He is healer." Mei whispered, "We need him."

The chamber vibrated, low hum pressing against their bones. Hale's operatives tightened their grip on rifles. Reed clenched his jaw, forcing himself to stay calm. Mei gasped, clutching her instruments. Sarah whispered another prayer. Taq whispered, "I will go." Mr. Black's eyes gleamed. "Yes."

Masks glowed brighter, effigies shifting. Sarah whispered another prayer. Taq whispered, "I will go." Reed clenched his jaw. "Stay sharp." Mei whispered, "It's alive." Hale frowned, jaw tight. "Secure the site." Mr. Black whispered, "Activate it."

Visions intensified. Reed saw his father, his childhood. Mei glimpsed fractals spiraling endlessly. Sarah saw rituals, sacrifices, spirits. Taq whispered prayers, invoking guardians. Hale's operatives shifted uneasily. Mr. Black's voice was steady. "It is prison. And power."

The altar pulsed, resonating with the aurora. Sarah whispered, "The wound is awake." Taq's voice was steady. "It must remain sealed." Mei's instruments spiked again. "It's stronger." Reed clenched his jaw. "We keep moving." Hale muttered, "Retrieve artifacts." Mr. Black's eyes gleamed. "Or opened."

The chamber vibrated, low hum pressing against their bones. Reed felt Lena's voice pressing against him. Mei gasped, clutching her head. "It's knowledge. Forbidden knowledge." Sarah trembled, eyes wide. "The ancestors warned of this." Taq whispered, "The wound must remain sealed." Mr. Black's voice was steady. "It demands release."

CHAPTER 12: THE OPENING

The chamber vibrated with anticipation, masks and effigies glowing faintly in the flickering light. Reed's jaw tightened, his voice sharp. "Don't do this." Sarah trembled, whispering another prayer. Mei's instruments buzzed, readings spiking wildly. Taq stood calm, raven feather glowing faintly. Mr. Black stepped forward, eyes gleaming. "It begins," he whispered.

He laid out devices—mathematical arrays etched into metal, circuits humming with power. He whispered chants, words stolen from indigenous ceremonies, twisted into formulas. His voice rose, blending prayer with calculation, rhythm with precision. The chamber pulsed, resonating with the aurora. Hale's operatives shifted uneasily, rifles raised. Reed clenched his jaw. "Stop." Mr. Black ignored him.

The altar glowed, glyphs shifting, spirals twisting. Masks stared, eyes alive with faint light. Effigies trembled, their forms shifting. Sarah gasped, breath ragged. "The seal is breaking." Taq whispered prayers, invoking Raven, Kushtaka, Thunderbird. His voice was steady, but his eyes burned with dread. "The wound is opening."

The chamber shook, stone groaning. Auroras flared, colors bleeding across the sky. Earth trembled, cracks splitting the floor. Operatives stumbled, rifles clattering. Mei gasped, clutching her instruments. "It's catastrophic." Reed clenched his jaw. "You've doomed us." Mr. Black's voice was steady. "I've freed us."

Visions flooded their minds. Reed saw Lena, her voice whispering his name. Mei glimpsed fractals spiraling endlessly, mathematics beyond comprehension. Sarah saw ancestors, spirits, rituals, sacrifices. Taq trembled, his body convulsing. A spirit pressed against him, voice sharp. "The seal is broken. The darkness returns."

Operatives screamed, rifles firing wildly. Shadows moved, spectral entities emerging. Their forms were twisted, half-human, half-animal, echoes of Kushtaka and Thunderbird. Auroras flared, colors bleeding across the chamber. Earth shook, stone splitting. Reed clenched his jaw. "Stay together." Mei gasped, clutching her instruments. "It's overwhelming."

Several operatives fell, consumed by shadows. Others screamed, driven mad, eyes wide, voices incoherent. Hale barked orders, voice sharp. "Hold formation!" Her operatives stumbled, rifles useless. Mr. Black's eyes gleamed. "It begins." Reed clenched his jaw. "You've killed them."

The chamber pulsed, resonating with the aurora. Sarah whispered another prayer, her voice trembling. "The ancestors warned of this." Taq convulsed, his body trembling. A spirit pressed against him, voice sharp. "The seal is broken. The darkness returns." His eyes glowed faintly, voice no longer his own.

Reed froze, breath ragged. "Taq?" Sarah gasped, breath sharp. "He is possessed." Mei whispered, "It's conduit. The spirit speaks through him." Hale frowned, jaw tight. "Control him." Mr. Black's voice was steady. "He is necessary."

The chamber shook, stone splitting. Auroras flared, colors bleeding across the sky. Shadows moved, spectral entities emerging. Operatives screamed, rifles firing wildly. Reed clenched his jaw. "Stay sharp." Mei gasped, clutching her instruments. "It's catastrophic."

Visions consumed them. Reed saw Lena, her voice whispering his name. Mei gasped, whispering equations. Sarah spoke in tongues, words older than the mountains. Taq whispered prayers, his voice not his own. "The seal is broken. The darkness returns." Mr. Black's eyes gleamed. "Yes."

The altar pulsed, resonating with the aurora. Glyphs glowed, spirals twisted. Masks stared, eyes alive with faint light. Effigies trembled, their forms shifting. Sarah gasped, breath ragged. "The wound is open." Taq's voice was steady, possessed. "The darkness returns."

Operatives fell, consumed by shadows. Others screamed, driven mad. Hale barked orders, voice sharp. "Hold formation!" Her operatives stumbled, rifles useless. Reed clenched his jaw. "You've doomed us." Mei gasped, clutching her instruments. "It's catastrophic." Mr. Black's voice was steady. "It begins."

The chamber vibrated, low hum pressing against their bones. Reed felt Lena's voice pressing against him. Mei gasped, clutching her head. "It's knowledge. Forbidden knowledge." Sarah trembled, eyes wide. "The ancestors warned of this." Taq whispered, possessed. "The seal is broken. The darkness returns."

Auroras flared, colors bleeding across the chamber. Earth shook, stone splitting. Shadows moved, spectral entities emerging. Operatives screamed, rifles firing wildly. Reed clenched his jaw. "Stay together." Mei gasped, clutching her instruments. "It's overwhelming."

Visions intensified. Reed saw his father, his childhood. Mei glimpsed fractals spiraling endlessly. Sarah saw rituals, sacrifices, spirits. Taq whispered prayers, his voice not his own. "The seal is broken. The darkness returns." Mr. Black's eyes gleamed. "Yes."

The altar pulsed, resonating with the aurora. Glyphs glowed, spirals twisted. Masks stared, eyes alive with faint light. Effigies trembled, their forms shifting. Sarah gasped, breath ragged. "The wound is open." Taq's voice was steady, possessed. "The darkness returns."

The chamber shook, stone splitting. Auroras flared, colors bleeding across the sky. Shadows moved, spectral entities emerging. Operatives screamed, rifles firing wildly. Reed clenched his jaw. "Stay sharp." Mei gasped, clutching her instruments. "It's catastrophic."

The apex of the pyramid glowed, light bleeding upward. Stone cracked, splitting open. Auroras flared, colors bleeding across the sky. A portal opened, vast and dark, its surface shimmering. Reed froze, breath ragged. Sarah gasped, whispering another prayer. Mei whispered, "It's open." Taq's voice was steady, possessed. "The darkness returns."

The chamber was heavy with silence, masks and effigies glowing faintly as if awakened by memory. Reed's jaw tightened, his voice sharp. "Don't do this." Sarah trembled, whispering another prayer. Mei's instruments buzzed, readings spiking wildly. Taq stood calm, raven feather glowing faintly. Mr. Black stepped forward, eyes gleaming. "The ritual begins," he whispered.

He laid out devices—mathematical arrays etched into metal, circuits humming with power. His voice rose, weaving indigenous chants with formulas, prayer with calculation. The chamber pulsed, resonating with the aurora. Hale's operatives shifted uneasily, rifles raised. Reed clenched his jaw. "Stop." Mr. Black ignored him, his words echoing like prophecy.

The altar glowed, glyphs shifting, spirals twisting. Masks stared, eyes alive with faint light. Effigies trembled, their forms shifting. Sarah gasped, breath ragged. "The seal is breaking." Taq whispered prayers, invoking Raven, Kushtaka, Thunderbird. His voice was steady, but his eyes burned with dread. "The wound is opening."

The chamber shook, stone groaning. Auroras flared, colors bleeding across the sky. Earth trembled, cracks splitting the floor. Operatives stumbled, rifles clattering. Mei gasped, clutching her instruments. "It's catastrophic." Reed clenched his jaw. "You've doomed us." Mr. Black's voice was steady. "I've freed us."

Visions flooded their minds. Reed saw Lena, her voice whispering his name. Mei glimpsed fractals spiraling endlessly, mathematics beyond comprehension. Sarah saw ancestors, spirits, rituals, sacrifices. Taq trembled, his body convulsing. A spirit pressed against him, voice sharp. "The seal is broken. The darkness returns."

Operatives screamed, rifles firing wildly. Shadows moved, spectral entities emerging. Their forms were twisted, half-human, half-animal, echoes of Kushtaka and Thunderbird. Auroras flared, colors bleeding across the chamber. Earth shook, stone splitting. Reed clenched his jaw. "Stay together." Mei gasped, clutching her instruments. "It's overwhelming."

Several operatives fell, consumed by shadows. Others screamed, driven mad, eyes wide, voices incoherent. Hale barked orders, voice sharp. "Hold formation!" Her operatives stumbled, rifles useless. Mr. Black's eyes gleamed. "It begins." Reed clenched his jaw. "You've killed them."

The chamber pulsed, resonating with the aurora. Sarah whispered another prayer, her voice trembling. "The ancestors warned of this." Taq convulsed, his body trembling. A spirit pressed against him, voice sharp. "The seal is broken. The darkness returns." His eyes glowed faintly, voice no longer his own.

Reed froze, breath ragged. "Taq?" Sarah gasped, breath sharp. "He is possessed." Mei whispered, "It's conduit. The spirit speaks through him." Hale frowned, jaw tight. "Control him." Mr. Black's voice was steady. "He is necessary."

The chamber shook, stone splitting. Auroras flared, colors bleeding across the sky. Shadows moved, spectral entities emerging. Operatives screamed, rifles firing wildly. Reed clenched his jaw. "Stay sharp." Mei gasped, clutching her instruments. "It's catastrophic."

Visions consumed them. Reed saw Lena, her voice whispering his name. Mei gasped, whispering equations. Sarah spoke in tongues, words older than the mountains. Taq whispered prayers, his voice not his own. "The seal is broken. The darkness returns." Mr. Black's eyes gleamed. "Yes."

The altar pulsed, resonating with the aurora. Glyphs glowed, spirals twisted. Masks stared, eyes alive with faint light. Effigies trembled, their forms shifting. Sarah gasped, breath ragged. "The wound is open." Taq's voice was steady, possessed. "The darkness returns."

Operatives fell, consumed by shadows. Others screamed, driven mad. Hale barked orders, voice sharp. "Hold formation!" Her operatives stumbled, rifles useless. Reed clenched his jaw. "You've doomed us." Mei gasped, clutching her instruments. "It's catastrophic." Mr. Black's voice was steady. "It begins."

The chamber vibrated, low hum pressing against their bones. Reed felt Lena's voice pressing against him. Mei gasped, clutching her head. "It's knowledge. Forbidden knowledge." Sarah trembled, eyes wide. "The ancestors warned of this." Taq whispered, possessed. "The seal is broken. The darkness returns."

Auroras flared, colors bleeding across the chamber. Earth shook, stone splitting. Shadows moved, spectral entities emerging. Operatives screamed, rifles firing wildly. Reed clenched his jaw. "Stay together." Mei gasped, clutching her instruments. "It's overwhelming."

Visions intensified. Reed saw his father, his childhood. Mei glimpsed fractals spiraling endlessly. Sarah saw rituals, sacrifices, spirits. Taq whispered prayers, his voice not his own. "The seal is broken. The darkness returns." Mr. Black's eyes gleamed. "Yes."

The altar pulsed, resonating with the aurora. Glyphs glowed, spirals twisted. Masks stared, eyes alive with faint light. Effigies trembled, their forms shifting. Sarah gasped, breath ragged. "The wound is open." Taq's voice was steady, possessed. "The darkness returns."

The chamber shook, stone splitting. Auroras flared, colors bleeding across the sky. Shadows moved, spectral entities emerging. Operatives screamed, rifles firing wildly. Reed clenched his jaw. "Stay sharp." Mei gasped, clutching her instruments. "It's catastrophic."

The chamber was alive with tension, lanterns flickering, shadows stretching unnaturally. Reed's voice cut through the hum. "Stop this now." Sarah trembled, whispering prayers, her eyes fixed on the altar. Mei's instruments screamed with data, numbers climbing off the scale. Hale's operatives shifted, rifles raised, unease spreading. Mr. Black stepped forward, calm, deliberate. "The seal will break," he said.

He set down devices—metallic arrays etched with spirals, circuits glowing faintly. His voice rose, weaving chants with equations, rhythm with calculation. The sound was wrong, too precise, too ancient. The chamber pulsed, glyphs glowing brighter. Hale frowned, jaw tight. "What are you doing?" Mr. Black didn't answer.

The altar lit up, spirals twisting, geometry bending. Masks

stared, their carved eyes glowing. Effigies trembled, their forms shifting. Sarah gasped, "The guardians are awake." Taq whispered prayers, his voice steady. "The wound is opening." Reed clenched his jaw. "You'll kill us all."

The floor shook, cracks splitting stone. Auroras flared, colors bleeding across the chamber. Operatives stumbled, rifles clattering. Mei gasped, clutching her instruments. "It's catastrophic." Reed barked, "Shut it down!" Mr. Black's eyes gleamed. "No. Let it through."

Visions slammed into them. Reed saw Lena, her voice whispering his name. Mei glimpsed endless fractals, spirals without end. Sarah saw ancestors, spirits, rituals, blood. Taq convulsed, his body trembling. A voice spoke through him, sharp and ancient. "The seal is broken. The darkness returns."

Operatives screamed, rifles firing wildly. Shadows moved, spectral entities emerging from the walls. Their forms twisted, half-human, half-animal, echoes of Kushtaka and Thunderbird. Hale barked orders, "Hold formation!" Her voice was drowned by screams. Reed clenched his jaw. "Stay together!"

The chamber pulsed, auroras bleeding across the stone. Sarah whispered another prayer, her voice breaking. "The ancestors warned of this." Taq's eyes glowed faintly, his voice no longer his own. "The seal is broken. The darkness returns." Mei gasped, "He's possessed." Mr. Black smiled. "He is conduit."

The ground split, stone tearing apart. Auroras flared, colors bleeding into impossible hues. Shadows poured from the cracks, entities shrieking. Operatives fell, consumed, their screams echoing. Hale's jaw tightened, but her eyes betrayed fear. Reed clenched his jaw. "You've doomed us."

Visions consumed them again. Reed saw his father, his childhood. Mei whispered equations, trembling. Sarah spoke in tongues, words older than the mountains. Taq whispered prayers, his voice not his own. "The seal is broken. The darkness returns." Mr. Black's voice was steady. "Yes."

The altar pulsed, glyphs glowing brighter. Masks stared, eyes alive with faint light. Effigies trembled, their forms shifting. Sarah gasped, "The wound is open." Taq's voice was steady, possessed. "The darkness returns." Reed clenched his jaw. "We have to stop this."

Operatives fell, consumed by shadows. Others screamed, driven mad, eyes wide, voices incoherent. Hale barked orders, "Hold formation!" Her operatives stumbled, rifles useless. Reed clenched his jaw. "You've killed them." Mei gasped, "It's catastrophic." Mr. Black's eyes gleamed. "It begins."

The chamber vibrated, low hum pressing against their bones. Reed felt Lena's voice pressing against him. Mei gasped, clutching her head. "It's knowledge. Forbidden knowledge." Sarah trembled, eyes wide. "The ancestors warned of this." Taq whispered, possessed. "The seal is broken. The darkness returns."

Auroras flared, colors bleeding across the chamber. Earth shook, stone splitting. Shadows moved, spectral entities emerging. Operatives screamed, rifles firing wildly. Reed clenched his jaw. "Stay sharp." Mei gasped, "It's overwhelming." Sarah whispered, "The wound is awake."

Visions intensified. Reed saw Lena, her voice whispering his name. Mei glimpsed fractals spiraling endlessly. Sarah saw rituals, sacrifices, spirits. Taq whispered prayers, his voice not his own. "The seal is broken. The darkness returns." Mr. Black's eyes gleamed. "Yes."

The altar pulsed, resonating with the aurora. Glyphs glowed, spirals twisted. Masks stared, eyes alive with faint light. Effigies trembled, their forms shifting. Sarah gasped,

"The wound is open." Taq's voice was steady, possessed. "The darkness returns."

The chamber shook, stone splitting. Auroras flared, colors bleeding across the sky. Shadows moved, spectral entities emerging. Operatives screamed, rifles firing wildly. Reed clenched his jaw. "Stay together." Mei gasped, "It's catastrophic." Hale's voice cracked. "Fall back!"

The apex of the pyramid glowed, light bleeding upward. Stone cracked, splitting open. Auroras flared, colors bleeding across the sky. A portal opened, vast and dark, its surface shimmering. Reed froze, breath ragged. Sarah gasped, whispering another prayer. Mei whispered, "It's open."

Taq's body convulsed, his voice sharp, ancient. "The seal is broken. The darkness returns." His eyes glowed faintly, his voice no longer his own. Reed clenched his jaw, forcing himself to stay calm. Sarah trembled, whispering another prayer. Mei gasped, "It's catastrophic." Mr. Black's eyes gleamed. "The way is open."

The chamber stretched endlessly, dominated by the altar and the portal above. Hale's operatives stood rigid, rifles raised, fear in their eyes. Reed clenched his jaw, breath ragged. Sarah whispered another prayer. Mei's curiosity burned, eyes wide. Taq whispered, possessed. "The darkness returns." Mr. Black's voice was steady. "Step through."

CHAPTER 13: THE OTHER SIDE

The portal swallowed them in silence, its surface shimmering like liquid shadow. Reed felt his body pulled apart, stretched across dimensions, then reassembled in a place that defied comprehension. Mei gasped, clutching her instruments, though they no longer registered anything recognizable. Sarah whispered prayers, her voice trembling. Taq stumbled, raven feather glowing faintly, his eyes wide. Mr. Black stepped forward, calm, his expression unreadable.

The landscape was surreal, a horizon that bent and folded upon itself. Mountains rose and fell in impossible arcs, rivers flowed upward into the sky, and time itself seemed fractured. Reed froze, breath ragged. "This isn't real," he muttered. Mei whispered, "It's beyond physics." Sarah trembled, whispering another prayer. Taq whispered, "It is the other side." Mr. Black's eyes gleamed. "It is truth."

Echoes moved across the landscape—shamans chanting, explorers wandering, mythic creatures shifting. Their forms were translucent, caught in endless cycles of suffering and transformation. Reed gasped, "They're trapped." Mei whispered, "Echoes. Residual consciousness." Sarah trembled, whispering, "Spirits." Taq's voice was steady. "They are warnings." Mr. Black's voice was calm. "They are proof."

Time flowed erratically, moments stretching and collapsing. Reed saw Lena, her voice whispering his name, then fading.

Mei glimpsed equations spiraling endlessly, fractals without end. Sarah saw ancestors, rituals, sacrifices. Taq whispered prayers, invoking Raven. Mr. Black's eyes gleamed. "The seal was never meant to last."

The entity emerged, vast and luminous, its form shifting between shadow and light. It was beautiful and terrifying, its presence overwhelming. Reed froze, breath ragged. "What is it?" Mei whispered, "A cosmic wanderer." Sarah trembled, whispering another prayer. Taq's voice was steady. "It was imprisoned." Mr. Black's voice was calm. "It was betrayed."

The entity communicated through visions, emotions flooding their minds. Reed saw worlds shaped and destroyed, civilizations rising and falling. Mei glimpsed mathematics woven into creation itself. Sarah saw ancestors sealing the entity, their voices sharp with fear. Taq whispered, "They gave everything to contain it." Mr. Black's voice was steady. "And now we free it."

Reed clenched his jaw, forcing himself to stay calm. "We can't control this." Mei gasped, clutching her instruments. "It's beyond comprehension." Sarah whispered another prayer. Taq's voice was steady. "It must remain sealed." Mr. Black's eyes gleamed. "It must be harnessed."

The landscape shifted, mountains collapsing, rivers reversing. Echoes screamed, their forms twisting. Reed froze, breath ragged. "It's unraveling." Mei whispered, "Reality is breaking." Sarah trembled, whispering another prayer. Taq whispered, "The wound spreads." Mr. Black's voice was calm. "It is awakening."

Visions consumed them again. Reed saw Lena, her voice whispering his name. Mei gasped, whispering equations. Sarah spoke in tongues, words older than the mountains. Taq whispered prayers, invoking guardians. Mr. Black's voice was steady. "It is power."

The entity loomed closer, its form shifting. Reed clenched his jaw. "We can't fight this." Mei whispered, "We can't understand it." Sarah trembled, whispering another prayer. Taq's voice was steady. "We can endure." Mr. Black's eyes gleamed. "We can rule."

The landscape pulsed, resonating with the entity's presence. Reed felt vibration beneath his skin, deep and resonant. Mei gasped, clutching her instruments. "It's rewriting reality." Sarah whispered, "The ancestors warned of this." Taq whispered, "The wound is awake." Mr. Black's voice was calm. "The wound is ours."

Echoes moved closer, shamans chanting, explorers screaming, mythic creatures shifting. Reed froze, breath ragged. "They're trapped in cycles." Mei whispered, "Endless suffering." Sarah trembled, whispering another prayer. Taq's voice was steady. "They are warnings." Mr. Black's voice was calm. "They are sacrifices."

The entity's voice pressed against them, emotions flooding their minds. Reed saw worlds collapsing. Mei glimpsed equations spiraling endlessly. Sarah saw ancestors sealing the entity. Taq whispered, "It was imprisoned." Mr. Black's voice was calm. "It was betrayed."

The landscape fractured, time collapsing. Reed froze, breath ragged. "We're breaking apart." Mei gasped, clutching her instruments. "It's unstable." Sarah whispered another prayer. Taq's voice was steady. "We must endure." Mr. Black's eyes gleamed. "We must embrace it."

Visions intensified. Reed saw Lena, her voice whispering his name. Mei glimpsed fractals spiraling endlessly. Sarah saw rituals, sacrifices, spirits. Taq whispered prayers, invoking guardians. Mr. Black's voice was steady. "It is power."

The entity loomed closer, its form overwhelming. Reed

clenched his jaw. "We can't stop this." Mei whispered, "We can't survive this." Sarah trembled, whispering another prayer. Taq's voice was steady. "We must endure." Mr. Black's eyes gleamed. "We must rule."

The landscape pulsed, resonating with the entity's presence. Reed felt vibration beneath his skin. Mei gasped, clutching her instruments. "It's rewriting reality." Sarah whispered, "The ancestors warned of this." Taq whispered, "The wound is awake." Mr. Black's voice was calm. "The wound is ours."

Echoes screamed, their forms twisting. Reed froze, breath ragged. "It's unraveling." Mei whispered, "Reality is breaking." Sarah trembled, whispering another prayer. Taq whispered, "The wound spreads." Mr. Black's voice was calm. "It is awakening."

The entity's voice pressed against them, emotions flooding their minds. Reed saw worlds collapsing. Mei glimpsed equations spiraling endlessly. Sarah saw ancestors sealing the entity. Taq whispered, "It was imprisoned." Mr. Black's voice was calm. "It was betrayed."

The portal swallowed them whole, its surface shimmering like liquid shadow. Reed felt himself torn apart, stretched across dimensions, then reassembled in a place that was neither earth nor sky. Mei gasped, clutching her instruments, though they no longer measured anything recognizable. Sarah whispered prayers, her voice trembling. Taq stumbled, raven feather glowing faintly, his eyes wide. Mr. Black stepped forward, calm, his expression unreadable.

The landscape was mythic, a horizon that bent and folded upon itself. Mountains rose in spirals, rivers flowed upward into the aurora, and time itself fractured into shards. Reed froze, breath ragged. "This isn't real," he muttered. Mei whispered, "It's beyond physics." Sarah trembled, whispering another prayer. Taq whispered, "It is the other side." Mr. Black's eyes gleamed. "It is truth."

Echoes moved across the terrain—ancient shamans chanting, explorers wandering, mythic creatures shifting. Their forms were translucent, caught in endless cycles of suffering and transformation. Reed gasped, "They're trapped." Mei whispered, "Residual consciousness. Fragments of those who came before." Sarah trembled, whispering, "Spirits." Taq's voice was steady. "They are warnings." Mr. Black's voice was calm. "They are sacrifices."

Time flowed erratically, moments stretching and collapsing. Reed saw Lena, her voice whispering his name, then fading. Mei glimpsed equations spiraling endlessly, fractals without end. Sarah saw ancestors sealing the entity, their voices sharp with fear. Taq whispered prayers, invoking Raven. Mr. Black's eyes gleamed. "The seal was never meant to last."

The entity emerged, vast and luminous, its form shifting between shadow and light. It was beautiful and terrifying, its presence overwhelming. Reed froze, breath ragged. "What is it?" Mei whispered, "A cosmic wanderer." Sarah trembled, whispering another prayer. Taq's voice was steady. "It was imprisoned." Mr. Black's voice was calm. "It was betrayed."

The entity spoke without words, flooding them with visions. Reed saw worlds shaped and destroyed, civilizations rising and falling. Mei glimpsed mathematics woven into creation itself. Sarah saw ancestors sealing the entity, their chants echoing like thunder. Taq whispered, "They gave everything to contain it." Mr. Black's voice was steady. "And now we free it."

Reed clenched his jaw, forcing himself to stay calm. "We can't control this." Mei gasped, clutching her instruments. "It's beyond comprehension." Sarah whispered another prayer. Taq's voice was steady. "It must remain sealed." Mr. Black's eyes gleamed. "It must be harnessed."

The landscape shifted, mountains collapsing, rivers reversing. Echoes screamed, their forms twisting. Reed froze, breath ragged. "It's unraveling." Mei whispered, "Reality is breaking." Sarah trembled, whispering another prayer. Taq whispered, "The wound spreads." Mr. Black's voice was calm. "It is awakening."

Visions consumed them again. Reed saw Lena, her voice whispering his name. Mei gasped, whispering equations. Sarah spoke in tongues, words older than the mountains. Taq whispered prayers, invoking guardians. Mr. Black's voice was steady. "It is power."

The entity loomed closer, its form shifting. Reed clenched his jaw. "We can't fight this." Mei whispered, "We can't understand it." Sarah trembled, whispering another prayer. Taq's voice was steady. "We can endure." Mr. Black's eyes gleamed. "We can rule."

The landscape pulsed, resonating with the entity's presence. Reed felt vibration beneath his skin, deep and resonant. Mei gasped, clutching her instruments. "It's rewriting reality." Sarah whispered, "The ancestors warned of this." Taq whispered, "The wound is awake." Mr. Black's voice was calm. "The wound is ours."

Echoes moved closer, shamans chanting, explorers screaming, mythic creatures shifting. Reed froze, breath ragged. "They're trapped in cycles." Mei whispered, "Endless suffering." Sarah trembled, whispering another prayer. Taq's voice was steady. "They are warnings." Mr. Black's voice was calm. "They are sacrifices."

The entity's voice pressed against them, emotions flooding their minds. Reed saw worlds collapsing. Mei glimpsed equations spiraling endlessly. Sarah saw ancestors sealing the entity. Taq whispered, "It was imprisoned." Mr. Black's voice was calm. "It was betrayed."

The landscape fractured, time collapsing. Reed froze, breath ragged. "We're breaking apart." Mei gasped, clutching her instruments. "It's unstable." Sarah whispered another prayer. Taq's voice was steady. "We must endure." Mr. Black's eyes gleamed. "We must embrace it."

Visions intensified. Reed saw his father, his childhood. Mei glimpsed fractals spiraling endlessly. Sarah saw rituals, sacrifices, spirits. Taq whispered prayers, invoking guardians. Mr. Black's voice was steady. "It is power."

The entity loomed closer, its form overwhelming. Reed clenched his jaw. "We can't stop this." Mei whispered, "We can't survive this." Sarah trembled, whispering another prayer. Taq's voice was steady. "We must endure." Mr. Black's eyes gleamed. "We must rule."

The landscape pulsed, resonating with the entity's presence. Reed felt vibration beneath his skin. Mei gasped, clutching her instruments. "It's rewriting reality." Sarah whispered, "The ancestors warned of this." Taq whispered, "The wound is awake." Mr. Black's voice was calm. "The wound is ours."

Echoes screamed, their forms twisting. Reed froze, breath ragged. "It's unraveling." Mei whispered, "Reality is breaking." Sarah trembled, whispering another prayer. Taq whispered, "The wound spreads." Mr. Black's voice was calm. "It is awakening."

The entity's voice pressed against them, emotions flooding their minds. Reed saw worlds collapsing. Mei glimpsed equations spiraling endlessly. Sarah saw ancestors sealing the entity. Taq whispered, "It was imprisoned." Mr. Black's voice was calm. "It was betrayed."

The landscape stretched endlessly, dominated by the entity's presence. Reed clenched his jaw, breath ragged. Sarah whispered another prayer. Mei's curiosity burned, eyes wide. Taq whispered, "We must endure." Mr. Black's eyes gleamed. "We must rule." The wound in the world awaited.

The portal ripped them through, bodies stretched across dimensions, then slammed into a place that defied comprehension. Reed staggered, lantern useless, breath ragged. Mei clutched her instruments, their screens flickering nonsense. Sarah whispered prayers, her voice trembling. Taq stumbled, raven feather glowing faintly. Mr. Black stood tall, calm, his eyes gleaming.

The landscape bent and folded, mountains spiraling upward, rivers flowing into the aurora. Time fractured, moments collapsing and stretching. Reed froze, jaw tight. "This isn't real." Mei whispered, "It's beyond physics." Sarah trembled, whispering another prayer. Taq whispered, "It is the other side." Mr. Black's voice was steady. "It is truth."

Echoes moved across the terrain—shamans chanting, explorers wandering, mythic creatures shifting. Their forms were translucent, caught in endless cycles of suffering. Reed gasped, "They're trapped." Mei whispered, "Residual consciousness." Sarah trembled, whispering, "Spirits." Taq's voice was steady. "They are warnings." Mr. Black's eyes gleamed. "They are sacrifices."

Visions slammed into them. Reed saw Lena, her voice whispering his name. Mei glimpsed fractals spiraling endlessly. Sarah saw ancestors sealing the entity, their chants echoing. Taq whispered prayers, invoking Raven. Mr. Black's voice was calm. "The seal was never meant to last."

The entity emerged, vast and luminous, its form shifting between shadow and light. It was beautiful and terrifying, its presence overwhelming. Reed froze, breath ragged. "What is it?" Mei whispered, "A cosmic wanderer." Sarah trembled, whispering another prayer. Taq's voice was steady. "It was imprisoned." Mr. Black's voice was calm. "It was betrayed."

The entity spoke without words, flooding them with visions. Reed saw worlds shaped and destroyed. Mei glimpsed mathematics woven into creation itself. Sarah saw ancestors sealing the entity, their voices sharp with fear. Taq whispered, "They gave everything to contain it." Mr. Black's voice was steady. "And now we free it."

The landscape shifted, mountains collapsing, rivers reversing. Echoes screamed, their forms twisting. Reed clenched his jaw. "It's unraveling." Mei whispered, "Reality is breaking." Sarah trembled, whispering another prayer. Taq whispered, "The wound spreads." Mr. Black's voice was calm. "It is awakening."

Visions consumed them again. Reed saw Lena, her voice whispering his name. Mei gasped, whispering equations. Sarah spoke in tongues, words older than the mountains. Taq whispered prayers, invoking guardians. Mr. Black's voice was steady. "It is power."

The entity loomed closer, its form overwhelming. Reed clenched his jaw. "We can't fight this." Mei whispered, "We can't understand it." Sarah trembled, whispering another prayer. Taq's voice was steady. "We must endure." Mr. Black's eyes gleamed. "We must rule."

The landscape pulsed, resonating with the entity's presence. Reed felt vibration beneath his skin. Mei gasped, clutching her instruments. "It's rewriting reality." Sarah whispered, "The ancestors warned of this." Taq whispered, "The wound is awake." Mr. Black's voice was calm. "The wound is ours."

Echoes moved closer, shamans chanting, explorers screaming, mythic creatures shifting. Reed froze, breath ragged. "They're trapped in cycles." Mei whispered, "Endless suffering." Sarah trembled, whispering another prayer. Taq's voice was steady. "They are warnings." Mr. Black's voice was calm. "They are sacrifices."

The entity's voice pressed against them, emotions flooding their minds. Reed saw worlds collapsing. Mei glimpsed equations spiraling endlessly. Sarah saw ancestors sealing the entity. Taq whispered, "It was imprisoned." Mr. Black's voice was calm. "It was betrayed."

The landscape fractured, time collapsing. Reed froze, breath ragged. "We're breaking apart." Mei gasped, clutching her instruments. "It's unstable." Sarah whispered another prayer. Taq's voice was steady. "We must endure." Mr. Black's eyes gleamed. "We must embrace it."

Visions intensified. Reed saw his father, his childhood. Mei glimpsed fractals spiraling endlessly. Sarah saw rituals, sacrifices, spirits. Taq whispered prayers, invoking guardians. Mr. Black's voice was steady. "It is power."

The entity loomed closer, its form overwhelming. Reed clenched his jaw. "We can't stop this." Mei whispered, "We can't survive this." Sarah trembled, whispering another prayer. Taq's voice was steady. "We must endure." Mr. Black's eyes gleamed. "We must rule."

The landscape pulsed, resonating with the entity's presence. Reed felt vibration beneath his skin. Mei gasped, clutching her instruments. "It's rewriting reality." Sarah whispered, "The ancestors warned of this." Taq whispered, "The wound is awake." Mr. Black's voice was calm. "The wound is ours."

Echoes screamed, their forms twisting. Reed froze, breath ragged. "It's unraveling." Mei whispered, "Reality is breaking." Sarah trembled, whispering another prayer. Taq whispered, "The wound spreads." Mr. Black's voice was calm. "It is awakening."

The entity's voice pressed against them, emotions flooding

their minds. Reed saw worlds collapsing. Mei glimpsed equations spiraling endlessly. Sarah saw ancestors sealing the entity. Taq whispered, "It was imprisoned." Mr. Black's voice was calm. "It was betrayed."

The landscape stretched endlessly, dominated by the entity's presence. Reed clenched his jaw, breath ragged. Sarah whispered another prayer. Mei's curiosity burned, eyes wide. Taq whispered, "We must endure." Mr. Black's eyes gleamed. "We must rule." The wound in the world awaited.

CHAPTER 14: THE BARGAIN

The entity loomed above them, its form shifting between shadow and light, beautiful and terrifying. Its presence pressed against their minds, flooding them with visions. Reed froze, breath ragged. Mei gasped, clutching her instruments. Sarah whispered prayers, her voice trembling. Taq stood calm, raven feather glowing faintly. Mr. Black's eyes gleamed, fixed on the entity.

The voice came without sound, emotions flooding their minds. "Release me fully," it whispered. "Grant me freedom, and I will give you knowledge and power beyond imagining. Refuse, and I will consume your minds and bodies." Reed clenched his jaw, forcing himself to stay calm. Mei trembled, curiosity burning. Sarah whispered another prayer. Taq's voice was steady. "It is a lie." Mr. Black's voice was calm. "It is truth."

Visions slammed into them. Reed saw Lena, her voice whispering his name. Mei glimpsed fractals spiraling endlessly, mathematics woven into creation. Sarah saw ancestors sealing the entity, their chants echoing. Taq whispered prayers, invoking Raven. Mr. Black's voice was steady. "It offers us everything."

Reed clenched his jaw. "It offers death." Mei gasped, clutching her instruments. "But the knowledge… it's beyond comprehension." Sarah trembled, whispering another prayer. Taq's voice was steady. "It is poison." Mr. Black's eyes gleamed.

"It is salvation."

The entity pressed harder, visions overwhelming. Reed saw worlds collapsing. Mei glimpsed equations spiraling endlessly. Sarah saw ancestors bleeding, sacrificing. Taq whispered, "They gave everything to contain it." Mr. Black's voice was calm. "And now we free it."

The clash of agendas sharpened. Reed sought survival, Mei sought knowledge, Sarah sought protection, Taq sought healing. Mr. Black sought dominion. The chamber pulsed, resonating with the aurora. The wound in the world awaited.

Sarah stepped forward, her voice trembling but steady. "There is another way." Reed frowned, skepticism faltering. Mei's eyes widened. "What?" Taq's voice was steady. "Speak." Mr. Black scoffed, dismissive. "There is no other way." Sarah's voice was calm. "A synthesis. Old and new."

She traced symbols, her fingers trembling. "Traditional chants. Mathematical patterns. Technological amplification. A ritual that combines them all." Reed clenched his jaw. "You think that will work?" Sarah nodded. "It must." Taq whispered, "It is balance." Mei gasped, "It's possible." Mr. Black's voice was sharp. "It is weakness."

The entity pressed harder, its voice sharp. "Release me. Rule with me. Or be consumed." Reed clenched his jaw. "We will resist." Mei trembled, whispering, "We must try." Sarah whispered another prayer. Taq's voice was steady. "We will seal it." Mr. Black's eyes gleamed. "We will free it."

The chamber vibrated, low hum pressing against their bones. Reed felt Lena's voice pressing against him. Mei gasped, clutching her head. "It's knowledge. Forbidden knowledge." Sarah trembled, whispering another prayer. Taq whispered, "It must remain sealed." Mr. Black's voice was calm. "It must be harnessed."

Masks glowed brighter, effigies shifting. Sarah whispered another prayer. Taq whispered, "I will go." Reed clenched his jaw. "Stay sharp." Mei whispered, "It's alive." Hale's operatives shifted uneasily, rifles raised. Mr. Black whispered, "Activate it."

Visions consumed them again. Reed saw his father, his childhood. Mei glimpsed fractals spiraling endlessly. Sarah saw rituals, sacrifices, spirits. Taq whispered prayers, invoking guardians. Mr. Black's voice was steady. "It is power."

The entity loomed closer, its form overwhelming. Reed clenched his jaw. "We can't stop this alone." Mei whispered, "We can't survive this without knowledge." Sarah trembled, whispering another prayer. Taq's voice was steady. "We must endure." Mr. Black's eyes gleamed. "We must rule."

The chamber pulsed, resonating with the aurora. Reed felt vibration beneath his skin. Mei gasped, clutching her instruments. "It's rewriting reality." Sarah whispered, "The ancestors warned of this." Taq whispered, "The wound is awake." Mr. Black's voice was calm. "The wound is ours."

Echoes screamed, their forms twisting. Reed froze, breath ragged. "It's unraveling." Mei whispered, "Reality is breaking." Sarah trembled, whispering another prayer. Taq whispered, "The wound spreads." Mr. Black's voice was calm. "It is awakening."

Sarah's voice rose, steady now. "We must work together. Old and new. Ceremony and science. Faith and calculation. Balance." Reed clenched his jaw. "We'll try." Mei whispered, "We can do this." Taq's voice was steady. "We must." Mr. Black's eyes gleamed. "You are fools."

The entity pressed harder, its voice sharp. "Release me. Rule with me. Or be consumed." Reed clenched his jaw. "We will resist." Mei trembled, whispering, "We must try." Sarah whispered another prayer. Taq's voice was steady. "We will seal it." Mr. Black's eyes gleamed. "We will free it."

The chamber vibrated, low hum pressing against their bones. Reed felt Lena's voice pressing against him. Mei gasped, clutching her head. "It's knowledge. Forbidden knowledge." Sarah trembled, whispering another prayer. Taq whispered, "It must remain sealed." Mr. Black's voice was calm. "It must be harnessed."

The entity towered above them, its form shifting between shadow and light, beautiful and terrifying. Its presence pressed against their minds, flooding them with visions of worlds collapsing and reborn. Reed froze, breath ragged. Mei gasped, clutching her instruments, though they no longer measured anything recognizable. Sarah whispered prayers, her voice trembling. Taq stood calm, raven feather glowing faintly. Mr. Black's eyes gleamed, fixed on the entity.

The voice came without sound, emotions flooding their minds. "Release me fully," it whispered. "Grant me freedom, and I will give you knowledge and power beyond imagining. Refuse, and I will consume your minds and bodies." Reed clenched his jaw, forcing himself to stay calm. Mei trembled, curiosity burning. Sarah whispered another prayer. Taq's voice was steady. "It is deception." Mr. Black's voice was calm. "It is promise."

Visions slammed into them. Reed saw Lena, her voice whispering his name. Mei glimpsed fractals spiraling endlessly, mathematics woven into creation. Sarah saw ancestors sealing the entity, their chants echoing like thunder. Taq whispered prayers, invoking Raven. Mr. Black's voice was steady. "It offers us everything."

Reed clenched his jaw. "It offers ruin." Mei gasped, clutching her instruments. "But the knowledge... it's beyond comprehension." Sarah trembled, whispering another prayer.

Taq's voice was steady. "It is poison." Mr. Black's eyes gleamed. "It is salvation."

The entity pressed harder, visions overwhelming. Reed saw civilizations rising and falling. Mei glimpsed equations spiraling endlessly, fractals without end. Sarah saw ancestors bleeding, sacrificing. Taq whispered, "They gave everything to contain it." Mr. Black's voice was calm. "And now we free it."

The clash of agendas sharpened. Reed sought survival, Mei sought knowledge, Sarah sought protection, Taq sought healing. Mr. Black sought dominion. The chamber pulsed, resonating with the aurora. The wound in the world awaited.

Sarah stepped forward, her voice trembling but steady. "There is another way." Reed frowned, skepticism faltering. Mei's eyes widened. "What?" Taq's voice was steady. "Speak." Mr. Black scoffed, dismissive. "There is no other way." Sarah's voice was calm. "A synthesis. Old and new."

She traced symbols, her fingers trembling. "Traditional chants. Mathematical patterns. Technological amplification. A ritual that combines them all." Reed clenched his jaw. "You think that will work?" Sarah nodded. "It must." Taq whispered, "It is balance." Mei gasped, "It's possible." Mr. Black's voice was sharp. "It is weakness."

The entity pressed harder, its voice sharp. "Release me. Rule with me. Or be consumed." Reed clenched his jaw. "We will resist." Mei trembled, whispering, "We must try." Sarah whispered another prayer. Taq's voice was steady. "We will seal it." Mr. Black's eyes gleamed. "We will free it."

The chamber vibrated, low hum pressing against their bones. Reed felt Lena's voice pressing against him. Mei gasped, clutching her head. "It's knowledge. Forbidden knowledge." Sarah trembled, whispering another prayer. Taq whispered, "It must remain sealed." Mr. Black's voice was calm. "It must be harnessed."

Masks glowed brighter, effigies shifting. Sarah whispered another prayer. Taq whispered, "I will go." Reed clenched his jaw. "Stay sharp." Mei whispered, "It's alive." Hale's operatives shifted uneasily, rifles raised. Mr. Black whispered, "Activate it."

Visions consumed them again. Reed saw his father, his childhood. Mei glimpsed fractals spiraling endlessly. Sarah saw rituals, sacrifices, spirits. Taq whispered prayers, invoking guardians. Mr. Black's voice was steady. "It is power."

The entity loomed closer, its form overwhelming. Reed clenched his jaw. "We can't stop this alone." Mei whispered, "We can't survive this without knowledge." Sarah trembled, whispering another prayer. Taq's voice was steady. "We must endure." Mr. Black's eyes gleamed. "We must rule."

The chamber pulsed, resonating with the aurora. Reed felt vibration beneath his skin. Mei gasped, clutching her instruments. "It's rewriting reality." Sarah whispered, "The ancestors warned of this." Taq whispered, "The wound is awake." Mr. Black's voice was calm. "The wound is ours."

Echoes screamed, their forms twisting. Reed froze, breath ragged. "It's unraveling." Mei whispered, "Reality is breaking." Sarah trembled, whispering another prayer. Taq whispered, "The wound spreads." Mr. Black's voice was calm. "It is awakening."

Sarah's voice rose, steady now. "We must work together. Old and new. Ceremony and science. Faith and calculation. Balance." Reed clenched his jaw. "We'll try." Mei whispered, "We can do this." Taq's voice was steady. "We must." Mr. Black's eyes gleamed. "You are fools."

The entity pressed harder, its voice sharp. "Release me. Rule with me. Or be consumed." Reed clenched his jaw. "We will resist." Mei trembled, whispering, "We must try." Sarah whispered another prayer. Taq's voice was steady. "We will seal it." Mr. Black's eyes gleamed. "We will free it."

The chamber vibrated, low hum pressing against their bones. Reed felt Lena's voice pressing against him. Mei gasped, clutching her head. "It's knowledge. Forbidden knowledge." Sarah trembled, whispering another prayer. Taq whispered, "It must remain sealed." Mr. Black's voice was calm. "It must be harnessed."

The entity loomed, its form shifting in jagged bursts of shadow and light. Its presence pressed against their minds, flooding them with visions. Reed staggered, breath ragged. Mei clutched her instruments, eyes wide. Sarah whispered prayers, her voice trembling. Taq stood calm, raven feather glowing faintly. Mr. Black's eyes gleamed, fixed on the entity.

The voice came without sound, slicing into their thoughts. "Release me fully. Grant me freedom, and I will give you knowledge and power beyond imagining. Refuse, and I will consume your minds and bodies." Reed clenched his jaw. "It's a trap." Mei trembled, whispering, "But the knowledge…" Sarah whispered another prayer. Taq's voice was steady. "It is poison." Mr. Black's voice was sharp. "It is salvation."

Visions slammed into them. Reed saw Lena, her voice whispering his name. Mei glimpsed fractals spiraling endlessly, mathematics woven into creation. Sarah saw ancestors sealing the entity, their chants echoing. Taq whispered prayers, invoking Raven. Mr. Black's voice was steady. "It offers us everything."

Reed barked, "It offers death." Mei gasped, clutching her instruments. "It's beyond comprehension." Sarah trembled, whispering another prayer. Taq's voice was steady. "It is deception." Mr. Black's eyes gleamed. "It is promise."

The entity pressed harder, visions overwhelming. Reed saw civilizations rising and falling. Mei glimpsed equations spiraling endlessly. Sarah saw ancestors bleeding, sacrificing. Taq whispered, "They gave everything to contain it." Mr. Black's voice was calm. "And now we free it."

The clash sharpened. Reed sought survival, Mei sought knowledge, Sarah sought protection, Taq sought healing. Mr. Black sought dominion. The chamber pulsed, resonating with the aurora. The wound in the world awaited.

Sarah stepped forward, her voice trembling but steady. "There is another way." Reed frowned, skepticism faltering. Mei's eyes widened. "What?" Taq's voice was steady. "Speak." Mr. Black scoffed, dismissive. "There is no other way." Sarah's voice was calm. "A synthesis. Old and new."

She traced symbols, her fingers trembling. "Traditional chants. Mathematical patterns. Technological amplification. A ritual that combines them all." Reed clenched his jaw. "You think that will work?" Sarah nodded. "It must." Taq whispered, "It is balance." Mei gasped, "It's possible." Mr. Black's voice was sharp. "It is weakness."

The entity pressed harder, its voice sharp. "Release me. Rule with me. Or be consumed." Reed clenched his jaw. "We will resist." Mei trembled, whispering, "We must try." Sarah whispered another prayer. Taq's voice was steady. "We will seal it." Mr. Black's eyes gleamed. "We will free it."

The chamber vibrated, low hum pressing against their bones. Reed felt Lena's voice pressing against him. Mei gasped, clutching her head. "It's knowledge. Forbidden knowledge." Sarah trembled, whispering another prayer. Taq whispered, "It must remain sealed." Mr. Black's voice was calm. "It must be harnessed."

Masks glowed brighter, effigies shifting. Sarah whispered

another prayer. Taq whispered, "I will go." Reed clenched his jaw. "Stay sharp." Mei whispered, "It's alive." Hale's operatives shifted uneasily, rifles raised. Mr. Black whispered, "Activate it."

Visions consumed them again. Reed saw his father, his childhood. Mei glimpsed fractals spiraling endlessly. Sarah saw rituals, sacrifices, spirits. Taq whispered prayers, invoking guardians. Mr. Black's voice was steady. "It is power."

The entity loomed closer, its form overwhelming. Reed clenched his jaw. "We can't stop this alone." Mei whispered, "We can't survive this without knowledge." Sarah trembled, whispering another prayer. Taq's voice was steady. "We must endure." Mr. Black's eyes gleamed. "We must rule."

The chamber pulsed, resonating with the aurora. Reed felt vibration beneath his skin. Mei gasped, clutching her instruments. "It's rewriting reality." Sarah whispered, "The ancestors warned of this." Taq whispered, "The wound is awake." Mr. Black's voice was calm. "The wound is ours."

Echoes screamed, their forms twisting. Reed froze, breath ragged. "It's unraveling." Mei whispered, "Reality is breaking." Sarah trembled, whispering another prayer. Taq whispered, "The wound spreads." Mr. Black's voice was calm. "It is awakening."

Sarah's voice rose, steady now. "We must work together. Old and new. Ceremony and science. Faith and calculation. Balance." Reed clenched his jaw. "We'll try." Mei whispered, "We can do this." Taq's voice was steady. "We must." Mr. Black's eyes gleamed. "You are fools."

The entity pressed harder, its voice sharp. "Release me. Rule with me. Or be consumed." Reed clenched his jaw. "We will resist." Mei trembled, whispering, "We must try." Sarah whispered another prayer. Taq's voice was steady. "We will seal it." Mr. Black's eyes gleamed. "We will free it."

The chamber vibrated, low hum pressing against their bones. Reed felt Lena's voice pressing against him. Mei gasped, clutching her head. "It's knowledge. Forbidden knowledge." Sarah trembled, whispering another prayer. Taq whispered, "It must remain sealed." Mr. Black's voice was calm. "It must be harnessed."

The chamber stretched endlessly, dominated by masks, drums, and effigies. Reed clenched his jaw, breath ragged. Sarah whispered another prayer. Mei's curiosity burned, eyes wide. Taq whispered, "We must endure." Mr. Black's eyes gleamed. "We must rule." The wound in the world awaited.

CHAPTER 15: THE RETURN

The ritual began with urgency, Sarah's voice rising in chants older than memory. Reed steadied her rhythm, his jaw tight, forcing himself to stay focused. Mei traced mathematical spirals into the air, her instruments buzzing, amplifying the cadence. Taq stood at the center, raven feather glowing faintly, his body trembling. Mr. Black moved closer, his eyes gleaming, his voice sharp. "Yes. Release it."

The chamber pulsed, resonating with the aurora. Masks glowed, effigies trembled, glyphs shifted. Sarah's chants blended with Mei's equations, rhythm and calculation weaving together. Reed clenched his jaw, forcing himself to stay calm. Taq whispered prayers, invoking Raven, Kushtaka, Thunderbird. Mr. Black's voice was steady. "It is ours."

The entity pressed harder, its voice sharp. "Release me. Rule with me. Or be consumed." Reed barked, "Seal it!" Mei gasped, clutching her instruments. "It's overwhelming." Sarah whispered another prayer. Taq's voice was steady. "We will endure." Mr. Black's eyes gleamed. "We will rule."

The chamber shook, stone splitting. Auroras flared, colors bleeding across the sky. Shadows moved, spectral entities emerging. Operatives screamed, rifles firing wildly. Reed clenched his jaw. "Stay sharp." Mei gasped, "It's catastrophic." Sarah trembled, whispering another prayer. Taq whispered, "The wound is awake."

Mr. Black stepped forward, his voice rising. "I accept the bargain. I release you fully." The entity surged, its presence overwhelming. Reed froze, breath ragged. "No!" Sarah gasped, whispering another prayer. Mei screamed, clutching her instruments. Taq's voice was steady. "It is betrayal."

The entity consumed Mr. Black, his body dissolving into shadow and light. His scream echoed, then vanished. Reed clenched his jaw, forcing himself to stay calm. Sarah trembled, whispering another prayer. Mei gasped, "He's gone." Taq whispered, "It is the price."

The ritual intensified, Sarah's chants rising, Mei's equations spiraling. Reed steadied their rhythm, his voice sharp. "Focus." Taq convulsed, his body trembling, spirit pressed against him. His voice shifted, ancient, sharp. "The seal weakens. The darkness returns." Reed clenched his jaw. "Hold on."

The chamber pulsed, resonating with the aurora. Masks glowed, effigies trembled, glyphs shifted. Sarah whispered another prayer. Mei gasped, clutching her instruments. Reed clenched his jaw. "We keep moving." Taq whispered, "I will endure."

Visions consumed them. Reed saw Lena, her voice whispering his name. Mei glimpsed fractals spiraling endlessly. Sarah saw ancestors sealing the entity. Taq whispered prayers, his voice not his own. "The seal is broken. The darkness returns." Reed clenched his jaw. "Seal it again."

The ritual reached its peak, chants and equations weaving together. Sarah's voice rose, Mei's instruments screamed, Reed steadied their rhythm. Taq convulsed, his spirit fracturing. His voice was sharp, ancient. "The seal weakens. The wound spreads." Reed clenched his jaw. "Hold on."

The entity pressed harder, its voice sharp. "Release me. Rule with me. Or be consumed." Reed barked, "Seal it!" Mei gasped, clutching her instruments. Sarah whispered another prayer. Taq whispered, "We will endure." Mr. Black was gone, consumed.

The chamber shook, stone splitting. Auroras flared, colors bleeding across the sky. Shadows moved, spectral entities emerging. Operatives screamed, rifles firing wildly. Reed clenched his jaw. "Stay sharp." Mei gasped, "It's catastrophic." Sarah trembled, whispering another prayer. Taq whispered, "The wound is awake."

The ritual succeeded, the entity weakening, its form fracturing. Reed froze, breath ragged. "It's working." Mei gasped, clutching her instruments. "It's stabilizing." Sarah whispered another prayer. Taq convulsed, his spirit fracturing. "I will endure."

The portal stabilized, its surface shimmering. Reed clenched his jaw. "We can return." Mei gasped, "It's open." Sarah whispered another prayer. Taq stumbled, his body trembling. "I will endure." Reed steadied him. "We're going home."

The chamber pulsed, resonating with the aurora. Masks dimmed, effigies stilled, glyphs faded. Reed clenched his jaw. "It's ending." Mei gasped, clutching her instruments. Sarah whispered another prayer. Taq whispered, "The wound is sealed."

The survivors stepped through the portal, their bodies pulled back into the physical world. Reed froze, breath ragged. Mei gasped, clutching her instruments. Sarah whispered another prayer. Taq stumbled, his body trembling. "I will endure."

The pyramid collapsed, stone splitting, energy spent. Hale's operatives evacuated, rifles abandoned. Reed clenched his jaw. "Move!" Mei gasped, clutching her instruments. Sarah whispered another prayer. Taq stumbled, his spirit fractured.

Reed steadied him. "We're going home."

The chamber shook, stone collapsing. Auroras faded, colors bleeding into darkness. Reed clenched his jaw. "It's ending." Mei gasped, "We're alive." Sarah whispered another prayer. Taq whispered, "I will endure." Reed steadied him. "We're going home."

The survivors emerged into the tundra, the pyramid collapsing behind them. Reed froze, breath ragged. Mei gasped, clutching her instruments. Sarah whispered another prayer. Taq stumbled, his body trembling. Reed steadied him. "We're alive."

The ritual began with solemn weight, Sarah's chants rising like echoes of forgotten ceremonies. Her voice carried the cadence of ancestors, weaving with Mei's spiraling equations that glowed faintly in the air. Reed steadied their rhythm, his jaw tight, forcing himself to stay focused. Taq stood at the center, raven feather glowing, his body trembling as spirits pressed against him. Mr. Black moved closer, his eyes gleaming, his voice sharp. "Yes. Release it."

The chamber pulsed, resonating with the aurora. Masks glowed, effigies trembled, glyphs shifted. Sarah's chants blended with Mei's equations, rhythm and calculation weaving together. Reed clenched his jaw, forcing himself to stay calm. Taq whispered prayers, invoking Raven, Kushtaka, Thunderbird. Mr. Black's voice was steady. "It is ours."

The entity pressed harder, its voice sharp. "Release me. Rule with me. Or be consumed." Reed barked, "Seal it!" Mei gasped, clutching her instruments. "It's overwhelming." Sarah whispered another prayer. Taq's voice was steady. "We will endure." Mr. Black's eyes gleamed. "We will rule."

The chamber shook, stone splitting. Auroras flared, colors bleeding across the sky. Shadows moved, spectral entities emerging. Operatives screamed, rifles firing wildly. Reed clenched his jaw. "Stay sharp." Mei gasped, "It's catastrophic." Sarah trembled, whispering another prayer. Taq whispered, "The wound is awake."

Mr. Black stepped forward, his voice rising. "I accept the bargain. I release you fully." The entity surged, its presence overwhelming. Reed froze, breath ragged. "No!" Sarah gasped, whispering another prayer. Mei screamed, clutching her instruments. Taq's voice was steady. "It is betrayal."

The entity consumed Mr. Black, his body dissolving into shadow and light. His scream echoed, then vanished. Reed clenched his jaw, forcing himself to stay calm. Sarah trembled, whispering another prayer. Mei gasped, "He's gone." Taq whispered, "It is the price."

The ritual intensified, Sarah's chants rising, Mei's equations spiraling. Reed steadied their rhythm, his voice sharp. "Focus." Taq convulsed, his body trembling, spirit pressed against him. His voice shifted, ancient, sharp. "The seal weakens. The darkness returns." Reed clenched his jaw. "Hold on."

The chamber pulsed, resonating with the aurora. Masks glowed, effigies trembled, glyphs shifted. Sarah whispered another prayer. Mei gasped, clutching her instruments. Reed clenched his jaw. "We keep moving." Taq whispered, "I will endure."

Visions consumed them. Reed saw Lena, her voice whispering his name. Mei glimpsed fractals spiraling endlessly. Sarah saw ancestors sealing the entity. Taq whispered prayers, his voice not his own. "The seal is broken. The darkness returns." Reed clenched his jaw. "Seal it again."

The ritual reached its peak, chants and equations weaving together. Sarah's voice rose, Mei's instruments screamed, Reed steadied their rhythm. Taq convulsed, his spirit fracturing.

His voice was sharp, ancient. "The seal weakens. The wound spreads." Reed clenched his jaw. "Hold on."

The entity pressed harder, its voice sharp. "Release me. Rule with me. Or be consumed." Reed barked, "Seal it!" Mei gasped, clutching her instruments. Sarah whispered another prayer. Taq whispered, "We will endure." Mr. Black was gone, consumed.

The chamber shook, stone splitting. Auroras flared, colors bleeding across the sky. Shadows moved, spectral entities emerging. Operatives screamed, rifles firing wildly. Reed clenched his jaw. "Stay sharp." Mei gasped, "It's catastrophic." Sarah trembled, whispering another prayer. Taq whispered, "The wound is awake."

The ritual succeeded, the entity weakening, its form fracturing. Reed froze, breath ragged. "It's working." Mei gasped, clutching her instruments. "It's stabilizing." Sarah whispered another prayer. Taq convulsed, his spirit fracturing. "I will endure."

The portal stabilized, its surface shimmering. Reed clenched his jaw. "We can return." Mei gasped, "It's open." Sarah whispered another prayer. Taq stumbled, his body trembling. "I will endure." Reed steadied him. "We're going home."

The chamber pulsed, resonating with the aurora. Masks dimmed, effigies stilled, glyphs faded. Reed clenched his jaw. "It's ending." Mei gasped, clutching her instruments. Sarah whispered another prayer. Taq whispered, "The wound is sealed."

The survivors stepped through the portal, their bodies pulled back into the physical world. Reed froze, breath ragged. Mei gasped, clutching her instruments. Sarah whispered another prayer. Taq stumbled, his body trembling. "I will endure."

The pyramid collapsed, stone splitting, energy spent. Hale's operatives evacuated, rifles abandoned. Reed clenched his jaw. "Move!" Mei gasped, clutching her instruments. Sarah whispered another prayer. Taq stumbled, his spirit fractured. Reed steadied him. "We're going home."

The chamber shook, stone collapsing. Auroras faded, colors bleeding into darkness. Reed clenched his jaw. "It's ending." Mei gasped, "We're alive." Sarah whispered another prayer. Taq whispered, "I will endure." Reed steadied him. "We're going home."

The survivors emerged into the tundra, the pyramid collapsing behind them. Reed froze, breath ragged. Mei gasped, clutching her instruments. Sarah whispered another prayer. Taq stumbled, his body trembling. Reed steadied him. "We're alive."

The chamber shook violently, stone splitting as auroras bled across the sky. Reed barked, "Hold the rhythm!" Sarah's chants rose, sharp and urgent. Mei's instruments screamed, numbers climbing off the scale. Taq convulsed at the center, raven feather glowing faintly. Mr. Black stepped forward, his voice rising. "Yes. Release it!"

The entity pressed harder, its voice slicing into their minds. "Grant me freedom. Rule with me. Or be consumed." Reed clenched his jaw. "Seal it!" Sarah whispered another prayer, her voice breaking. Mei gasped, clutching her instruments. Taq's voice shifted, ancient. "The seal weakens. The darkness returns." Mr. Black's eyes gleamed. "It is ours."

The chamber pulsed, glyphs glowing brighter, effigies trembling. Reed steadied Sarah's rhythm, forcing himself to stay calm. Mei traced spirals, her equations weaving into the chants. Taq convulsed, his spirit fracturing. Mr. Black's voice rose. "I accept the bargain. I release you fully."

The entity surged, its presence overwhelming. Reed froze, breath ragged. "No!" Sarah gasped, whispering another prayer. Mei screamed, clutching her instruments. Taq's voice was sharp, ancient. "It is betrayal." Mr. Black's body dissolved into shadow and light, his scream echoing, then vanishing.

Reed clenched his jaw, forcing himself to stay calm. "He's gone." Sarah trembled, whispering another prayer. Mei gasped, "Consumed." Taq whispered, "It is the price." The chamber shook, stone splitting. Auroras flared, colors bleeding across the sky. Shadows moved, spectral entities shrieking.

The ritual intensified, Sarah's chants rising, Mei's equations spiraling. Reed steadied their rhythm, his voice sharp. "Focus." Taq convulsed, his body trembling, spirit pressed against him. His voice shifted, ancient, sharp. "The seal weakens. The wound spreads." Reed clenched his jaw. "Hold on."

The entity pressed harder, its voice sharp. "Release me. Rule with me. Or be consumed." Reed barked, "Seal it!" Mei gasped, clutching her instruments. Sarah whispered another prayer. Taq whispered, "We will endure." Mr. Black was gone, consumed.

The chamber shook, stone splitting. Auroras flared, colors bleeding across the sky. Shadows moved, spectral entities emerging. Operatives screamed, rifles firing wildly. Reed clenched his jaw. "Stay sharp." Mei gasped, "It's catastrophic." Sarah trembled, whispering another prayer. Taq whispered, "The wound is awake."

The ritual peaked, chants and equations weaving together. Sarah's voice rose, Mei's instruments screamed, Reed steadied their rhythm. Taq convulsed, his spirit fracturing. His voice was sharp, ancient. "The seal weakens. The wound spreads." Reed clenched his jaw. "Hold on."

The entity fractured, its form breaking apart. Reed

froze, breath ragged. "It's working." Mei gasped, clutching her instruments. "It's stabilizing." Sarah whispered another prayer. Taq convulsed, his spirit fracturing. "I will endure."

The portal stabilized, its surface shimmering. Reed clenched his jaw. "We can return." Mei gasped, "It's open." Sarah whispered another prayer. Taq stumbled, his body trembling. "I will endure." Reed steadied him. "We're going home."

The chamber pulsed, resonating with the aurora. Masks dimmed, effigies stilled, glyphs faded. Reed clenched his jaw. "It's ending." Mei gasped, clutching her instruments. Sarah whispered another prayer. Taq whispered, "The wound is sealed."

The survivors stepped through the portal, their bodies pulled back into the physical world. Reed froze, breath ragged. Mei gasped, clutching her instruments. Sarah whispered another prayer. Taq stumbled, his body trembling. "I will endure."

The pyramid collapsed, stone splitting, energy spent. Hale's operatives evacuated, rifles abandoned. Reed clenched his jaw. "Move!" Mei gasped, clutching her instruments. Sarah whispered another prayer. Taq stumbled, his spirit fractured. Reed steadied him. "We're going home."

The chamber shook, stone collapsing. Auroras faded, colors bleeding into darkness. Reed clenched his jaw. "It's ending." Mei gasped, "We're alive." Sarah whispered another prayer. Taq whispered, "I will endure." Reed steadied him. "We're going home."

The survivors emerged into the tundra, the pyramid collapsing behind them. Reed froze, breath ragged. Mei gasped, clutching her instruments. Sarah whispered another prayer. Taq stumbled, his body trembling. Reed steadied him. "We're alive."

The aurora faded, the sky darkened, silence returned. Reed clenched his jaw, breath ragged. Mei gasped, "We survived." Sarah whispered another prayer. Taq whispered, "The wound is sealed." Reed steadied him. "We're going home."

The tundra stretched endlessly, the pyramid collapsing into ruin. Reed clenched his jaw, breath ragged. Sarah whispered another prayer. Mei's curiosity burned, eyes wide. Taq whispered, "I will endure." Reed steadied him. "We're alive." The wound in the world awaited.

CHAPTER 16: THE COVER-UP

The tundra lay silent, the pyramid collapsed into ruin, its energy spent. Hale stood at the edge of the wreckage, her coat snapping in the wind, eyes sharp. Her operatives gathered, shaken, rifles abandoned. Reed steadied Taq, his body trembling, spirit fractured. Mei clutched her instruments, eyes wide. Sarah whispered prayers, her voice trembling. Hale's jaw tightened. "No one will know."

She orchestrated the cover-up with precision, her voice sharp. "This was a natural disaster. Nothing more. All evidence is classified." Operatives nodded, fear in their eyes. Reed clenched his jaw, forcing himself to stay calm. "You can't bury this." Hale's eyes narrowed. "Watch me."

Reed was debriefed, his voice sharp. "We saw everything. The entity. The ritual. The collapse." Officials leaned forward, their faces unreadable. Hale's voice cut through. "You will say nothing. If you speak, you will be prosecuted." Reed clenched his jaw, forcing himself to stay calm. "You're afraid." Hale's eyes narrowed. "I'm in control."

Mei was approached quietly, her instruments confiscated. A shadowy figure whispered, "Your knowledge is valuable. Join us." Mei froze, breath ragged. "What do you mean?" The figure's voice was calm. "A government agency. Research. Power. You will serve." Mei trembled, curiosity burning. "And if I refuse?" The figure's eyes gleamed. "You won't."

Sarah returned to her community, her voice trembling but steady. She carried the weight of visions, chants, and sacrifices. Elders listened, their faces solemn. "You have seen what was sealed," they whispered. Sarah nodded. "It is awake. But we sealed it again." Elders whispered prayers, their voices sharp. "You must preserve this knowledge." Sarah's jaw tightened. "I will."

Taq lay in recovery, his body trembling, spirit fractured. His grandmother sat beside him, her voice calm. "You are wounded, but you are healer." Taq whispered, "The entity pressed against me. It spoke. The seal is broken. The balance disturbed." His grandmother's eyes gleamed. "The ancestors commend your bravery. But the wound lingers."

Visions haunted Taq, spirits pressing against him. Raven whispered, "You endured." Kushtaka whispered, "You sacrificed." Thunderbird whispered, "You are wounded healer." Taq trembled, his voice sharp. "The balance is disturbed." His grandmother whispered prayers, her voice steady. "You will restore it."

Reed clenched his jaw, haunted by Lena's voice. He whispered, "We sealed it. But at what cost?" Sarah's voice was calm. "At the cost of sacrifice." Mei trembled, whispering equations. "At the cost of knowledge." Taq whispered, "At the cost of balance." Hale's voice was sharp. "At the cost of truth."

The cover-up spread, reports fabricated. "Avalanche. Natural disaster. Nothing unusual." Files were sealed, evidence destroyed. Reed clenched his jaw. "It's a lie." Hale's voice was calm. "It's control." Mei whispered, "It's manipulation." Sarah whispered prayers. "It's betrayal." Taq whispered, "It's disturbance."

Officials leaned forward, their voices sharp. "You will remain silent." Reed clenched his jaw. "You can't bury this." Hale's eyes narrowed. "I already have." Mei trembled, whispering, "You're afraid." Sarah whispered another prayer. Taq whispered, "The spirits know."

The tundra lay silent, the pyramid collapsed into ruin. Hale's operatives evacuated, rifles abandoned. Reed steadied Taq, his body trembling. Mei clutched her instruments, eyes wide. Sarah whispered prayers, her voice trembling. Hale's jaw tightened. "No one will know."

Visions haunted them all. Reed saw Lena, her voice whispering his name. Mei glimpsed fractals spiraling endlessly. Sarah saw ancestors sealing the entity. Taq whispered prayers, invoking guardians. Hale's voice was sharp. "It is buried."

The cover-up deepened, files sealed, evidence destroyed. Reed clenched his jaw. "It's betrayal." Mei whispered, "It's manipulation." Sarah whispered prayers. "It's deception." Taq whispered, "It's disturbance." Hale's voice was calm. "It's control."

Officials leaned forward, their voices sharp. "You will remain silent." Reed clenched his jaw. "You can't bury this." Hale's eyes narrowed. "I already have." Mei trembled, whispering, "You're afraid." Sarah whispered another prayer. Taq whispered, "The spirits know."

The tundra stretched endlessly, silence pressing against them. Reed clenched his jaw, breath ragged. Mei gasped, clutching her instruments. Sarah whispered another prayer. Taq whispered, "The wound is sealed, but balance disturbed." Hale's voice was calm. "It is buried."

Taq's grandmother whispered prayers, her voice steady. "You are wounded healer. You will restore balance." Taq trembled, his voice sharp. "The entity lingers. The visions remain." His grandmother's eyes gleamed. "The ancestors commend your bravery. But the wound lingers."

Reed clenched his jaw, haunted by Lena's voice. "We sealed it. But at what cost?" Sarah whispered, "At the cost of sacrifice." Mei trembled, whispering equations. "At the cost of knowledge." Taq whispered, "At the cost of balance." Hale's voice was sharp. "At the cost of truth."

The aurora faded, the sky darkened, silence returned. Reed clenched his jaw, breath ragged. Mei gasped, "We survived." Sarah whispered another prayer. Taq whispered, "The wound is sealed, but balance disturbed." Hale's voice was calm. "It is buried."

The tundra lay silent, the pyramid collapsed into ruin, its energy spent. Hale stood at the edge of the wreckage, her coat snapping in the wind, eyes sharp. Her operatives gathered, shaken, rifles abandoned. Reed steadied Taq, his body trembling, spirit fractured. Mei clutched her instruments, eyes wide. Sarah whispered prayers, her voice trembling. Hale's jaw tightened. "No one will know."

She orchestrated the cover-up with precision, her voice sharp. "This was a natural disaster. Nothing more. All evidence is classified." Operatives nodded, fear in their eyes. Reed clenched his jaw, forcing himself to stay calm. "You can't bury this." Hale's eyes narrowed. "Watch me."

Reed was debriefed, his voice sharp. "We saw everything. The entity. The ritual. The collapse." Officials leaned forward, their faces unreadable. Hale's voice cut through. "You will say nothing. If you speak, you will be prosecuted." Reed clenched his jaw, forcing himself to stay calm. "You're afraid." Hale's eyes narrowed. "I'm in control."

Mei was approached quietly, her instruments confiscated. A shadowy figure whispered, "Your knowledge is valuable. Join us." Mei froze, breath ragged. "What do you mean?" The figure's voice was calm. "A government agency. Research. Power. You will serve." Mei trembled, curiosity burning. "And if I refuse?" The figure's eyes gleamed. "You won't."

Sarah returned to her community, her voice trembling but steady. She carried the weight of visions, chants, and sacrifices. Elders listened, their faces solemn. "You have seen what was sealed," they whispered. Sarah nodded. "It is awake. But we sealed it again." Elders whispered prayers, their voices sharp. "You must preserve this knowledge." Sarah's jaw tightened. "I will."

Taq lay in recovery, his body trembling, spirit fractured. His grandmother sat beside him, her voice calm. "You are wounded, but you are healer." Taq whispered, "The entity pressed against me. It spoke. The seal is broken. The balance disturbed." His grandmother's eyes gleamed. "The ancestors commend your bravery. But the wound lingers."

Visions haunted Taq, spirits pressing against him. Raven whispered, "You endured." Kushtaka whispered, "You sacrificed." Thunderbird whispered, "You are wounded healer." Taq trembled, his voice sharp. "The balance is disturbed." His grandmother whispered prayers, her voice steady. "You will restore it."

Reed clenched his jaw, haunted by Lena's voice. He whispered, "We sealed it. But at what cost?" Sarah's voice was calm. "At the cost of sacrifice." Mei trembled, whispering equations. "At the cost of knowledge." Taq whispered, "At the cost of balance." Hale's voice was sharp. "At the cost of truth."

The cover-up spread, reports fabricated. "Avalanche. Natural disaster. Nothing unusual." Files were sealed, evidence destroyed. Reed clenched his jaw. "It's a lie." Hale's voice was calm. "It's control." Mei whispered, "It's manipulation." Sarah whispered prayers. "It's betrayal." Taq whispered, "It's disturbance."

Officials leaned forward, their voices sharp. "You will remain silent." Reed clenched his jaw. "You can't bury this." Hale's eyes narrowed. "I already have." Mei trembled, whispering, "You're afraid." Sarah whispered another prayer. Taq whispered, "The spirits know."

The tundra lay silent, the pyramid collapsed into ruin. Hale's operatives evacuated, rifles abandoned. Reed steadied Taq, his body trembling. Mei clutched her instruments, eyes wide. Sarah whispered prayers, her voice trembling. Hale's jaw tightened. "No one will know."

Visions haunted them all. Reed saw Lena, her voice whispering his name. Mei glimpsed fractals spiraling endlessly. Sarah saw ancestors sealing the entity. Taq whispered prayers, invoking guardians. Hale's voice was sharp. "It is buried."

The cover-up deepened, files sealed, evidence destroyed. Reed clenched his jaw. "It's betrayal." Mei whispered, "It's manipulation." Sarah whispered prayers. "It's deception." Taq whispered, "It's disturbance." Hale's voice was calm. "It's control."

Officials leaned forward, their voices sharp. "You will remain silent." Reed clenched his jaw. "You can't bury this." Hale's eyes narrowed. "I already have." Mei trembled, whispering, "You're afraid." Sarah whispered another prayer. Taq whispered, "The spirits know."

The tundra stretched endlessly, silence pressing against them. Reed clenched his jaw, breath ragged. Mei gasped, clutching her instruments. Sarah whispered another prayer. Taq whispered, "The wound is sealed, but balance disturbed." Hale's voice was calm. "It is buried."

Taq's grandmother whispered prayers, her voice steady. "You are wounded healer. You will restore balance." Taq trembled, his voice sharp. "The entity lingers. The visions remain." His grandmother's eyes gleamed. "The ancestors commend your bravery. But the wound lingers."

Reed clenched his jaw, haunted by Lena's voice. "We sealed it. But at what cost?" Sarah whispered, "At the cost of sacrifice." Mei trembled, whispering equations. "At the cost of knowledge." Taq whispered, "At the cost of balance." Hale's voice was sharp. "At the cost of truth."

The tundra was silent, the pyramid collapsed into ruin. Hale stood at the edge, her coat snapping in the wind, eyes sharp. Operatives gathered, shaken, rifles abandoned. Reed steadied Taq, his body trembling, spirit fractured. Mei clutched her instruments, eyes wide. Sarah whispered prayers, her voice trembling. Hale's jaw tightened. "No one will know."

She moved quickly, her voice sharp. "This was a natural disaster. Avalanche. Nothing more." Operatives nodded, fear in their eyes. Reed clenched his jaw. "You can't bury this." Hale's eyes narrowed. "Watch me."

Reed was debriefed under harsh lights, his voice sharp. "We saw everything. The entity. The ritual. The collapse." Officials leaned forward, faces unreadable. Hale's voice cut through. "You will say nothing. If you speak, you will be prosecuted." Reed clenched his jaw. "You're afraid." Hale's eyes narrowed. "I'm in control."

Mei was approached quietly, her instruments confiscated. A shadowy figure whispered, "Your knowledge is valuable. Join us." Mei froze, breath ragged. "What do you mean?" The figure's voice was calm. "A government agency. Research. Power. You will serve." Mei trembled, curiosity burning. "And if I refuse?" The figure's eyes gleamed. "You won't."

Sarah returned to her community, her voice trembling but steady. She carried the weight of visions, chants, and sacrifices.

Elders listened, solemn. "You have seen what was sealed," they whispered. Sarah nodded. "It is awake. But we sealed it again." Elders whispered prayers. "You must preserve this knowledge." Sarah's jaw tightened. "I will."

Taq lay in recovery, his body trembling, spirit fractured. His grandmother sat beside him, her voice calm. "You are wounded, but you are healer." Taq whispered, "The entity pressed against me. It spoke. The seal is broken. The balance disturbed." His grandmother's eyes gleamed. "The ancestors commend your bravery. But the wound lingers."

Visions haunted Taq, spirits pressing against him. Raven whispered, "You endured." Kushtaka whispered, "You sacrificed." Thunderbird whispered, "You are wounded healer." Taq trembled, his voice sharp. "The balance is disturbed." His grandmother whispered prayers. "You will restore it."

Reed clenched his jaw, haunted by Lena's voice. "We sealed it. But at what cost?" Sarah's voice was calm. "At the cost of sacrifice." Mei trembled, whispering equations. "At the cost of knowledge." Taq whispered, "At the cost of balance." Hale's voice was sharp. "At the cost of truth."

The cover-up spread, reports fabricated. "Avalanche. Natural disaster. Nothing unusual." Files sealed, evidence destroyed. Reed clenched his jaw. "It's a lie." Hale's voice was calm. "It's control." Mei whispered, "It's manipulation." Sarah whispered prayers. "It's betrayal." Taq whispered, "It's disturbance."

Officials leaned forward, voices sharp. "You will remain silent." Reed clenched his jaw. "You can't bury this." Hale's eyes narrowed. "I already have." Mei trembled, whispering, "You're afraid." Sarah whispered another prayer. Taq whispered, "The spirits know."

The tundra stretched endlessly, silence pressing against them. Reed clenched his jaw, breath ragged. Mei gasped, clutching her instruments. Sarah whispered another prayer. Taq whispered, "The wound is sealed, but balance disturbed." Hale's voice was calm. "It is buried."

Taq's grandmother whispered prayers, her voice steady. "You are wounded healer. You will restore balance." Taq trembled, his voice sharp. "The entity lingers. The visions remain." His grandmother's eyes gleamed. "The ancestors commend your bravery. But the wound lingers."

Reed clenched his jaw, haunted by Lena's voice. "We sealed it. But at what cost?" Sarah whispered, "At the cost of sacrifice." Mei trembled, whispering equations. "At the cost of knowledge." Taq whispered, "At the cost of balance." Hale's voice was sharp. "At the cost of truth."

The aurora faded, the sky darkened, silence returned. Reed clenched his jaw, breath ragged. Mei gasped, "We survived." Sarah whispered another prayer. Taq whispered, "The wound is sealed, but balance disturbed." Hale's voice was calm. "It is buried."

The tundra stretched endlessly, the pyramid collapsed into ruin. Reed clenched his jaw, breath ragged. Sarah whispered another prayer. Mei's curiosity burned, eyes wide. Taq whispered, "I will endure." Hale's eyes gleamed. "No one will know."

Visions haunted them all. Reed saw Lena, her voice whispering his name. Mei glimpsed fractals spiraling endlessly. Sarah saw ancestors sealing the entity. Taq whispered prayers, invoking guardians. Hale's voice was sharp. "It is buried."

The cover-up deepened, files sealed, evidence destroyed. Reed clenched his jaw. "It's betrayal." Mei whispered, "It's manipulation." Sarah whispered prayers. "It's deception." Taq whispered, "It's disturbance." Hale's voice was calm. "It's control."

Officials leaned forward, their voices sharp. "You will remain silent." Reed clenched his jaw. "You can't bury this." Hale's eyes narrowed. "I already have." Mei trembled, whispering, "You're afraid." Sarah whispered another prayer. Taq whispered, "The spirits know."

The tundra stretched endlessly, silence pressing against them. Reed clenched his jaw, breath ragged. Mei gasped, clutching her instruments. Sarah whispered another prayer. Taq whispered, "The wound is sealed, but balance disturbed." Hale's voice was calm. "It is buried."

CHAPTER 17: THE SURVIVORS

Reed returned to his old life, but nothing felt familiar anymore. Nights were broken by visions of Lena whispering his name, shadows pressing against his walls. He woke drenched in sweat, heart pounding, convinced someone was watching. Every flicker of light outside his window felt like surveillance. He clenched his jaw, whispering, "They're still here."

Paranoia grew, gnawing at him. He noticed cars parked too long, strangers lingering near his building. Conversations felt scripted, eyes too sharp. Reed muttered, "They know." He carried the weight of Hale's threat, the silence forced upon him. His nightmares bled into waking hours, leaving him restless, haunted.

Mei buried herself in research, her instruments scattered across her desk. Equations spiraled across notebooks, diagrams filled walls. She whispered, "There must be a pattern." Yet the deeper she dug, the stranger the sources became. Esoteric texts, forbidden grimoires, fragments of myth. She trembled, whispering, "It's all connected."

Her colleagues noticed her obsession, whispering behind closed doors. Mei ignored them, her eyes burning with curiosity. She traced symbols, compared chants to fractals, mapped rituals to equations. "It's science," she muttered, "but it's more." She felt herself slipping, drawn into shadows of knowledge.

Sarah chose another path, her voice rising in classrooms and gatherings. She became a storyteller, weaving her experiences into lessons. Children listened, wide-eyed, as she spoke of spirits, ancestors, and balance. "Knowledge must be preserved," she said. Elders nodded, their voices solemn. "You carry the burden."

Her stories blended memory and myth, ritual and warning. She spoke of the wound in the world, the necessity of humility. "We must respect the land," she whispered. "We must honor the spirits." Her voice carried weight, echoing across generations. Sarah became a teacher, a guardian of memory.

Taq struggled, his body weakened, spirit fractured. He whispered prayers, his voice trembling. "The wound lingers." His grandmother sat beside him, her voice calm. "You are wounded healer. You will restore balance." Taq nodded, his eyes burning with determination. "I will prepare them."

He began training a new generation of shamans, his voice steady despite pain. "You must learn the chants. You must honor the guardians. You must endure." Young voices echoed his words, their eyes wide with fear and hope. Taq whispered, "The balance must be restored."

Reed's paranoia deepened, his nights broken by whispers. He muttered, "They're watching." He carried the weight of Hale's threat, the silence forced upon him. His nightmares bled into waking hours, leaving him restless, haunted. He clenched his jaw, whispering, "It's not over."

Mei's obsession grew, her notebooks filled with spirals. She whispered, "It's all connected." She traced chants to equations, rituals to fractals. Her eyes burned with curiosity, her voice sharp. "It's science. It's myth. It's truth." She trembled, whispering, "It's forbidden."

Sarah's voice carried across generations, her stories blending memory and myth. "We must respect the land. We must honor the spirits." Children listened, elders nodded. Sarah whispered, "The wound lingers, but we endure." Her voice became anchor, her lessons became legacy.

Taq's training intensified, his voice sharp despite pain. "You must endure. You must honor. You must restore." Young voices echoed, their chants rising. Taq whispered, "The balance must be restored." His grandmother's voice was calm. "You are wounded healer."

Reed clenched his jaw, haunted by Lena's voice. "We sealed it. But at what cost?" His paranoia gnawed, his nights broken. He whispered, "They're watching." His breath ragged, his eyes sharp. "It's not over."

Mei trembled, her notebooks filled with spirals. She whispered, "It's forbidden." Her curiosity burned, her voice sharp. "It's science. It's myth. It's truth." She felt herself slipping, drawn into shadows of knowledge.

Sarah whispered prayers, her voice steady. "We must honor the spirits. We must preserve the knowledge." Her stories carried weight, her lessons echoed. "We endure." Elders nodded, children listened. Sarah became guardian of memory.

Taq whispered prayers, his voice trembling. "The wound lingers." His training continued, his voice sharp. "You must endure. You must restore." Young voices echoed, their chants rising. Taq whispered, "Balance must be restored."

Reed's paranoia sharpened, his nights broken. He whispered, "They're watching." His breath ragged, his eyes sharp. "It's not over." Hale's threat lingered, silence pressing against him. Reed clenched his jaw. "They know."

Mei's obsession consumed her, her notebooks filled with

spirals. She whispered, "It's forbidden." Her curiosity burned, her voice sharp. "It's science. It's myth. It's truth." She trembled, whispering, "It's all connected."

Sarah's voice carried, her lessons echoed. "We must honor. We must endure." Children listened, elders nodded. Sarah whispered, "The wound lingers, but we endure." Her voice became anchor, her lessons became legacy.

Taq whispered prayers, his voice trembling. "The wound lingers." His training continued, his voice sharp. "You must endure. You must restore." Young voices echoed, their chants rising. Taq whispered, "Balance must be restored."

Reed returned to his old life, but the world felt altered, as though the wound in Alaska had followed him. His nights were broken by visions of Lena whispering his name, shadows pressing against his walls. He woke drenched in sweat, heart pounding, convinced unseen watchers lingered nearby. Every flicker of light outside his window felt like surveillance. He clenched his jaw, whispering, "The spirits are not done with me."

Paranoia grew, gnawing at him. He noticed cars parked too long, strangers lingering near his building. Conversations felt scripted, eyes too sharp. Reed muttered, "The balance is disturbed." He carried the weight of Hale's threat, the silence forced upon him. His nightmares bled into waking hours, leaving him restless, haunted, as though ancestral voices demanded vigilance.

Mei buried herself in research, her instruments scattered across her desk. Equations spiraled across notebooks, diagrams filled walls. She whispered, "There must be a pattern." Yet the deeper she dug, the stranger the sources became. Esoteric texts, forbidden grimoires, fragments of myth. She trembled, whispering, "The ancestors encoded this knowledge."

Her colleagues noticed her obsession, whispering behind closed doors. Mei ignored them, her eyes burning with curiosity. She traced symbols, compared chants to fractals, mapped rituals to equations. "It is science," she muttered, "but it is also ceremony." She felt herself slipping, drawn into shadows of knowledge, as though guided by unseen hands.

Sarah chose another path, her voice rising in classrooms and gatherings. She became a storyteller, weaving her experiences into lessons. Children listened, wide-eyed, as she spoke of spirits, ancestors, and balance. "Knowledge must be preserved," she said. Elders nodded, their voices solemn. "You carry the burden."

Her stories blended memory and myth, ritual and warning. She spoke of the wound in the world, the necessity of humility. "We must respect the land," she whispered. "We must honor the spirits." Her voice carried weight, echoing across generations. Sarah became a teacher, a guardian of memory, her words like chants binding the community together.

Taq struggled, his body weakened, spirit fractured. He whispered prayers, his voice trembling. "The wound lingers." His grandmother sat beside him, her voice calm. "You are wounded healer. You will restore balance." Taq nodded, his eyes burning with determination. "I will prepare them."

He began training a new generation of shamans, his voice steady despite pain. "You must learn the chants. You must honor the guardians. You must endure." Young voices echoed his words, their eyes wide with fear and hope. Taq whispered, "The balance must be restored." His grandmother's voice was steady. "The ancestors walk with you."

Reed's paranoia deepened, his nights broken by whispers. He muttered, "They're watching." He carried the weight of Hale's threat, the silence forced upon him. His nightmares bled into waking hours, leaving him restless, haunted. He clenched his jaw, whispering, "The spirits demand vigilance."

Mei's obsession grew, her notebooks filled with spirals. She whispered, "It is all connected." She traced chants to equations, rituals to fractals. Her eyes burned with curiosity, her voice sharp. "It is science. It is myth. It is truth." She trembled, whispering, "It is forbidden knowledge."

Sarah's voice carried across generations, her stories blending memory and myth. "We must respect the land. We must honor the spirits." Children listened, elders nodded. Sarah whispered, "The wound lingers, but we endure." Her voice became anchor, her lessons became legacy.

Taq's training intensified, his voice sharp despite pain. "You must endure. You must honor. You must restore." Young voices echoed, their chants rising. Taq whispered, "The balance must be restored." His grandmother's voice was calm. "You are wounded healer."

Reed clenched his jaw, haunted by Lena's voice. "We sealed it. But at what cost?" His paranoia gnawed, his nights broken. He whispered, "The balance is disturbed." His breath ragged, his eyes sharp. "It is not over."

Mei trembled, her notebooks filled with spirals. She whispered, "It is forbidden." Her curiosity burned, her voice sharp. "It is science. It is myth. It is truth." She felt herself slipping, drawn into shadows of knowledge, as though ancestors guided her hand.

Sarah whispered prayers, her voice steady. "We must honor the spirits. We must preserve the knowledge." Her stories carried weight, her lessons echoed. "We endure." Elders nodded, children listened. Sarah became guardian of memory, her words like chants binding the wound.

Taq whispered prayers, his voice trembling. "The wound

lingers." His training continued, his voice sharp. "You must endure. You must restore." Young voices echoed, their chants rising. Taq whispered, "Balance must be restored." His grandmother's voice was calm. "The ancestors commend your bravery."

Reed's paranoia sharpened, his nights broken. He whispered, "They're watching." His breath ragged, his eyes sharp. "It is not over." Hale's threat lingered, silence pressing against him. Reed clenched his jaw. "The spirits know."

Mei's obsession consumed her, her notebooks filled with spirals. She whispered, "It is forbidden." Her curiosity burned, her voice sharp. "It is science. It is myth. It is truth." She trembled, whispering, "It is all connected."

Sarah's voice carried, her lessons echoed. "We must honor. We must endure." Children listened, elders nodded. Sarah whispered, "The wound lingers, but we endure." Her voice became anchor, her lessons became legacy.

Taq whispered prayers, his voice trembling. "The wound lingers." His training continued, his voice sharp. "You must endure. You must restore." Young voices echoed, their chants rising. Taq whispered, "Balance must be restored." His grandmother's voice was calm. "The ancestors walk with you."

Reed jolted awake, sweat soaking his sheets. The dream was always the same—Lena whispering his name, shadows pressing against him. He sat up, scanning the room, convinced someone was watching. A car idled outside too long. A figure lingered near the corner. Reed muttered, "They're here."

Paranoia gnawed at him. Conversations felt scripted, eyes too sharp. He clenched his jaw, whispering, "The government isn't finished." Hale's threat echoed in his mind. Silence was demanded, but silence was impossible. Reed's nightmares bled into daylight, leaving him restless, haunted.

Mei buried herself in research, her desk buried in notebooks and screens. Equations spiraled across pages, diagrams filled walls. "There must be a pattern," she whispered. But the deeper she dug, the stranger the sources became. Esoteric texts. Forbidden grimoires. Symbols that matched the chants. She trembled, whispering, "It's all connected."

Her colleagues noticed, whispering behind closed doors. Mei ignored them, her eyes burning with obsession. She traced spirals, compared chants to fractals, mapped rituals to equations. "It's science," she muttered. "But it's more." She felt herself slipping, drawn into shadows of knowledge.

Sarah chose another path, her voice rising in classrooms and gatherings. She became a storyteller, weaving her experiences into lessons. Children listened, wide-eyed, as she spoke of spirits, ancestors, and balance. "Knowledge must be preserved," she said. Elders nodded, solemn. "You carry the burden."

Her stories blended memory and myth, ritual and warning. She spoke of the wound in the world, the necessity of humility. "Respect the land," she whispered. "Honor the spirits." Her voice carried weight, echoing across generations. Sarah became a teacher, a guardian of memory.

Taq struggled, his body weakened, spirit fractured. He whispered prayers, his voice trembling. "The wound lingers." His grandmother sat beside him, her voice calm. "You are wounded healer. You will restore balance." Taq nodded, his eyes burning. "I will prepare them."

He began training a new generation of shamans, his voice steady despite pain. "Learn the chants. Honor the guardians. Endure." Young voices echoed, their eyes wide with fear and hope. Taq whispered, "The balance must be restored." His grandmother's voice was steady. "The ancestors walk with you."

Reed's paranoia deepened. He muttered, "They're watching." He carried Hale's threat, silence pressing against him. His nightmares bled into waking hours, leaving him restless, haunted. He clenched his jaw. "It's not over."

Mei's obsession grew, notebooks filled with spirals. She whispered, "It's forbidden." Her curiosity burned, her voice sharp. "It's science. It's myth. It's truth." She trembled, whispering, "It's all connected."

Sarah's voice carried across generations, her stories blending memory and myth. "Respect the land. Honor the spirits." Children listened, elders nodded. Sarah whispered, "The wound lingers, but we endure." Her voice became anchor, her lessons became legacy.

Taq's training intensified, his voice sharp despite pain. "Endure. Honor. Restore." Young voices echoed, their chants rising. Taq whispered, "Balance must be restored." His grandmother's voice was calm. "You are wounded healer."

Reed clenched his jaw, haunted by Lena's voice. "We sealed it. But at what cost?" His paranoia gnawed, his nights broken. He whispered, "They're watching." His breath ragged, his eyes sharp. "It's not over."

Mei trembled, her notebooks filled with spirals. She whispered, "It's forbidden." Her curiosity burned, her voice sharp. "It's science. It's myth. It's truth." She felt herself slipping, drawn into shadows of knowledge.

Sarah whispered prayers, her voice steady. "Honor the spirits. Preserve the knowledge." Her stories carried weight, her lessons echoed. "We endure." Elders nodded, children listened. Sarah became guardian of memory.

Taq whispered prayers, his voice trembling. "The wound

lingers." His training continued, his voice sharp. "Endure. Restore." Young voices echoed, their chants rising. Taq whispered, "Balance must be restored."

Reed's paranoia sharpened, his nights broken. He whispered, "They're watching." His breath ragged, his eyes sharp. "It's not over." Hale's threat lingered, silence pressing against him. Reed clenched his jaw. "They know."

Mei's obsession consumed her, notebooks filled with spirals. She whispered, "It's forbidden." Her curiosity burned, her voice sharp. "It's science. It's myth. It's truth." She trembled, whispering, "It's all connected."

Sarah's voice carried, her lessons echoed. "Honor. Endure." Children listened, elders nodded. Sarah whispered, "The wound lingers, but we endure." Her voice became anchor, her lessons became legacy.

Reed jolted awake, heart hammering. The dream was always the same—Lena's voice calling from the dark, shadows pressing against him. He scanned the room, convinced someone was there. A car idled too long outside. A figure lingered near the corner. He muttered, "They're watching."

Paranoia stalked him through the day. Conversations felt rehearsed, eyes lingered too long. He clenched his jaw, whispering, "The government isn't finished." Hale's threat echoed in his mind. Silence demanded, silence enforced. Reed's nightmares bled into daylight, leaving him restless, hunted.

Mei drowned herself in research, her desk buried under notebooks and glowing screens. Equations spiraled across pages, diagrams covered walls. "There has to be a pattern," she whispered. But the deeper she dug, the stranger the sources became—esoteric texts, forbidden grimoires, symbols that matched the chants. She trembled, whispering, "It's all connected."

Her colleagues whispered about her obsession. Mei ignored them, eyes burning with fixation. She traced spirals, compared chants to fractals, mapped rituals to equations. "It's science," she muttered. "But it's more." She felt herself slipping, drawn into shadows of knowledge, as if the entity had left fingerprints on her mind.

Sarah chose another path. She stood before classrooms, gatherings, circles of children and elders. Her voice rose, weaving memory into myth. "We must respect the land. We must honor the spirits." Children listened, wide-eyed. Elders nodded, solemn. Sarah's words carried weight, binding community together.

Her stories blended warning and hope. She spoke of the wound in the world, the necessity of humility. "Balance must be preserved," she whispered. "The spirits demand it." Her voice became anchor, her lessons became legacy. Sarah transformed trauma into teaching.

Taq struggled, his body weakened, spirit fractured. He whispered prayers, his voice trembling. "The wound lingers." His grandmother sat beside him, her voice calm. "You are wounded healer. You will restore balance." Taq nodded, determination burning through pain. "I will prepare them."

He began training a new generation of shamans. His voice was steady, though his hands shook. "Learn the chants. Honor the guardians. Endure." Young voices echoed, their eyes wide with fear and hope. Taq whispered, "Balance must be restored." His grandmother's voice was steady. "The ancestors walk with you."

Reed's paranoia deepened. He muttered, "They're watching." Hale's threat pressed against him like a blade. His nightmares bled into waking hours, leaving him restless, haunted. He clenched his jaw. "It's not over."

Mei's obsession grew. Her notebooks filled with spirals, her walls covered in symbols. She whispered, "It's forbidden." Her curiosity burned, her voice sharp. "It's science. It's myth. It's truth." She trembled, whispering, "It's all connected."

Sarah's voice carried across generations. "Respect the land. Honor the spirits." Children listened, elders nodded. Sarah whispered, "The wound lingers, but we endure." Her voice became anchor, her lessons became legacy.

Taq's training intensified. His voice was sharp despite pain. "Endure. Honor. Restore." Young voices echoed, their chants rising. Taq whispered, "Balance must be restored." His grandmother's voice was calm. "You are wounded healer."

Reed clenched his jaw, haunted by Lena's voice. "We sealed it. But at what cost?" His paranoia gnawed, his nights broken. He whispered, "They're watching." His breath ragged, his eyes sharp. "It's not over."

Mei trembled, her notebooks filled with spirals. She whispered, "It's forbidden." Her curiosity burned, her voice sharp. "It's science. It's myth. It's truth." She felt herself slipping, drawn deeper into shadows of knowledge.

Sarah whispered prayers, her voice steady. "Honor the spirits. Preserve the knowledge." Her stories carried weight, her lessons echoed. "We endure." Elders nodded, children listened. Sarah became guardian of memory.

Taq whispered prayers, his voice trembling. "The wound lingers." His training continued, his voice sharp. "Endure. Restore." Young voices echoed, their chants rising. Taq whispered, "Balance must be restored." His grandmother's voice was calm. "The ancestors commend your bravery."

Reed's paranoia sharpened, his nights broken. He whispered, "They're watching." His breath ragged, his eyes sharp. "It's not over." Hale's threat lingered, silence pressing against him. Reed clenched his jaw. "They know."

Mei's obsession consumed her. Notebooks filled with spirals, walls covered in symbols. She whispered, "It's forbidden." Her curiosity burned, her voice sharp. "It's science. It's myth. It's truth." She trembled, whispering, "It's all connected."

Sarah's voice carried, her lessons echoed. "Honor. Endure." Children listened, elders nodded. Sarah whispered, "The wound lingers, but we endure." Her voice became anchor, her lessons became legacy.

Taq whispered prayers, his voice trembling. "The wound lingers." His training continued, his voice sharp. "Endure. Restore." Young voices echoed, their chants rising. Taq whispered, "Balance must be restored." His grandmother's voice was calm. "The ancestors walk with you."

CHAPTER 18: THE CULTISTS

The ruins of the pyramid lay silent, but silence was never safety. In the shadows of collapsed stone, figures gathered, cloaked and whispering. They traced symbols into the snow, their voices low, rhythmic. A leader stepped forward, his eyes gleaming beneath a hood. He called himself the Black Prophet.

The Black Prophet spoke of enlightenment, of gateways between worlds. His voice was calm, persuasive, carrying weight. "The ritual was interrupted," he whispered. "But it can be completed. The entity awaits." His followers nodded, their faces hidden. They believed him, believed the promise of power.

Rumors spread through local communities. Strange ceremonies in the woods. Disappearances of disaffected youth. Symbols carved into trees, painted onto walls. Sarah heard whispers, her jaw tightening. "The cult is moving," she muttered. Reed clenched his jaw. "They're recruiting."

The cult infiltrated quietly, blending into gatherings, whispering promises. "The pyramid is gateway," they said. "The entity is salvation." Some listened, drawn by charisma, by mystery. Others turned away, fearful. But the cult grew, its reach spreading.

The Black Prophet claimed knowledge passed down from shamans and visitors from the stars. His voice was sharp, persuasive. "The ancestors knew. The entity is truth. We will finish what they began." His followers chanted, their voices rising. "We will open the wound."

Symbols appeared across the tundra—spirals, glyphs, marks of power. Reed noticed them, his paranoia sharpening. "They're signaling," he muttered. Mei traced the spirals, her curiosity burning. "It's ritual language." Sarah whispered prayers. "It is corruption." Taq's voice was steady. "It is danger."

The cult's ceremonies grew bolder. Fires burned in the night, chants echoed across the tundra. Disappearances multiplied, families whispered of missing sons and daughters. Reed clenched his jaw. "They're building an army." Mei trembled, whispering, "They're building a ritual." Sarah whispered prayers. "They're building destruction."

The Black Prophet stood before his followers, his voice sharp. "The entity was betrayed. We will free it. We will rule." His words carried weight, his charisma undeniable. Followers chanted, their voices rising. "We will open the wound."

Sarah listened to elders, their voices solemn. "We have seen this before," they whispered. "False prophets. Corruption. Danger." Sarah nodded, her jaw tight. "We must resist." Elders whispered prayers. "We must endure."

Reed's paranoia sharpened. He muttered, "They're watching us." Mei's curiosity burned. "They're rewriting the ritual." Sarah whispered prayers. "They're corrupting the chants." Taq's voice was steady. "They're disturbing the balance."

The cult spread symbols across towns, cryptic marks on doors, spirals on walls. Reed clenched his jaw. "It's infiltration." Mei whispered, "It's communication." Sarah whispered prayers. "It's corruption." Taq whispered, "It is warning."

The Black Prophet's voice carried across gatherings. "The entity is salvation. The pyramid is gateway. We will finish the ritual." His followers chanted, their voices sharp. "We will open the wound."

Disappearances continued, families whispered of missing children. Reed clenched his jaw. "They're recruiting." Mei trembled, whispering, "They're sacrificing." Sarah whispered prayers. "They're betraying." Taq whispered, "They're disturbing balance."

The cult's ceremonies grew darker. Fires burned, chants echoed, symbols glowed. Reed froze, breath ragged. "It's happening again." Mei whispered, "They're rebuilding the ritual." Sarah whispered prayers. "They're awakening the wound." Taq whispered, "They're calling the entity."

The Black Prophet raised his hands, his voice sharp. "The entity awaits. We will free it. We will rule." His followers chanted, their voices rising. "We will open the wound."

Sarah whispered prayers, her voice trembling. "We must resist." Reed clenched his jaw. "We must fight." Mei whispered, "We must understand." Taq's voice was steady. "We must restore balance."

The cult spread symbols across the tundra, spirals glowing faintly. Reed clenched his jaw. "It's infiltration." Mei whispered, "It's communication." Sarah whispered prayers. "It's corruption." Taq whispered, "It is warning."

The Black Prophet's voice carried, sharp and persuasive. "The entity was betrayed. We will free it. We will rule." His followers chanted, their voices rising. "We will open the wound."

Sarah listened to elders, their voices solemn. "We have seen this before," they whispered. "False prophets. Corruption. Danger." Sarah nodded, her jaw tight. "We must resist." Elders whispered prayers. "We must endure."

The ruins of the pyramid lay silent, but silence was never

safety. In the shadows of collapsed stone, figures gathered, cloaked and whispering. They traced spirals into the snow, their voices low, rhythmic. A leader stepped forward, his eyes gleaming beneath a hood. He called himself the Black Prophet, claiming lineage from shamans and star-walkers.

The Black Prophet spoke of enlightenment, of gateways between worlds. His voice carried the cadence of ritual, persuasive and heavy with promise. "The ritual was interrupted," he whispered. "But it can be completed. The entity awaits." His followers bowed, believing his words were prophecy. They saw him as chosen, a vessel of ancient power.

Rumors spread through villages and towns. Strange ceremonies in the woods. Disappearances of disaffected youth. Symbols carved into trees, painted onto walls. Elders whispered, "The old corruption returns." Sarah listened, her jaw tightening. "The cult is moving," she muttered. Reed clenched his jaw. "They're recruiting."

The cult infiltrated quietly, blending into gatherings, whispering promises. "The pyramid is gateway," they said. "The entity is salvation." Some listened, drawn by charisma, by mystery. Others turned away, fearful. But the cult grew, its reach spreading like shadow across the tundra.

The Black Prophet claimed knowledge passed down from shamans and visitors from the stars. His voice was sharp, persuasive. "The ancestors knew. The entity is truth. We will finish what they began." His followers chanted, their voices rising. "We will open the wound."

Symbols appeared across the tundra—spirals, glyphs, marks of power. Reed noticed them, his paranoia sharpening. "They're signaling," he muttered. Mei traced the spirals, her curiosity burning. "It's ritual language." Sarah whispered prayers. "It is corruption." Taq's voice was steady. "It is danger."

The cult's ceremonies grew bolder. Fires burned in the night, chants echoed across the tundra. Disappearances multiplied, families whispered of missing sons and daughters. Elders spoke of imbalance, of spirits disturbed. Reed clenched his jaw. "They're building an army." Mei trembled, whispering, "They're building a ritual." Sarah whispered prayers. "They're building destruction."

The Black Prophet stood before his followers, his voice sharp. "The entity was betrayed. We will free it. We will rule." His words carried weight, his charisma undeniable. Followers chanted, their voices rising. "We will open the wound."

Sarah listened to elders, their voices solemn. "We have seen this before," they whispered. "False prophets. Corruption. Danger." Sarah nodded, her jaw tight. "We must resist." Elders whispered prayers. "We must endure."

Reed's paranoia sharpened. He muttered, "They're watching us." Mei's curiosity burned. "They're rewriting the ritual." Sarah whispered prayers. "They're corrupting the chants." Taq's voice was steady. "They're disturbing the balance."

The cult spread symbols across towns, cryptic marks on doors, spirals on walls. Reed clenched his jaw. "It's infiltration." Mei whispered, "It's communication." Sarah whispered prayers. "It's corruption." Taq whispered, "It is warning."

The Black Prophet's voice carried across gatherings. "The entity is salvation. The pyramid is gateway. We will finish the ritual." His followers chanted, their voices sharp. "We will open the wound."

Disappearances continued, families whispered of missing children. Reed clenched his jaw. "They're recruiting." Mei trembled, whispering, "They're sacrificing." Sarah whispered prayers. "They're betraying." Taq whispered, "They're disturbing balance."

The cult's ceremonies grew darker. Fires burned, chants echoed, symbols glowed. Reed froze, breath ragged. "It's happening again." Mei whispered, "They're rebuilding the ritual." Sarah whispered prayers. "They're awakening the wound." Taq whispered, "They're calling the entity."

The Black Prophet raised his hands, his voice sharp. "The entity awaits. We will free it. We will rule." His followers chanted, their voices rising. "We will open the wound."

Sarah whispered prayers, her voice trembling. "We must resist." Reed clenched his jaw. "We must fight." Mei whispered, "We must understand." Taq's voice was steady. "We must restore balance."

The cult spread symbols across the tundra, spirals glowing faintly. Reed clenched his jaw. "It's infiltration." Mei whispered, "It's communication." Sarah whispered prayers. "It's corruption." Taq whispered, "It is warning."

The Black Prophet's voice carried, sharp and persuasive. "The entity was betrayed. We will free it. We will rule." His followers chanted, their voices rising. "We will open the wound."

Sarah listened to elders, their voices solemn. "We have seen this before," they whispered. "False prophets. Corruption. Danger." Sarah nodded, her jaw tight. "We must resist." Elders whispered prayers. "We must endure."

The tundra stretched endlessly, symbols glowing faintly. Reed clenched his jaw, breath ragged. Mei's curiosity burned, eyes wide. Sarah whispered prayers, her voice trembling. Taq whispered, "The cult is danger." The Black Prophet's eyes gleamed. "The wound awaits."

The ruins of the pyramid smoldered under the aurora, but silence was deceptive. Figures moved in the shadows, cloaked, deliberate. They traced spirals into the snow, their voices low, rhythmic. A leader stepped forward, his hood concealing his face. His voice cut through the cold. "I am the Black Prophet."

He spoke of gateways, of enlightenment, of power. His words were sharp, persuasive, carrying weight. "The ritual was interrupted," he whispered. "But it can be completed. The entity awaits." Followers bowed, their faces hidden. They believed him, believed the promise of salvation.

Rumors spread quickly. Strange ceremonies in the woods. Disappearances of disaffected youth. Symbols carved into trees, painted onto walls. Sarah heard whispers, her jaw tightening. "The cult is moving," she muttered. Reed clenched his jaw. "They're recruiting."

The cult infiltrated quietly, blending into gatherings, whispering promises. "The pyramid is gateway," they said. "The entity is salvation." Some listened, drawn by charisma, by mystery. Others turned away, fearful. But the cult grew, its reach spreading like wildfire.

The Black Prophet claimed knowledge passed down from shamans and visitors from the stars. His voice was sharp, persuasive. "The ancestors knew. The entity is truth. We will finish what they began." His followers chanted, their voices rising. "We will open the wound."

Symbols appeared across the tundra—spirals, glyphs, marks of power. Reed noticed them, paranoia sharpening. "They're signaling," he muttered. Mei traced the spirals, her curiosity burning. "It's ritual language." Sarah whispered prayers. "It is corruption." Taq's voice was steady. "It is danger."

The cult's ceremonies grew bolder. Fires burned in the night, chants echoed across the tundra. Disappearances multiplied, families whispered of missing sons and daughters. Reed clenched his jaw. "They're building an army." Mei trembled, whispering, "They're building a ritual." Sarah whispered prayers. "They're building destruction."

The Black Prophet stood before his followers, his voice sharp. "The entity was betrayed. We will free it. We will rule." His words carried weight, his charisma undeniable. Followers chanted, their voices rising. "We will open the wound."

Sarah listened to elders, their voices solemn. "We have seen this before," they whispered. "False prophets. Corruption. Danger." Sarah nodded, her jaw tight. "We must resist." Elders whispered prayers. "We must endure."

Reed's paranoia sharpened. He muttered, "They're watching us." Mei's curiosity burned. "They're rewriting the ritual." Sarah whispered prayers. "They're corrupting the chants." Taq's voice was steady. "They're disturbing the balance."

The cult spread symbols across towns, cryptic marks on doors, spirals on walls. Reed clenched his jaw. "It's infiltration." Mei whispered, "It's communication." Sarah whispered prayers. "It's corruption." Taq whispered, "It is warning."

The Black Prophet's voice carried across gatherings. "The entity is salvation. The pyramid is gateway. We will finish the ritual." His followers chanted, their voices sharp. "We will open the wound."

Disappearances continued, families whispered of missing children. Reed clenched his jaw. "They're recruiting." Mei trembled, whispering, "They're sacrificing." Sarah whispered prayers. "They're betraying." Taq whispered, "They're disturbing balance."

The cult's ceremonies grew darker. Fires burned, chants echoed, symbols glowed. Reed froze, breath ragged. "It's happening again." Mei whispered, "They're rebuilding the ritual." Sarah whispered prayers. "They're awakening the wound." Taq whispered, "They're calling the entity."

The Black Prophet raised his hands, his voice sharp. "The entity awaits. We will free it. We will rule." His followers chanted, their voices rising. "We will open the wound."

Sarah whispered prayers, her voice trembling. "We must resist." Reed clenched his jaw. "We must fight." Mei whispered, "We must understand." Taq's voice was steady. "We must restore balance."

The cult spread symbols across the tundra, spirals glowing faintly. Reed clenched his jaw. "It's infiltration." Mei whispered, "It's communication." Sarah whispered prayers. "It's corruption." Taq whispered, "It is warning."

The Black Prophet's voice carried, sharp and persuasive. "The entity was betrayed. We will free it. We will rule." His followers chanted, their voices rising. "We will open the wound."

Sarah listened to elders, their voices solemn. "We have seen this before," they whispered. "False prophets. Corruption. Danger." Sarah nodded, her jaw tight. "We must resist." Elders whispered prayers. "We must endure."

CHAPTER 19: THE LITTLE PEOPLE

Sarah listened to whispers carried on the wind—stories of "little people" appearing near the ruins of the pyramid. Elders spoke of Ircenrraat, beings who lived between worlds, guardians of balance. Their voices were solemn, warning. "They are mischievous, but protective," one elder said. Sarah nodded, her jaw tight. "They are watching."

She traveled across villages, gathering stories. Witnesses spoke of small figures darting through the snow, vanishing into shadows. Hunters claimed they were saved from storms by unseen hands. Travelers whispered of tools stolen, paths blocked, warnings given. Sarah wrote everything down, her notebook filling with fragments of myth.

The cult's symbols appeared near these sightings—spirals carved into trees, glyphs painted onto stones. Sarah frowned, her breath ragged. "They are connected." Elders whispered prayers. "The little people resist corruption." Sarah nodded. "They are guardians."

She interviewed a hunter who claimed he saw them sabotage a cult ceremony. "They knocked over the fire, scattered the symbols, vanished into the snow," he whispered. Sarah's eyes widened. "They are intervening." Elders nodded, solemn. "They protect the land."

The Black Prophet's followers whispered of interference. "The little ones sabotage us," they muttered. "They are enemies." The Prophet's voice was sharp. "They are obstacles. We will silence them." His followers nodded, their chants rising. "We will open the wound."

Sarah traced the stories, mapping sightings to cult activity. The patterns aligned—where the cult gathered, the little people appeared. Mischief, sabotage, protection. Sarah whispered, "They are guardians of balance." Elders nodded. "They are warning us."

She listened to an elder's tale, voice trembling. "Long ago, the little people sealed wounds in the world. They guarded the land, kept spirits at bay. They are protectors." Sarah wrote every word, her jaw tight. "They are still here."

Reed clenched his jaw, listening. "They're real?" Sarah nodded. "They are guardians." Mei trembled, whispering, "They are myth." Taq's voice was steady. "They are balance." Reed muttered, "They are warning us."

The cult's ceremonies grew darker, fires burning, chants echoing. Symbols glowed faintly, spirals spreading. Sarah whispered prayers. "The little people will resist." Elders nodded. "They will protect."

Witnesses spoke of strange encounters—tools stolen, paths blocked, warnings given. Sarah wrote everything down, her notebook filling with fragments of myth. "They are mischievous," she whispered. "But they are guardians." Elders nodded. "They are balance."

The Black Prophet's voice carried, sharp. "The little ones are enemies. They resist us. We will silence them." His followers chanted, their voices rising. "We will open the wound."

Sarah whispered prayers, her voice trembling. "They are guardians. They resist corruption." Reed clenched his jaw. "They are allies." Mei trembled, whispering, "They are myth." Taq's voice was steady. "They are balance."

The tundra stretched endlessly, symbols glowing faintly. Sarah traced the patterns, her notebook filling. "They are connected," she whispered. Elders nodded. "They are guardians."

She listened to another tale, voice trembling. "The little people saved travelers, guided them home. They are protectors." Sarah wrote every word, her jaw tight. "They are still here."

Reed clenched his jaw, haunted. "They are warning us." Mei trembled, whispering, "They are myth." Sarah whispered prayers. "They are guardians." Taq's voice was steady. "They are balance."

The cult's ceremonies grew darker, fires burning, chants echoing. Symbols glowed faintly, spirals spreading. Sarah whispered prayers. "The little people will resist." Elders nodded. "They will protect."

Witnesses spoke of sabotage—fires knocked over, symbols scattered, chants broken. Sarah wrote everything down, her notebook filling with fragments of myth. "They are intervening," she whispered. Elders nodded. "They are guardians."

The Black Prophet's voice carried, sharp. "They are enemies. They resist us. We will silence them." His followers chanted, their voices rising. "We will open the wound."

Sarah whispered prayers, her voice trembling. "They are guardians. They resist corruption." Reed clenched his jaw. "They are allies." Mei trembled, whispering, "They are myth." Taq's voice was steady. "They are balance."

Sarah listened closely to the elders, their voices carrying the weight of centuries. They spoke of the Ircenrraat, the "little people," who lived between worlds. Mischievous, protective, elusive, they were said to guard the land from imbalance. "They are not myth," one elder whispered. "They are guardians." Sarah nodded, her notebook open. "They are watching."

She traveled across villages, gathering stories. Hunters spoke of being saved from storms by unseen hands. Travelers recalled paths blocked, tools stolen, warnings given. Each account carried echoes of protection, of intervention. Sarah wrote every word, her jaw tight. "They are resisting corruption."

The cult's symbols appeared near these sightings—spirals carved into trees, glyphs painted onto stones. Sarah frowned, her breath ragged. "They are connected." Elders whispered prayers. "The little people resist the Black Prophet." Sarah nodded. "They are guardians of balance."

One hunter described sabotage. "They knocked over the fire, scattered the symbols, vanished into the snow," he whispered. Sarah's eyes widened. "They are intervening." Elders nodded, solemn. "They protect the land."

The Black Prophet's followers whispered of interference. "The little ones sabotage us," they muttered. "They are enemies." The Prophet's voice was sharp. "They are obstacles. We will silence them." His followers chanted, their voices rising. "We will open the wound."

Sarah traced the stories, mapping sightings to cult activity. The patterns aligned—where the cult gathered, the little people appeared. Mischief, sabotage, protection. Sarah whispered, "They are guardians of balance." Elders nodded. "They are warning us."

She listened to an elder's tale, voice trembling. "Long ago, the little people sealed wounds in the world. They guarded the land, kept spirits at bay. They are protectors." Sarah wrote every word, her jaw tight. "They are still here."

Reed clenched his jaw, listening. "They're real?" Sarah nodded. "They are guardians." Mei trembled, whispering, "They are myth." Taq's voice was steady. "They are balance." Reed muttered, "They are warning us."

The cult's ceremonies grew darker, fires burning, chants echoing. Symbols glowed faintly, spirals spreading. Sarah whispered prayers. "The little people will resist." Elders nodded. "They will protect."

Witnesses spoke of strange encounters—tools stolen, paths blocked, warnings given. Sarah wrote everything down, her notebook filling with fragments of myth. "They are mischievous," she whispered. "But they are guardians." Elders nodded. "They are balance."

The Black Prophet's voice carried, sharp. "The little ones are enemies. They resist us. We will silence them." His followers chanted, their voices rising. "We will open the wound."

Sarah whispered prayers, her voice trembling. "They are guardians. They resist corruption." Reed clenched his jaw. "They are allies." Mei trembled, whispering, "They are myth." Taq's voice was steady. "They are balance."

The tundra stretched endlessly, symbols glowing faintly. Sarah traced the patterns, her notebook filling. "They are connected," she whispered. Elders nodded. "They are guardians."

She listened to another tale, voice trembling. "The little people saved travelers, guided them home. They are protectors." Sarah wrote every word, her jaw tight. "They are still here."

Reed clenched his jaw, haunted. "They are warning us." Mei trembled, whispering, "They are myth." Sarah whispered prayers. "They are guardians." Taq's voice was steady. "They are balance."

The cult's ceremonies grew darker, fires burning, chants echoing. Symbols glowed faintly, spirals spreading. Sarah whispered prayers. "The little people will resist." Elders nodded. "They will protect."

Witnesses spoke of sabotage—fires knocked over, symbols scattered, chants broken. Sarah wrote everything down, her notebook filling with fragments of myth. "They are intervening," she whispered. Elders nodded. "They are guardians."

The Black Prophet's voice carried, sharp. "They are enemies. They resist us. We will silence them." His followers chanted, their voices rising. "We will open the wound."

Sarah whispered prayers, her voice trembling. "They are guardians. They resist corruption." Reed clenched his jaw. "They are allies." Mei trembled, whispering, "They are myth." Taq's voice was steady. "They are balance."

Sarah moved quickly, her notebook clutched tight, chasing rumors across the tundra. Villagers whispered of figures darting through the snow, vanishing into shadows. Hunters claimed unseen hands pulled them from storms. Travelers spoke of tools stolen, paths blocked, warnings given. Sarah's jaw tightened. "They're real."

She pressed elders for details. Their voices were solemn, heavy with memory. "The Ircenrraat are mischievous, but they protect," one said. "They guard the land." Sarah nodded, her breath sharp. "They're resisting the cult." Elders whispered prayers. "They are guardians."

Symbols appeared near sightings—spirals carved into trees, glyphs painted onto stones. Sarah frowned, tracing them with her fingers. "The cult is here." Elders whispered, "The little people resist corruption." Sarah wrote quickly. "They are intervening."

A hunter described sabotage. "They knocked over the fire, scattered the symbols, vanished into the snow," he whispered. Sarah's eyes widened. "They're disrupting ceremonies." Elders nodded. "They protect the land."

The Black Prophet's followers muttered of interference. "The little ones sabotage us," they said. "They are enemies." The Prophet's voice was sharp, commanding. "They are obstacles. We will silence them." His followers chanted, "We will open the wound."

Sarah mapped sightings against cult activity. The patterns aligned perfectly. Where the cult gathered, the little people appeared. Mischief, sabotage, protection. Sarah whispered, "They are guardians of balance." Elders nodded. "They are warning us."

She listened to an elder's tale, voice trembling. "Long ago, the little people sealed wounds in the world. They guarded the land, kept spirits at bay. They are protectors." Sarah wrote every word, her jaw tight. "They are still here."

Reed clenched his jaw, listening. "They're real?" Sarah nodded. "They are guardians." Mei trembled, whispering, "They are myth." Taq's voice was steady. "They are balance." Reed muttered, "They are warning us."

The cult's ceremonies grew darker. Fires burned, chants echoed across the tundra. Symbols glowed faintly, spirals spreading. Sarah whispered prayers. "The little people will resist." Elders nodded. "They will protect."

Witnesses spoke of strange encounters—tools stolen, paths blocked, warnings given. Sarah wrote everything down, her notebook filling with fragments of myth. "They are mischievous," she whispered. "But they are guardians." Elders nodded. "They are balance."

The Black Prophet's voice carried, sharp. "The little ones are enemies. They resist us. We will silence them." His followers chanted, their voices rising. "We will open the wound."

Sarah whispered prayers, her voice trembling. "They are guardians. They resist corruption." Reed clenched his jaw. "They are allies." Mei trembled, whispering, "They are myth." Taq's voice was steady. "They are balance."

The tundra stretched endlessly, symbols glowing faintly. Sarah traced the patterns, her notebook filling. "They are connected," she whispered. Elders nodded. "They are guardians."

Another tale emerged—travelers saved, guided home by unseen hands. "They are protectors," the elder said. Sarah wrote every word, her jaw tight. "They are still here."

Reed clenched his jaw, haunted. "They are warning us." Mei trembled, whispering, "They are myth." Sarah whispered prayers. "They are guardians." Taq's voice was steady. "They are balance."

The cult's ceremonies grew darker, fires burning, chants echoing. Symbols glowed faintly, spirals spreading. Sarah whispered prayers. "The little people will resist." Elders nodded. "They will protect."

Witnesses spoke of sabotage—fires knocked over, symbols scattered, chants broken. Sarah wrote everything down, her notebook filling with fragments of myth. "They are intervening," she whispered. Elders nodded. "They are guardians."

The Black Prophet's voice carried, sharp. "They are enemies. They resist us. We will silence them." His followers chanted, their voices rising. "We will open the wound."

Sarah whispered prayers, her voice trembling. "They are guardians. They resist corruption." Reed clenched his jaw. "They are allies." Mei trembled, whispering, "They are myth." Taq's voice was steady. "They are balance."

The tundra stretched endlessly, symbols glowing faintly. Sarah traced the patterns, her notebook filling. "They are connected," she whispered. Elders nodded. "They are guardians." The little people watched, unseen, protecting the land.

CHAPTER 20: THE AURORA'S SONG

The aurora blazed across the night sky, brighter than ever before. Colors bled into each other—green, violet, crimson—shimmering like a living tapestry. Taq stood beneath it, raven feather in hand, his body trembling. He whispered prayers, his voice sharp. "It is bridge. It is song." The lights pulsed, resonating with his spirit.

Visions consumed him. He saw the cult gathering, fires burning, chants rising. He saw spirals carved into stone, symbols glowing faintly. He saw the Black Prophet, his voice sharp, commanding. "We will open the wound." Taq convulsed, his spirit pressed against him. "It is danger."

The aurora shifted, revealing ancestors. Their voices echoed, solemn. "You must resist. You must restore balance." Taq whispered, "I will endure." Raven whispered, "You are wounded healer." Thunderbird whispered, "You are guardian." Kushtaka whispered, "You are balance."

Taq's visions sharpened. He saw Sarah, her voice rising in classrooms, her stories binding community. He saw Mei, her notebooks filled with spirals, her curiosity burning. He saw Reed, haunted, paranoid, but determined. The aurora whispered, "They are allies." Taq nodded. "We will resist."

Guided by spirits, Taq assembled a coalition. Shamans gathered, elders whispered prayers, outsiders listened. Sarah stood beside him, her voice steady. "We must preserve knowledge." Mei trembled, her eyes burning. "We must understand." Reed clenched his jaw. "We must fight."

The coalition formed, voices blending. Shamans chanted, elders prayed, outsiders listened. Sarah whispered, "We must honor the land." Mei whispered, "We must trace the patterns." Reed whispered, "We must resist." Taq whispered, "We must restore balance."

The aurora pulsed, resonating with their voices. Spirits whispered, "You are guardians. You are balance." Taq trembled, his voice sharp. "We will endure." Sarah's voice was calm. "We will preserve." Mei's voice was sharp. "We will understand." Reed's voice was steady. "We will fight."

Visions consumed Taq again. He saw the cult preparing a second ritual, fires burning, chants rising. He saw symbols glowing, spirals spreading. He saw the Black Prophet, his voice sharp. "We will open the wound." Taq convulsed, his spirit fracturing. "We must resist."

The coalition planned a counter-ritual. Shamans traced chants, elders whispered prayers, Mei mapped equations. Sarah blended memory and myth, her voice rising. Reed clenched his jaw, his paranoia sharpening. "We must stop them." Taq whispered, "We must restore balance."

The aurora blazed, brighter than ever. Spirits whispered, "You are guardians. You are balance." Taq trembled, his voice sharp. "We will endure." Sarah whispered, "We will preserve." Mei whispered, "We will understand." Reed whispered, "We will fight."

The coalition gathered, voices blending. Shamans chanted, elders prayed, outsiders listened. Sarah whispered, "We must honor the land." Mei whispered, "We must trace the patterns." Reed whispered, "We must resist." Taq whispered, "We must restore balance."

Visions consumed Taq again. He saw the cult gathering, fires burning, chants rising. He saw spirals carved into stone, symbols glowing faintly. He saw the Black Prophet, his voice sharp. "We will open the wound." Taq convulsed, his spirit fracturing. "We must resist."

The aurora pulsed, resonating with their voices. Spirits whispered, "You are guardians. You are balance." Taq trembled, his voice sharp. "We will endure." Sarah's voice was calm. "We will preserve." Mei's voice was sharp. "We will understand." Reed's voice was steady. "We will fight."

The coalition planned carefully. Shamans traced chants, elders whispered prayers, Mei mapped equations. Sarah blended memory and myth, her voice rising. Reed clenched his jaw, his paranoia sharpening. "We must stop them." Taq whispered, "We must restore balance."

The aurora blazed, brighter than ever. Spirits whispered, "You are guardians. You are balance." Taq trembled, his voice sharp. "We will endure." Sarah whispered, "We will preserve." Mei whispered, "We will understand." Reed whispered, "We will fight."

The coalition gathered, voices blending. Shamans chanted, elders prayed, outsiders listened. Sarah whispered, "We must honor the land." Mei whispered, "We must trace the patterns." Reed whispered, "We must resist." Taq whispered, "We must restore balance."

Visions consumed Taq again. He saw the cult preparing a second ritual, fires burning, chants rising. He saw symbols glowing, spirals spreading. He saw the Black Prophet, his voice sharp. "We will open the wound." Taq convulsed, his spirit fracturing. "We must resist."

The aurora pulsed, resonating with their voices. Spirits whispered, "You are guardians. You are balance." Taq trembled, his voice sharp. "We will endure." Sarah's voice was calm. "We will preserve." Mei's voice was sharp. "We will understand." Reed's voice was steady. "We will fight."

The aurora blazed across the night sky, brighter than any living memory. Colors bled into each other—green, violet, crimson—woven like threads of a vast tapestry. Taq stood beneath it, raven feather in hand, his body trembling. He whispered prayers, his voice steady despite pain. "It is bridge. It is song." The lights pulsed, resonating with his spirit, as though ancestors were speaking through the sky.

Visions consumed him. He saw the cult gathering, fires burning, chants rising. Spirals carved into stone, glyphs glowing faintly. The Black Prophet's voice rang out, sharp, commanding. "We will open the wound." Taq convulsed, his spirit pressed against him. "It is danger," he whispered.

The aurora shifted, revealing ancestral figures. Their voices echoed, solemn, layered with centuries of memory. "You must resist. You must restore balance." Raven whispered, "You are wounded healer." Thunderbird whispered, "You are guardian." Kushtaka whispered, "You are balance." Taq bowed his head. "I will endure."

Taq's visions sharpened. He saw Sarah, her voice rising in classrooms, her stories binding community. He saw Mei, her notebooks filled with spirals, her curiosity burning. He saw Reed, haunted, paranoid, but determined. The aurora whispered, "They are allies." Taq nodded. "We will resist together."

Guided by spirits, Taq assembled a coalition. Shamans gathered, elders whispered prayers, outsiders listened. Sarah stood beside him, her voice steady. "We must preserve knowledge." Mei trembled, her eyes burning. "We must understand." Reed clenched his jaw. "We must fight."

The coalition formed, voices blending. Shamans chanted, elders prayed, outsiders listened. Sarah whispered, "We must honor the land." Mei whispered, "We must trace the patterns." Reed whispered, "We must resist." Taq whispered, "We must restore balance."

The aurora pulsed, resonating with their voices. Spirits whispered, "You are guardians. You are balance." Taq trembled, his voice sharp. "We will endure." Sarah's voice was calm. "We will preserve." Mei's voice was sharp. "We will understand." Reed's voice was steady. "We will fight."

Visions consumed Taq again. He saw the cult preparing a second ritual, fires burning, chants rising. Symbols glowing, spirals spreading. The Black Prophet's voice rang out. "We will open the wound." Taq convulsed, his spirit fracturing. "We must resist."

The coalition planned a counter-ritual. Shamans traced chants, elders whispered prayers, Mei mapped equations. Sarah blended memory and myth, her voice rising. Reed clenched his jaw, his paranoia sharpening. "We must stop them." Taq whispered, "We must restore balance."

The aurora blazed, brighter than ever. Spirits whispered, "You are guardians. You are balance." Taq trembled, his voice sharp. "We will endure." Sarah whispered, "We will preserve." Mei whispered, "We will understand." Reed whispered, "We will fight."

The coalition gathered, voices blending. Shamans chanted, elders prayed, outsiders listened. Sarah whispered, "We must honor the land." Mei whispered, "We must trace the patterns." Reed whispered, "We must resist." Taq whispered, "We must restore balance."

Visions consumed Taq again. He saw the cult gathering, fires burning, chants rising. Spirals carved into stone, glyphs glowing faintly. The Black Prophet's voice rang out. "We will open the wound." Taq convulsed, his spirit fracturing. "We must resist."

The aurora pulsed, resonating with their voices. Spirits whispered, "You are guardians. You are balance." Taq trembled, his voice sharp. "We will endure." Sarah's voice was calm. "We will preserve." Mei's voice was sharp. "We will understand." Reed's voice was steady. "We will fight."

The coalition planned carefully. Shamans traced chants, elders whispered prayers, Mei mapped equations. Sarah blended memory and myth, her voice rising. Reed clenched his jaw, his paranoia sharpening. "We must stop them." Taq whispered, "We must restore balance."

The aurora blazed, brighter than ever. Spirits whispered, "You are guardians. You are balance." Taq trembled, his voice sharp. "We will endure." Sarah whispered, "We will preserve." Mei whispered, "We will understand." Reed whispered, "We will fight."

The coalition gathered, voices blending. Shamans chanted, elders prayed, outsiders listened. Sarah whispered, "We must honor the land." Mei whispered, "We must trace the patterns." Reed whispered, "We must resist." Taq whispered, "We must restore balance."

Visions consumed Taq again. He saw the cult preparing a second ritual, fires burning, chants rising. Symbols glowing, spirals spreading. The Black Prophet's voice rang out. "We will open the wound." Taq convulsed, his spirit fracturing. "We must resist."

The aurora pulsed, resonating with their voices. Spirits whispered, "You are guardians. You are balance." Taq trembled, his voice sharp. "We will endure." Sarah's voice was calm. "We will preserve." Mei's voice was sharp. "We will understand."

Reed's voice was steady. "We will fight."

The aurora ripped across the sky, violent streaks of green and crimson tearing through the night. Taq stood alone, raven feather trembling in his hand. His breath came sharp, his body convulsing. "It's alive," he whispered. The lights pulsed, bending the air, pressing against his spirit.

Visions slammed into him. The cult gathered, fires burning, chants rising. Spirals carved into stone, glyphs glowing faintly. The Black Prophet's voice cut through. "We will open the wound." Taq staggered, clutching his chest. "It's danger. It's coming."

The aurora shifted, faces appearing in the light. Ancestors stared down, their eyes burning. "Resist," they whispered. "Restore balance." Raven's voice echoed. "You are wounded healer." Thunderbird roared. "You are guardian." Kushtaka hissed. "You are balance." Taq bowed his head. "I will endure."

The visions sharpened. Sarah appeared, her voice rising in classrooms, her stories binding community. Mei hunched over notebooks, spirals filling every page. Reed stood in shadows, paranoid, hunted, but unbroken. The aurora whispered, "They are allies." Taq clenched his jaw. "We will resist together."

Guided by spirits, Taq moved quickly. He called shamans, elders, outsiders. Sarah stood beside him, her voice steady. "We must preserve knowledge." Mei trembled, her eyes burning. "We must understand." Reed clenched his jaw. "We must fight."

The coalition formed, voices blending. Shamans chanted, elders prayed, outsiders listened. Sarah whispered, "Honor the land." Mei whispered, "Trace the patterns." Reed whispered, "Resist." Taq whispered, "Restore balance."

The aurora pulsed, brighter, sharper. Spirits pressed against them, voices layered. "You are guardians. You are balance." Taq trembled, his voice sharp. "We will endure." Sarah's voice was calm. "We will preserve." Mei's voice was sharp. "We will understand." Reed's voice was steady. "We will fight."

Visions consumed Taq again. The cult prepared a second ritual, fires burning, chants rising. Symbols glowed, spirals spread. The Black Prophet raised his hands. "We will open the wound." Taq convulsed, his spirit fracturing. "We must resist."

The coalition planned a counter-ritual. Shamans traced chants, elders whispered prayers, Mei mapped equations. Sarah blended memory and myth, her voice rising. Reed clenched his jaw, paranoia sharpening. "We must stop them." Taq whispered, "We must restore balance."

The aurora blazed, violent and alive. Spirits whispered, "You are guardians. You are balance." Taq trembled, his voice sharp. "We will endure." Sarah whispered, "We will preserve." Mei whispered, "We will understand." Reed whispered, "We will fight."

The coalition gathered, voices blending. Shamans chanted, elders prayed, outsiders listened. Sarah whispered, "Honor the land." Mei whispered, "Trace the patterns." Reed whispered, "Resist." Taq whispered, "Restore balance."

The aurora surged, visions sharper. The cult gathered, fires burning, chants rising. Spirals carved into stone, glyphs glowing faintly. The Black Prophet's voice rang out. "We will open the wound." Taq convulsed, his spirit fracturing. "We must resist."

The aurora pulsed, resonating with their voices. Spirits whispered, "You are guardians. You are balance." Taq trembled, his voice sharp. "We will endure." Sarah's voice was calm. "We will preserve." Mei's voice was sharp. "We will understand." Reed's voice was steady. "We will fight."

The coalition planned carefully. Shamans traced chants, elders whispered prayers, Mei mapped equations. Sarah blended memory and myth, her voice rising. Reed clenched his jaw, paranoia sharpening. "We must stop them." Taq whispered, "We must restore balance."

The aurora blazed, brighter than ever. Spirits whispered, "You are guardians. You are balance." Taq trembled, his voice sharp. "We will endure." Sarah whispered, "We will preserve." Mei whispered, "We will understand." Reed whispered, "We will fight."

The coalition gathered, voices blending. Shamans chanted, elders prayed, outsiders listened. Sarah whispered, "Honor the land." Mei whispered, "Trace the patterns." Reed whispered, "Resist." Taq whispered, "Restore balance."

Visions consumed Taq again. He saw the cult preparing a second ritual, fires burning, chants rising. Symbols glowing, spirals spreading. The Black Prophet's voice rang out. "We will open the wound." Taq convulsed, his spirit fracturing. "We must resist."

The aurora pulsed, resonating with their voices. Spirits whispered, "You are guardians. You are balance." Taq trembled, his voice sharp. "We will endure." Sarah's voice was calm. "We will preserve." Mei's voice was sharp. "We will understand." Reed's voice was steady. "We will fight."

The tundra stretched endlessly, aurora blazing. Taq whispered prayers, his voice trembling. "We will resist." Sarah whispered, "We will preserve." Mei whispered, "We will understand." Reed whispered, "We will fight." The coalition stood together, guardians of balance.

CHAPTER 21: THE GATHERING STORM

The tundra groaned under the weight of a storm. Winds howled, snow lashed, lightning split the sky. At the pyramid site, fires burned defiantly, cultists chanting in unison. The Black Prophet raised his hands, his voice sharp. "The alignment is here. The wound will open." His followers roared, their chants echoing across the ice.

The celestial alignment had begun. Stars shifted, aurora blazed, the sky itself seemed to fracture. Seismic tremors rippled through the ground, fissures opening in the ice. Cultists pressed forward, their voices rising. "We will open the wound." The storm intensified, blizzards swirling, chaos unleashed.

The government task force moved in, their vehicles grinding across ice. Soldiers disembarked, rifles ready, faces grim. Commanders barked orders, but arguments erupted —conflicting agendas, bureaucratic infighting. "Contain the cult," one shouted. "Secure the site," another demanded. Confusion spread, their unity fractured.

Reed returned to Alaska, a fugitive, breath ragged. He moved through shadows, paranoia sharpening his senses. He whispered, "They're watching." But he pressed forward, determined. He carried warnings, his voice sharp. "The cult is preparing. The storm is here." His eyes burned with urgency.

He found Sarah and Mei, their voices steady. Sarah

whispered prayers, her jaw tight. "We must resist." Mei trembled, her notebooks filled with spirals. "We must understand." Reed clenched his jaw. "We must fight." Their voices blended, determination rising.

Taq's coalition gathered, shamans chanting, elders whispering prayers. The aurora blazed above, spirits pressing against them. Taq's voice was sharp. "The cult is danger. The balance is disturbed." Elders nodded, solemn. "We must restore." Shamans whispered, "We must resist."

The storm intensified, blizzards swirling, lightning splitting the sky. Cultists pressed forward, their chants rising. The Black Prophet's voice carried. "The wound will open." Government soldiers stumbled, their unity fractured. Reed clenched his jaw. "We must stop them."

Sarah's voice rose, weaving memory and myth. "We must honor the land. We must preserve balance." Mei traced spirals, her curiosity burning. "We must understand the ritual." Taq whispered prayers, his voice trembling. "We must restore." Reed's voice was sharp. "We must fight."

The pyramid site became battlefield. Cultists chanted, soldiers advanced, storm raged. Lightning split the sky, fissures opened in the ice. Spirits pressed against the world, their voices echoing. "Balance must be restored." Taq trembled, his voice sharp. "We will endure."

Government commanders argued, their voices sharp. "Contain the cult." "Secure the site." "Protect the civilians." Confusion spread, their unity fractured. Soldiers hesitated, their rifles shaking. Reed clenched his jaw. "They're failing." Sarah whispered prayers. "We must resist."

The Black Prophet raised his hands, his voice sharp. "The alignment is here. The wound will open." His followers roared, their chants echoing. Symbols glowed faintly, spirals spreading. Mei trembled, whispering, "It's happening." Taq whispered, "We must restore."

The storm grew violent, blizzards swirling, lightning splitting the sky. Seismic tremors rippled through the ground, fissures opening. Cultists pressed forward, their chants rising. Government soldiers stumbled, their unity fractured. Reed clenched his jaw. "We must fight."

Sarah's voice rose, weaving memory and myth. "We must honor the land. We must preserve balance." Mei traced spirals, her curiosity burning. "We must understand the ritual." Taq whispered prayers, his voice trembling. "We must restore." Reed's voice was sharp. "We must resist."

The pyramid site became chaos. Cultists chanted, soldiers advanced, storm raged. Lightning split the sky, fissures opened in the ice. Spirits pressed against the world, their voices echoing. "Balance must be restored." Taq trembled, his voice sharp. "We will endure."

Government commanders argued, their voices sharp. "Contain the cult." "Secure the site." "Protect the civilians." Confusion spread, their unity fractured. Soldiers hesitated, their rifles shaking. Reed clenched his jaw. "They're failing." Sarah whispered prayers. "We must resist."

The Black Prophet's voice carried, sharp. "The alignment is here. The wound will open." His followers roared, their chants echoing. Symbols glowed faintly, spirals spreading. Mei trembled, whispering, "It's happening." Taq whispered, "We must restore."

The storm grew violent, blizzards swirling, lightning splitting the sky. Seismic tremors rippled through the ground, fissures opening. Cultists pressed forward, their chants rising. Government soldiers stumbled, their unity fractured. Reed clenched his jaw. "We must fight."

Sarah's voice rose, weaving memory and myth. "We must honor the land. We must preserve balance." Mei traced spirals, her curiosity burning. "We must understand the ritual." Taq whispered prayers, his voice trembling. "We must restore." Reed's voice was sharp. "We must resist."

The tundra trembled as the celestial alignment began. Stars shifted, aurora blazed, and the sky itself seemed to fracture. Winds howled, snow lashed, lightning split the heavens. Elders whispered, "It is omen. It is storm." Shamans bowed their heads. "The balance is disturbed."

At the pyramid site, fires burned defiantly, cultists chanting in unison. The Black Prophet raised his hands, his voice sharp. "The alignment is here. The wound will open." His followers roared, their chants echoing across the ice. Symbols glowed faintly, spirals spreading. "We will finish what was begun."

The aurora pulsed, resonating with ancestral voices. Spirits pressed against the world, whispering warnings. "The wound must not open. Balance must be restored." Taq trembled, his voice sharp. "We will endure." Elders nodded, solemn. "We must resist."

Government task forces moved in, their vehicles grinding across ice. Soldiers disembarked, rifles ready, faces grim. Commanders barked orders, but arguments erupted—conflicting agendas, bureaucratic infighting. "Contain the cult," one shouted. "Secure the site," another demanded. Confusion spread, their unity fractured.

Reed returned to Alaska, a fugitive, breath ragged. He moved through shadows, paranoia sharpening his senses. He whispered, "They're watching." But he pressed forward, determined. He carried warnings, his voice sharp. "The cult is preparing. The storm is here." His eyes burned with urgency.

He found Sarah and Mei, their voices steady. Sarah

whispered prayers, her jaw tight. "We must resist." Mei trembled, her notebooks filled with spirals. "We must understand." Reed clenched his jaw. "We must fight." Their voices blended, determination rising.

Taq's coalition gathered, shamans chanting, elders whispering prayers. The aurora blazed above, spirits pressing against them. Taq's voice was sharp. "The cult is danger. The balance is disturbed." Elders nodded, solemn. "We must restore." Shamans whispered, "We must resist."

The storm intensified, blizzards swirling, lightning splitting the sky. Cultists pressed forward, their chants rising. The Black Prophet's voice carried. "The wound will open." Government soldiers stumbled, their unity fractured. Reed clenched his jaw. "We must stop them."

Sarah's voice rose, weaving memory and myth. "We must honor the land. We must preserve balance." Mei traced spirals, her curiosity burning. "We must understand the ritual." Taq whispered prayers, his voice trembling. "We must restore." Reed's voice was sharp. "We must fight."

The pyramid site became battlefield. Cultists chanted, soldiers advanced, storm raged. Lightning split the sky, fissures opened in the ice. Spirits pressed against the world, their voices echoing. "Balance must be restored." Taq trembled, his voice sharp. "We will endure."

Government commanders argued, their voices sharp. "Contain the cult." "Secure the site." "Protect the civilians." Confusion spread, their unity fractured. Soldiers hesitated, their rifles shaking. Reed clenched his jaw. "They're failing." Sarah whispered prayers. "We must resist."

The Black Prophet raised his hands, his voice sharp. "The alignment is here. The wound will open." His followers roared, their chants echoing. Symbols glowed faintly, spirals spreading. Mei trembled, whispering, "It's happening." Taq whispered, "We must restore."

The storm grew violent, blizzards swirling, lightning splitting the sky. Seismic tremors rippled through the ground, fissures opening. Cultists pressed forward, their chants rising. Government soldiers stumbled, their unity fractured. Reed clenched his jaw. "We must fight."

Sarah's voice rose, weaving memory and myth. "We must honor the land. We must preserve balance." Mei traced spirals, her curiosity burning. "We must understand the ritual." Taq whispered prayers, his voice trembling. "We must restore." Reed's voice was sharp. "We must resist."

The pyramid site became chaos. Cultists chanted, soldiers advanced, storm raged. Lightning split the sky, fissures opened in the ice. Spirits pressed against the world, their voices echoing. "Balance must be restored." Taq trembled, his voice sharp. "We will endure."

Government commanders argued, their voices sharp. "Contain the cult." "Secure the site." "Protect the civilians." Confusion spread, their unity fractured. Soldiers hesitated, their rifles shaking. Reed clenched his jaw. "They're failing." Sarah whispered prayers. "We must resist."

The Black Prophet's voice carried, sharp. "The alignment is here. The wound will open." His followers roared, their chants echoing. Symbols glowed faintly, spirals spreading. Mei trembled, whispering, "It's happening." Taq whispered, "We must restore."

The storm grew violent, blizzards swirling, lightning splitting the sky. Seismic tremors rippled through the ground, fissures opening. Cultists pressed forward, their chants rising. Government soldiers stumbled, their unity fractured. Reed clenched his jaw. "We must fight."

Sarah's voice rose, weaving memory and myth. "We must honor the land. We must preserve balance." Mei traced spirals, her curiosity burning. "We must understand the ritual." Taq whispered prayers, his voice trembling. "We must restore." Reed's voice was sharp. "We must resist."

The tundra shook under the storm. Winds screamed, snow slashed sideways, lightning ripped the sky. At the pyramid site, fires burned defiantly, cultists chanting in rhythm. The Black Prophet raised his hands, his voice cutting through chaos. "The alignment is here. The wound will open." His followers roared, their chants echoing across the ice.

The celestial alignment began. Stars shifted, aurora blazed, the sky fractured. Tremors rippled through the ground, fissures opening in the ice. Cultists pressed forward, their voices rising. "We will open the wound." The storm intensified, blizzards swirling, chaos unleashed.

Government task force vehicles crawled across the ice, headlights cutting through snow. Soldiers disembarked, rifles raised, faces grim. Commanders barked orders, but arguments erupted—contain the cult, secure the site, protect civilians. Confusion spread, unity fractured. Radios crackled with conflicting commands.

Reed returned to Alaska, a fugitive, breath ragged. He moved through shadows, paranoia sharpening his senses. "They're watching," he muttered. But he pressed forward, determined. He carried warnings, his voice sharp. "The cult is preparing. The storm is here." His eyes burned with urgency.

He found Sarah and Mei, their voices steady. Sarah whispered prayers, her jaw tight. "We must resist." Mei trembled, her notebooks filled with spirals. "We must understand." Reed clenched his jaw. "We must fight." Their voices blended, determination rising.

Taq's coalition gathered, shamans chanting, elders whispering prayers. The aurora blazed above, spirits pressing against them. Taq's voice was sharp. "The cult is danger. The balance is disturbed." Elders nodded, solemn. "We must restore." Shamans whispered, "We must resist."

The storm intensified, blizzards swirling, lightning splitting the sky. Cultists pressed forward, their chants rising. The Black Prophet's voice carried. "The wound will open." Government soldiers stumbled, their unity fractured. Reed clenched his jaw. "We must stop them."

Sarah's voice rose, weaving memory and myth. "We must honor the land. We must preserve balance." Mei traced spirals, her curiosity burning. "We must understand the ritual." Taq whispered prayers, his voice trembling. "We must restore." Reed's voice was sharp. "We must fight."

The pyramid site became battlefield. Cultists chanted, soldiers advanced, storm raged. Lightning split the sky, fissures opened in the ice. Spirits pressed against the world, their voices echoing. "Balance must be restored." Taq trembled, his voice sharp. "We will endure."

Government commanders argued, their voices sharp. "Contain the cult." "Secure the site." "Protect the civilians." Confusion spread, their unity fractured. Soldiers hesitated, rifles shaking. Reed clenched his jaw. "They're failing." Sarah whispered prayers. "We must resist."

The Black Prophet raised his hands, his voice sharp. "The alignment is here. The wound will open." His followers roared, their chants echoing. Symbols glowed faintly, spirals spreading. Mei trembled, whispering, "It's happening." Taq whispered, "We must restore."

The storm grew violent, blizzards swirling, lightning splitting the sky. Seismic tremors rippled through the ground, fissures opening. Cultists pressed forward, their chants rising. Government soldiers stumbled, their unity fractured. Reed clenched his jaw. "We must fight."

Sarah's voice rose, weaving memory and myth. "We must honor the land. We must preserve balance." Mei traced spirals, her curiosity burning. "We must understand the ritual." Taq whispered prayers, his voice trembling. "We must restore." Reed's voice was sharp. "We must resist."

The pyramid site became chaos. Cultists chanted, soldiers advanced, storm raged. Lightning split the sky, fissures opened in the ice. Spirits pressed against the world, their voices echoing. "Balance must be restored." Taq trembled, his voice sharp. "We will endure."

Government commanders argued, their voices sharp. "Contain the cult." "Secure the site." "Protect the civilians." Confusion spread, their unity fractured. Soldiers hesitated, rifles shaking. Reed clenched his jaw. "They're failing." Sarah whispered prayers. "We must resist."

The Black Prophet's voice carried, sharp. "The alignment is here. The wound will open." His followers roared, their chants echoing. Symbols glowed faintly, spirals spreading. Mei trembled, whispering, "It's happening." Taq whispered, "We must restore."

The storm grew violent, blizzards swirling, lightning splitting the sky. Seismic tremors rippled through the ground, fissures opening. Cultists pressed forward, their chants rising. Government soldiers stumbled, their unity fractured. Reed clenched his jaw. "We must fight."

Sarah's voice rose, weaving memory and myth. "We must honor the land. We must preserve balance." Mei traced spirals, her curiosity burning. "We must understand the ritual." Taq whispered prayers, his voice trembling. "We must restore."

Reed's voice was sharp. "We must resist."

The tundra stretched endlessly, storm raging, aurora blazing. Cultists pressed forward, soldiers stumbled, spirits pressed against the world. Reed clenched his jaw, breath ragged. Sarah whispered prayers, her voice trembling. Mei's curiosity burned, eyes wide. Taq whispered, "Balance must be restored." The Black Prophet's eyes gleamed. "The wound awaits."

CHAPTER 22: THE SIEGE

The cultists swarmed the pyramid, torches blazing against the storm. Their chants rose, spirals carved into stone glowing faintly. The Black Prophet stood at the center, his voice sharp. "The seal will break. The entity will rise." His followers roared, their voices echoing across the tundra.

Government task force vehicles surrounded the site, headlights cutting through snow. Soldiers disembarked, rifles raised, faces grim. Commanders barked orders, their voices sharp. "Contain the cult. Secure the site." But confusion spread, agendas clashed, unity fractured. Radios crackled with conflicting commands.

Gunfire erupted, bullets tearing through the storm. Cultists pressed forward, their chants rising. Symbols glowed brighter, spirals spreading. Lightning split the sky, fissures opened in the ice. Spirits pressed against the world, their voices echoing. "Balance must be restored."

The environment itself turned hostile. Ice fissures widened, avalanches thundered, spectral apparitions flickered. Soldiers stumbled, rifles shaking. Cultists roared, their chants unbroken. Reed clenched his jaw, breath ragged. "It's chaos." Sarah whispered prayers, her voice trembling. "It is storm."

Taq's coalition moved quietly, slipping through shadows. Shamans whispered chants, elders prayed, outsiders listened. Taq's voice was sharp. "We must infiltrate. We must restore balance." Sarah nodded, her jaw tight. "We must resist." Mei trembled, her eyes burning. "We must understand." Reed clenched his jaw. "We must fight."

The pyramid became fortress. Cultists occupied chambers, symbols glowing faintly. Traps were laid, illusions conjured. The Black Prophet's voice carried. "The wound will open." His followers chanted, their voices sharp. "We will finish the ritual."

Government soldiers advanced, gunfire echoing. Cultists resisted, their chants rising. Lightning split the sky, fissures opened in the ice. Spirits pressed against the world, their voices echoing. "Balance must be restored." Taq whispered prayers, his voice trembling. "We will endure."

The siege intensified, chaos spreading. Soldiers fired, cultists chanted, storm raged. Avalanches thundered, spectral apparitions flickered. Reed clenched his jaw. "We must stop them." Sarah whispered prayers. "We must resist." Mei traced spirals, her curiosity burning. "We must understand." Taq whispered, "We must restore."

The Black Prophet raised his hands, his voice sharp. "The seal will break. The entity will rise." His followers roared, their chants echoing. Symbols glowed faintly, spirals spreading. Mei trembled, whispering, "It's happening." Taq whispered, "We must resist."

The pyramid's labyrinth unfolded, corridors twisting, illusions shifting. Taq's coalition moved carefully, their voices steady. Shamans whispered chants, elders prayed, outsiders listened. Sarah's voice rose, weaving memory and myth. "We must honor the land." Reed clenched his jaw. "We must fight." Mei whispered, "We must understand."

The siege became chaos. Soldiers fired, cultists chanted, storm raged. Lightning split the sky, fissures opened in the ice. Spirits pressed against the world, their voices echoing. "Balance must be restored." Taq trembled, his voice sharp. "We will endure."

Government commanders argued, their voices sharp. "Contain the cult." "Secure the site." "Protect the civilians." Confusion spread, their unity fractured. Soldiers hesitated, rifles shaking. Reed clenched his jaw. "They're failing." Sarah whispered prayers. "We must resist."

The Black Prophet's voice carried, sharp. "The seal will break. The entity will rise." His followers roared, their chants echoing. Symbols glowed faintly, spirals spreading. Mei trembled, whispering, "It's happening." Taq whispered, "We must restore."

The labyrinth deepened, corridors twisting, illusions shifting. Taq's coalition pressed forward, their voices steady. Shamans whispered chants, elders prayed, outsiders listened. Sarah's voice rose, weaving memory and myth. "We must honor the land." Reed clenched his jaw. "We must fight." Mei whispered, "We must understand."

The siege grew violent, chaos spreading. Soldiers fired, cultists chanted, storm raged. Avalanches thundered, spectral apparitions flickered. Reed clenched his jaw. "We must stop them." Sarah whispered prayers. "We must resist." Mei traced spirals, her curiosity burning. "We must understand." Taq whispered, "We must restore."

The Black Prophet raised his hands, his voice sharp. "The seal will break. The entity will rise." His followers roared, their chants echoing. Symbols glowed faintly, spirals spreading. Mei trembled, whispering, "It's happening." Taq whispered, "We must resist."

The pyramid's labyrinth unfolded further, corridors twisting, illusions shifting. Taq's coalition moved carefully, their voices steady. Shamans whispered chants, elders prayed, outsiders listened. Sarah's voice rose, weaving memory and myth. "We must honor the land." Reed clenched his jaw. "We must fight." Mei whispered, "We must understand."

The siege became chaos. Soldiers fired, cultists chanted, storm raged. Lightning split the sky, fissures opened in the ice. Spirits pressed against the world, their voices echoing. "Balance must be restored." Taq trembled, his voice sharp. "We will endure."

The pyramid loomed like a wounded titan, its stones trembling under chants. Cultists occupied its chambers, torches blazing, spirals glowing faintly. The Black Prophet raised his hands, his voice sharp. "The seal will break. The entity will rise." His followers roared, their voices echoing. Elders whispered, "It is corruption. It is danger."

The government task force surrounded the site, their vehicles grinding across ice. Soldiers disembarked, rifles raised, faces grim. Commanders barked orders, but arguments erupted—contain the cult, secure the site, protect civilians. Confusion spread, their unity fractured. Shamans whispered, "They are blind to balance."

Gunfire erupted, bullets tearing through the storm. Cultists pressed forward, their chants rising. Symbols glowed brighter, spirals spreading. Lightning split the sky, fissures opened in the ice. Spirits pressed against the world, their voices echoing. "Balance must be restored."

The environment itself turned hostile. Avalanches thundered, spectral apparitions flickered, ice fissures widened. Soldiers stumbled, rifles shaking. Cultists roared, their chants unbroken. Reed clenched his jaw, breath ragged. "It is chaos." Sarah whispered prayers, her voice trembling. "It is storm."

Taq's coalition moved quietly, slipping through shadows.

Shamans whispered chants, elders prayed, outsiders listened. Taq's voice was sharp. "We must infiltrate. We must restore balance." Sarah nodded, her jaw tight. "We must resist." Mei trembled, her eyes burning. "We must understand." Reed clenched his jaw. "We must fight."

The pyramid became fortress, its chambers twisting like labyrinth. Cultists occupied corridors, illusions shifting. The Black Prophet's voice carried. "The wound will open." His followers chanted, their voices sharp. "We will finish the ritual." Elders whispered, "It is corruption."

Government soldiers advanced, gunfire echoing. Cultists resisted, their chants rising. Lightning split the sky, fissures opened in the ice. Spirits pressed against the world, their voices echoing. "Balance must be restored." Taq whispered prayers, his voice trembling. "We will endure."

The siege intensified, chaos spreading. Soldiers fired, cultists chanted, storm raged. Avalanches thundered, spectral apparitions flickered. Reed clenched his jaw. "We must stop them." Sarah whispered prayers. "We must resist." Mei traced spirals, her curiosity burning. "We must understand." Taq whispered, "We must restore."

The Black Prophet raised his hands, his voice sharp. "The seal will break. The entity will rise." His followers roared, their chants echoing. Symbols glowed faintly, spirals spreading. Mei trembled, whispering, "It is happening." Taq whispered, "We must resist."

The labyrinth deepened, corridors twisting, illusions shifting. Taq's coalition pressed forward, their voices steady. Shamans whispered chants, elders prayed, outsiders listened. Sarah's voice rose, weaving memory and myth. "We must honor the land." Reed clenched his jaw. "We must fight." Mei whispered, "We must understand."

The siege became chaos. Soldiers fired, cultists chanted, storm raged. Lightning split the sky, fissures opened in the ice. Spirits pressed against the world, their voices echoing. "Balance must be restored." Taq trembled, his voice sharp. "We will endure."

Government commanders argued, their voices sharp. "Contain the cult." "Secure the site." "Protect the civilians." Confusion spread, their unity fractured. Soldiers hesitated, rifles shaking. Reed clenched his jaw. "They are failing." Sarah whispered prayers. "We must resist."

The Black Prophet's voice carried, sharp. "The seal will break. The entity will rise." His followers roared, their chants echoing. Symbols glowed faintly, spirals spreading. Mei trembled, whispering, "It is happening." Taq whispered, "We must restore."

The labyrinth unfolded further, corridors twisting, illusions shifting. Taq's coalition moved carefully, their voices steady. Shamans whispered chants, elders prayed, outsiders listened. Sarah's voice rose, weaving memory and myth. "We must honor the land." Reed clenched his jaw. "We must fight." Mei whispered, "We must understand."

The siege grew violent, chaos spreading. Soldiers fired, cultists chanted, storm raged. Avalanches thundered, spectral apparitions flickered. Reed clenched his jaw. "We must stop them." Sarah whispered prayers. "We must resist." Mei traced spirals, her curiosity burning. "We must understand." Taq whispered, "We must restore."

The Black Prophet raised his hands, his voice sharp. "The seal will break. The entity will rise." His followers roared, their chants echoing. Symbols glowed faintly, spirals spreading. Mei trembled, whispering, "It is happening." Taq whispered, "We must resist."

The pyramid's labyrinth twisted endlessly, corridors shifting, illusions pressing. Taq's coalition pressed forward, their voices steady. Shamans whispered chants, elders prayed, outsiders listened. Sarah's voice rose, weaving memory and myth. "We must honor the land." Reed clenched his jaw. "We must fight." Mei whispered, "We must understand."

The siege became storm. Soldiers fired, cultists chanted, spirits pressed against the world. Lightning split the sky, fissures opened in the ice. Taq trembled, his voice sharp. "We will endure." Sarah whispered prayers. "We must resist." Reed clenched his jaw. "We must fight." Mei whispered, "We must understand."

The pyramid burned with torchlight, shadows twisting across its fractured stones. Cultists surged through the chambers, their chants pounding like war drums. The Black Prophet stood at the apex, his voice cutting through the storm. "The seal will break. The entity will rise." His followers roared, their voices echoing across the tundra.

Government vehicles screeched to a halt, headlights slicing through snow. Soldiers poured out, rifles raised, boots crunching on ice. Commanders barked orders, but radios crackled with confusion. "Contain the cult." "Secure the site." "Protect civilians." Arguments erupted, unity fractured. The siege began in chaos.

Gunfire ripped through the storm. Bullets tore into cultists, but chants did not falter. Spirals glowed brighter, symbols pulsed against stone. Lightning split the sky, fissures opened in the ice. Spirits pressed against the world, their voices echoing. "Balance must be restored."

The environment turned hostile. Avalanches thundered down slopes, spectral apparitions flickered in the storm. Soldiers stumbled, rifles shaking. Cultists roared, their chants unbroken. Reed clenched his jaw, breath ragged. "It's chaos." Sarah whispered prayers, her voice trembling. "It is storm."

Taq's coalition moved in silence, slipping through shadows. Shamans whispered chants, elders prayed, outsiders followed. Taq's voice was sharp. "We must infiltrate. We must restore balance." Sarah nodded, her jaw tight. "We must resist." Mei trembled, her eyes burning. "We must understand." Reed clenched his jaw. "We must fight."

The pyramid became fortress. Cultists occupied corridors, illusions shifting like smoke. Traps snapped shut, symbols glowed faintly. The Black Prophet's voice carried. "The wound will open." His followers chanted, their voices sharp. "We will finish the ritual."

Government soldiers advanced, gunfire echoing. Cultists resisted, their chants rising. Lightning split the sky, fissures widened. Spirits pressed against the world, their voices echoing. "Balance must be restored." Taq whispered prayers, his voice trembling. "We will endure."

The siege intensified, chaos spreading. Soldiers fired, cultists chanted, storm raged. Avalanches thundered, spectral apparitions flickered. Reed clenched his jaw. "We must stop them." Sarah whispered prayers. "We must resist." Mei traced spirals, her curiosity burning. "We must understand." Taq whispered, "We must restore."

The Black Prophet raised his hands, his voice sharp. "The seal will break. The entity will rise." His followers roared, their chants echoing. Symbols glowed faintly, spirals spreading. Mei trembled, whispering, "It's happening." Taq whispered, "We must resist."

The labyrinth unfolded, corridors twisting, illusions pressing. Taq's coalition pressed forward, their voices steady. Shamans whispered chants, elders prayed, outsiders listened.

Sarah's voice rose, weaving memory and myth. "We must honor the land." Reed clenched his jaw. "We must fight." Mei whispered, "We must understand."

The siege became chaos. Soldiers fired, cultists chanted, storm raged. Lightning split the sky, fissures opened in the ice. Spirits pressed against the world, their voices echoing. "Balance must be restored." Taq trembled, his voice sharp. "We will endure."

Government commanders argued, their voices sharp. "Contain the cult." "Secure the site." "Protect the civilians." Confusion spread, their unity fractured. Soldiers hesitated, rifles shaking. Reed clenched his jaw. "They're failing." Sarah whispered prayers. "We must resist."

The Black Prophet's voice carried, sharp. "The seal will break. The entity will rise." His followers roared, their chants echoing. Symbols glowed faintly, spirals spreading. Mei trembled, whispering, "It's happening." Taq whispered, "We must restore."

The labyrinth deepened, corridors twisting, illusions shifting. Taq's coalition pressed forward, their voices steady. Shamans whispered chants, elders prayed, outsiders listened. Sarah's voice rose, weaving memory and myth. "We must honor the land." Reed clenched his jaw. "We must fight." Mei whispered, "We must understand."

The siege grew violent, chaos spreading. Soldiers fired, cultists chanted, storm raged. Avalanches thundered, spectral apparitions flickered. Reed clenched his jaw. "We must stop them." Sarah whispered prayers. "We must resist." Mei traced spirals, her curiosity burning. "We must understand." Taq whispered, "We must restore."

The Black Prophet raised his hands, his voice sharp. "The seal will break. The entity will rise." His followers roared, their chants echoing. Symbols glowed faintly, spirals spreading. Mei trembled, whispering, "It's happening." Taq whispered, "We must resist."

The pyramid's labyrinth twisted endlessly, corridors shifting, illusions pressing. Taq's coalition pressed forward, their voices steady. Shamans whispered chants, elders prayed, outsiders listened. Sarah's voice rose, weaving memory and myth. "We must honor the land." Reed clenched his jaw. "We must fight." Mei whispered, "We must understand."

The siege became storm. Soldiers fired, cultists chanted, spirits pressed against the world. Lightning split the sky, fissures opened in the ice. Taq trembled, his voice sharp. "We will endure." Sarah whispered prayers. "We must resist." Reed clenched his jaw. "We must fight." Mei whispered, "We must understand."

The tundra stretched endlessly, storm raging, aurora blazing. Cultists pressed forward, soldiers stumbled, spirits pressed against the world. Reed clenched his jaw, breath ragged. Sarah whispered prayers, her voice trembling. Mei's curiosity burned, eyes wide. Taq whispered, "Balance must be restored." The Black Prophet's eyes gleamed. "The wound awaits."

CHAPTER 23: THE FINAL RITUAL

The heart of the pyramid pulsed with unnatural light. Torches flickered, shadows stretched, walls trembled. The Black Prophet stood before an altar, ancient artifacts arrayed around him. Forbidden texts lay open, their glyphs glowing faintly. His voice was sharp, commanding. "The seal will break. The entity will rise." His followers roared, their chants echoing.

The ritual began. Spirals carved into stone glowed, symbols shifted, chants rose. Human sacrifices were dragged forward, their cries swallowed by the storm. The Black Prophet raised his hands, his voice sharp. "The wound will open." Reality bent, time looped, perspectives shifted. Language fractured, logic dissolved.

The entity stirred. Its presence pressed against the world, distorting space. Shadows twisted, walls bent, voices echoed in impossible layers. Soldiers stumbled, rifles shaking. Cultists roared, their chants unbroken. Reed clenched his jaw, breath ragged. "It's happening." Sarah whispered prayers, her voice trembling. "It is danger."

Taq's coalition pressed forward, slipping through the labyrinth. Shamans whispered chants, elders prayed, outsiders followed. Illusions shifted, corridors twisted, traps snapped shut. Taq's voice was sharp. "We must endure." Sarah nodded, her jaw tight. "We must resist." Mei trembled, her eyes burning. "We must understand." Reed clenched his jaw. "We must fight."

The Black Prophet raised forbidden texts, his voice sharp. "The entity is truth. The wound will open." His followers chanted, their voices rising. Symbols glowed faintly, spirals spreading. The entity pressed harder, reality fracturing. Time looped, perspectives shifted, language dissolved.

Taq convulsed, visions consuming him. Ancestors whispered, their voices solemn. "You must resist. You must restore balance." Raven whispered, "You are wounded healer." Thunderbird roared, "You are guardian." Kushtaka hissed, "You are balance." Taq bowed his head. "I will endure."

Sarah's voice rose, weaving memory and myth. "We must honor the land. We must preserve balance." Her words carried weight, binding community. Elders nodded, solemn. "We must endure." Children listened, their eyes wide. Sarah whispered, "We must resist."

Mei traced spirals, her notebooks filled with equations. "It is science. It is myth. It is truth." Her voice was sharp, her curiosity burning. She mapped chants to fractals, rituals to equations. "It is pattern. It is connection." She trembled, whispering, "We must understand."

Reed clenched his jaw, haunted. "They're watching." His paranoia sharpened, his breath ragged. But his determination burned. "We must fight." His voice was sharp, his eyes steady. "We must resist."

The confrontation began. Taq's coalition faced the Black Prophet, voices rising. Shamans chanted, elders prayed, outsiders listened. The Black Prophet's voice carried. "The wound will open." Taq's voice was sharp. "Balance must be restored."

The entity pressed harder, reality fracturing. Time looped,

perspectives shifted, language dissolved. Shadows twisted, walls bent, voices echoed in impossible layers. Soldiers stumbled, rifles shaking. Cultists roared, their chants unbroken. Reed clenched his jaw. "We must fight."

Sarah's voice rose, weaving memory and myth. "We must honor the land. We must preserve balance." Her words carried weight, binding community. Elders nodded, solemn. "We must endure." Children listened, their eyes wide. Sarah whispered, "We must resist."

Mei traced spirals, her notebooks filled with equations. "It is science. It is myth. It is truth." Her voice was sharp, her curiosity burning. She mapped chants to fractals, rituals to equations. "It is pattern. It is connection." She trembled, whispering, "We must understand."

Taq convulsed, visions consuming him. Ancestors whispered, their voices solemn. "You must resist. You must restore balance." Raven whispered, "You are wounded healer." Thunderbird roared, "You are guardian." Kushtaka hissed, "You are balance." Taq bowed his head. "I will endure."

The Black Prophet raised forbidden texts, his voice sharp. "The entity is truth. The wound will open." His followers chanted, their voices rising. Symbols glowed faintly, spirals spreading. The entity pressed harder, reality fracturing. Time looped, perspectives shifted, language dissolved.

The confrontation escalated. Taq's coalition pressed forward, voices rising. Shamans chanted, elders prayed, outsiders listened. The Black Prophet's voice carried. "The wound will open." Taq's voice was sharp. "Balance must be restored."

The entity pressed harder, reality fracturing. Shadows twisted, walls bent, voices echoed in impossible layers. Soldiers stumbled, rifles shaking. Cultists roared, their chants unbroken. Reed clenched his jaw. "We must fight." Sarah whispered prayers. "We must resist." Mei whispered, "We must understand." Taq whispered, "We must restore."

The heart of the pyramid glowed with ancient power, its stones trembling under chants. Torches flickered, shadows stretched, walls bent. The Black Prophet stood before the altar, artifacts arrayed around him. Forbidden texts lay open, glyphs glowing faintly. His voice carried the cadence of prophecy. "The seal will break. The entity will rise." Elders whispered, "It is corruption. It is danger."

The ritual began. Spirals carved into stone glowed, symbols shifted, chants rose. Human sacrifices were dragged forward, their cries swallowed by storm. The Black Prophet raised his hands, his voice sharp. "The wound will open." Reality bent, time looped, perspectives fractured. Language dissolved, logic unraveled.

The entity stirred, pressing against the world. Shadows twisted, walls bent, voices echoed in impossible layers. Soldiers stumbled, rifles shaking. Cultists roared, their chants unbroken. Reed clenched his jaw, breath ragged. "It is happening." Sarah whispered prayers, her voice trembling. "It is danger."

Taq's coalition pressed forward, slipping through labyrinth corridors. Shamans whispered chants, elders prayed, outsiders followed. Illusions shifted, traps snapped shut, symbols glowed faintly. Taq's voice was sharp. "We must endure." Sarah nodded, her jaw tight. "We must resist." Mei trembled, her eyes burning. "We must understand." Reed clenched his jaw. "We must fight."

The Black Prophet raised forbidden texts, his voice sharp. "The entity is truth. The wound will open." His followers chanted, their voices rising. Symbols glowed faintly, spirals spreading. The entity pressed harder, reality fracturing. Time looped, perspectives shifted, language dissolved.

Taq convulsed, visions consuming him. Ancestors whispered, their voices solemn. "You must resist. You must restore balance." Raven whispered, "You are wounded healer." Thunderbird roared, "You are guardian." Kushtaka hissed, "You are balance." Taq bowed his head. "I will endure."

Sarah's voice rose, weaving memory and myth. "We must honor the land. We must preserve balance." Her words carried weight, binding community. Elders nodded, solemn. "We must endure." Children listened, their eyes wide. Sarah whispered, "We must resist."

Mei traced spirals, her notebooks filled with equations. "It is science. It is myth. It is truth." Her voice was sharp, her curiosity burning. She mapped chants to fractals, rituals to equations. "It is pattern. It is connection." She trembled, whispering, "We must understand."

Reed clenched his jaw, haunted. "They are watching." His paranoia sharpened, his breath ragged. But his determination burned. "We must fight." His voice was sharp, his eyes steady. "We must resist."

The confrontation began. Taq's coalition faced the Black Prophet, voices rising. Shamans chanted, elders prayed, outsiders listened. The Black Prophet's voice carried. "The wound will open." Taq's voice was sharp. "Balance must be restored."

The entity pressed harder, reality fracturing. Time looped, perspectives shifted, language dissolved. Shadows twisted, walls bent, voices echoed in impossible layers. Soldiers stumbled, rifles shaking. Cultists roared, their chants unbroken. Reed clenched his jaw. "We must fight."

Sarah's voice rose, weaving memory and myth. "We must honor the land. We must preserve balance." Her words carried weight, binding community. Elders nodded, solemn. "We must endure." Children listened, their eyes wide. Sarah whispered, "We must resist."

Mei traced spirals, her notebooks filled with equations. "It is science. It is myth. It is truth." Her voice was sharp, her curiosity burning. She mapped chants to fractals, rituals to equations. "It is pattern. It is connection." She trembled, whispering, "We must understand."

Taq convulsed, visions consuming him. Ancestors whispered, their voices solemn. "You must resist. You must restore balance." Raven whispered, "You are wounded healer." Thunderbird roared, "You are guardian." Kushtaka hissed, "You are balance." Taq bowed his head. "I will endure."

The Black Prophet raised forbidden texts, his voice sharp. "The entity is truth. The wound will open." His followers chanted, their voices rising. Symbols glowed faintly, spirals spreading. The entity pressed harder, reality fracturing. Time looped, perspectives shifted, language dissolved.

The confrontation escalated. Taq's coalition pressed forward, voices rising. Shamans chanted, elders prayed, outsiders listened. The Black Prophet's voice carried. "The wound will open." Taq's voice was sharp. "Balance must be restored."

The entity pressed harder, reality fracturing. Shadows twisted, walls bent, voices echoed in impossible layers. Soldiers stumbled, rifles shaking. Cultists roared, their chants unbroken. Reed clenched his jaw. "We must fight." Sarah whispered prayers. "We must resist." Mei whispered, "We must understand." Taq whispered, "We must restore."

The pyramid's heart pulsed like a living wound. Torches flared, shadows stretched, walls bent under pressure. The Black Prophet stood at the altar, artifacts gleaming, forbidden texts open. His voice cut through the chaos. "The seal will break. The entity will rise." His followers roared, their chants pounding like war drums.

The ritual surged. Spirals carved into stone glowed, symbols shifted, chants rose. Human sacrifices were dragged forward, their cries swallowed by the storm. The Black Prophet raised his hands, his voice sharp. "The wound will open." Reality buckled, time looped, perspectives fractured. Language dissolved, logic unraveled.

The entity stirred. Its presence pressed against the world, distorting space. Shadows twisted, walls bent, voices echoed in impossible layers. Soldiers stumbled, rifles shaking. Cultists roared, their chants unbroken. Reed clenched his jaw, breath ragged. "It's happening." Sarah whispered prayers, her voice trembling. "It is danger."

Taq's coalition pressed forward, slipping through the labyrinth. Shamans whispered chants, elders prayed, outsiders followed. Illusions shifted, corridors twisted, traps snapped shut. Taq's voice was sharp. "We must endure." Sarah nodded, her jaw tight. "We must resist." Mei trembled, her eyes burning. "We must understand." Reed clenched his jaw. "We must fight."

The Black Prophet raised forbidden texts, his voice sharp. "The entity is truth. The wound will open." His followers chanted, their voices rising. Symbols glowed faintly, spirals spreading. The entity pressed harder, reality fracturing. Time looped, perspectives shifted, language dissolved.

Taq convulsed, visions consuming him. Ancestors whispered, their voices solemn. "You must resist. You must restore balance." Raven whispered, "You are wounded healer." Thunderbird roared, "You are guardian." Kushtaka hissed, "You are balance." Taq bowed his head. "I will endure."

Sarah's voice rose, weaving memory and myth. "We must honor the land. We must preserve balance." Her words carried weight, binding community. Elders nodded, solemn. "We must endure." Children listened, their eyes wide. Sarah whispered, "We must resist."

Mei traced spirals, her notebooks filled with equations. "It is science. It is myth. It is truth." Her voice was sharp, her curiosity burning. She mapped chants to fractals, rituals to equations. "It is pattern. It is connection." She trembled, whispering, "We must understand."

Reed clenched his jaw, haunted. "They're watching." His paranoia sharpened, his breath ragged. But his determination burned. "We must fight." His voice was sharp, his eyes steady. "We must resist."

The confrontation erupted. Taq's coalition faced the Black Prophet, voices rising. Shamans chanted, elders prayed, outsiders listened. The Black Prophet's voice carried. "The wound will open." Taq's voice was sharp. "Balance must be restored."

The entity pressed harder, reality fracturing. Time looped, perspectives shifted, language dissolved. Shadows twisted, walls bent, voices echoed in impossible layers. Soldiers stumbled, rifles shaking. Cultists roared, their chants unbroken. Reed clenched his jaw. "We must fight."

Sarah's voice rose, weaving memory and myth. "We must honor the land. We must preserve balance." Her words carried weight, binding community. Elders nodded, solemn. "We must endure." Children listened, their eyes wide. Sarah whispered, "We must resist."

Mei traced spirals, her notebooks filled with equations. "It is science. It is myth. It is truth." Her voice was sharp, her curiosity burning. She mapped chants to fractals, rituals to equations. "It is pattern. It is connection." She trembled, whispering, "We must understand."

Taq convulsed, visions consuming him. Ancestors whispered, their voices solemn. "You must resist. You must restore balance." Raven whispered, "You are wounded healer." Thunderbird roared, "You are guardian." Kushtaka hissed, "You are balance." Taq bowed his head. "I will endure."

The Black Prophet raised forbidden texts, his voice sharp. "The entity is truth. The wound will open." His followers chanted, their voices rising. Symbols glowed faintly, spirals spreading. The entity pressed harder, reality fracturing. Time looped, perspectives shifted, language dissolved.

The confrontation escalated. Taq's coalition pressed forward, voices rising. Shamans chanted, elders prayed, outsiders listened. The Black Prophet's voice carried. "The wound will open." Taq's voice was sharp. "Balance must be restored."

The entity pressed harder, reality fracturing. Shadows twisted, walls bent, voices echoed in impossible layers. Soldiers stumbled, rifles shaking. Cultists roared, their chants unbroken. Reed clenched his jaw. "We must fight." Sarah whispered prayers. "We must resist." Mei whispered, "We must understand." Taq whispered, "We must restore."

The pyramid trembled, aurora blazing above. The Black Prophet's eyes gleamed. "The wound awaits." Taq's coalition stood together, voices blending. "We will endure. We will resist. We will understand. We will fight." Spirits pressed against the world, their voices echoing. "Balance must be restored."

CHAPTER 24: THE SHAMAN'S SACRIFICE

The pyramid shook, its stones cracking under the weight of the ritual. The entity pressed harder, reality fracturing, voices echoing in impossible layers. Taq convulsed, visions consuming him. Ancestors whispered, their voices solemn. "You must resist. You must restore balance." Raven whispered, "You are wounded healer." Thunderbird roared, "You are guardian." Kushtaka hissed, "You are balance." Taq bowed his head. "I will endure."

He realized the truth. The seal could not be restored by chants alone. The entity's energy had to be redirected, absorbed, contained. Only a vessel could channel it, only a sacrifice could restore balance. Taq's voice was sharp. "It must be me." Elders trembled, their voices breaking. "You will be destroyed." Taq nodded. "I will endure."

The aurora blazed above, brighter than ever. Colors bled into each other, shimmering like a living tapestry. Taq whispered prayers, his voice trembling. "I will offer myself." Spirits pressed against him, their voices solemn. "You are chosen. You are balance." Taq bowed his head. "I will endure."

Sarah's voice rose, weaving memory and myth. "We will anchor you. We will preserve balance." Her words carried weight, binding community. Elders nodded, solemn. "We will endure." Children listened, their eyes wide. Sarah whispered, "We will resist."

Mei traced spirals, her notebooks filled with equations. "We will anchor you with patterns. We will stabilize the ritual." Her voice was sharp, her curiosity burning. She mapped chants to fractals, rituals to equations. "It is pattern. It is connection." She trembled, whispering, "We will understand."

Reed clenched his jaw, haunted. "I will fight. I will hold them back." His paranoia sharpened, his breath ragged. But his determination burned. "We must resist." His voice was sharp, his eyes steady. "We must fight."

The ritual began. Taq stood at the altar, his body trembling. Sarah's voice rose, weaving chants. Mei traced spirals, her equations glowing faintly. Reed fired into the storm, cultists falling. The Black Prophet roared, his voice sharp. "The wound will open." Taq whispered, "Balance must be restored."

The entity pressed harder, reality fracturing. Time looped, perspectives shifted, language dissolved. Shadows twisted, walls bent, voices echoed in impossible layers. Taq convulsed, his spirit fracturing. "I will endure." Sarah whispered prayers. "We will anchor you." Mei whispered, "We will stabilize." Reed clenched his jaw. "We will fight."

Agony consumed Taq. His body burned, his spirit torn apart. Visions of past and future surged—ancestors whispering, descendants crying, worlds collapsing. He saw the wound opening, the entity rising, the land breaking. He screamed, his voice sharp. "I will endure."

Sarah's voice rose, weaving chants. "Honor the land. Preserve balance." Her words carried weight, binding community. Elders nodded, solemn. "We must endure." Children listened, their eyes wide. Sarah whispered, "We must resist."

Mei traced spirals, her equations glowing faintly. "It is pattern. It is connection." Her voice was sharp, her curiosity burning. She mapped chants to fractals, rituals to equations. "We will stabilize." She trembled, whispering, "We must understand."

Reed fired into the storm, cultists falling. Government soldiers stumbled, their unity fractured. The Black Prophet roared, his voice sharp. "The wound will open." Reed clenched his jaw. "We must fight." His voice was sharp, his eyes steady. "We must resist."

Taq's body convulsed, his spirit fracturing. Agony consumed him, his voice trembling. "I will endure." Ancestors whispered, their voices solemn. "You are wounded healer. You are guardian. You are balance." Taq bowed his head. "I will endure."

The entity pressed harder, reality fracturing. Shadows twisted, walls bent, voices echoed in impossible layers. Taq screamed, his body burning. "I will endure." Sarah whispered prayers. "We will anchor you." Mei whispered, "We will stabilize." Reed clenched his jaw. "We will fight."

Agony consumed Taq, his body torn apart. His spirit dispersed, visions consuming him. He saw ancestors, descendants, worlds collapsing, worlds restored. He whispered, "Balance must be restored." His body shattered, his spirit rising.

The aurora blazed, brighter than ever. Colors bled into each other, shimmering like a living tapestry. Taq's spirit dispersed into the lights, his voice echoing. "I will endure." Spirits whispered, "You are balance. You are guardian." The aurora pulsed, resonating with his sacrifice.

Sarah collapsed, her voice trembling. "He is gone." Mei trembled, her eyes burning. "He is dispersed." Reed clenched his jaw, breath ragged. "He endured." Elders whispered, their voices solemn. "He is balance."

The pyramid trembled, its stones cracking. The seal restored, the wound closed. The entity pressed against the world, then vanished. The aurora blazed, brighter than ever. Spirits whispered, "Balance must be restored." Taq's voice echoed faintly. "I will endure."

The pyramid groaned like a wounded beast, its stones trembling under the weight of the ritual. The entity pressed harder, reality bending, voices echoing in impossible layers. Taq convulsed, visions consuming him. Ancestors whispered, their voices solemn. "The wound must be sealed. Balance must be restored." Raven whispered, "You are wounded healer." Thunderbird roared, "You are guardian." Kushtaka hissed, "You are balance."

Taq understood. The chants, the prayers, the equations—they were not enough. The seal demanded a vessel, a bridge between worlds. Only sacrifice could restore balance. His voice was steady, though his body shook. "It must be me." Elders trembled, their voices breaking. "You will be destroyed." Taq bowed his head. "I will endure."

The aurora blazed above, brighter than any living memory. Colors bled into each other, weaving a tapestry of spirit and sky. Taq whispered prayers, his voice trembling. "I will offer myself." Spirits pressed against him, their voices solemn. "You are chosen. You are balance." Taq bowed his head. "I will endure."

Sarah's voice rose, weaving memory and myth. "We will anchor you. We will preserve balance." Her words carried weight, binding community. Elders nodded, solemn. "We will endure." Children listened, their eyes wide. Sarah whispered, "We will resist."

Mei traced spirals, her notebooks filled with equations. "We will anchor you with patterns. We will stabilize the ritual." Her voice was sharp, her curiosity burning. She mapped chants to fractals, rituals to equations. "It is pattern. It is connection." She trembled, whispering, "We will understand."

Reed clenched his jaw, haunted. "I will fight. I will hold them back." His paranoia sharpened, his breath ragged. But his determination burned. "We must resist." His voice was sharp, his eyes steady. "We must fight."

The ritual began anew. Taq stood at the altar, his body trembling. Sarah's chants rose, weaving memory and myth. Mei traced spirals, her equations glowing faintly. Reed fired into the storm, cultists falling. The Black Prophet roared, his voice sharp. "The wound will open." Taq whispered, "Balance must be restored."

The entity pressed harder, reality fracturing. Time looped, perspectives shifted, language dissolved. Shadows twisted, walls bent, voices echoed in impossible layers. Taq convulsed, his spirit fracturing. "I will endure." Sarah whispered prayers. "We will anchor you." Mei whispered, "We will stabilize." Reed clenched his jaw. "We will fight."

Agony consumed Taq. His body burned, his spirit torn apart. Visions of past and future surged—ancestors whispering, descendants crying, worlds collapsing. He saw the wound opening, the entity rising, the land breaking. He screamed, his voice sharp. "I will endure."

Sarah's voice rose, weaving chants. "Honor the land. Preserve balance." Her words carried weight, binding community. Elders nodded, solemn. "We must endure." Children listened, their eyes wide. Sarah whispered, "We must resist."

Mei traced spirals, her equations glowing faintly. "It is pattern. It is connection." Her voice was sharp, her curiosity burning. She mapped chants to fractals, rituals to equations.

"We will stabilize." She trembled, whispering, "We must understand."

Reed fired into the storm, cultists falling. Government soldiers stumbled, their unity fractured. The Black Prophet roared, his voice sharp. "The wound will open." Reed clenched his jaw. "We must fight." His voice was sharp, his eyes steady. "We must resist."

Taq's body convulsed, his spirit fracturing. Agony consumed him, his voice trembling. "I will endure." Ancestors whispered, their voices solemn. "You are wounded healer. You are guardian. You are balance." Taq bowed his head. "I will endure."

The entity pressed harder, reality fracturing. Shadows twisted, walls bent, voices echoed in impossible layers. Taq screamed, his body burning. "I will endure." Sarah whispered prayers. "We will anchor you." Mei whispered, "We will stabilize." Reed clenched his jaw. "We will fight."

Agony consumed Taq, his body torn apart. His spirit dispersed, visions consuming him. He saw ancestors, descendants, worlds collapsing, worlds restored. He whispered, "Balance must be restored." His body shattered, his spirit rising.

The aurora blazed, brighter than ever. Colors bled into each other, weaving a tapestry of spirit and sky. Taq's spirit dispersed into the lights, his voice echoing. "I will endure." Spirits whispered, "You are balance. You are guardian." The aurora pulsed, resonating with his sacrifice.

Sarah collapsed, her voice trembling. "He is gone." Mei trembled, her eyes burning. "He is dispersed." Reed clenched his jaw, breath ragged. "He endured." Elders whispered, their voices solemn. "He is balance."

The pyramid trembled, its stones cracking. The seal

restored, the wound closed. The entity pressed against the world, then vanished. The aurora blazed, brighter than ever. Spirits whispered, "Balance must be restored." Taq's voice echoed faintly. "I will endure."

The pyramid shook violently, stones cracking, torches sputtering. The entity pressed harder, reality buckling. Time looped, voices echoed in impossible layers. Taq staggered, clutching his chest. "It must be me." His voice cut through the chaos. Elders gasped, their voices breaking. "You will be destroyed." Taq's jaw tightened. "I will endure."

The aurora ripped across the sky, violent streaks of green and crimson. Colors bled into each other, shimmering like fire. Taq raised the raven feather, his body trembling. "I will offer myself." Spirits pressed against him, voices layered. "You are chosen. You are balance." Taq bowed his head. "I will endure."

Sarah's voice rose, sharp, urgent. "We will anchor you." Her chants cut through the storm, weaving memory and myth. Elders joined, their voices trembling. "Preserve balance." Sarah's jaw tightened. "We will resist."

Mei scribbled furiously, spirals filling her notebook. Equations glowed faintly, mapped to chants. "We will stabilize." Her voice was sharp, her curiosity burning. "It is pattern. It is connection." She trembled, whispering, "We must understand."

Reed fired into the storm, bullets tearing through cultists. His breath came ragged, paranoia sharpening his aim. "I'll hold them back." His voice was sharp, his eyes steady. "We must fight."

The ritual surged. Taq stood at the altar, his body convulsing. Sarah's chants rose, Mei's equations pulsed, Reed's gunfire echoed. The Black Prophet roared, his voice sharp. "The wound will open." Taq screamed, "Balance must be restored."

The entity pressed harder, reality fracturing. Shadows twisted, walls bent, voices echoed in impossible layers. Taq convulsed, his spirit fracturing. "I will endure." Sarah whispered prayers. "We will anchor you." Mei whispered, "We will stabilize." Reed clenched his jaw. "We will fight."

Agony consumed Taq. His body burned, his spirit torn apart. Visions surged—ancestors whispering, descendants crying, worlds collapsing. He saw the wound opening, the entity rising, the land breaking. He screamed, his voice sharp. "I will endure."

Sarah's chants cut through the storm. "Honor the land. Preserve balance." Her words carried weight, binding community. Elders nodded, solemn. "We must endure." Sarah's jaw tightened. "We must resist."

Mei's spirals glowed, equations pulsing. "It is pattern. It is connection." Her voice was sharp, her curiosity burning. "We will stabilize." She trembled, whispering, "We must understand."

Reed fired again, cultists falling. Government soldiers stumbled, their unity fractured. The Black Prophet roared, his voice sharp. "The wound will open." Reed clenched his jaw. "We must fight."

Taq's body convulsed, his spirit fracturing. Agony consumed him, his voice trembling. "I will endure." Ancestors whispered, their voices solemn. "You are wounded healer. You are guardian. You are balance." Taq bowed his head. "I will endure."

The entity pressed harder, reality fracturing. Shadows twisted, walls bent, voices echoed in impossible layers. Taq screamed, his body burning. "I will endure." Sarah whispered prayers. "We will anchor you." Mei whispered, "We will stabilize." Reed clenched his jaw. "We will fight."

Agony consumed Taq, his body torn apart. His spirit dispersed, visions consuming him. He saw ancestors, descendants, worlds collapsing, worlds restored. He whispered, "Balance must be restored." His body shattered, his spirit rising.

The aurora blazed, violent and alive. Colors bled into each other, shimmering like fire. Taq's spirit dispersed into the lights, his voice echoing. "I will endure." Spirits whispered, "You are balance. You are guardian." The aurora pulsed, resonating with his sacrifice.

Sarah collapsed, her voice trembling. "He is gone." Mei trembled, her eyes burning. "He is dispersed." Reed clenched his jaw, breath ragged. "He endured." Elders whispered, their voices solemn. "He is balance."

The pyramid cracked, stones collapsing. The seal restored, the wound closed. The entity pressed against the world, then vanished. The aurora blazed, brighter than ever. Spirits whispered, "Balance must be restored." Taq's voice echoed faintly. "I will endure."

The tundra stretched endlessly, storm fading, aurora blazing. Survivors stood together, their voices trembling. Sarah whispered prayers. "We must preserve." Mei whispered, "We must understand." Reed clenched his jaw. "We must fight." Elders whispered, "We must endure." The aurora pulsed, resonating with Taq's sacrifice.

CHAPTER 25: THE AFTERMATH

The pyramid groaned, its stones splitting, cracks racing across its surface. The aurora blazed overhead, pulsing with Taq's dispersed spirit. With a final shudder, the structure collapsed inward, sealing the portal. Dust and snow billowed, swallowing torches, chants, and screams. The wound was closed. Balance restored.

Survivors staggered across the tundra, their voices trembling. Sarah whispered prayers, her jaw tight. "He is gone." Mei trembled, her eyes burning. "He is dispersed." Reed clenched his jaw, breath ragged. "He endured." Elders whispered, their voices solemn. "He is balance."

The cult fractured, its members scattered. Some fled into the storm, their chants broken. Others collapsed, their voices silenced. The Black Prophet vanished into shadows, his fate uncertain. Government soldiers pressed forward, rifles raised, faces grim. "Contain survivors. Secure the site."

The government issued orders, their voices sharp. "Arrest fugitives. Interrogate witnesses. Control narrative." Reed was seized, his wrists bound. "You are fugitive. You are traitor." He clenched his jaw, his voice sharp. "I resisted." Soldiers dragged him away.

Mei was approached by officials, their voices calm. "You are scientist. You are valuable." They offered her a place in a secretive institute. "You will study. You will preserve."

Mei trembled, her curiosity burning. "I will understand." She nodded, her voice sharp. "I will endure."

Sarah returned to her community, her voice steady. Elders welcomed her, children listened. "You are keeper. You are elder." She whispered prayers, weaving memory and myth. "We must honor the land. We must preserve balance." Her words carried weight, binding community.

The government issued a sanitized report. "It was disaster. It was terrorism. It was storm." Their voices were sharp, their narrative controlled. Evidence was erased, records destroyed. The true story vanished from official archives. Only survivors remembered.

Oral tradition preserved truth. Elders whispered, children listened, shamans prayed. Sarah's voice rose, weaving memory and myth. "We must endure. We must resist. We must preserve." Her words carried weight, binding community.

Reed sat in interrogation rooms, his voice sharp. "It was ritual. It was entity. It was wound." Officials dismissed him, their voices cold. "It was storm. It was terrorism." Reed clenched his jaw, his voice trembling. "It was truth."

Mei studied in secretive halls, her notebooks filled with spirals. Equations mapped to chants, rituals to fractals. "It is science. It is myth. It is truth." Her voice was sharp, her curiosity burning. She whispered, "We must understand."

Sarah traveled to villages, her voice steady. She shared stories, weaving memory and myth. "We must honor the land. We must preserve balance." Elders nodded, solemn. Children listened, their eyes wide. Sarah whispered, "We must endure."

The cult disbanded, its members scattered. Some institutionalized, their voices silenced. Others fled, their chants broken. The Black Prophet's fate remained uncertain, his shadow lingering. Elders whispered, "He will return."

Shamans prayed, "We must resist."

The government tightened control, their voices sharp. "It was disaster. It was terrorism. It was storm." Reports circulated, evidence erased. Survivors whispered, their voices trembling. "It was ritual. It was entity. It was wound."

Sarah's voice rose, weaving memory and myth. "We must honor the land. We must preserve balance." Her words carried weight, binding community. Elders nodded, solemn. "We must endure." Children listened, their eyes wide. Sarah whispered, "We must resist."

Mei published papers, her voice sharp. "It is science. It is myth. It is truth." She challenged paradigms, proposed new models. "It is pattern. It is connection." Her curiosity burned, her voice trembling. "We must understand."

Reed, disgraced, found solace in teaching. His voice was sharp, his eyes haunted. "We must resist. We must endure." Students listened, their eyes wide. Reed whispered, "We must fight."

The pyramid was gone, erased from maps. The tundra stretched endlessly, aurora blazing. Survivors whispered prayers, their voices trembling. "We must preserve. We must understand. We must resist. We must endure." The aurora pulsed, resonating with Taq's sacrifice.

The government's report echoed, its voice sharp. "It was disaster. It was terrorism. It was storm." Survivors whispered, their voices trembling. "It was ritual. It was entity. It was wound." Elders nodded, solemn. "We must preserve truth."

The pyramid collapsed inward, its stones folding like a dying star. The aurora blazed above, carrying Taq's spirit into the sky. Dust and snow swallowed the ruins, leaving no trace of the wound. Elders whispered, "The seal is restored. Balance returns." Shamans bowed their heads. "The sacrifice is complete."

Survivors stood in silence, their voices trembling. Sarah whispered prayers, her jaw tight. "He is gone." Mei trembled, her eyes burning. "He is dispersed." Reed clenched his jaw, breath ragged. "He endured." Elders whispered, "He is balance."

The cult fractured, its chants broken. Some fled into the storm, their voices silenced. Others collapsed, their faith shattered. The Black Prophet vanished into shadows, his fate uncertain. Elders whispered, "His shadow lingers." Shamans prayed, "We must resist."

Government soldiers pressed forward, rifles raised, faces grim. "Contain survivors. Secure the site." Their voices were sharp, their orders absolute. Reed was seized, his wrists bound. "You are fugitive. You are traitor." He clenched his jaw, his voice trembling. "I resisted."

Mei was approached by officials, their voices calm. "You are scientist. You are valuable." They offered her a place in a secretive institute. "You will study. You will preserve." Mei trembled, her curiosity burning. "I will understand." She nodded, her voice sharp. "I will endure."

Sarah returned to her community, her voice steady. Elders welcomed her, children listened. "You are keeper. You are elder." She whispered prayers, weaving memory and myth. "We must honor the land. We must preserve balance." Her words carried weight, binding community.

The government issued a report, its voice sharp. "It was disaster. It was terrorism. It was storm." Their narrative was controlled, their evidence erased. Records vanished, archives cleansed. The true story was silenced. Elders whispered, "Truth survives in memory."

Oral tradition preserved what the state erased. Elders whispered, children listened, shamans prayed. Sarah's voice rose, weaving memory and myth. "We must endure. We must resist. We must preserve." Her words carried weight, binding community.

Reed sat in interrogation rooms, his voice sharp. "It was ritual. It was entity. It was wound." Officials dismissed him, their voices cold. "It was storm. It was terrorism." Reed clenched his jaw, his voice trembling. "It was truth."

Mei studied in secretive halls, her notebooks filled with spirals. Equations mapped to chants, rituals to fractals. "It is science. It is myth. It is truth." Her voice was sharp, her curiosity burning. She whispered, "We must understand."

Sarah traveled to villages, her voice steady. She shared stories, weaving memory and myth. "We must honor the land. We must preserve balance." Elders nodded, solemn. Children listened, their eyes wide. Sarah whispered, "We must endure."

The cult disbanded, its members scattered. Some institutionalized, their voices silenced. Others fled, their chants broken. The Black Prophet's fate remained uncertain, his shadow lingering. Elders whispered, "He will return." Shamans prayed, "We must resist."

The government tightened control, its voice sharp. "It was disaster. It was terrorism. It was storm." Reports circulated, evidence erased. Survivors whispered, their voices trembling. "It was ritual. It was entity. It was wound."

Sarah's voice rose, weaving memory and myth. "We must honor the land. We must preserve balance." Her words carried weight, binding community. Elders nodded, solemn. "We must endure." Children listened, their eyes wide. Sarah whispered, "We must resist."

Mei published papers, her voice sharp. "It is science. It is myth. It is truth." She challenged paradigms, proposed new models. "It is pattern. It is connection." Her curiosity burned, her voice trembling. "We must understand."

Reed, disgraced, found solace in teaching. His voice was sharp, his eyes haunted. "We must resist. We must endure." Students listened, their eyes wide. Reed whispered, "We must fight."

The pyramid was gone, erased from maps. The tundra stretched endlessly, aurora blazing. Survivors whispered prayers, their voices trembling. "We must preserve. We must understand. We must resist. We must endure." The aurora pulsed, resonating with Taq's sacrifice.

The government's report echoed, its voice sharp. "It was disaster. It was terrorism. It was storm." Survivors whispered, their voices trembling. "It was ritual. It was entity. It was wound." Elders nodded, solemn. "We must preserve truth."

The pyramid collapsed in a roar, stones splitting, dust exploding outward. The aurora blazed overhead, violent streaks of green and crimson tearing through the sky. Survivors staggered, shielding their eyes. The wound was sealed. The entity was gone. Balance restored.

Sarah dropped to her knees, breath ragged. "He is gone." Her voice cracked, but her eyes burned. Mei trembled, clutching her notebook. "He is dispersed." Reed clenched his jaw, fists tight. "He endured." Elders whispered, their voices solemn. "He is balance."

Cultists scattered, their chants broken. Some fled into the storm, their torches extinguished. Others collapsed, their faith shattered. The Black Prophet vanished into shadows, his voice echoing faintly. "The wound awaits." His fate remained uncertain.

Government soldiers surged forward, rifles raised. "Contain survivors. Secure the site." Their voices were sharp, their movements precise. Reed was seized, his wrists bound. "You are fugitive. You are traitor." He spat blood, his voice sharp. "I resisted."

Mei was pulled aside, officials whispering. "You are scientist. You are valuable." They offered her a place in a secretive institute. "You will study. You will preserve." Mei's eyes burned, her voice trembling. "I will understand."

Sarah returned to her community, her voice steady. Elders embraced her, children listened. "You are keeper. You are elder." She whispered prayers, weaving memory and myth. "We must honor the land. We must preserve balance." Her words carried weight, binding community.

The government issued its report, cold and sanitized. "It was disaster. It was terrorism. It was storm." Their narrative was sharp, their evidence erased. Records vanished, archives cleansed. The true story silenced.

Survivors whispered, their voices trembling. "It was ritual. It was entity. It was wound." Elders nodded, solemn. "Truth survives in memory." Shamans prayed, their voices sharp. "We must resist."

Reed sat in interrogation rooms, his voice sharp. "It was ritual. It was entity. It was wound." Officials dismissed him, their voices cold. "It was storm. It was terrorism." Reed clenched his jaw, his voice trembling. "It was truth."

Mei studied in secretive halls, her notebooks filled with spirals. Equations mapped to chants, rituals to fractals. "It is science. It is myth. It is truth." Her voice was sharp, her curiosity burning. She whispered, "We must understand."

Sarah traveled to villages, her voice steady. She shared stories, weaving memory and myth. "We must honor the land. We must preserve balance." Elders nodded, solemn. Children listened, their eyes wide. Sarah whispered, "We must endure."

The cult disbanded, its members scattered. Some institutionalized, their voices silenced. Others fled, their chants broken. The Black Prophet's fate remained uncertain, his shadow lingering. Elders whispered, "He will return." Shamans prayed, "We must resist."

The government tightened control, its voice sharp. "It was disaster. It was terrorism. It was storm." Reports circulated, evidence erased. Survivors whispered, their voices trembling. "It was ritual. It was entity. It was wound."

Sarah's voice rose, weaving memory and myth. "We must honor the land. We must preserve balance." Her words carried weight, binding community. Elders nodded, solemn. "We must endure." Children listened, their eyes wide. Sarah whispered, "We must resist."

Mei published papers, her voice sharp. "It is science. It is myth. It is truth." She challenged paradigms, proposed new models. "It is pattern. It is connection." Her curiosity burned, her voice trembling. "We must understand."

Reed, disgraced, found solace in teaching. His voice was sharp, his eyes haunted. "We must resist. We must endure." Students listened, their eyes wide. Reed whispered, "We must fight."

The pyramid was gone, erased from maps. The tundra stretched endlessly, aurora blazing. Survivors whispered prayers, their voices trembling. "We must preserve. We must understand. We must resist. We must endure." The aurora pulsed, resonating with Taq's sacrifice.

The government's report echoed, its voice sharp. "It was disaster. It was terrorism. It was storm." Survivors whispered, their voices trembling. "It was ritual. It was entity. It was wound." Elders nodded, solemn. "We must preserve truth."

The tundra held silence, aurora blazing. Sarah whispered prayers. Mei traced spirals. Reed clenched his jaw. Elders whispered. "Balance must be restored." Taq's voice echoed faintly. "I will endure."

CHAPTER 26: THE RAVEN'S LEGACY

Sarah stood before her community, the aurora blazing above. Her voice was steady, weaving memory and myth. "We must honor the land. We must preserve balance." Elders nodded, solemn. Children listened, their eyes wide. Sarah whispered, "We must endure."

She traveled to villages, her voice carrying across tundra. Schools welcomed her, artists gathered, activists listened. She shared stories, weaving chants and visions. "Taq endured. Taq restored balance." Her words carried weight, binding community.

Songs were composed, their melodies echoing Raven's cry. Carvings were etched, spirals glowing faintly. Digital archives preserved chants, equations, visions. Sarah whispered, "We must remember." Elders nodded, solemn. "We must resist."

The motif of Raven recurred, its wings spread across stories. Raven was trickster, survivor, guardian. Raven was transformation, survival, storytelling. Sarah's voice rose, weaving memory and myth. "Raven endures. Raven preserves."

Mei's curiosity burned, her notebooks filled with spirals. She published papers, her voice sharp. "It is science. It is myth. It is truth." She challenged paradigms, proposed new models. "It is pattern. It is connection." Her voice trembled. "We must understand."

She advocated collaboration, her voice steady. "Scientists must listen. Communities must speak. Knowledge must merge." Her words carried weight, binding worlds. Elders nodded, solemn. "We must endure."

Her papers spread, their equations mapped to chants. Institutes listened, paradigms shifted. "It is science. It is myth. It is truth." Mei whispered, "We must understand."

Reed, disgraced, found solace in teaching. His voice was sharp, his eyes haunted. "We must resist. We must endure." Students listened, their eyes wide. Reed whispered, "We must fight."

He mentored investigators, his voice steady. "Truth must survive. Balance must be restored." His words carried weight, binding generations. Students nodded, solemn. "We must endure."

Sarah collaborated with artists, her voice steady. Songs echoed, carvings glowed, archives pulsed. "We must preserve. We must resist." Her words carried weight, binding community.

Mei collaborated with scientists, her voice sharp. Equations mapped to chants, rituals to fractals. "We must understand. We must endure." Her words carried weight, binding worlds.

Reed collaborated with students, his voice steady. "We must resist. We must fight." His words carried weight, binding generations. Students whispered, "We must endure."

The motif of Raven spread, its wings across villages. Raven was transformation, survival, storytelling. Raven was balance, guardian, healer. Sarah whispered, "Raven endures."

Songs echoed across tundra, their melodies sharp. Carvings glowed faintly, spirals spreading. Archives pulsed, their voices steady. "We must preserve. We must resist." Elders nodded, solemn. "We must endure."

Mei's papers challenged paradigms, her voice sharp. "It is science. It is myth. It is truth." Her words carried weight, binding worlds. Scientists listened, their voices trembling. "We must understand."

Reed's teachings spread, his voice steady. "We must resist. We must endure." His words carried weight, binding generations. Students whispered, "We must fight."

Sarah stood beneath the aurora, its colors shimmering like wings across the night. Her voice rose in cadence with the lights, weaving memory and myth. "We must honor the land. We must preserve balance." Elders nodded, solemn. Children listened, their eyes wide. Sarah whispered, "We must endure."

She traveled from village to village, carrying the story like a sacred bundle. In schools, she spoke of Taq's sacrifice. In longhouses, she recited chants that bound the past to the present. Artists carved spirals into wood and stone, their hands guided by her words. "Taq endured. Taq restored balance."

Songs were composed, their melodies echoing Raven's cry. Dancers moved in circles, their steps tracing spirals. Digital archives preserved chants and visions, ensuring the story would not be erased. Sarah whispered, "We must remember." Elders nodded, solemn. "We must resist."

The Raven appeared again and again, its wings spread across stories. Raven was trickster, survivor, guardian. Raven was transformation, survival, storytelling. Sarah's voice rose, weaving memory and myth. "Raven endures. Raven preserves."

Mei's notebooks filled with spirals, equations mapped to chants. She published papers, her voice sharp. "It is science. It is myth. It is truth." She challenged paradigms, proposed new models. "It is pattern. It is connection." Her voice trembled. "We must understand."

She advocated collaboration, her voice steady. "Scientists must listen. Communities must speak. Knowledge must merge." Her words carried weight, binding worlds. Elders nodded, solemn. "We must endure."

Her work spread, her papers translated into many languages. Institutes listened, paradigms shifted. "It is science. It is myth. It is truth." Mei whispered, "We must understand."

Reed, disgraced, withdrew from the public eye. His voice was sharp, his eyes haunted. "We must resist. We must endure." He found solace in teaching, mentoring the next generation. Students listened, their eyes wide. Reed whispered, "We must fight."

He told them fragments of the truth, careful but insistent. "There are wounds in the world. There are guardians. There are sacrifices." His words carried weight, binding generations. Students nodded, solemn. "We must endure."

Sarah collaborated with artists, her voice steady. Songs echoed, carvings glowed, archives pulsed. "We must preserve. We must resist." Her words carried weight, binding community.

Mei collaborated with scientists, her voice sharp. Equations mapped to chants, rituals to fractals. "We must understand. We must endure." Her words carried weight, binding worlds.

Reed collaborated with students, his voice steady. "We must resist. We must fight." His words carried weight, binding generations. Students whispered, "We must endure."

The motif of Raven spread, its wings across villages. Raven was transformation, survival, storytelling. Raven was balance, guardian, healer. Sarah whispered, "Raven endures."

Songs echoed across tundra, their melodies sharp. Carvings glowed faintly, spirals spreading. Archives pulsed, their voices steady. "We must preserve. We must resist." Elders nodded, solemn. "We must endure."

Mei's papers challenged paradigms, her voice sharp. "It is science. It is myth. It is truth." Her words carried weight, binding worlds. Scientists listened, their voices trembling. "We must understand."

Reed's teachings spread, his voice steady. "We must resist. We must endure." His words carried weight, binding generations. Students whispered, "We must fight."

Sarah's voice rose, weaving memory and myth. "We must honor the land. We must preserve balance." Her words carried weight, binding community. Elders nodded, solemn. "We must endure."

Sarah stood beneath the aurora, its colors tearing across the sky like fire. Her voice cut through the silence. "We must remember." Elders leaned forward, children froze, activists scribbled notes. She spoke of Taq, of sacrifice, of balance. Her words hit like blows.

She traveled fast, village to village, school to school. Crowds gathered, restless, hungry for truth. She told them of the wound, the entity, the shaman who endured. "He gave everything. We must honor him." Her voice was sharp, unyielding.

Artists carved spirals into wood and stone. Musicians struck drums, their rhythms echoing Raven's wings. Digital archives flickered alive, preserving chants and visions. Sarah whispered, "We will not be erased." The people answered, "We will endure."

The Raven appeared everywhere. Painted on walls, etched

into carvings, sung in chants. Raven was trickster, survivor, guardian. Raven was transformation, survival, story. Sarah's voice rose. "Raven endures. Raven preserves."

Mei's notebooks overflowed with spirals, equations mapped to chants. She published papers, her voice sharp. "It is science. It is myth. It is truth." Her words spread, shaking institutions. "It is pattern. It is connection."

She stood before scientists, her voice steady. "You must listen. You must merge knowledge. You must respect." Her words cut through silence. Some scoffed, others trembled. Mei pressed forward. "We must understand."

Her work spread like fire. Institutes debated, paradigms cracked. "It is science. It is myth. It is truth." Mei whispered, "We must endure."

Reed, disgraced, found classrooms instead of battlefields. His voice was sharp, his eyes haunted. "We must resist. We must endure." Students leaned in, their eyes wide. Reed whispered, "We must fight."

He told them fragments, careful but relentless. "There are wounds in the world. There are guardians. There are sacrifices." His words landed heavy. Students nodded, solemn. "We must endure."

Sarah collaborated with artists. Songs echoed, carvings glowed, archives pulsed. "We must preserve. We must resist." Her voice was sharp, her presence unshakable.

Mei collaborated with scientists. Equations mapped to chants, rituals to fractals. "We must understand. We must endure." Her voice was sharp, her conviction unbreakable.

Reed collaborated with students. "We must resist. We must fight." His voice was sharp, his lessons unforgettable. Students whispered, "We must endure."

The Raven spread across villages, its wings painted on walls. Raven was transformation, survival, story. Raven was balance, guardian, healer. Sarah whispered, "Raven endures."

Songs echoed across tundra, their rhythms sharp. Carvings glowed faintly, spirals spreading. Archives pulsed, their voices steady. "We must preserve. We must resist." Elders nodded. "We must endure."

Mei's papers hit journals like thunder. "It is science. It is myth. It is truth." Her words carried weight, binding worlds. Scientists listened, their voices trembling. "We must understand."

Reed's teachings spread underground. "We must resist. We must endure." His words carried weight, binding generations. Students whispered, "We must fight."

Sarah's voice rose, weaving memory and myth. "We must honor the land. We must preserve balance." Her words carried weight, binding community. Elders nodded. "We must endure."

The aurora blazed, Raven's wings shimmering. Sarah whispered prayers. Mei traced spirals. Reed clenched his jaw. Elders whispered. "Balance must be restored."

And in the lights above, faint but unbroken, Taq's voice echoed. "I will endure."

CHAPTER 27: THE SPIRITS' RETURN

The aurora blazed across the night sky, shimmering like a living bridge. Elders whispered, "It is Taq." Shamans bowed their heads, their voices trembling. "He has returned." Children pointed, their eyes wide. "The lights are alive." The community gathered, their voices hushed.

Taq's spirit moved through the aurora, his voice echoing in dreams. Grandmothers stirred in sleep, hearing his words. "Be vigilant. Be humble. The wound is sealed, but danger lingers." Shamans trembled, their visions filled with spirals. "He is guardian. He is balance."

The dreams spread, carried from house to house. Hunters woke with visions of caribou. Children whispered of Raven's wings. Elders spoke of Kushtaka's hiss. "The spirits are near. The land is alive." The community listened, their voices solemn.

A potlatch was declared, a feast of remembrance. Families gathered, gifts exchanged, stories told. Elders spoke of Taq's sacrifice, their voices trembling. "He gave himself. He restored balance." Shamans prayed, their chants rising. "We must honor him."

The feast began, drums pounding, dancers moving in circles. Songs echoed, their melodies sharp. Carvings glowed faintly, spirals spreading. Sarah whispered prayers, her voice steady. "We must preserve." Mei traced spirals, her curiosity burning. "We must understand." Reed clenched his jaw. "We must endure."

The potlatch carried stories, weaving memory and myth. Elders spoke of Raven, trickster and guardian. "Raven endures. Raven preserves." Children listened, their eyes wide. "Raven is balance." Shamans whispered, "Raven is transformation."

Taq's spirit moved through the aurora, his voice echoing. "You must resist. You must restore balance." Ancestors whispered, their voices solemn. "He is guardian. He is healer." The aurora pulsed, resonating with his sacrifice.

The spirits of the land returned. Ravens circled, their cries sharp. Caribou moved through tundra, their presence steady. Little people flickered at the edges of vision, their laughter faint. Elders whispered, "The land is alive." Shamans bowed their heads. "Balance is restored."

Sarah's voice rose, weaving memory and myth. "We must honor the land. We must preserve balance." Her words carried weight, binding community. Elders nodded, solemn. "We must endure." Children listened, their eyes wide. Sarah whispered, "We must resist."

Mei traced spirals, her notebooks filled with equations. "It is science. It is myth. It is truth." Her voice was sharp, her curiosity burning. She mapped chants to fractals, rituals to equations. "It is pattern. It is connection." She trembled, whispering, "We must understand."

Reed clenched his jaw, haunted. "We must resist. We must endure." His voice was sharp, his eyes steady. Students listened, their eyes wide. Reed whispered, "We must fight."

The potlatch continued, gifts exchanged, stories told. Elders spoke of Taq, their voices trembling. "He gave himself. He restored balance." Shamans prayed, their chants rising. "We must honor him."

The aurora blazed, brighter than ever. Colors bled into each other, shimmering like fire. Taq's spirit dispersed into lights, his voice echoing. "I will endure." Spirits whispered, "You are balance. You are guardian."

Sarah collapsed, her voice trembling. "He is gone." Mei trembled, her eyes burning. "He is dispersed." Reed clenched his jaw, breath ragged. "He endured." Elders whispered, their voices solemn. "He is balance."

The spirits pressed against the world, their voices echoing. "Balance must be restored." Ravens cried, caribou moved, little people laughed. The land was alive, its presence renewed. Shamans bowed their heads. "We must endure."

Sarah's voice rose, weaving memory and myth. "We must honor the land. We must preserve balance." Her words carried weight, binding community. Elders nodded, solemn. "We must endure." Children listened, their eyes wide. Sarah whispered, "We must resist."

Mei traced spirals, her equations glowing faintly. "It is science. It is myth. It is truth." Her voice was sharp, her curiosity burning. "We must understand." Her words carried weight, binding worlds.

Reed clenched his jaw, his voice sharp. "We must resist. We must endure." His words carried weight, binding generations. Students whispered, "We must fight."

The aurora shimmered like a living tapestry, its colors weaving across the night sky. Elders whispered, "It is Taq." Shamans bowed their heads, their voices trembling. "He has returned." Children pointed, their eyes wide. "The lights are alive." The community gathered, their voices hushed.

Taq's spirit moved through the aurora, his voice echoing in dreams. Grandmothers stirred in sleep, hearing his words. "Be vigilant. Be humble. The wound is sealed, but danger lingers." Shamans trembled, their visions filled with spirals. "He is guardian. He is balance."

The dreams spread, carried from house to house. Hunters woke with visions of caribou. Children whispered of Raven's wings. Elders spoke of Kushtaka's hiss. "The spirits are near. The land is alive." The community listened, their voices solemn.

A potlatch was declared, a feast of remembrance. Families gathered, gifts exchanged, stories told. Elders spoke of Taq's sacrifice, their voices trembling. "He gave himself. He restored balance." Shamans prayed, their chants rising. "We must honor him."

The feast began, drums pounding, dancers moving in circles. Songs echoed, their melodies sharp. Carvings glowed faintly, spirals spreading. Sarah whispered prayers, her voice steady. "We must preserve." Mei traced spirals, her curiosity burning. "We must understand." Reed clenched his jaw. "We must endure."

The potlatch carried stories, weaving memory and myth. Elders spoke of Raven, trickster and guardian. "Raven endures. Raven preserves." Children listened, their eyes wide. "Raven is balance." Shamans whispered, "Raven is transformation."

Taq's spirit moved through the aurora, his voice echoing. "You must resist. You must restore balance." Ancestors whispered, their voices solemn. "He is guardian. He is healer." The aurora pulsed, resonating with his sacrifice.

The spirits of the land returned. Ravens circled, their cries sharp. Caribou moved through tundra, their presence steady. Little people flickered at the edges of vision, their laughter faint. Elders whispered, "The land is alive." Shamans bowed their heads. "Balance is restored."

Sarah's voice rose, weaving memory and myth. "We must honor the land. We must preserve balance." Her words carried weight, binding community. Elders nodded, solemn. "We must endure." Children listened, their eyes wide. Sarah whispered, "We must resist."

Mei traced spirals, her notebooks filled with equations. "It is science. It is myth. It is truth." Her voice was sharp, her curiosity burning. She mapped chants to fractals, rituals to equations. "It is pattern. It is connection." She trembled, whispering, "We must understand."

Reed clenched his jaw, haunted. "We must resist. We must endure." His voice was sharp, his eyes steady. Students listened, their eyes wide. Reed whispered, "We must fight."

The potlatch continued, gifts exchanged, stories told. Elders spoke of Taq, their voices trembling. "He gave himself. He restored balance." Shamans prayed, their chants rising. "We must honor him."

The aurora blazed, brighter than ever. Colors bled into each other, shimmering like fire. Taq's spirit dispersed into lights, his voice echoing. "I will endure." Spirits whispered, "You are balance. You are guardian."

Sarah collapsed, her voice trembling. "He is gone." Mei trembled, her eyes burning. "He is dispersed." Reed clenched his jaw, breath ragged. "He endured." Elders whispered, their voices solemn. "He is balance."

The spirits pressed against the world, their voices echoing. "Balance must be restored." Ravens cried, caribou moved, little people laughed. The land was alive, its presence renewed. Shamans bowed their heads. "We must endure."

Sarah's voice rose, weaving memory and myth. "We must honor the land. We must preserve balance." Her words carried weight, binding community. Elders nodded, solemn. "We must endure." Children listened, their eyes wide. Sarah whispered, "We must resist."

Mei traced spirals, her equations glowing faintly. "It is science. It is myth. It is truth." Her voice was sharp, her curiosity burning. "We must understand." Her words carried weight, binding worlds.

Reed clenched his jaw, his voice sharp. "We must resist. We must endure." His words carried weight, binding generations. Students whispered, "We must fight."

The aurora ripped across the sky, violent streaks of green and crimson tearing through the night. The tundra shook, the air electric. Elders froze, their voices sharp. "It is Taq." Shamans bowed, trembling. "He has returned." Children pointed, their eyes wide. "The lights are alive."

Dreams spread like wildfire. Grandmothers stirred, hearing his voice. "Be vigilant. Be humble. Danger lingers." Hunters woke with visions of caribou. Children whispered of Raven's wings. Elders spoke of Kushtaka's hiss. The community listened, their voices sharp.

A potlatch was declared, urgent and immediate. Families gathered, gifts exchanged, stories told. Elders spoke of Taq's sacrifice, their voices trembling. "He gave himself. He restored balance." Shamans prayed, chants rising. "We must honor him."

Drums pounded, dancers moved in spirals. Songs echoed, sharp and relentless. Carvings glowed faintly, spirals spreading. Sarah whispered prayers, her voice steady. "We must preserve." Mei traced spirals, her curiosity burning. "We must understand." Reed clenched his jaw. "We must endure."

Stories cut through the feast, weaving memory and myth. Elders spoke of Raven, trickster and guardian. "Raven endures.

Raven preserves." Children listened, their eyes wide. "Raven is balance." Shamans whispered, "Raven is transformation."

The aurora pulsed, Taq's voice echoing. "You must resist. You must restore balance." Ancestors whispered, their voices solemn. "He is guardian. He is healer." The lights shimmered, resonating with his sacrifice.

Spirits pressed against the land. Ravens circled, their cries sharp. Caribou moved through tundra, steady and unbroken. Little people flickered at the edges of vision, laughter faint. Elders whispered, "The land is alive." Shamans bowed. "Balance is restored."

Sarah's voice rose, urgent and sharp. "We must honor the land. We must preserve balance." Her words carried weight, binding community. Elders nodded, solemn. "We must endure." Children listened, their eyes wide. Sarah whispered, "We must resist."

Mei traced spirals, her notebooks glowing faintly. "It is science. It is myth. It is truth." Her voice was sharp, her curiosity burning. She mapped chants to fractals, rituals to equations. "It is pattern. It is connection." She whispered, "We must understand."

Reed clenched his jaw, haunted but steady. "We must resist. We must endure." His voice was sharp, his eyes unyielding. Students listened, their eyes wide. Reed whispered, "We must fight."

The potlatch surged, gifts exchanged, stories told. Elders spoke of Taq, their voices trembling. "He gave himself. He restored balance." Shamans prayed, chants rising. "We must honor him."

The aurora blazed, violent and alive. Colors bled into each other, shimmering like fire. Taq's spirit dispersed into lights, his voice echoing. "I will endure." Spirits whispered, "You are balance. You are guardian."

Sarah collapsed, her voice trembling. "He is gone." Mei trembled, her eyes burning. "He is dispersed." Reed clenched his jaw, breath ragged. "He endured." Elders whispered, their voices solemn. "He is balance."

The spirits pressed harder, their voices sharp. "Balance must be restored." Ravens cried, caribou moved, little people laughed. The land was alive, its presence renewed. Shamans bowed, their voices trembling. "We must endure."

Sarah's voice rose, weaving memory and myth. "We must honor the land. We must preserve balance." Her words carried weight, binding community. Elders nodded, solemn. "We must endure." Children listened, their eyes wide. Sarah whispered, "We must resist."

Mei traced spirals, her equations glowing faintly. "It is science. It is myth. It is truth." Her voice was sharp, her curiosity burning. "We must understand." Her words carried weight, binding worlds.

Reed clenched his jaw, his voice sharp. "We must resist. We must endure." His words carried weight, binding generations. Students whispered, "We must fight."

The aurora blazed, Raven's wings shimmering. Sarah whispered prayers. Mei traced spirals. Reed clenched his jaw. Elders whispered. "Balance must be restored."

CHAPTER 28: THE NEW GENERATION

The tundra stretched silent, the aurora burning overhead. Years had passed since the collapse of the black pyramid, but its legend endured. Elders whispered its story, scientists debated its anomalies, explorers traced its echoes. A new generation emerged, restless and curious. "We must learn. We must endure."

Aana was young, her eyes sharp, her spirit restless. She wandered the tundra, guided by visions. Ravens circled above, their cries sharp. She followed spirals carved into stone, her breath ragged. "It is calling."

She discovered a hidden cache, buried beneath ice. Artifacts gleamed, journals lay wrapped in cloth. Taq's handwriting trembled across pages. Sarah's chants echoed in ink. Aana's hands shook. "It is truth."

She read of sacrifice, of balance, of wounds. She traced spirals, her eyes burning. "I must endure." Elders whispered, "She is apprentice." Shamans bowed their heads. "She is chosen."

Visions consumed her. Ancestors whispered, their voices solemn. "You must resist. You must restore balance." Raven whispered, "You are apprentice." Thunderbird roared, "You are guardian." Kushtaka hissed, "You are balance."

Mentors guided her, their voices sharp. "You must learn.

You must endure." Scientists taught her equations, shamans taught her chants. Explorers showed her maps, elders told her stories. Aana whispered, "I will endure."

She joined expeditions, her voice steady. Remote sites called, their stones trembling. Spirals glowed faintly, anomalies spread. "It is wound. It is danger." Aana's jaw tightened. "We must resist."

The cycle began again. Discovery, danger, renewal. Aana's journey mirrored the past. She was apprentice, she was seeker, she was guardian. The aurora blazed, her voice sharp. "I will endure."

She carried journals close, her breath ragged. Taq's words echoed, Sarah's chants pulsed. "Balance must be restored." Aana whispered, "I will endure." Elders nodded, solemn. "She is chosen."

Her visions grew sharper, her nights restless. Ancestors whispered, their voices solemn. "You must resist. You must restore balance." Raven whispered, "You are apprentice." Thunderbird roared, "You are guardian." Kushtaka hissed, "You are balance."

She stood before mentors, her voice steady. "I will endure." Scientists nodded, their voices sharp. "You must understand." Shamans bowed, their voices trembling. "You must resist." Explorers whispered, "You must fight."

The tundra stretched endlessly, aurora blazing. Aana's footsteps echoed, her breath ragged. "It is calling." Ravens circled, their cries sharp. Carvings glowed faintly, spirals spreading. "It is wound."

She pressed forward, her voice sharp. "I will endure." Elders whispered, "She is chosen." Shamans bowed, their voices trembling. "She is apprentice." Scientists nodded, their voices sharp. "She is seeker."

Her journey mirrored the past, its rhythm sharp. Discovery, danger, renewal. Aana's voice rose, weaving memory and myth. "Balance must be restored." The aurora pulsed, its rhythm heavy. "She will endure."

She carried artifacts, journals, chants. Her hands shook, her eyes burned. "It is truth." Elders whispered, "She is apprentice." Shamans bowed, their voices trembling. "She is chosen."

The cycle continued, its rhythm sharp. Aana pressed forward, her voice steady. "I will endure." Ravens cried, caribou moved, little people laughed. "Balance must be restored."

Her visions consumed her, their presence heavy. Ancestors whispered, their voices solemn. "You must resist. You must restore balance." Raven whispered, "You are apprentice." Thunderbird roared, "You are guardian." Kushtaka hissed, "You are balance."

She stood beneath the aurora, its colors shimmering. Her voice was sharp, her spirit restless. "I will endure." Elders nodded, solemn. "She is chosen." Shamans bowed, their voices trembling. "She is apprentice."

The tundra stretched beneath the aurora, its colors shimmering like ancestral fire. Elders whispered, "The story endures." Shamans bowed their heads, their voices trembling. "The sacrifice is remembered." Children listened, their eyes wide. "The lights are alive."

Years passed, but the legend of the black pyramid did not fade. It was carried in chants, preserved in carvings, whispered in dreams. Scientists debated anomalies, explorers traced echoes, communities guarded memory. "We must endure. We must resist."

Aana was young, her spirit restless. She wandered the tundra, guided by visions. Ravens circled above, their cries sharp. Spirals glowed faintly on stone, their presence undeniable. "It is calling."

She discovered a hidden cache, buried beneath ice. Artifacts gleamed, journals lay wrapped in cloth. Taq's handwriting trembled across pages. Sarah's chants echoed in ink. Aana's hands shook. "It is truth."

She read of sacrifice, of balance, of wounds. She traced spirals, her eyes burning. "I must endure." Elders whispered, "She is apprentice." Shamans bowed their heads. "She is chosen."

Visions consumed her, their presence heavy. Ancestors whispered, their voices solemn. "You must resist. You must restore balance." Raven whispered, "You are apprentice." Thunderbird roared, "You are guardian." Kushtaka hissed, "You are balance."

Mentors guided her, their voices sharp. "You must learn. You must endure." Scientists taught her equations, shamans taught her chants. Explorers showed her maps, elders told her stories. Aana whispered, "I will endure."

She joined expeditions, her voice steady. Remote sites called, their stones trembling. Spirals glowed faintly, anomalies spread. "It is wound. It is danger." Aana's jaw tightened. "We must resist."

The cycle began again, its rhythm sharp. Discovery, danger, renewal. Aana's journey mirrored the past. She was apprentice, she was seeker, she was guardian. The aurora blazed, her voice sharp. "I will endure."

She carried journals close, her breath ragged. Taq's words echoed, Sarah's chants pulsed. "Balance must be restored." Aana whispered, "I will endure." Elders nodded, solemn. "She is chosen."

Her visions grew sharper, her nights restless. Ancestors whispered, their voices solemn. "You must resist. You must restore balance." Raven whispered, "You are apprentice." Thunderbird roared, "You are guardian." Kushtaka hissed, "You are balance."

She stood before mentors, her voice steady. "I will endure." Scientists nodded, their voices sharp. "You must understand." Shamans bowed, their voices trembling. "You must resist." Explorers whispered, "You must fight."

The tundra stretched endlessly, aurora blazing. Aana's footsteps echoed, her breath ragged. "It is calling." Ravens circled, their cries sharp. Carvings glowed faintly, spirals spreading. "It is wound."

She pressed forward, her voice sharp. "I will endure." Elders whispered, "She is chosen." Shamans bowed, their voices trembling. "She is apprentice." Scientists nodded, their voices sharp. "She is seeker."

Her journey mirrored the past, its rhythm sharp. Discovery, danger, renewal. Aana's voice rose, weaving memory and myth. "Balance must be restored." The aurora pulsed, its rhythm heavy. "She will endure."

She carried artifacts, journals, chants. Her hands shook, her eyes burned. "It is truth." Elders whispered, "She is apprentice." Shamans bowed, their voices trembling. "She is chosen."

The cycle continued, its rhythm sharp. Aana pressed forward, her voice steady. "I will endure." Ravens cried, caribou moved, little people laughed. "Balance must be restored."

Her visions consumed her, their presence heavy. Ancestors whispered, their voices solemn. "You must resist. You must restore balance." Raven whispered, "You are apprentice." Thunderbird roared, "You are guardian." Kushtaka hissed,

"You are balance."

She stood beneath the aurora, its colors shimmering. Her voice was sharp, her spirit restless. "I will endure." Elders nodded, solemn. "She is chosen." Shamans bowed, their voices trembling. "She is apprentice."

The tundra was silent, the aurora ripping across the sky like fire. Years had passed, but the legend of the black pyramid still burned. Elders whispered, scientists argued, explorers searched. A new generation rose, restless. "We must endure."

Aana was young, her eyes sharp, her spirit restless. She wandered the tundra, visions pulling her forward. Ravens circled overhead, their cries cutting the air. Spirals glowed faintly on stone. Her breath came ragged. "It is calling."

She found the cache buried beneath ice. Artifacts gleamed, journals wrapped in cloth. Taq's handwriting trembled across pages. Sarah's chants pulsed in ink. Aana's hands shook. "It is truth."

She read of sacrifice, balance, wounds. She traced spirals, her eyes burning. "I must endure." Elders whispered, "She is apprentice." Shamans bowed, trembling. "She is chosen."

Visions hit her hard, sharp and relentless. Ancestors whispered, voices layered. "You must resist. You must restore balance." Raven whispered, "You are apprentice." Thunderbird roared, "You are guardian." Kushtaka hissed, "You are balance."

Mentors stepped forward, their voices sharp. "Learn. Endure." Scientists gave her equations, shamans gave her chants. Explorers showed maps, elders told stories. Aana whispered, "I will endure."

She joined expeditions, her voice steady. Remote sites called, stones trembling. Spirals glowed faintly, anomalies spread. "It is wound. It is danger." Aana's jaw tightened. "We must resist."

The cycle surged again. Discovery. Danger. Renewal. Aana's journey mirrored the past. Apprentice. Seeker. Guardian. The aurora blazed, her voice sharp. "I will endure."

She carried journals close, her breath ragged. Taq's words echoed, Sarah's chants pulsed. "Balance must be restored." Aana whispered, "I will endure." Elders nodded. "She is chosen."

Her visions sharpened, nights restless. Ancestors whispered, voices solemn. "You must resist. You must restore balance." Raven whispered, "You are apprentice." Thunderbird roared, "You are guardian." Kushtaka hissed, "You are balance."

She stood before mentors, her voice steady. "I will endure." Scientists nodded. "You must understand." Shamans bowed. "You must resist." Explorers whispered. "You must fight."

The tundra stretched endlessly, aurora blazing. Aana's footsteps echoed, her breath ragged. "It is calling." Ravens circled, cries sharp. Carvings glowed faintly, spirals spreading. "It is wound."

She pressed forward, her voice sharp. "I will endure." Elders whispered, "She is chosen." Shamans bowed. "She is apprentice." Scientists nodded. "She is seeker."

Her journey mirrored the past, its rhythm sharp. Discovery. Danger. Renewal. Aana's voice rose, weaving memory and myth. "Balance must be restored." The aurora pulsed, heavy. "She will endure."

She carried artifacts, journals, chants. Her hands shook, her eyes burned. "It is truth." Elders whispered, "She is apprentice." Shamans bowed. "She is chosen."

The cycle continued, its rhythm sharp. Aana pressed forward, her voice steady. "I will endure." Ravens cried, caribou moved, little people laughed. "Balance must be restored."

Her visions consumed her, relentless. Ancestors whispered, voices solemn. "You must resist. You must restore balance." Raven whispered, "You are apprentice." Thunderbird roared, "You are guardian." Kushtaka hissed, "You are balance."

She stood beneath the aurora, its colors tearing across the sky. Her voice was sharp, her spirit restless. "I will endure." Elders nodded. "She is chosen." Shamans bowed. "She is apprentice."

The tundra stretched silent, aurora blazing. Aana whispered prayers, her voice sharp. "Balance must be restored." Ravens circled, cries sharp. The aurora pulsed, heavy. "She will endure."

CHAPTER 29: THE UNANSWERED QUESTIONS

The tundra lay quiet, but silence did not mean peace. Strange lights flickered at the horizon, faint spirals etched into the snow. Hunters whispered of voices in the wind. Elders frowned, their voices trembling. "The wounds remain."

Satellite images revealed anomalies, sharp and undeniable. Spirals carved into wilderness, auroras blazing brighter than memory. Scientists debated, their voices sharp. "It is anomaly. It is danger." Shamans bowed their heads. "It is wound."

Mei received a message, cryptic and sharp. "There are others. There are pyramids. There are nodes." Her hands trembled, her eyes burned. "It is network. It is danger." She whispered, "We must understand."

She traced spirals in her notebooks, equations glowing faintly. "It is science. It is myth. It is truth." Her voice was sharp, her curiosity burning. "We must endure." Elders nodded, solemn. "We must resist."

Reed was old, his voice trembling. He sat at a desk, his hands shaking. He wrote a memoir, blending fact and fiction. "It was ritual. It was wound. It was balance." His words carried weight.

He sent copies to colleagues, elders, shamans. "Preserve truth. Resist erasure." His voice was sharp, his eyes haunted.

"We must endure." Elders nodded, solemn. "We must remember."

The anomalies spread, their presence undeniable. Spirals glowed faintly, auroras blazed brighter. Scientists argued, shamans prayed, explorers searched. "It is wound. It is danger." Mei whispered, "It is truth."

Ambiguity lingered, its presence sharp. Was it myth? Was it science? Was it truth? Reed whispered, "It is mystery." His voice trembled. "It endures."

Communities whispered, their voices trembling. "It is wound. It is balance." Elders whispered, "It is cycle." Shamans bowed their heads. "We must resist."

Mei traced spirals, her equations glowing faintly. "It is science. It is myth. It is truth." Her voice was sharp, her curiosity burning. "We must understand." Her words carried weight, binding worlds.

Reed's memoir spread, its rhythm sharp. Students read, elders listened, scientists debated. "It is truth. It is mystery." Reed whispered, "It endures." His voice trembled. "It is cycle."

The aurora blazed, its colors shimmering. Mei whispered prayers, her voice sharp. "We must understand." Reed whispered, "We must endure." Elders bowed their heads. "We must resist."

The anomalies pulsed, their rhythm heavy. Spirals spread, auroras blazed. "It is wound. It is danger." Shamans bowed, their voices trembling. "It is cycle."

Mei's message echoed, sharp and heavy. "There are others. There are pyramids. There are nodes." Her voice trembled. "It is network. It is danger." Elders whispered, "It is truth."

Reed's memoir closed, his voice trembling. "It is mystery. It endures." His words carried weight, binding generations.

Students whispered, "We must endure." Elders nodded, solemn. "We must resist."

The tundra stretched silent, aurora blazing. Spirals glowed faintly, anomalies spread. "It is wound. It is danger." Mei whispered, "It is truth." Reed whispered, "It is mystery."

Ambiguity lingered, its presence sharp. Was it myth? Was it science? Was it truth? Elders whispered, "It is cycle." Shamans bowed, their voices trembling. "We must resist."

The tundra lay beneath the aurora, its colors shimmering like ancestral fire. Elders whispered, "Balance was restored, but the story is not finished." Shamans bowed their heads, their voices trembling. "The wounds remain." Children listened, their eyes wide. "The lights are alive."

Years passed, but anomalies persisted. Satellite images revealed spirals etched into wilderness, auroras blazing brighter than memory. Scientists debated, their voices sharp. "It is anomaly. It is danger." Shamans whispered, "It is wound. It is cycle."

Mei received a message, cryptic and heavy. "There are others. There are pyramids. There are nodes." Her hands trembled, her eyes burned. "It is network. It is danger." She whispered, "We must understand."

She traced spirals in her notebooks, equations glowing faintly. "It is science. It is myth. It is truth." Her voice was sharp, her curiosity burning. "We must endure." Elders nodded, solemn. "We must resist."

Reed was old, his voice trembling. He sat at a desk, his hands shaking. He wrote a memoir, blending fact and fiction. "It was ritual. It was wound. It was balance." His words carried weight, binding generations.

He sent copies to colleagues, elders, shamans. "Preserve

truth. Resist erasure." His voice was sharp, his eyes haunted. "We must endure." Elders nodded, solemn. "We must remember."

The anomalies spread, their presence undeniable. Spirals glowed faintly, auroras blazed brighter. Scientists argued, shamans prayed, explorers searched. "It is wound. It is danger." Mei whispered, "It is truth."

Ambiguity lingered, its presence sharp. Was it myth? Was it science? Was it truth? Reed whispered, "It is mystery." His voice trembled. "It endures."

Communities whispered, their voices trembling. "It is wound. It is balance." Elders whispered, "It is cycle." Shamans bowed their heads. "We must resist."

Mei traced spirals, her equations glowing faintly. "It is science. It is myth. It is truth." Her voice was sharp, her curiosity burning. "We must understand." Her words carried weight, binding worlds.

Reed's memoir spread, its rhythm solemn. Students read, elders listened, scientists debated. "It is truth. It is mystery." Reed whispered, "It endures." His voice trembled. "It is cycle."

The aurora blazed, its colors shimmering. Mei whispered prayers, her voice sharp. "We must understand." Reed whispered, "We must endure." Elders bowed their heads. "We must resist."

The anomalies pulsed, their rhythm heavy. Spirals spread, auroras blazed. "It is wound. It is danger." Shamans bowed, their voices trembling. "It is cycle."

Mei's message echoed, sharp and heavy. "There are others. There are pyramids. There are nodes." Her voice trembled. "It is network. It is danger." Elders whispered, "It is truth."

Reed's memoir closed, his voice trembling. "It is mystery.

It endures." His words carried weight, binding generations. Students whispered, "We must endure." Elders nodded, solemn. "We must resist."

The tundra stretched silent, aurora blazing. Spirals glowed faintly, anomalies spread. "It is wound. It is danger." Mei whispered, "It is truth." Reed whispered, "It is mystery."

Ambiguity lingered, its presence sharp. Was it myth? Was it science? Was it truth? Elders whispered, "It is cycle." Shamans bowed, their voices trembling. "We must resist."

The aurora pulsed, its rhythm heavy. Ravens cried, caribou moved, little people laughed. "Balance must be restored." Elders whispered, "It is cycle." Shamans bowed. "It endures."

Satellite images flickered across screens, anomalies sharp and undeniable. Spirals carved into wilderness, auroras blazing brighter than memory. Scientists froze, their voices sharp. "It is anomaly. It is danger." Shamans whispered, "It is wound."

Mei's phone buzzed, a message appearing without sender. "There are others. There are pyramids. There are nodes." Her breath caught, her hands trembling. "It is network. It is danger." She whispered, "We must understand."

She traced spirals in her notebooks, equations glowing faintly. "It is science. It is myth. It is truth." Her voice was sharp, her curiosity burning. "We must endure." Elders nodded, solemn. "We must resist."

Reed sat alone, his desk cluttered, his hands shaking. He wrote furiously, words spilling across pages. "It was ritual. It was wound. It was balance." His voice trembled, his eyes haunted. "It endures."

He bound the memoir, copies stacked. He sent them to colleagues, elders, shamans. "Preserve truth. Resist erasure."

His voice was sharp, his breath ragged. "We must endure." Elders whispered, "We must remember."

The anomalies spread, their rhythm heavy. Spirals glowed faintly, auroras blazed brighter. Scientists argued, shamans prayed, explorers searched. "It is wound. It is danger." Mei whispered, "It is truth."

Ambiguity pressed hard, its presence sharp. Was it myth? Was it science? Was it truth? Reed whispered, "It is mystery." His voice trembled. "It endures."

Communities whispered, their voices trembling. "It is wound. It is balance." Elders whispered, "It is cycle." Shamans bowed their heads. "We must resist."

Mei traced spirals, her equations pulsing. "It is science. It is myth. It is truth." Her voice was sharp, her curiosity burning. "We must understand." Her words carried weight, binding worlds.

Reed's memoir spread, its rhythm sharp. Students read, elders listened, scientists debated. "It is truth. It is mystery." Reed whispered, "It endures." His voice trembled. "It is cycle."

The aurora blazed, its colors violent. Mei whispered prayers, her voice sharp. "We must understand." Reed whispered, "We must endure." Elders bowed their heads. "We must resist."

The anomalies pulsed, their rhythm heavy. Spirals spread, auroras blazed. "It is wound. It is danger." Shamans bowed, their voices trembling. "It is cycle."

Mei's message echoed, sharp and heavy. "There are others. There are pyramids. There are nodes." Her voice trembled. "It is network. It is danger." Elders whispered, "It is truth."

Reed's memoir closed, his voice trembling. "It is mystery. It endures." His words carried weight, binding generations. Students whispered, "We must endure." Elders nodded, solemn. "We must resist."

The tundra stretched silent, aurora blazing. Spirals glowed faintly, anomalies spread. "It is wound. It is danger." Mei whispered, "It is truth." Reed whispered, "It is mystery."

Ambiguity lingered, its presence sharp. Was it myth? Was it science? Was it truth? Elders whispered, "It is cycle." Shamans bowed, their voices trembling. "We must resist."

The aurora pulsed, its rhythm heavy. Ravens cried, caribou moved, little people laughed. "Balance must be restored." Elders whispered, "It is cycle." Shamans bowed. "It endures."

Mei traced spirals, her voice sharp. "We must understand." Reed whispered, "We must endure." Elders bowed their heads. "We must resist." The aurora blazed, its rhythm heavy. "It endures."

CHAPTER 30: THE BLACK PYRAMID ENDURES

The tundra stretched silent, its vastness unbroken. Snow buried ruins, ice sealed wounds. The black pyramid lay dormant beneath layers of frost, its stones hidden from sight. Ravens circled overhead, their cries sharp and unsettling. Elders whispered, "It endures."

The aurora shimmered, its colors weaving across the sky like ancestral fire. The lights pulsed, their rhythm heavy, echoing the heartbeat of the land. Shamans bowed their heads, their voices trembling. "It is sealed. It is balance." Children listened, their eyes wide. "The lights are alive."

A vision rose, sharp and heavy. The entity stirred, dormant but watchful. Its presence pressed against the land, woven into tundra and stone. "It is wound. It is guardian." Elders whispered, "It endures." Shamans bowed, their voices solemn. "We must resist."

Sarah's voice echoed in memory, weaving chants and myth. "We must honor the land. We must preserve balance." Mei whispered, "We must understand." Reed whispered, "We must endure." Their words carried weight, binding generations.

The aurora pulsed, its rhythm sharp. Ravens cried, caribou moved, little people laughed. The land was alive, its presence renewed. "Balance must be restored." Elders whispered, "It is cycle." Shamans bowed, their voices trembling. "It endures."

The entity remained, silent but present. Dormant, watchful, unbroken. Its essence seeped into soil, into stone, into ice. "It endures." Elders whispered, "It is wound. It is guardian." Shamans bowed, their voices solemn. "We must resist."

The story closed, its rhythm heavy. Awe and humility filled the tundra. Humanity was small, cosmic forces vast. But community endured, tradition endured, storytelling endured. Elders whispered, "We must remember."

The motif of the black pyramid returned, its presence undeniable. Wound and guardian, danger and balance. "It endures." Elders whispered, "It is cycle." Shamans bowed, their voices trembling. "We must resist."

The aurora blazed, its colors shimmering. Ravens circled, their cries sharp. The tundra stretched silent, its presence heavy. "Balance must be restored." Elders whispered, "It is cycle." Shamans bowed. "It endures."

A final vision rose, sharp and heavy. The entity stirred, dormant but watchful. Its presence pressed against the land. "It endures." The aurora pulsed, its rhythm heavy. "I will endure."

The tundra stretched endlessly, its silence unbroken. Ravens cried, their wings cutting the air. Caribou moved across snow, steady and unyielding. Little people flickered at the edges of vision, laughter faint. Elders whispered, "The land is alive."

The aurora shimmered, its colors weaving across sky. Shamans bowed, their voices trembling. "It is sealed. It is balance." Children listened, their eyes wide. "The lights are alive." Elders whispered, "It endures."

The entity pressed against memory, its presence

undeniable. Dormant, watchful, silent. "It endures." Elders whispered, "It is wound. It is guardian." Shamans bowed, their voices solemn. "We must resist."

Sarah's voice echoed, weaving chants and myth. "We must honor the land. We must preserve balance." Mei whispered, "We must understand." Reed whispered, "We must endure." Their words carried weight, binding generations.

The aurora pulsed, its rhythm sharp. Ravens cried, caribou moved, little people laughed. The land was alive, its presence renewed. "Balance must be restored." Elders whispered, "It is cycle." Shamans bowed, their voices trembling. "It endures."

The entity remained, silent but present. Dormant, watchful, unbroken. Its essence seeped into soil, into stone, into ice. "It endures." Elders whispered, "It is wound. It is guardian." Shamans bowed, their voices solemn. "We must resist."

The story closed, its rhythm heavy. Awe and humility filled the tundra. Humanity was small, cosmic forces vast. But community endured, tradition endured, storytelling endured. Elders whispered, "We must remember."

The motif of the black pyramid returned, its presence undeniable. Wound and guardian, danger and balance. "It endures." Elders whispered, "It is cycle." Shamans bowed, their voices trembling. "We must resist."

The tundra stretched beneath the aurora, its colors shimmering like ancestral fire. Snow buried the ruins, ice sealed the stones. The black pyramid lay dormant, hidden but unforgotten. Elders whispered, "It endures." Shamans bowed their heads, their voices trembling. "It is sealed. It is balance."

The aurora shimmered, its rhythm heavy. The lights pulsed like chants carried across generations. Children listened, their eyes wide. "The lights are alive." Elders whispered, "It is cycle." Shamans bowed, their voices solemn. "We must resist."

A vision rose, sharp and heavy. The entity stirred, dormant but watchful. Its presence pressed against the land, woven into tundra and stone. "It is wound. It is guardian." Ancestors whispered, "It endures." Shamans bowed, their voices trembling. "It is balance."

Sarah's voice echoed in memory, weaving chants and myth. "We must honor the land. We must preserve balance." Mei whispered, "We must understand." Reed whispered, "We must endure." Their words carried weight, binding generations.

The aurora pulsed, its rhythm solemn. Ravens cried, caribou moved, little people laughed. The land was alive, its presence renewed. Elders whispered, "Balance must be restored." Shamans bowed, their voices trembling. "It endures."

The entity remained, silent but present. Dormant, watchful, unbroken. Its essence seeped into soil, into stone, into ice. "It endures." Elders whispered, "It is wound. It is guardian." Shamans bowed, their voices solemn. "We must resist."

The story closed, its rhythm heavy. Awe and humility filled the tundra. Humanity was small, cosmic forces vast. But community endured, tradition endured, storytelling endured. Elders whispered, "We must remember."

The motif of the black pyramid returned, its presence undeniable. Wound and guardian, danger and balance. "It endures." Elders whispered, "It is cycle." Shamans bowed, their voices trembling. "We must resist."

The aurora blazed, its colors shimmering. Ravens circled, their cries sharp. The tundra stretched silent, its presence heavy. "Balance must be restored." Elders whispered, "It is cycle." Shamans bowed. "It endures."

A final vision rose, solemn and heavy. The entity stirred, dormant but watchful. Its presence pressed against the land.

"It endures." The aurora pulsed, its rhythm heavy. "I will endure."

The tundra stretched endlessly, its silence unbroken. Ravens cried, their wings cutting the air. Caribou moved across snow, steady and unyielding. Little people flickered at the edges of vision, laughter faint. Elders whispered, "The land is alive."

The aurora shimmered, its colors weaving across sky. Shamans bowed, their voices trembling. "It is sealed. It is balance." Children listened, their eyes wide. "The lights are alive." Elders whispered, "It endures."

The entity pressed against memory, its presence undeniable. Dormant, watchful, silent. "It endures." Elders whispered, "It is wound. It is guardian." Shamans bowed, their voices solemn. "We must resist."

Sarah's voice echoed, weaving chants and myth. "We must honor the land. We must preserve balance." Mei whispered, "We must understand." Reed whispered, "We must endure." Their words carried weight, binding generations.

The aurora pulsed, its rhythm solemn. Ravens cried, caribou moved, little people laughed. The land was alive, its presence renewed. "Balance must be restored." Elders whispered, "It is cycle." Shamans bowed, their voices trembling. "It endures."

The entity remained, silent but present. Dormant, watchful, unbroken. Its essence seeped into soil, into stone, into ice. "It endures." Elders whispered, "It is wound. It is guardian." Shamans bowed, their voices solemn. "We must resist."

The story closed, its rhythm heavy. Awe and humility filled the tundra. Humanity was small, cosmic forces vast. But community endured, tradition endured, storytelling endured. Elders whispered, "We must remember."

The motif of the black pyramid returned, its presence

undeniable. Wound and guardian, danger and balance. "It endures." Elders whispered, "It is cycle." Shamans bowed, their voices trembling. "We must resist."

The tundra was silent, the aurora ripping across the sky like fire. Snow buried ruins, ice sealed wounds. The black pyramid lay dormant beneath layers of frost, its stones hidden but unbroken. Ravens circled overhead, their cries sharp. "It endures."

The aurora blazed, violent streaks tearing through the night. Lights pulsed, their rhythm heavy, echoing the heartbeat of the land. Shamans bowed, trembling. "It is sealed. It is balance." Elders whispered, "It endures." Children froze, their eyes wide.

A vision hit hard, sharp and relentless. The entity stirred, dormant but watchful. Its presence pressed against the land, woven into tundra and stone. "It is wound. It is guardian." Ancestors whispered, "It endures." Shamans bowed, their voices trembling.

Sarah's voice echoed in memory, clipped and sharp. "Honor the land. Preserve balance." Mei whispered, "Understand." Reed whispered, "Endure." Their words cut through silence, binding generations.

The aurora pulsed, its rhythm jagged. Ravens cried, caribou moved, little people laughed. The land was alive, its presence undeniable. "Balance must be restored." Elders whispered, "It is cycle." Shamans bowed, their voices trembling.

The entity remained, silent but present. Dormant, watchful, unbroken. Its essence seeped into soil, into stone, into ice. "It endures." Elders whispered, "It is wound. It is guardian." Shamans bowed, their voices solemn.

The story closed, its rhythm sharp. Awe and humility filled the tundra. Humanity was small, cosmic forces vast. But community endured, tradition endured, storytelling endured. Elders whispered, "We must remember."

The motif of the black pyramid returned, heavy and undeniable. Wound and guardian, danger and balance. "It endures." Elders whispered, "It is cycle." Shamans bowed, their voices trembling.

The aurora blazed, violent and alive. Ravens circled, their cries sharp. The tundra stretched silent, its presence heavy. "Balance must be restored." Elders whispered, "It is cycle." Shamans bowed.

A final vision rose, jagged and heavy. The entity stirred, dormant but watchful. Its presence pressed against the land. "It endures." The aurora pulsed, its rhythm violent. "I will endure."

The tundra stretched endlessly, silence unbroken. Ravens cried, wings cutting the air. Caribou moved across snow, steady and unyielding. Little people flickered at the edges of vision, laughter faint. Elders whispered, "The land is alive."

The aurora shimmered, its colors tearing across sky. Shamans bowed, their voices trembling. "It is sealed. It is balance." Children listened, their eyes wide. "The lights are alive." Elders whispered, "It endures."

The entity pressed against memory, its presence undeniable. Dormant, watchful, silent. "It endures." Elders whispered, "It is wound. It is guardian." Shamans bowed, their voices solemn.

Sarah's voice echoed, clipped and sharp. "Honor the land. Preserve balance." Mei whispered, "Understand." Reed whispered, "Endure." Their words carried weight, binding generations.

The aurora pulsed, jagged and violent. Ravens cried, caribou moved, little people laughed. The land was alive, its presence renewed. "Balance must be restored." Elders whispered, "It is cycle." Shamans bowed, trembling.

The entity remained, silent but present. Dormant, watchful, unbroken. Its essence seeped into soil, into stone, into ice. "It endures." Elders whispered, "It is wound. It is guardian." Shamans bowed, solemn.

The story closed, its rhythm sharp. Awe and humility filled the tundra. Humanity was small, cosmic forces vast. But community endured, tradition endured, storytelling endured. Elders whispered, "We must remember."

The motif of the black pyramid returned, heavy and undeniable. Wound and guardian, danger and balance. "It endures." Elders whispered, "It is cycle." Shamans bowed, trembling.

The aurora blazed, violent and alive. Ravens circled, cries sharp. The tundra stretched silent, its presence heavy. "Balance must be restored." Elders whispered, "It is cycle." Shamans bowed.

The final vision rose, jagged and heavy. The entity stirred, dormant but watchful. Its presence pressed against the land. "It endures." The aurora pulsed, violent and sharp. "I will endure."

EPILOGUE: BENEATH THE ICE

The tundra stretched silent, its vastness unbroken. Snow drifted endlessly, covering scars, sealing wounds. The black pyramid lay buried, hidden beneath ice and stone. Ravens circled overhead, their cries sharp. Elders whispered, "It endures."

The aurora shimmered, its colors weaving across the sky like ancestral fire. Lights pulsed, their rhythm heavy, echoing the heartbeat of the land. Shamans bowed their heads, their voices trembling. "It is sealed. It is balance." Children listened, their eyes wide. "The lights are alive."

Generations passed, but the story remained. Carvings glowed faintly, spirals etched into stone. Songs carried memory, chants preserved sacrifice. "We must endure. We must resist." Elders whispered, "It is cycle." Shamans bowed, their voices solemn.

Aana's journals joined Taq's, Sarah's, Reed's. Their words bound together, a lineage of guardians. "It was wound. It was balance. It endures." Communities listened, their voices trembling. "We must remember."

The aurora pulsed, its rhythm solemn. Ravens cried, caribou moved, little people laughed. The land was alive, its presence renewed. Elders whispered, "Balance must be restored." Shamans bowed, their voices trembling. "It endures."

The entity remained, silent but present. Dormant, watchful, unbroken. Its essence seeped into soil, into stone, into ice. "It endures." Elders whispered, "It is wound. It is guardian." Shamans bowed, their voices solemn.

The story closed, its rhythm heavy. Awe and humility filled the tundra. Humanity was small, cosmic forces vast. But community endured, tradition endured, storytelling endured. Elders whispered, "We must remember."

The motif of the black pyramid returned, its presence undeniable. Wound and guardian, danger and balance. "It endures." Elders whispered, "It is cycle." Shamans bowed, their voices trembling. "We must resist."

The aurora blazed, its colors shimmering. Ravens circled, their cries sharp. The tundra stretched silent, its presence heavy. "Balance must be restored." Elders whispered, "It is cycle." Shamans bowed. "It endures."

A final vision rose, solemn and heavy. The entity stirred, dormant but watchful. Its presence pressed against the land. "It endures." The aurora pulsed, its rhythm heavy. "I will endure."

The tundra stretched endlessly, silence unbroken. Ravens cried, wings cutting the air. Caribou moved across snow, steady and unyielding. Little people flickered at the edges of vision, laughter faint. Elders whispered, "The land is alive."

The aurora shimmered, its colors weaving across sky. Shamans bowed, their voices trembling. "It is sealed. It is balance." Children listened, their eyes wide. "The lights are alive." Elders whispered, "It endures."

The entity pressed against memory, its presence undeniable. Dormant, watchful, silent. "It endures." Elders whispered, "It is wound. It is guardian." Shamans bowed, their voices solemn. "We must resist."

Sarah's voice echoed, weaving chants and myth. "We must honor the land. We must preserve balance." Mei whispered, "We must understand." Reed whispered, "We must endure." Their words carried weight, binding generations.

The aurora pulsed, its rhythm solemn. Ravens cried, caribou moved, little people laughed. The land was alive, its presence renewed. "Balance must be restored." Elders whispered, "It is cycle." Shamans bowed, their voices trembling. "It endures."

The entity remained, silent but present. Dormant, watchful, unbroken. Its essence seeped into soil, into stone, into ice. "It endures." Elders whispered, "It is wound. It is guardian." Shamans bowed, their voices solemn. "We must resist."

The story closed, its rhythm heavy. Awe and humility filled the tundra. Humanity was small, cosmic forces vast. But community endured, tradition endured, storytelling endured. Elders whispered, "We must remember."

The motif of the black pyramid returned, its presence undeniable. Wound and guardian, danger and balance. "It endures." Elders whispered, "It is cycle." Shamans bowed, their voices trembling. "We must resist."

The aurora blazed, its colors shimmering. Ravens circled, their cries sharp. The tundra stretched silent, its presence heavy. "Balance must be restored." Elders whispered, "It is cycle." Shamans bowed. "It endures."

The final vision rose, solemn and heavy. The entity stirred, dormant but watchful. Its presence pressed against the land. "It endures." The aurora pulsed, its rhythm heavy. "I will endure."

The tundra stretched beneath the aurora, its colors shimmering like ancestral fire. Snow drifted endlessly, covering scars, sealing wounds. The black pyramid lay dormant, hidden beneath ice and stone. Ravens circled overhead, their cries sharp. Elders whispered, "It endures."

The aurora shimmered, its rhythm heavy. Lights pulsed like chants carried across generations. Shamans bowed their heads, their voices trembling. "It is sealed. It is balance." Children listened, their eyes wide. "The lights are alive."

Generations passed, but the story remained. Carvings glowed faintly, spirals etched into stone. Songs carried memory, chants preserved sacrifice. "We must endure. We must resist." Elders whispered, "It is cycle." Shamans bowed, their voices solemn.

Aana's journals joined Taq's, Sarah's, Reed's. Their words bound together, a lineage of guardians. "It was wound. It was balance. It endures." Communities listened, their voices trembling. "We must remember."

The aurora pulsed, its rhythm solemn. Ravens cried, caribou moved, little people laughed. The land was alive, its presence renewed. Elders whispered, "Balance must be restored." Shamans bowed, their voices trembling. "It endures."

The entity remained, silent but present. Dormant, watchful, unbroken. Its essence seeped into soil, into stone, into ice. "It endures." Elders whispered, "It is wound. It is guardian." Shamans bowed, their voices solemn.

The story closed, its rhythm heavy. Awe and humility filled the tundra. Humanity was small, cosmic forces vast. But community endured, tradition endured, storytelling endured. Elders whispered, "We must remember."

The motif of the black pyramid returned, its presence undeniable. Wound and guardian, danger and balance. "It endures." Elders whispered, "It is cycle." Shamans bowed, their voices trembling. "We must resist."

The aurora blazed, its colors shimmering. Ravens circled, their cries sharp. The tundra stretched silent, its presence heavy. "Balance must be restored." Elders whispered, "It is cycle." Shamans bowed. "It endures."

A final vision rose, solemn and heavy. The entity stirred, dormant but watchful. Its presence pressed against the land. "It endures." The aurora pulsed, its rhythm heavy. "I will endure."

The tundra stretched endlessly, silence unbroken. Ravens cried, wings cutting the air. Caribou moved across snow, steady and unyielding. Little people flickered at the edges of vision, laughter faint. Elders whispered, "The land is alive."

The aurora shimmered, its colors weaving across sky. Shamans bowed, their voices trembling. "It is sealed. It is balance." Children listened, their eyes wide. "The lights are alive." Elders whispered, "It endures."

The entity pressed against memory, its presence undeniable. Dormant, watchful, silent. "It endures." Elders whispered, "It is wound. It is guardian." Shamans bowed, their voices solemn. "We must resist."

Sarah's voice echoed, weaving chants and myth. "We must honor the land. We must preserve balance." Mei whispered, "We must understand." Reed whispered, "We must endure." Their words carried weight, binding generations.

The aurora pulsed, its rhythm solemn. Ravens cried, caribou moved, little people laughed. The land was alive, its presence renewed. "Balance must be restored." Elders whispered, "It is cycle." Shamans bowed, their voices trembling. "It endures."

The entity remained, silent but present. Dormant, watchful, unbroken. Its essence seeped into soil, into stone, into ice. "It endures." Elders whispered, "It is wound. It is guardian."

Shamans bowed, their voices solemn. "We must resist."

The story closed, its rhythm heavy. Awe and humility filled the tundra. Humanity was small, cosmic forces vast. But community endured, tradition endured, storytelling endured. Elders whispered, "We must remember."

The motif of the black pyramid returned, its presence undeniable. Wound and guardian, danger and balance. "It endures." Elders whispered, "It is cycle." Shamans bowed, their voices trembling. "We must resist."

THE END
By: **Michael James**

To Find Much More Visit Website Below & Thanks 4 Reading

https://sites.google.com/view/michael-james-books/books

ABOUT THE AUTHOR

Michael James

Michael James is a raw and honest author who writes straight from the heart. From surviving childhood trauma to battling addiction and discovering spiritual truth, he brings powerful life experiences into every book. His work ranges from emotional memoirs to deep research on ancient civilizations and the mysteries of our world. Michael believes in writing with purpose—and sharing real stories that might help someone else make it through.

He is the author of Taken On My Birthday, Fading Silence, Understanding Mayan Mysteries, The Keys of Thoth, and more.

Author's Note

In 2007, my life changed forever. I suffered a terrible fall down a flight of steps, fracturing my skull and temple in three places. For seven days, I lay in a coma — suspended between this world and somewhere else. When I finally opened my eyes again, I knew I wasn't the same person who had fallen.

Something had shifted. My mind felt different. I carried with me knowledge, impressions, and insights that I couldn't explain through ordinary means. It was as if a door had opened in my consciousness, revealing patterns, connections, and truths that had been hidden from me before.

Since that moment, I've felt an unshakable drive to put these discoveries into words — to research, to question, and to share. Writing became more than a passion; it became a calling. Through these books, I seek to explore mysteries both ancient and modern: the stories hidden in sacred texts, the messages written in stone and circle, the echoes left behind by civilizations that still speak to us if we're willing to listen.

This journey is not just mine — it belongs to every reader who has ever felt there is more to life, more to history, and more to the universe than what we are told. If you are holding this book, then perhaps some part of you has felt the same pull. Together, we walk into these mysteries — not for easy answers, but for deeper understanding.

BOOKS BY THIS AUTHOR

Ashfall Watchers: The Yellowstone Awakening (Global Disaster Scenarios Book 4) Kindle Edition

When the earth remembers, humanity forgets how small it truly is.

Yellowstone has always been a place of wonder — geysers, wildlife, and the illusion of permanence. But beneath its steaming basins, something ancient stirs. Seismographs record a heartbeat. Geysers erupt out of rhythm. Birds fall silent at noon. And in the night sky, strange lights flicker like omens.

Scientists dismiss the signs as anomalies. Officials bury the warnings in bureaucratic language. Tourists keep coming, unaware that the ground beneath their feet is shifting toward catastrophe. But a handful of watchers — rangers, locals, and those who have seen too much to ignore — begin to piece together the truth.

The mountain is not just restless. It is waking.

As storms darken the Rockies and a dome of heat warps the skies, the first tremors of an extinction-level event ripple outward. What rises from Yellowstone's depths will test not only human survival, but the fragile line between science, myth, and something far older than civilization itself.

Ashfall Watchers: The Yellowstone Awakening is the opening chapter of a visionary apocalyptic saga — where geology becomes prophecy, and the day fire remembers may be the day humanity forgets hope.

Understanding Petra: The Hidden City Of Stone (Understanding Lost Knowledge) Kindle Edition

Understanding Petra: The Hidden City of Stone
Lost Civilizations, Ancient Engineering, and the Spiritual Legacy of the Nabataeans

Carved into crimson cliffs and hidden for centuries beneath the desert sands, Petra stands as one of humanity's most breathtaking enigmas. Once a thriving crossroads of trade and worship, it has whispered across millennia through its temples, tombs, and winding Siq — the serpent's mouth of stone that guards its heart.

In this powerful exploration, Understanding Petra unveils the lost world of the Nabataeans — the mysterious architects, traders, and spiritual engineers who transformed desert rock into living memory. Discover how their mastery of water, geometry, and celestial alignment built a city that defied both time and empire.

From the rediscovery by Johann Ludwig Burckhardt to the coded messages hidden in Petra's inscriptions, this book guides readers through myth, archaeology, and the deeper metaphysical purpose of this sacred city. Was Petra merely a trading hub — or a temple of cosmic design, where stone itself became divine?

Richly detailed and deeply evocative, Understanding Petra: The Hidden City of Stone reveals the convergence of faith, architecture, and forgotten science — a journey into the desert where the Earth still remembers heaven.

Yellowstone & The World Averting Global Disaster (Global Disaster Scenarios Book 1) Kindle Edition

When Yellowstone's restless heart awakens, humanity's survival hinges on a daring alliance of science, tradition, and global will. From the steaming vents of Norris Geyser Basin to high-altitude command hubs in Reykjavik, cryogenic slurries freeze magma pathways while acoustic arrays send counter-harmonic pulses deep into Earth's molten core. Across six continents, emergency brigades drill evacuation corridors, tribal custodians infuse ancestral wisdom, and quantum-powered models forecast every rumble.

In Yellowstone & The World: Averting Global Disaster, follow Leah Santos and her team of engineers, geologists, and indigenous partners as they race to outsmart nature's most formidable supervolcano. Witness the invention of self-healing freeze gels, drone-deployed micro-injectors, and metamaterial speakers—and feel the global stakes soar as satellite constellations and community sensor networks stitch every tremor and plume into a unified tapestry of defense.

This is more than a technical thriller; it's a testament to collective resilience and the promise of shared stewardship. Whether you're drawn to cutting-edge cryogenics or the quiet power of tribal ceremonies, this epic chronicle proves that when the world listens—with humility, respect, and relentless ingenuity—it can hold back Earth's most ancient fury. The next pulse beneath our feet may be unstoppable, but united, we stand ready.

The Solar Tempest (Global Disaster Scenarios Book 3) Kindle Edition

The Solar Tempest
Book Three of the Global Disaster Scenarios

The storm was only the beginning.

When the Sun unleashed its fury, the Earth was remade in fire and silence. Cities melted into glass, oceans boiled into vapor, and the sky itself fractured into ribbons of light. From the ruins, humanity clawed its way back — smaller, quieter, and forever changed.

Now, decades later, the survivors live beneath skies that shimmer with auroras even at noon. Children are born with eyes that flicker with static, their very blood humming with the residue of the storm. To some, they are a blessing — the dawn of a new humanity. To others, they are a warning of what still sleeps above.

Elara, the last great chronicler of the storm, has devoted her life to listening to the Sun's pulse. What she discovers is more than data — it is memory. The Sun has not forgotten what it unleashed. It dreams, and in its dreams lie both mercy and fire.

As whispers of another cycle stir, humanity must decide: will they resist the rhythm of a world reborn, or learn to live within it?

The Solar Tempest is a haunting vision of survival and transformation — a story of storms that never truly end, and of a species learning to find its place in the dream of a living cosmos.

The Crimson Gate Of Petra Kindle Edition

The Crimson Gate of Petra
An Ancient Mystery. A Forbidden God. A City That Breathes.

Beneath the timeless rose-red cliffs of Petra lies something far older than civilization itself. When Dr. Amara Khalid, a brilliant linguist and archaeologist, leads a multinational team to explore a newly discovered void beneath the Treasury, she believes she's about to rewrite history. Instead, she awakens it.

The Bedouin whisper of Dushara — a god carved in stone, sealed away by those who once worshipped him. At first, Amara dismisses the legends as myth. But when the canyon hums with a living vibration, when the rock begins to breathe, when her instruments detect a heartbeat deep beneath the desert floor… she realizes some doors were never meant to be opened.

As the sands rise and the world trembles, ancient songs return to the air — songs that reshape flesh and stone alike. The city of Petra begins to move, statues whisper prayers, and across the globe, red dust spreads like a plague. Humanity's oldest god is stirring, and time itself bends around his awakening.

Now, Amara must uncover the truth of the Seven Gates of the Earth before the Crimson Gate opens completely — or the desert will remember all who walk upon it.

A haunting blend of archaeology, mythology, and cosmic horror, The Crimson Gate of Petra will leave you questioning what truly sleeps beneath the sands.

Understanding Forgotten Magic (Understanding Lost Knowledge) Kindle Edition

Understanding Forgotten Magic
By Michael James

Unlock the hidden truths of ancient power.

For centuries, magic—both white and black—has been whispered about, feared, and misunderstood. Understanding Forgotten Magic peels back the veil between myth and reality, revealing the origins, evolution, and real-world practices behind humanity's oldest mystical traditions. From sacred rites of protection and healing to shadowy arts of influence and desire, this book explores how magic once shaped civilizations—and how its essence still lingers today.

Discover:

The historical roots of white and black magic across ancient cultures.

The connection between intent, energy, and manifestation.

Forgotten rituals, charms, and spiritual symbols that carried real power.

Insights into modern money spells and prosperity workings that echo ancient techniques.

The thin line between benevolent and forbidden magic—and how to walk it with wisdom.

Whether you're a curious seeker, a student of the occult,

or someone searching for practical insight into the unseen forces of the universe, Understanding Forgotten Magic offers a captivating journey through the mysteries that time tried to erase.

Step into the forgotten. Rediscover the power that once moved worlds.

The Pole Shift (Global Disaster Scenarios Book 2) Kindle Edition

The Pole Shift
Book Two in the Global Disaster Scenarios Series
By Michael James

When Earth's magnetic field begins to falter, science turns into survival.

As the poles slip into chaos, compasses spin uselessly, storms rage with unnatural fury, and technology collapses under a sky alive with static and fire. Governments fall into panic, scientists scramble for answers, and the military races to save what's left of civilization. Amid the confusion, NASA and global defense forces launch a desperate mission—evacuate the last survivors to orbit before Earth's surface becomes uninhabitable.

But as humanity watches from above, the planet continues to unravel. Lightning storms tear across continents, magnetic fields twist oceans into violent tempests, and solar flares ignite the upper atmosphere. The Earth that once sustained life becomes an unpredictable wasteland. And just when hope begins to fade, one signal from the ground changes everything…

Now, the survivors aboard the ISS must risk everything to return home and restore a dying planet. With Earth's magnetic poles shifting uncontrollably and time running out, humanity faces its greatest test yet: reclaiming the world it nearly destroyed.

The Pole Shift is a breathtaking journey through global catastrophe and human resilience—a bold vision of science, survival, and rebirth on a planet forever changed.

Understanding Ancient Power (Understanding Lost Knowledge) Kindle Edition

A bold reimagining of monuments as living technologies, The Nodes of Memory traces pyramids from Giza to the Yucatán, the Alaskan tundra to submerged reefs and canyon terraces—and listens for the practical wisdom they teach. This is not a book of lost-civilization headlines. It is a field guide to repair, timing, and the human institutions that make endurance possible.

A fresh premise: Pyramids and terraces are civic instruments—calendars, storehouses, observatories, and social protocols—designed to teach communities how to wait, survive, and pass knowledge on.

A humane methodology: Grounded in archaeology, craft lore, and indigenous stewardship, the book insists that curiosity be paired with consent and reversibility.

Practical prescriptions: Apprenticeship funding, maintenance trusts, reversible design standards, and community data sovereignty become actionable policy tools, not abstract ideals.

Urgent relevance: As climates shift and coasts drown, these

ancient practices offer low-tech, scalable lessons for resilience and ethical conservation.

For readers who want history that helps us act—and for practitioners seeking frameworks that respect people as much as stone—this book reframes heritage as an engine of practical continuity. Open it to learn how to listen, how to repair, and how to build institutions that last.

Earth's Hidden Highways Ley Lines And Ufo Corridors Kindle Edition

Earth's Hidden Highways Ley Lines and UFO Corridors

Beneath the surface of our planet lies a forgotten architecture — a global grid of energy lines, ancient monuments, and unexplained aerial phenomena. From the spiral etched into the mesa near Skinwalker Ranch to the magnetic bluestones of Stonehenge and the towering geometry of the Great Pyramid, this book uncovers a planetary-scale system that may have been designed to open gateways between worlds.

Blending field research, mythic storytelling, and cutting-edge theory, Earth's Hidden Highways explores how ley lines, megalithic structures, and UFO hotspots may form a unified network — one that pulses with electromagnetic resonance, acoustic harmonics, and cosmic alignment. Each chapter dives deeper into the possibility that these sites are not isolated mysteries, but interconnected nodes in a vast, ancient machine.

Are these corridors guiding energy — or something else? Are the anomalies we witness today echoes of a system reawakening?

This is a book for seekers, skeptics, and scientists alike — a journey across continents and dimensions, revealing the hidden highways that have shaped our skies, our myths, and perhaps our future.

Understanding Skinwalkers & Wormholes (Understanding Lost Knowledge) Kindle Edition

Beneath the windswept mesa of Skinwalker Ranch, something ancient hums. It pulses through the Triangle, the spiral stones, and the hidden chamber below — a rhythm older than human memory, yet tuned to respond to those who dare to listen.

When a team of investigators decodes the first harmonic "handshake," they unlock a bridge between worlds — a living network of gateways, each governed by a silent intelligence. But the deeper they explore, the more they realize the bridge is no passive conduit. It is a gatekeeper. It decides what passes through… and what must never cross.

From the eerie glow of the aerial anomaly to the impossible symmetry of phenomena unfolding in two places at once, Understanding Skinwalkers & Wormholes blends rigorous research with cinematic narrative to explore the intersection of Native legend, cutting-edge physics, and the uncharted mechanics of wormholes.

As the network expands to link with a foreign lattice, the team witnesses matter duplicated across worlds, environmental conditions shared in real time, and a final transmission that could reopen the bridge — once, and only once. The choice to use it will change everything.

Part field report, part speculative science, and part mythic mystery, this book takes you inside the hum — where the boundaries between folklore and physics dissolve, and the question is no longer what the machine is, but why it chose to reveal itself now.

Broken Wings Kindle Edition

Some scars are visible. Others are carried deep inside. Both tell a story of survival.

Broken Wings is a powerful true-to-life series that brings together two unforgettable journeys of resilience.

Taken on My Birthday reveals the shattering moment a child is torn from his mother's arms on his fourth birthday, thrust into foster care after years of abuse. From age four to eight, state custody became both a cage and a crucible—shaping a boy who refused to be broken.

Fading Silence chronicles the aftermath of a devastating fall in 2007 that fractured a skull in three places and left its survivor in a seven-day coma. Waking meant not only relearning life after brain surgery, but also confronting addiction and clawing back from the edge toward recovery.

Together, these stories form the foundation of Broken Wings —a series about pain, survival, and the unyielding fight to reclaim your voice. It is a testament to the strength it takes to rise when the world has tried to silence you.

For readers of memoirs that cut to the bone, Broken Wings is not just a story—it's proof that even in the darkest chapters, hope can still take flight.

The Shadows Of Skinwalker Ranch Kindle Edition

On a lonely stretch of land in northeastern Utah lies one of the most infamous paranormal hotbeds in the world.

For generations, Skinwalker Ranch has been a place of fear and fascination. UFO sightings, glowing orbs, mutilated cattle, vanishing portals, and beings that seem to step out of nightmare have all been reported on this cursed land. To the Navajo, it is a place tainted by shapeshifters. To scientists and investigators, it is a riddle that refuses to be solved.

The Shadows of Skinwalker Ranch takes you deep into the unsettling history and ongoing mysteries of this enigmatic property. Drawing from legend, testimony, and research, it uncovers why the ranch continues to draw those searching for answers—and why so many leave with more questions than before.

If you've ever wondered what lies beyond the veil of the ordinary, step into the shadows… but beware—some who enter never truly return.

Understanding The Book Of Enoch (Understanding Lost Knowledge) Kindle Edition

Understanding The Book of Enoch A Visionary Exploration of Ancient Mysteries and Cosmic Networks

Long before the flood, before the towers fell and the stars were named, the Watchers descended. Their secrets were buried. Their warnings were sealed. But the Book of Enoch remembers.

In this immersive and genre-defying work, Alex unravels the mysteries of Enoch's lost text — not as static scripture, but as a living map of planetary-scale networks, ley lines, and cosmic corridors. From the architecture of the heavens to the transmission of forbidden knowledge, this book journeys through ancient structures, UFO phenomena, and mythic patterns that stretch across time and space.

Blending folklore, science, and speculative theory, Understanding The Book of Enoch treats the text not as a relic, but as a ritual — a multidimensional signal encoded in story. Each chapter is a gateway, each insight a thread in the great weave of hidden history.

Whether you're a student of ancient texts, a seeker of cosmic truth, or a lover of mythic storytelling, this book invites you to walk the path Enoch walked — and see the world as the Watchers once did.

Understanding The Sumerians (Understanding Lost Knowledge) Kindle Edition

From the Cradle of Civilization Comes the Story of Humanity's First Great Cities

Before Egypt's pyramids rose or Rome's legions marched, the Sumerians built the world's first urban civilization in the fertile lands between the Tigris and Euphrates. Understanding the Sumerians takes you deep into their cities, temples, and marketplaces, revealing how they mastered agriculture, invented writing, codified laws, and wove myth and religion into every aspect of life.

Through vivid, historically grounded storytelling, this book explores:

The rise of city-states and the divine kings who ruled them

The ingenuity of irrigation, trade networks, and craftsmanship

The pantheon of gods, creation myths, and the Sumerian vision of the cosmos

Daily life — from bread ovens and beer brewing to festivals and diplomacy

Drawing on archaeological evidence, translated cuneiform texts, and the latest scholarship, Understanding the Sumerians brings to life a civilization whose innovations still shape our world. Whether you are a history enthusiast, a student of ancient cultures, or simply curious about where so much of human society began, this is your guide to the people who turned clay and river water into the foundations of civilization.

Step into the streets of Ur, stand before the ziggurats of Uruk, and meet the people who first taught the world how to live together.

Printed in Dunstable, United Kingdom